A whimsy about the author.

What should have been:

Petra Ceason was born on Friday 21 June 1972, on the right side of the tracks in a small town in Somerset, South-west of Bath. She was the first member of her family for several generations to fail to get into an Academically Biased institution, which left a severe, but deeply hidden open wound, until she was emergency blind dated with an older man. Although the wound took years to heal, Easteruprising O'Grady packed it with salve and sewed the edges back tightly together, on their first date.

Consequently she embarked on a passionate, friendly, Sexual Education Affair with Pi, until Mr. Right came knocking barely two months later. They were married when he graduated, and she joined him in the 'Frozen North', where they now live, with their two children, on the Estate he manages.

Pi, now retired, and with no children of his own that he is aware of, is a God Parent of each of the youngsters, and a regular, and eagerly awaited, welcome-visitor to the house.

What is:

Delia, Chef In A Wheelchair is chronologically parallel with more than a dozen novels and novellas about the personnel of West Novochester.

Also by Petra Ceason

West Novochester Chronicles Group
Karen, The Girl Who Would Be A Plumber.
Rita--Who?
Janie, Mechanic On A Motorbike.

Rough Cut
Rosalind And Timothy, An Essay In Deflated Self Worth.

Almost Finished
Richard, Jim And Friends, Finance And Fine Art.
Frank, An Essay On Health.

Work Related to Creative Writing Course, {available.}
Collected Short Stories And Pomes,
{And No. It's Not A Typo.}

Work in Progress
Anna, CEO In Short Socks.
Ash And Cindy.
Fred And Louise, Reluctant Athletes
Jennifer And Sylvie, Flouting Convention, But Politely.
Jill.
Pealle, Sporty Sparks.
Shelley And William, Autistic Artist.
Shirley And John, Monta's Secret Weapon.
Stewart And Jean, The Different.

Autobiography {Whimsy (in progress)}
Writes En Passion

Petra Ceason

Delia, Chef In A Wheelchair

Double-Sausage

Delia, Chef In A Wheelchair

First paperback edition printed 2017 in the United Kingdom

A catalogue record for this book is available from the British Library.

ISBN 978-0-9930419-1-4

    Published by Double-Sausage.

For more copies of this book, please contact the distributor, on line book facilitator, Lulu: www.lulu.com {from there the UK page can be chosen; click on the Old Glory Flag choose the Union Flag.}

Designed and Set by Petra Ceason: www.petraceason.co.uk
    This website carries a link direct to books by Petra Ceason.

Printed in Great Britain.

Acknowledgements:
    My thanks to Renée Cuthbertson for helpful comments.

This book is fiction! There are some real places mentioned, and some with similar names in Warwickshire, but they are present here merely as a backdrop. The events in this book never took place there. Although every precaution has been taken in the preparation of this book, the publisher and author assume no responsibility for errors or omissions. Neither is any liability assumed for damages resulting from the use of this information contained herein. In particular the Laws of Man, and possibly Physics may occasionally have been ignored. 'Delia' has not been professionally edited, please forgive any errors.

Author's Comment

The Events in this story are fictitious; any similarity to things that really happened is purely accidental--

Except for The Carol Concert.

The Carol Concert {Chapter Twenty-seven} is one of himself's favourite memories of his teaching career.

To those who turned up resentful and glum-faced to-endure, but stayed bright-eyed and tuned-in,

to sing; and whistle; and stamp;

I know you enjoyed it, now you can join with me in:

'Delia', Thank you for suggesting it,

'Enid', Thank you for agreeing to it.

Most of the Characters are fictitious. Except for Delia {who in real life was neither older than her classmates, nor in a wheelchair, nor to the best of my knowledge a trainee chef,} and her group of friends.

Also Big Mamma, Anna Monta, Jean Ripson, Enid Macey.

You may recognise yourselves, if so I hope you're pleased.

One half of the inspiration for Bill Carpenter is dead and sadly missed. The poisoned troll will almost certainly not recognise themself, but anyone who knew either of them will.

Anyone who knows my home city, or East Warwickshire will recognise either {or both} settings, but, since I started writing Delia, West Novochester has been demolished {2010} and replaced by a newer building.

For Mildred Patterson, it is payback time! Enough said!

My Characters' wild-child character traits, freethinking and non-mainstream exploits are very largely their own, not those of the real person who inspired the character. All the views expressed by all the characters in this book are their own, but some of them definitely are mine too.

This First Commercial Edition published by Double-Sausage™.

{In memory of the Ancestor who, had he ever owned a boat,would have called it, The Double-Sausage.}

Petra Ceason

2017.

Acknowledgements

I write separate scenes and join them up later, with invisible mending of varying quality. When J. K. Rowling acknowledged that was how she wrote 'The Philosopher's Stone,'it gave me heart to learn that the other writer who wrote at least one of her books this way was on her way to being a Billionaire. It's a PUSILLANIMOUs little American billion; of course, but what the floppies!

I, for one, wouldn't mind being ninety-nine p in the £1 behind her.

To all those authors over the years who have given me so much pleasure a sincere and heartfelt thank you.

Arthur Ransome; Dick Francis; Robert A. Heinlein; Reginald Hill; Jane Austen; Lew Matthews; Manning O'Brine; Dornford Yeats; John Wyndham; C. S. Forester; J. K. Rowling to name but a few.

I have tried to credit you when I knowingly referred to your work. When I missed, it was innocently done, please forgive. With so many wonderful stories buried in my cortex, I must have used variations on your ideas some time.

Where I did so without credits, it was unintentional and anyway, imitation is the sincerest form of flattery, even when done by accident.

Often between writing and getting a scene to the printer, I too have seen one of my plot lines appear on the small screen.

One of my heroines asks of her boss,

"Have you got my brain bugged?"[1]

There are times when I think mine is.

Anyway,Thank You! And where necessary,

Sorry,

Petra Ceason 2017.

---

1   Karen Robinson. Karen, the Girl That Would Be A Plumber

For:

Rachael Elizabeth Lloyd,
who had the temerity to ask
for her purchase, to be gift wrapped.

And Susan Burn,
who created a character that
I mistakenly thought was disabled,
but when the misunderstanding was cleared up,
kindly donated the wheelchair to me.

As a direct consequence of these actions,
Delia, slumbering in the wings,
heard her cue, woke up and took centre stage.

Any incorrect possessive or
omitted character apostrophes are typos,
not bad grammar,
as are any faulty its; your; or who's;
and down to me.
But, for content,
as always:
Don't blame me,
blame Petra.
She did it, all I did
was hit the keys

Mervyn Waine

Sex

Parasites outnumber non-parasites in the World by many to one. It's the nature of things.

Any animal or plant behaviour that occurs regularly is likely to be targeted by parasites for their own devices. As an ecologist I cannot think of any behaviour where also I cannot quote an example of parasitic exploitation.

Sex is no different.
    From the misguided souls who consider it sinful, all the way down to those troublesome life forms called viruses, which are scarcely any more advanced than complex chemical compound groups, sex is under attack for a multitude of hidden agendas.

Petra can fight the ignorance and allow me to be sybaritic and ignore the venereal diseases in her books, but Dear Reader, please do not ignore them in life.

Sex is not sinful, it is neither wrong, nor likely to kill you, but the parasitic hangers-on are!
    Sex is lovely; please keep it that way by practising safe sex always.

Jennifer Jackson

Delia, Chef In A Wheelchair

Midlogue as a Prologue:
26 July 1986

To trip over a dead body on your big day was not the best of the Wedding Presents. To be in the frame as principal suspect for the murder before you had reached your marriage bed, was decidedly the worst.

Chapter 1
Old Endings: Tyne-dale Summer 1982
Delia

What was to become the most momentous day in Delia Summers life so far began with no hint of being special. As she limped inelegantly into the bathroom to get her towel from the messy and disarrayed airing cupboard, her thoughts were of mild annoyance,

Why do boys always leave a trail of wreckage behind them?

She refolded and straightened the contents, until the cupboard was tidy. As she reached out to close the door, her cousin's call rang up the stairs,

"Come on. Why do girls always take ages?"

"I'm coming, I was ready before you, it's your mess I'm, like, cleaning away."

The reply was a banging door. Grandma's voice reached her faintly,

"You're still young, you need a wife and those children need a mother."

Delia grabbed her towel and swimming bag and came down the stairs one at a time on the awkward right leg lead. Unobserved, she coped with the last six in a {strictly forbidden} single bound. Her Dad called to her, no doubt pointedly changing the subject from his lack of spouse,

"Delia! You've left your clump in here and I've tripped over it twice."

She stepped through to the kitchen, disguising the limp as best she could, which increased the pain greatly. The younger of her brothers helpfully lifted her shoes up for her.

"Sorry Dad. Thanks Robbie, I'm off, I'll be back to cook dinner." She took the shoes and, on her way out, stowed them away in the porch.

Grandma looked at the swimming bag over the top of her glasses, her voice carried from the kitchen, full of tut,

"You know they're skinny-dipping."

Batty old woman, she thought. *Usually okay, but sometimes a total control freak--*

"So big deal."

"She's not a child any more, she'll be a teenager soon."

"She's fourteen now Nanna, they're in the bath together every night and I'd much rather--"

Thanks Dad. She grabbed the banging door and secured it properly. Ben was already mounted, pedals cocked,

"Race you."

"Oh yes, with you already on your bike and, like, twenty start."

"See you there then." He pushed off and a moment later was flying down the farm track towards the gate. Delia hobbled over and retrieved her more girly bike from the hut. Holding the old and oily cylinder-padlock fastidiously, she pressed it together and the shackle clicked into place. It was only as she tested it that she realised the shackle had slipped down the outside of the lock, because although it stayed shut with a straight pull, it sprang open when her checking twisted it.

"Broken brake-blocks!" she snarled. "Bent ones!" She refastened the padlock correctly. By now, she had to lose valuable seconds wiping her hands on the rough wood of the shed.

Because she would be washing it later anyway, she wiped the last few stains off on her towel and stuffed it back into her bag which she clipped onto the pannier. She checked the blocks on the right pedal that corrected the difference in the length of her legs. There was a slight wobble and so she lost yet another few seconds tightening the wing nuts. A moment later, she was in hot pursuit, out of the farm gate and along the quiet country lane. Ben was waiting for her at the road junction.

"I thought you'd gone," she called as she closed up.

"More fun with you next to me, besides --"

He waved generally down the road just out of her sight. She braked hard to a halt beside him; a herd of Friesians was being moved from one field to another. The steaming river of shuffling black and white bodies filled the narrow lane from wall to hedge.

"I take it you can't jump your bike fifty metres, like, over live cows."

"No, now had it been only forty-five --"

As the last of the cows ambled good naturedly out of their way, the youngsters kicked hard up the little rise through the wood that surrounded Loblom Lake on all sides and down the other side, past the fashionable east shore. The first of the swarm of day visitors from the conurbations of Lower Tyne-dale had already arrived. It wouldn't be long before a sudden unexpected sneeze at one end of the shoreline, would ripple through the crowd and spill drink, half a mile away, at the other.

The young cousins, with solitude in wide-open spaces in mind, pedalled past with barely a glance. They were heading for a peninsula, to all intents a solidly wooded island, which stuck out from the southern shore of the lake, several minutes cycling away. Their destination had some supreme advantages. Despite the 'island' being in plain sight from many viewpoints, the access to it was very difficult to find and, once inside, the solidity of the trees was revealed to be merely an illusion. At the next road junction, they turned right and cycled westwards until the hedge, fence and ditch, barring their way in, merged to barely a depression by the roadside. As soon as they could, they entered the Loblom Lake Nature Reserve and doubled back through the widely spaced trees, on a steep diagonal.

Ahead lay an almost solid Rhododendron wall, which bordered most of the accessible shoreline of the lake. The trees were arranged in a ragged line. Their dense foliage and huge blowsy blooms cascaded out in vast overlapping spherical caps, an undisciplined line of showgirls in crinolines, each striving to outdo her neighbour. Ben slowed, scanning the wanton display,

"I never know which one it is."

"It's the next one, opposite the tree with the, like, lovely bark."

"They all look the same to me."

"That's because you, like, don't look properly."

Ben hopped off his still moving bike and ran it into the big Rhododendron. He reached under and pulled a sweeping branch aside, revealing that the tree was a huge hollow dome.

"I'll hold, you squeeze under"

Once inside Delia could push the branch up, to allow her cousin also to squeeze under.

"Thanks," they said to each other as they crossed the large space and in through a second, smaller Rhododendron.

As they crossed a damp ditch, all that separated the 'island' from the shore, glimpses of open water could be seen on both sides. Incongruously, the squelching path they trod seemed well below the adjacent water level.

A few steps on, the path climbed into a narrow tunnel through bare twigs and branches.

"This passage gets smaller each year, or, like, am I bigger?"

"Yes."

"Yes, which?"

"Your choice. Dew undisturbed, nobody here."

"There never is."

The tunnel lightened, widened and grew leaves. The peat underfoot was replaced by thin sad grass, which rapidly became lush as they stepped back into sunlight. Suddenly, a green grassy glade opened up ahead. It was a bit smaller than a tennis court and almost completely covered in short, thick, lush, deep-green grass.

A few rocky outcrops sprinkled erratically across it sporadically interrupted the sward. A small cairn of stones and some tree stumps, covered in moss and lichen and decades old, lay over to their right.

A thin but solid belt of mixed forest surrounded the glade on all sides except ahead and slightly to the left, where a dense bed of Great Reed Mace ended in a rough earth beach with glinting water lapping gently onto it. The rocky, leaf-strewn bed of the lake, lovely to look at, but hard on the feet, reached out to banks of milfoil.

Several pairs of coots paddled about in the middle distance, teaching their broods survival tactics.

"Do you think the people who made the pathway are, like, still around?" Delia waved at the beach ahead of them that narrowed and disappeared among the fringe of trees. From previous visits, the cousins knew that it formed a pathway all around the peninsula, reappearing on the far side of the clearing, beside the cairn.

"Grown up, old and sedate, not interested in skinny-dipping any more, or even generations, long gone."

"I know they're happy we play here, I can feel it, like, in the trees and the land."

"Yes, it's a happy place. I'll race you into the water."

"No you won't, we, like, check for sharks first."

Boy and girl shed their clothes into a loose, twin-peaked pile and put their old trainers on as protection against stones, bottles and the odd rogue railway carriage.

"Ready?"

"Yeah."

Together they worked their way out through the deep, dense-forest of Great Reed Mace, at the edge of the lake. Ben kept pace with Delia, in case she needed him to lean on.

They searched out and followed a broken, rugged, L shaped path, composed of large flat rocks placed so that they just didn't break the surface. The short leg perpendicular to the island they left overgrown, but when they turned parallel with the shore, they hauled up all the young Reed Mace sprouts that encroached onto the path.

From the island, the reed bed still looked solid, but for any adventurers who picked their way through the first four or five metres, suddenly, to the right, a long wide path to deep water

19

opened up.

Of course, everything is relative, deep for Loblom is one metre.

At right angles from the end of the path, which stuck out like a jetty, a channel stretched away into the lake.

Although the milfoil on each side was already reaching its summer tendrils into the space, the channel was wide and clear, almost exactly as they had last seen it, nearly nine months ago. The main difference was the addition of the new carpet of last year's leaves. There were no broken bottles, dead prams or other inanimate sharks, to savage unwary bathers.

"It's safe," he said.

Delia surveyed the channel and donned her flippers.

"Yes safe," she replied and dived in with a flat racing dive. She surfaced immediately after, fitted her face mask, adjusted her snorkel and cruised the surface studying the bottom of the lake. Despite being equidistant from dozens of crowded picnic sites, they were completely alone and, binocular assistance apart, unobserved.

Ben waded in after her and, side-by-side, they swam a substantial part of the length of the lake and back, almost completely submerged, breathing through their snorkels, the entire time.

Later, while they were sitting on the jetty, Ben asked her about her new skill.

"Where did you learn to dive like that?"

"Swimming course."

"Teach me how."

"It's just a question of keeping your legs straight, hang on I'll, like, get a stick." She dropped her flippers and mask down and retrieved a stem with an impressive cigar on top of it, then held it out parallel to the water's edge, just below knee height.

"Dive clean over the stick, pretend you're diving onto a bed, or you'll, like, go too deep."

Ben obeyed her with a neat dive, ruined, as always, by him jackknifing his knees just as he was about to touch the water. Delia made sure they hit the stick.

"You did that deliberately, hit my legs."

"Yes, to make you straighten them."

Ben splashed her, two handed, a pair of scything snakes of water straight into her face.

"Oh. You piglet." Delia soaked him in retaliation using full kicks of her left leg.

Ben had to turn his back and then approached her protecting his face.

"Right I'm going to get you."

"You'll never catch me." She was already limping away along the causeway.

"Cheeky baggage! I'm going to tickle you till you squeal for mercy," he called as he climbed out and chased after her.

"Yah. Boo. Sucks. All mouth and no trousers."

Safely on dry land Delia accelerated away, galloping on a left leg lead, only to have the weak right foot crumple and bring her down. She broke her fall with a firm hand slap and rolled onto the grass.

"Yah. Boo. Suc-Ow."

Ben pounced upon her, but gently, concerned,

"Are you all right?"

"The foot's okay. Just, like, grit in my hand." She held it up, studded with small black stones. Together they brushed them away, a few had to be eased out, although none had broken through, they were smarting; Delia winced away slightly, from the touch.

"I'll kiss it better." He sensuously kissed each depression on her palm, plump lipped. "And the foot?"

"It's not crocked, not, like, good either, mind."

He took the small, twisted appendage and gently removed the tiny trainer, then sensuously kissed and caressed it. Delia was ready to yank it away, but he was making no effort to carry out the threat to tickle her into submission.

"She doesn't take care of you, not as she should. You're precious, but I'll look after you."

Delia fondly watched him pleasuring her. The delicate touches felt warm and fluffy in her tummy. His eyes glanced up to hers, pausing for hardly a moment on her naked sex and proud breasts, demonstrating that they needed no bra for support.

"There did that help?"

"Magic. But, like, now other places need better."

"Where?"

She leaned forward, grabbed his head cupping his face in her hands and kissed him full on the lips, voluptuous and pouty, like in the films, expecting him to pull away in disgust.

Instead, he pushed her down, under him and kissed her back.

It was lovely.

Incredible.

Exciting, fluffy and wonderful.

She opened her eyes and looked at him, he was as excited as she was.

She kissed him again and he kissed her back.

The girl slender arms, wheelchair powerful beyond their size, hugged him hard to her,

She spread and enfolded him, snugly wriggling against his wriggling body.

Oh that was nice.

He did it again.

That was really nice.

He did it again. Then suddenly stopped, she guessed he was unsure of her reaction.

"Wriggle like that again."

"Like that?"

"Yes, it's nice."

"Ugh--This--Like this?"

"It's lovely--Oh--Ooh."

"Am I hurting you?"

"No!--Don't stop--Don't Stop--Don't Stop--Ooh."

The activity slowed and stopped, presently to be replaced by deep relaxed breathing.

Delia woke up and gently kissed his sleeping face. After a minute or so the kisses were returned and she could feel him hard against her again.

"Wriggly Kiss me again."

22

"It's not the same."

"Your thing's not in me. Last time it was in me, like, inside me--Let me--Now, push in--Yes that's it. Is it nice now?"

"Yes--Yes--Can I push harder?"

"Hard--Quick--Anything."

"I'm really not hurting you?"

"No anythi--Ooh--Oh, anything you like--Oh--Oh--Don't stop, keep doing it--Don't stop--Oh--Ooh."

Slowly their heart-rates and breathing returned to normal, and reality intruded, for Delia.

Something as Earth Movingly Wonderful as that has to be really, seriously naughty, she thought, but couldn't bring herself to mention it. Nevertheless, in spite of her suspicious reservations, Wriggly Kisses became a standard feature of any quality time the pair spent alone.

"Oh, look at the time. Come on get ready, I have to be home to, like, cook the tea."

They packed up mid afternoon in preparation to return to Ben's home.

"Why do you have to cook tea?"

"I don't have to; I want to. I'm going to be a cook when I, like, grow up."

"All girls cook."

"A Cook. A chef in a restaurant. My own restaurant. That's why I'm doing all those, like, missed years, I need all that missed schooling."

"Huh, right. I'd leave tomorrow if I could."

"You'll feel differently this time next year."

"Huh!"

Despite it being entirely her own choice, the five years ahead of her was causing Delia much anxiety.

Warwickshire Summer 1982

Lovers

That the large, grey, middle-aged woman was not enjoying herself was obvious, her feelings, radiating out in waves of displeasure, were spoiling the East Warwickshire Charity Masked Ball for everyone around her. Her partner coped by withdrawing from her vicinity, like everyone else.

"Hello. I thought it was you." Although the masks stayed firmly in place on both faces, the recognition was mutual and so was the pleasure.

"Oh, hello. Just circulating a bit." Whilst glancing back.

"It's okay, she's not looking this way. Take me to the bar, get us some fresh drinks, then we can walk in the garden."

Several darker places in the garden already had couples in occupation. The new pair walked on. That their oblivion was merely apparent, became obvious when a particularly dark corner was discovered to be available, they slid into it without discussion.

The conversation was commiserative and supporting.

"She doesn't mean it. Just doesn't think of the pain she's causing."

"It's all right. Don't get upset, let me hold you, make you feel better. There. Don't upset yourself, you've done nothing wrong."

The comforting caresses worked their magic, the strong emotions swung, without warning, from one extreme to the other, a situation obvious to both instantly.

"Sorry. Just does it's own thing."

"It's all right, I don't mind, don't pull away, cuddle up. I really don't mind; it's a compliment in a way. I'd like to help, if you'll let me."

"Oh."

The intimate caress had been a shock, but the caressed, obediently, didn't pull away.

"There, this is what you need, some tender physical care, cuddle up, I'm going to give him what he wants."

Emboldened, the caresses became more intimate and mutual,

"Oh! You--"

"Of course! Don't worry. Don't stop, it was lovely, do it, do it again--Yes--Yes, Ooh, that was nice."

The clothing barriers were loosened enough to provide unfettered access.

"Oh--Oh--Ugh--Thank you, that was nice. You were right, that was exactly what I needed. Just, like being a teenager again."

"I liked it too. I want to do it again, no not right now, but soon. Will you meet me, come with me? I have a place we could go to, secluded, private; we could do it properly--I mean really properly, take our time, make love to each other."

"I don't know. Just, it--"

"Just come with me. Try it. If you decide you can't, at least we'll have tried it. I'm doing this for me too."

Shopping And Learning: Summer 1982

Delia

The holiday ended and the Summers family, father, daughter and two younger boys, returned home to Novochester.

Shopping for her new School Uniform and a full range of quality Mathematical instruments occupied an entire afternoon. Delia arranged for her Dad to pick her up from the cut through behind the line of bus shelters serving the country buses out west. Dave had had to work, so instead of going with her, he'd issued a stream of instructions.

"I'll leave the uniform to you, but get good stuff that'll last. Wool and cotton, none of your man made rubbish. Schools are full of drawing pins and staples and cracked chairs that--"

"I thought it was, like, being left to me?"

"Okay, but the instruments and pencils and that, go to the Art and Craft suppliers downtown, not the one next to the University and buy good stuff, quality stuff. A pair of compasses costing less than a fiver is landfill, pick out an assistant who seems to know things and ask him 'Which one would you prefer?'If you like it, buy it."

"I know."

"And don't forget inks. We'll get you some pens at the weekend and a special one for--"

"Dad I know! Go to work. Pick me up at six."

* * *

The uniform was packed in a capacious bag and left waiting for her at the department store's loading bay. This was a procedure so standard that several of the warehousemen who worked on the dock greeted Delia by name when she appeared. This left the wheelchair largely uncluttered for the long run down to the Art and Craft suppliers and the difficult manoeuvring in the cramped shop.

* * *

Drawing instruments were displayed in an illuminated cabinet like jewellery and were in three ranges, landfill, intermediate and architect.

Delia ignored the first, of which to be fair to the shop there wasn't much and the last, but several sets of the intermediate price range were eye-catching. Two individual compasses were particularly attractive, but one was dangerously near her Dad's 'don't buy' guide price.

"May I, like, have a look at those two--Thanks--The cheaper one does more, extension arm for bigger circles and an ink fitting as well as lead. What am I getting for my extra money if I buy the expensive one?"

The assistant removed the compasses from their cases,

"Open and close this one--Now this one."

"Ah. 'Nuff said. Have you got this one, but with, like, all the extras?"

"No. But hang on a sec."

The assistant disappeared into the back. While Delia waited, she replaced the cheaper item and closed the box.

"There's this." The assistant returned proffering a leatherette case. "You pull the pins at the front out sideways." He did so and laid the case down. Delia raised the lid. The contents lay each in their own purpose-cut depression in an elastic medium, which receded and returned slightly as it was pushed and released. The entire inside was lined with luxurious black velvet.

"Wow." She lifted out one pair of compasses and opened them. Silky smooth, if anything the best so far, she nodded and looked at him, "I've got the good news, what's the, like, bad?"

Outside, the impending cloudburst hadn't yet seriously started. Delia powered her way through the narrow Victorian walkway down to the Bus Station. The girls in the skimpy tops, short skirts and fuck-me boots were putting their umbrellas up.

"Hi Delia, your Dad's been around, he'll be back in five minutes."

"Oh, thanks."

"Oh, here's the rent," said the other girl and scuttled across the pavement. She dived into the cruising car, folding her umbrella at the last moment.

As the door closed behind her, the vehicle accelerated smoothly away; the wheels had never stopped rolling. Another car slowed abruptly, a tiny girl catapulted out, shut the car door behind her and fled for cover under a child's transparent-cowl umbrella.

"Hi Sam."

"Hi. Your Dad's been around, he'll be back in," Samantha looked at her watch. "Oh, ten minutes ago."

"Gillian told me he'd been, he'll be back."

"Do me a favour Delia. Look away now."

"Okay."

Obediently she spun her chair around, but the advert for Irish stout that she stared into, was nearly a mirror. Samantha scurried back across the pavement and, like Gillian before her, dived into the slowing car, closing her umbrella and the door almost simultaneously. Delia slowly turned around again and watched her Junior School Head Teacher's car vanish into the murk, with the tiny girl on board.

"Well at least he's not, like, cheating on a wife," she murmured to herself. Another car slowed. "My Dad," she called to another girl who had made to cross over to it and propelled herself across towards the back of the stopping hatchback. Dave opened the boot as she collapsed the chair, he stowed it away, closed the boot and just failed to beat his daughter into their seats.

"The girls told me you'd been."

"Twice."

"Sorry about that."

"No problem. That girl who used to be in your class? She's a real beauty now."

"Gillian, yes, but I used to be in her class Dad, before those useless operations, she's still in that class, it's, like, me that's not."

There was a pause.

"I think you'll love what I've bought and we've got a parcel to pick up, like, from the loading bay." Dave nodded and the difficult moment passed.

After tea Delia modelled the clothes and then placed the leatherette case on her father's knee. He pulled the pins and opened it up.

"Nice." He selected one of the compasses and opened it. "Very nice. Did you have to re-mortgage the house?"

"What will you, like, settle for?"

"This won't have cost much less than a pony. Two compasses, extensions, three spring bows, pen attachments, divider attachments, spares, tools. More, thirty quid?"

"It was more, but it was, like, in a sale, they wanted fifteen, but I got them down to twelve by buying the rest of my stuff there too."

"Which is what you were going to do anyway."

"He must have been prepared to sell it for twelve, I didn't, like, hold a gun at his head."

* * *

A few days later, Dave Summers dropped his daughter off to camp out overnight in her best friend's back garden. It would be their last great adventure, before joining the Big School.

The little two-girl tent had a useful front extension, for cooking in the rain.

"We won't need the extension. Like, no rain."

"We're going to erect it though, so that we know how when the time comes," Kim insisted. "It would be just like the thing to have to do it for the first time, with Hurricane Lorna lashing the landscape."

"Point!"

The sausages browned up nicely on the paraffin stove and Kim presented Delia with her sandwiches oozing sweet pickle as instructed.

The pair had just finished their supper when,

"Shit! Here's Natasha, pretend you're asleep, it's disgusting."

"What's disgusting?"

"She'll bring Hugo around the back of the summerhouse to shag him. She squeals and he grunts, it's disgusting."

Kim slammed her head under her pillow, using it to muffle her ears. Delia withdrew into the shadow, against the tent wall.

The back wall of the summerhouse was suddenly picked out in much sharper detail as the dazzling effect of the badly designed, light-pollution-generating-street-lamp, was shut off.

Delia watched, listened and learned.

Kim's big sister slid into view towing her boy with her. They snuggled up and began kissing, when he shoved his hands up her front, she helped him, popping her bra up over her small breasts. Then, his hand was up her skirt, Delia could see his arm moving as he rubbed. Suddenly they disengaged, Delia thought they must be going, but it was only to allow Hugo to loosen his trousers and push them down. Natasha meanwhile had wriggled her knickers down and stepped out of a leg. She eased her skirt up around her waist revealing the knickers clumped around one knee like a bobble. Delia had to stifle a gasp. Hugo's thing was sticking up hard, just like Ben's did when they had wriggly kisses. Natasha caressed it and Hugo rubbed her again. Suddenly, she pulled him hard to her, Hugo crouched down a bit and slid in between his girl, snuggled, readjusted and began thrusting into her in a smooth rhythm. Natasha squealed and Hugo grunted, just as Kim had said they would. The activity peaked, slowed and stopped. Delia watched from her hiding place, immobile and shocked, as the pair checked their clothes before retreating, back towards the house.

So that's what it is.

She and Ben had been doing it.

Something as good as that had to be, in the words of the old song, illegal, immoral, or destined to make you fat.

Or, in my case, all three; eventually, she thought.

Her instinct to keep quiet about it generally had been correct.

But, now she couldn't even tell her best friend.

Disgusting? No, Kim, it's lovely, but you'll have to find that out for yourself.

Natasha and Hugo had disappeared; Kim was still buried

under her pillow.

If grandma--, she crushed that line of thought, but the next was barely any better,

Oh Delia, where do you go from here? You'll have to stop. But, you can't can you; you've been eagerly awaiting the next time, ever since the last time. You'll have to stop!

She nudged Kim,

"They've gone," she said.

* * *

On the first morning of term at the big School, Kim pushed the wheelchair up the hill, allowing her friend to walk slowly beside it.

"Why is uphill easier than down?"

"Down and the flat! I really don't know; it just is. Downhill's a pain. It may be, like, the angle my foot has to make, at the ankle. A steep downhill's worse than stairs."

Their destination came bobbing into view as the pair breasted the rise.

This is it. Delia took deep breaths to calm the adrenaline rush; they helped with the throbbing foot too. *Go for it!* They stopped, Kim lifted their schoolbags out of the wheelchair and Delia sank gratefully into it and gathered the bags back to her. Kim watched her friend anxiously,

"You okay?"

"Yes. Fine. Wagons Yoh!" She replied whilst pointing at the School.

New Beginnings: Warwickshire Summer 1982

Lovers

The car, with the lovers on board, pulled into the farm gateway, ahead lay a barn, substantial, stone built, with a slate roof.

"It's large and structurally sound. I'm thinking of buying, converting it into a cottage, selling it on. There's plenty more available. I could build up a little business. Come on, I got everything ready." Inside, the air-bed and pillows took the hardness from the floor. "You need to give it a proper try, that's the only way you'll find out."

"I know. Just, do it to me, you do it to me. Then--"

"All right. Come on let me undress you--Well you might be unsure, but your body isn't."

"I know. Just, I am enjoying this. Do it."

Their tender lovemaking was a spectacular success, if their mutual pleasure were to be taken as the criterion. Their post coital talk eventually centred on the barn.

"What's stopping you? Just, buy it and try it."

"Money. I haven't got enough. Mother would want to know where it had gone, all sorts of niggles and bother."

"I've got some. Just, if we were partners, as well as lovers, we could do it together. How much do we need?"

"I can probably get it for ten thousand and another thirty thousand to convert it and build the road, possibly a bit less, then I could sell it for fifty, fifty-five with luck. I've got twenty, I need another twenty-thousand, to be sure."

The discussion of timescale, renovations, even colour schemes that followed, had them both understanding that agreement had been reached. Presently loving caresses began to interfere with the discussion,

"Ooh. Somebody is getting interested in what's going on again. You be on top this time--Feel me and get me ready."

Soon afterwards, they swapped places and rôles and triumphantly scaled the heights again. They got dressed and removed and stored the home comforts away in the car.

"I'll look into buying a little company, see what it would cost. We need to hide our involvement in it, as well as each other. Particularly, I must not be seen to be involved, conflict of interest and all that."

"Yes. Just, be careful."

"I will. I won't do anything without consulting you, I promise. You ring me, at the office, I can talk there, if I'm out leave a message from--from Roger. If you ring at four, I'm usually in at four."

Chapter 2
New Beginnings: Tyne-dale September 1982
Delia

West Novochester was a huge sprawling building standing in its own grounds, near the top of the hill, just off Airport Way.

"The highest point west of the Urals," Mr Pling would tell them sagely later. Pointing out an accidental fact of Geographical trivia, which meant the views to the east and north were eye-catching. On frosty mornings, the snow-covered, glacier-decapitated whale-back of The Cheviot, about forty miles away, formed a spectacular centrepiece. To the south and west the views were obstructed by even higher, highest points west of the Urals, but their Geography teacher usually failed to mention those. From a distance, the School looked impressive. From any viewpoint, the three, three-story wings nearest to you, reached out vaguely towards three cardinal points of the compass, with a fourth, always out of sight behind them.

Up close, the stretch marks were showing.

"Typical!" exclaimed Delia. "We join a new School and it's, like, as stressed as the old one."

Kim did a double take, stopping the chair,

"How d'y'mean?"

"Mobile classrooms sardined into any corner big enough to

take them."

"You mean stressed out because it's successful?"

Delia nodded,

"It's bursting at the seams. That wing is, like, a panic built extension." The builder's daughter was looking with educated eyes, she leaned forward and pointed to the newer part of the School. "The land's totally unsuitable. It's bordering on the unacceptable." The Southern end of the pale building with its dark blue panels was thrusting into the hillside.

"I can see what you mean."

"It's a giant pig, like, after truffles."

"What made you choose Novochester?" Kim replied, giggling. "I'm glad you did, but what was it?"

"Happy School. Did you visit any others? To, like, look around."

"Yes."

"What did you think of Baileyford?"

"Didn't like it, oppressive, crowding in on you"

"I wouldn't go in, not, like, inside the building, it's a weeping School. It didn't publish any exam results this year, I don't wonder why."

The pair walked along the side of the field to the School Gate. The Stone-Built Gatepost Entrance, that straddled the roadway in, was situated incongruously in the middle of nowhere, with no hedge or fence on either side of it.

"Where do we go again?"

"South Block, presumably this is it here, we make like a truffle."

"Yes, look everyone seems to be drifting this way."

"Everyone seems your age too, like, where's all the big people?"

A few minutes later the new First-Year was ushered into the building, through four pairs of French Windows, leading directly onto an assembly hall, which was comfortably twice as large as that of their Junior School.

Several teachers were standing by the doors into the School corridor at the far end of the hall. Kim eased Delia through the throng to join them. When they saw the approaching chair, people moved out of their way; most of them staring wide eyed.

A chunky little brunette edged into the crowded hall, apparently looking for someone she knew.

"Hello Rosalind."

The girl turned towards the friendly voice, glancing downwards automatically,

"Oh, Delia? Hello, are you here too?"

"Yeah."

"I mean--I know you're here, I mean First Year?"

"Yeah," replied the girl in the wheelchair again. "I missed some years with the leg, need to catch up." She introduced the girls to each other and. "Oh we're, like, on."

The meeting was called to order, which didn't take much doing; nearly everyone wanted to hear what was going on. The broad outline of the activities of their first day was introduced and a list of names read out.

"Those pupils go with Miss Algood."

A pretty, comfortably plump lady held her hand up and walked slowly out of the door as children from all over the room drifted towards her.

The third list began: Ingrid Addams, James Cragg, Robert Davison, -- Marjorie Gately, Kimberley Hart, Carly Helendale, Jennifer Jackson, -- The girls waited anxiously, -- Rosalind Schelle, Delia Summers, -- They grinned at each other, -- Fred Waston, Jeannette Wilshon go with Mr Bryant. The tallest of the teachers, bronzed, blonde and blue eyed, with an incongruously plain, lived-in face, held his hand up and he too, walked slowly out of the hall, turned sharply right and outside onto the yard. He stopped and turned,

"Girls in twos down here," he held his left arm out in front of him, raised his right arm and added. "Boys in twos down here." It took a minute and a couple of glares, but eventually he was satisfied. "What is your name?"

The girl at the front of the queue, realising that she was being spoken to answered,

"Carly Sir."

"That is South Block," he said; pointing at the building behind them. "Inside the School, there is a one way system in operation. You can come over to South Block any way you like, but you must return to the main block across the yard, never through the School. So obeying that rule, lead across the yard to the far corner please Carly, then stop and wait for me when you get there."

The girls set off and Delia heard Mr Bryant organising the boys to follow them. It took another three, wait-for-mes, before the group arrived at his classroom.

Inside; the building was also showing the characteristic stress signs of a successful School. The flat roof, Sixties trendy and now way past its replace by date, sucked almost the entire repair and maintenance budget into a rash of small felt patches, like a Code Napoleon attempt to cope with symptoms that only a pitched roof would cure. Occasionally their way was obstructed by a bin, or bucket in the corridor. Some of them were still catching the drips seeping through from the previous day's downpour. Mr Bryant stopped their progress and drew attention to them.

"When you are walking through the School and you come across a bucket, walk around it, you will notice everyone else does too. It is bad enough that the roof leaks, we do not want the floor tiles lifting too, so walk around them. Also, this corridor was built to take four hundred pupils. We now have four times that many, so there are safety issues, particularly for younger, smaller pupils and, believe me, that is you. You might have been the top dogs at Junior School; you are back down on the bottom now. The rest of the School comes back tomorrow, you will never see it this empty again. So obey the one-way system, walk on the left and never push into a crowd, stay away until it thins out. It is your safety that is on the line!"

The rapacious roof left no money for paint, replacement of doors so warped that one might question whether they were made from unseasoned wood, or the correction of drainage problems that seemed to date from the construction of the South Wing extension.

The fabric of the building was so poor that words like

corruption, bribes, or kickbacks might occur to you; but all the locals knew that the cause was the flagrant demonstration of inept incompetence, to an unbelievable level, by the L.E.A., housed a safe four miles away.

Having created the problem; of course, they made a point of rarely coming to see the place and never visiting during crises.

What the School did have, was a committed, enthusiastic and caring Staff led by a Head Teacher who set the tone and mucked in to help. So West Novochester, only the un-clued-up ever put 'Comprehensive School' in the name, was oversubscribed by a factor of two, with potential students ignoring the peeling paint, but noting instead the smiling faces and general feeling of expectation of good things to come, today.

When at last they reached it, Mr Bryant indicated his door,

"Line up. Girls on the left, boys on the right." Eagerly obeying the first instruction heard, without listening to the rest, meant several pupils got it wrong. A girl with the most astonishing shade of flame-red hair gently redirected a wayward boy, while Mr Bryant glared at a couple of tall, suave boys who mocked a girl standing beside them. The door was unlocked and the pupils were directed to sit at tables, in groups of six. Delia collapsed her chair and stood it against the wall by the door, then hobbled over to sit by her friend, swinging and planting the built up shoe pedantically, to avoid colliding with legs, table or human.

"I'm Carly, this is Jeanette," said a smiling red-brunette with impossibly green eyes with vertically slit pupils, whilst flicking her thumb at a bronzed, blonde, beauty beside her.

"Marjorie."

"Ingrid."

"Delia."

"Kim."

Silence pervaded the room, like a subtle perfume.

Andrew Bryant surveyed the thirty children sitting mice like, grouped around tables, in front of him.

"Good," he said. "That was not bad at all for a first try. That is how we begin every period. The lessons themselves will vary. Hopefully, some of them will be good. But we always begin and end, collected together as a class."

Delia was entranced; he was already a special friend. No comment about the wheelchair, the twisted foot, or the helper; that was just fine. He knew everybody would be feeling strange. He'd kept himself in check, giving them time to correct errors, time to get used to him, time to learn that when he said jump, the only reply allowed was 'How high?' She had this mental picture of a tiger, with sheathed claws.

By morning break-time, the group around their table had decided they liked each other enough to stay together outside. Another table also remained with each other as a group, with Rosalind, marshalling her troops, to the obvious quiet amusement of the flame-top. Delia quite liked the pretty, slightly plump, bossy girl, despite her name and short fuse. Besides Jennifer, Rosalind's group included a pair of twins, Jill and Jo, so identical that they wore name-plaques over their tie knots, two more girls, Jane and Sadie, good naturedly went with the flow.

The tall and suave boys who had mocked an errant classmate approached their group. Sophistication bathed them like the glow in the dark of that misjudged advert and they had Delia and Kim in their sights. Delia saw them coming from somewhere west of Ireland and made her decision instantly. They were everything she rejected. She pointedly turned and exaggerated the hobble of a few steps away, to pick at a loose piece of brick and the taller lad seamlessly turned his attention to Marjorie.

The dates were arranged, with Delia's back demonstrating her vote, but her ears traitorously registering every detail, Robert Davison had hooked Kim and she was swimming eagerly towards his net. Mission accomplished, the boys left. Delia turned around, Kim was glowing and Marjorie looked really pleased. Delia bit down hard on her annoyance.

"Well?"

She tried to evade by edging past, but Kim insisted,

"Well?"

"Your choice, it's your life. But, he won't make you happy. No!"

Kim's protest stalled.

"Like, you wanted my opinion, you've got it, I'd love to be proved wrong. No more bets please! Lets talk about something else."

At lunchtime, Mr. Bryant held Delia back, in her chair.

"I have been looking at the timetable. Most of it is on the ground floor. Languages is two flights of stairs, but you can get there across the yard on ramps, if you want to. The Sciences are the problem; it is four flights of stairs. Twice a week. And Art, once a week."

"I can do four flights of stairs Sir, it just, like, takes me longer."

"We have made you a little card."

He placed it in front of her; it was white with a neat border, it read,

Please excuse

Delia Summers

if she is a few minutes late.
Please return this card.

The card was printed and securely laminated. Delia's name had been hand-written in a neat script.

"It is a standard issue card for special occasions, mostly you hand it in to the next teacher. It says so on the card, yours says to give it back."

"Oh. I'll try not to need it."

"Good girl. How are you coping with the age gap? Eleven to fourteen is a big three years."

"No problem, I don't think about it any more, like, used to it. And anyway, I'm a wild little eight-year old in some things, on my bike, climbi--"

"And twenty-something in others?"

She just tilted her head giving him the eyes.

"Okay, just like everybody else, unless there is something obviously wrong, I will assume you are managing. When you need help, shout loud and shout clearly. Can I ask, is the bike prescribed exercise?"

"Yes, Sir, like, non weight bearing."

Mr. Bryant nodded,

"Good. Lunchtime, I think."

Priorities: September 1982

Amelia

On the evening of the first day back after the Summer Holiday, PE specialist, keen English teacher and trainee Year Tutor, Andrew Bryant, returned home to his wife. Amelia greeted her husband on the doorstep with a kiss and drew him through to the kitchen to talk while she dished up their tea. His new class was an urgent priority. Was the next five years going to be rewarding, or a trashing battle?

"So what are they like?"

"Interesting. Does the name Schelle mean anything to you?"

"Questioned often, but neither arrested nor charged?"

"That is he, I have got his only daughter, only child, Rosalind. You could be forgiven for thinking that she is a beautiful, spoilt bitch, but I have it on a three-line whip that she is not. A year ago she was really nice, then something happened."

"Oh dear."

"Yes, it is always the first thought, is it not? But, the Junior School checked it out. It does not hang together."

"How not?"

He picked up the plates and carried them through to the table.

"Her Dad is often away on business, it began while he was away and if anything she is more settled when he is home and so the first thought is a long-odds, also-ran at the moment. I was seeded a minder for her, Jennifer Jackson, but Rosalind picked her up herself. Jennifer is an astonishing redhead. Not ginger, not bottle, but her very own bright red and a natural carer."

"Handy."

"The Keener twins, Jill and Jo, they are identical. A shapely little dish of a Mathematical genius, who hates Maths--"

"What?"

"Her Junior School could not keep up with her, they are worried they might have turned her off. It is okay; Stewart will take her into Mafematica."

"Any fans?"

"The first day is usually too early to tell, but not this year, there is a fan, slightly plump, but already growing it off. She is very pretty and authentic smitten, she has got it real bad, she is the one that you wrote the card for; she is in a wheelchair."

Amelia's eyes doubled in size.

"You've got three storeys!"

"She manages, it is not all the time, or even most of the time, lunchtime and when she gets tired, towards the end of the day. She just plods slowly up the stairs when she has to. She lost some schooling, so she is three years older than the rest, she does not look it, specifically, other than being taller and stacked. The boys are a mixed bunch, from quiet and mature, to knows he is the gift to the World."

"I used to hate them, going around in pairs with the nicest girls tagging after them to be doormats for fucking and fucked not that well either."

"There are two and they are already auditioning the doormats, but I am delighted to say that the girls who are responding are not the ones coming across as the nicest."

Buried Bodies: September 1982

Delia

The first chaotic week ended, by which time the school day had settled into a pattern. Every morning, Carly would come in from her reconnoitre down the girl's gymnasium corridor shaking her head sadly. Rosalind would fuss over her chicks unnecessarily. At ten past nine they would set off in phalanx formation to try to avoid being trampled in the human river flowing relentlessly along the corridors. Mr Bryant had been correct about the crowds and sizes of the pupils. Inside the corridors, Fifth Formers looked gigantic. Mostly, at those times when she needed her chair, Delia commuted from room to room outside the building, if she could, and quickly learned which areas to avoid entirely at lesson change. These were the stairwells and doorways where several flows of traffic came together and the one-way system saved lives daily.

Living in a wheelchair attracted plenty of attention. Being good looking, with a friendly outgoing personality, a quick brain and an ability to make lightning fast decisions, meant that the moths, once attracted, tended to stay around the candle, to get to know it better. It quickly became apparent that she also could keep secrets, so later, when the candle rolled in among gossiping moths, even those of her own age and older, in toilets and other meeting places, things were often said that maybe shouldn't have been said; and definitely wouldn't have been said in her presence, if it had been almost any other First-Year, instead of Delia.

Snippets varied from the seriously mundane,
    "--Smiffy borrowed Davison's bike. Without asking of course. Lost the pump, broke two spokes and picked up a slow puncture in the front tyre. If Davison ever finds out who borrowed it, he'll--"

to the seriously illegal,
    "--and have you heard, Georgie's got to leave, go to the

preggie unit."

"I didn't know she had a boyfriend."

"She hasn't. She baby sits for the next door neighbour; he's thirty-two."

"Oops, he could be in serious shit if the social --."

and,

"--so Mrs Peeze's boyfriend brought her home in his truck, he drives for The Goldsmiths?"

"Yes."

"And he left the truck open and that Hopkins, the younger one? First-Year."

"Evil little git."

"Yes, that one. He slid his hand in through the window, there were some silver chains on a display card behind a curtain--"

Plunging In: Warwickshire September 1982

Lovers

"Hello."

The reply of,

"It's me," produced an immediate change from professional to personal mode.

"Oh, hello. We got it. We got it for eight. Well, Ternimal Investments got it for eight, subject to contract of course, but I'm fairly sure. What about that builder of yours, is he really as good as you were saying?"

"There's a problem. Just, he's not cheap and he's not quick and he knows me and mine."

"Dangerous."

"Yes. Just, I've been having a rethink. There's one I've heard good reports of, reasonable quick job for cash money, I guess some of it doesn't go through the books."

"That would give us a buried body, if we ever needed one."

"Exactly. Just, we could conduct the business by telephone and through the Building Inspector. Never any need for us to get involved, personally, with contractors and stuff."

"I'll let you know when it's ours, so you can start telephoning. In the meantime, do you fancy checking it out again? This evening for instance?"

"I thought you'd never ask."

The Different: Tyne-dale September 1982

Delia

1AB quickly sussed out their teachers, The Good, The Bad, The Idle, The Weak, The Gullible, The Poser. A few fell into no simple category, Andrew Bryant, his friend and fellow First-Year Form Tutor, Stewart Baques and the Head, Ashley Deeps. The best way to describe them was, The Different.

The class also quickly sussed out Delia. Bad behaviour would get an admonishing look, then a pointed ruler and if that was ignored, a dressing down worthy of any Sergeant Major. With Carly, Rosalind and the rest of their troops, prepared to back the older girl completely, few dressings down were required after September. Their young, unsure and painfully shy, History teacher, received the brunt of the first message. As soon as he saw who it was, Jimmy Cragg began putting himself about, shouting, jumping, pulling hair.

"Cragg shut it!"

His reply of,

"What's the matter with ye? Boot!" Got the attention of most of the class.

"You! You're the matter! Back in your kennel or you'll be, like, looking for your dick!"

"What'll ye de like?"

"Anything she likes Cragg, because the rest of us will be holding you down," said Carly.

The message, that he'd allied everyone against him, got through, he began to wheedle,

"I know him. He's soft. We can have some fun."

"We're here to learn, you as well. Behave decently and learn, or change schools, you've, like, got a choice."

"Huh!"

"And an apology." Fred Waston normally didn't get involved in trouble, so his interjection carried significant weight.

"--Sorry."

47

"And you Delia." Murmured Jennifer.

"I wouldn't harm your dick; I would grass you for scrumping Pastor Benne's Apples. Sorry for threatening your dick, I just, like, need you to behave."

"That's fine then," summarised Jennifer.

"No, it's not, she'd grass me!"

"No, that's okay, I'd do that, can we all go back to work now?" replied the redhead, into a dumbfounded silence.

The class returned to their seats and sat waiting.

"Er, Right," said the astonished teacher. "Er, Saxon Britain. Er, by the start of the second millennium, which was 1001 AD. Remember that when the Media tells you the next millennium starts in the year 2000, they are lying, knowingly lying[2]; it is 2001. Well, by 1001 AD, Britain was still divided into several kingdoms. Can anyone name any of--"

On the second Tuesday of term, Rosalind was fussing about, unnecessarily getting her friends organised and Mr Bryant wanted to begin,

"Queen Bee, will you please let, I have a register to mark and much administration to do."

"Sorry Sir."

"Right, thank you. Ingrid?"

"Sir."

Because the name fitted so well up front and because, if you wanted to get at her, you could substitute the B for Bitch, instead of Bee for Bee, Rosalind's nickname stuck. Although only a few of the staff used it to her face, most of the students used it behind her back and for over four years, rarely fondly.

Mr Bryant took them for Personal and Social Education and got them to write up a personal Biography, including, where I want to be in ten years time.

Delia put her pen to the paper several times to write a

2   They did **exactly** that, and got away with it! The biggest Media Lie during my lifetime. Biggest that is until the Tsunami of Spin, Exaggerations, Lies, Damned Lies and Statistics associated with engineering the Brexit vote. *P.C.*

plausible lie, then went for it, truthfully.

Later, when Andrew marked the books, which had been laid on the pile open at the work, he turned to the front to see who had written,

I want my own restaurant, specialising in top quality English food and I want it complete with Michelin Stars.

and praised her quietly later for doing so.

"Well done Delia, do not worry if it takes you longer than a decade for the stars, I am sure you will get them, eventually."

Mr Baques took them for Chemistry.

"Right pay close attention to everything that goes on in this lesson, remembering it correctly next time will get merit marks. Open your exercise books and put the heading, 'Famous Scientists'." He reached forward and ostentatiously pressed the buttons on a tape recorder, clanged his bin twice and banged his blackboard three times.

"The single most important skill for a Scientist to have is to be truthful. You might think that obvious, but sadly, the prize is to the winner and second is nowhere. Can anyone give me an example from life?--Sporting examples are good for winner takes all--Yes Jennifer." He pressed the stop button.

"Everybody in this room will know The Toon won the FA Cup three times in five years, not many of us will be able to name the runners up."

"Well? The opponents anyone, all three of them?--A good example Jennifer, well done, just for the record, can you?"

"No Sir."[3]

Mr Baques nodded and continued,

"So the temptation, to win at all costs, is so great that people

---

3   Chronologically, Blackpool, Arsenal and Manchester City. Blackpool won it two years after their defeat and Manchester City the year after. The Gunners had to wait longer, but -- *P.C.*

cut corners, make intuitive deductions and occasionally see what they want to see, instead of what's there. Sometimes they may even be tempted to use other people's ideas. How many of you know the name Rosalind Franklin?"

Jennifer's hand went up.

"One." He surveyed the blank faces. "That's one more than I normally get. The names Watson and Crick?" This time there was a forest of hands. "Good. Jennifer can you explain the connection?"

"Dr. Franklin was working on DNA at the same time as Watson and Crick and had X-ray photographs that showed the helix, somehow she hadn't published the implications. The photographs were the missing piece in their theories for the other two. Watson and Crick took a punt, and published, and won the Nobel Prize. Nobody remembers it was Franklin's photographs, or the contribution of other people, Gosling or Wilkins or Pauling."

"Rosalind Franklin wanted to be sure and it cost her dear; Newton held up publishing about Gravity, because he couldn't prove his theory."

The redhead's hand was up again.

"Jennifer?" Again he pressed the buttons.

"Galileo didn't publish his results on acceleration, that distance travelled was proportional to time taken, because they didn't quite fit the equations. His friends said, 'Publish it's just experimental error.' He knew better."

"Tell me more, why didn't they fit?"

"It was his equations that were wrong."

"Merit Mark. Yes, Sadie?"

"It's time squared."

"Merit Mark. Anyone else?" Eager to gain merit marks, but unaware of why the other two had been given, the rest of their classmates were looking stunned. Mr Baques pressed his buttons again.

"The message I'm trying to get across is that it is vital to observe correctly and not be tempted into bending the results to fit. Even though by doing so you might get there first. For every Watson and Crick, there are a hundred alchemists who will turn lead into gold for you. Not! It's also a good idea to have a colleague to bounce ideas off, Dr Franklin was a loner, working alone is not usually good scientific--"

The lab technician ran into the lab squealing,

"I can't do this, I haven't got the time; it's only ten minutes to lesson change." He was wearing a top hat with a 10/6 sticker in the hatband.

"Get out!" shouted Mr. Baques, then pointed out of the window. "Oh! Is that a fire? Oh thank goodness it's not, just a lorry changing gear. Exercise books!--Write the names of five famous scientists, any famous scientists. Everybody should be able to do it; we've mentioned eight in the lesson. Now what they are famous for--"

Presently the lesson ended.

When they came into the room for their next Science lesson, there were papers on their desks.

Chapter 3
Paying Attention, Fan-Male And Female: Autumn Term 1982

Delia

"Leave your papers absolutely alone, don't touch them, instead listen carefully, I will play you the tape I made during the last lesson, It's only a minute and a half, then I will ask questions." He pressed buttons on a tape recorder:

Two bangs on the blackboard were followed by three clangs on the bin and that by Mr Baques voice,

"The single most important skill for a Scientist to have is to be truthful. You might think that obvious, but sadly, the prize is to the winner and second is nowhere. Can anyone give me an example from life?--Sporting examples are good for winner takes all--Yes Jennifer."

"Galileo didn't publish his results on motion, that distance travelled was proportional to time taken, because they didn't quite fit the equations. His friends said, 'Publish it's just experimental error.'He knew better."

"Tell me more, why didn't they fit?"

"It's time squared."

"Merit Mark. Yes, Sadie?"

"It was his equations that were wrong."

"Merit Mark. Anyone else?"

Mr Baques stopped the tape.

"Right, all the questions are about last lesson, you will see most of them begin, 'Last lesson.' Put your name on the top and answer the questions in the space provided. Turn your papers over and begin."

The questions were so easy it wasn't true.

'Last lesson: What was the first thing Mr Baques did after switching on the tape?'

'Last lesson: What was the last thing Mr Baques did before speaking?'

'Last lesson: Who got the merit mark for saying? "It's time squared?"'Delia stopped,

Wait a minute, something's not right here. She read through the rest, returned to the top and changed her answers.

'Last lesson: What did Sadie get her merit mark for?'

'Last lesson: What time did Mr Rickaby run in?

'Last lesson: Mr Rickaby's hat had a sticker with 1016 hanging from the brim. Rewrite correctly.'

'Last lesson: What was on fire?'

'Write a sentence about this exercise, stating an important, relevant fact about it.'

Delia reread her answers carefully, the only one she wasn't sure about was the time Mr Rickaby ran in, it can't have been with only ten minutes left, she squashed 'about' in front of her answer.

After a little thought, she wrote,

The evidence was tampered with,

and is, therefore, unreliable.

as her final sentence.

Delia, along with five others, earned a merit mark for getting more than seven right answers and her final sentence correct, but Jennifer earned two for getting everything right, even to the time of Mr. Rickaby's part, she'd checked on her watch. {pp394}

Three weeks later, when Mr Rickaby and Miss Algood interrupted Mr. Baques lesson with a sword fight, Delia not only jotted down notes immediately afterwards, but also kept looking about her, so she, as well as Jennifer, recorded the time; saw Mr Baques change his jacket; and hide a microscope. They both scored two merit marks for all answers correct the following lesson.

It must have been about this time that Mr Baques first called the tall, dark, quietly dominant, born leader in his form, by the nickname Big Mamma.

The name fitted so well that it wasn't long before everyone did, pupils and staff alike, although to her face she was usually Shirley, Shirley Jayne Swyfte.

She too, inevitably, collected a comet tail of admirers, but whoever else was around, the inner circle was Anna; blonde and pretty heir apparent to the Monta Industries Empire; Samantha, the tiny working girl; and her barely any bigger friend Kerry; Laura, the tallest and most stunningly beautiful girl in the School; and a couple more blondes, Sally; and Shelley a dual personality, autistic savant of few words, who's alter ego drew and painted sex. A bowl of fruit, Seascape or even a single mountain rising out of mist, were all dripping with pulsating sex, made even more vibrant, because they appeared to move.

With the best will in the World, people are not always available for their commitments and one Art lesson, they had Mr Bryant on relief for their usual teacher. It was all arranged beforehand, so the pupils had their work and knew what to do. Delia could see that her friend was getting agitated and with whom and that Mr Bryant was about ready to jump in. She decided to get in first,

"Kim, what's the problem, between, like, you and Rosalind?"

"She gives me dirty looks. She's done it again. She's always doing it."

"She's not looking at you," whispered Jennifer. "It's her eyes, they look sideways, to her right, so she seems to be looking at you when really she's looking past you," she graphically flicked the red bunches sideways. "Have you never noticed how often people she's talking to, turn to look behind them?"

"I do it continually, look over my shoulder and she's talking to me, but she, like, never looks at me."

"She is, it just doesn't feel like it. If you give her a chance, she'll tell you herself. She's looking at the Ash tree," she pointed out of the window. "She's drawing it."

The tree, easily identifiable from its surroundings, was taking shape on Rosalind's paper.

"I'll do it," Delia said to Kim. "You're too cross, leave it to me, you, like, just listen." Delia hobbled over and stood across the table from, but directly in front of Queen-Bee.

Rosalind looked up, scowled at her and then moving in angry, jerky movements, rubbed out part of a branch on her tree. She looked up and scowled at Delia again. Then, she redrew a small part of the scene.

"I came across because I thought you were looking at me, I thought you, like, wanted something." Almost the whole class was waiting for Rosalind's answer. They got it, before she spoke.

She looked up, startled. She obviously hadn't even known Delia was standing almost in touching distance. Her head turned, her focus shortening down, her attention was clearly over Delia's right shoulder.

"No. I'm drawing that tree," she pointed straight at the tree while her eyes darted momentarily to Delia.

"You're giving it dirty looks."

The scowl returned,

"It keeps growing extra bits, I look away to draw it and when I look back, it's grown extra bits!"

The whole class burst out laughing. Rosalind glanced about, confused,

"What?"

"It's true then. You don't look at what you're, like, looking at."

"I do." She turned her head to her left, slowly her eyes drifted, presently they were looking at Delia. "You probably think I'm looking at you now."

"Yes."

Rosalind rotated the other way, until she was looking out of the left corners of her eyes.

"I'm still looking at you."

Delia shook her head, extending her right arm out sideways. "No. Over here."

"The World is full of Mad People who don't know when I'm looking at them."

"Mad people and me Queen Bee," interrupted Mr. Bryant. "But, it does give an idea how misunderstandings can occur and wars start for no reason. Are you quite satisfied now?" His eyes roamed over everyone, but the principal had turned away.

He collared her later,

"Well?"

Kim didn't answer.

"Well?" he insisted strongly. "At least you are not still claiming she gives you dirty looks. I have a class-full of pretty girls, with the World at their feet, but two of them walk around all day with their faces tripping them up. You nearly made a big mistake today, you hate yourself Kim and by accident you nearly took that hatred out on the only other girl in your class, who is as unhappy as you."

That got through; she reared up ready for battle.

"Oh yes she is, Rosalind hates herself, just as you do. And, for the record, when she takes it out on other people I tackle her about it too." Delia reached out and linked her friend.

"I'll try to talk some sense into her, Sir."

"You do that and while you are on, tell her how often Jennifer has to talk some sense into Rosalind."

They walked together, Delia pace, in silence, presently the arm she was holding relaxed.

"Go on then."

"No need, like, you've already done it."

"I'm sorry."

"If you need somebody to shout at, shout at me, I won't, like, take any notice."

"Does Rosalind hate herself, d'y'think?"

"Bad, worse than you. She might kill herself one day and she probably knows how."

"Yes, she's top of Chemistry."

"So shout at me, not her, then you won't have a death, like, on your conscience."

"I'm sorry."

"It's, like, okay."

The following day they all met at the bottom door of East Block. There was an uncomfortable silence for a few seconds, broken suddenly when Robert Davison barged into the group, spoiling for a fight and challenged Rosalind.

"What you giving Kim dirty looks for?"

Shocked, angry and totally wrong emotioned, Kim spluttered, "She's not."

Rosalind squared up, claws out.

"Eh. What for?" Before Queen Bee could reply, Kim pushed between them,

"She's not. What's the matter with you?"

Jennifer pulled Rosalind away from Robert's threatening fists, his shouts followed her. Kim grabbed his arms, he shrugged her off and in short order they were shouting at each other. Delia turned away,

I only hope I don't ever end up fighting with my man like that.

The row followed the same predictable pattern as all the rest, after a couple of days sulking, Robert allowed Kim to apologise to him and friendly relations were restored.

At registration Carly bounced into the form room, bursting with news,

"The lists are up for netball trials." She hastily extricated her pen from her pencil case. "Who else besides me and Jeanette?"

"Us two!"

"Me!

"Me," said Delia, Ingrid and Marjorie simultaneously.

Carly hurried away, pen rampant, before the elusive lists vanished again.

The six friends turned up to the hockey and netball trials, but things didn't quite go according to plan. It was a tightly controlled but excited group that turned up for trials, Delia in her wheelchair earned some questioning looks, and not just from the pupils. As they trooped out to the court the first niggles of doubt flickered in the Delia's head. A dozen girls were clustered around Mrs. Stonker like close buddies. They were the ones nominated to carry the balls and slings, and the teacher knew all their names, but repeatedly had to ask other girls for theirs. The buddies were split up into two teams, and those left over were instructed to wait at the side to be called

"Aren't we going to warm up?" Said Delia and was ignored.

"Well I have to," the disabled girl added and heaved herself out of her chair and began a complicated warm-up exercise routine. Kim joined her while watching her friend in a concerned manner. The other four joined in. From time to time team members were exchanged with buddies on the touchline. Eventually, Carly was called in.

" Helendale take over centre."

" I'm a shooter miss."

" You are what I tell you; you are centre. You what's your name? Girl with the bad foot?"

"Delia Summers Miss"

"You play goalkeeper."

"I'm a Wing Attack, Marjorie is our goalkeeper, Miss."

"I told you, I decide who plays where."

After a few minutes more Mrs. Stonker called them all together and gave them her squad talk.

"Right I've seen enough--"

"Miss we haven't been on court," said Ingrid waving at herself and Jeanette.

"I've seen enough to make up my mind, it's not enough to be good you have to look good too, there are other things as well, Deportment, Breeding. They all matter. Don't ask why you were dropped, think it through instead, if the cap fits you, wear it."

Delia glanced down at her right foot. It was encased in a trainer three sizes smaller than the left, with the toe pointed to the ground as usual, to allow her to stand straight.

She un-looped the red sling from around her shoulder and dropped it into the slings box beside the netball post. She looked Mrs. Stonker straight in the eye and adjusted an imaginary cap,

"I wear it with pride, Miss." Then she turned and limped away.

Carly peeled her sling off, the other four also dropped their slings into the box,

"Six of your very best players are walking off the court, Miss, and you haven't even **seen** two of them play."

When Mrs Stonker declined to reply to Carly's reprimand, they all followed Delia, without another word.

It was the week before half term, when the first occasion that the unusual openness and candour about their sexuality occurred. It was something that became a familiar characteristic of the Year. There were many girls having lunch on the grass, Delia, while waiting for her friends, was chatting to Rosalind's little group.

Queen Bee arrived late and sat down with,

"I've just come down from Mr Baques' classroom, Sally's just asked Shirley and them who's virgins and they're telling her." Sadie Parker half surfaced out of 'Famous Mathematicians' and whilst still reading, stuck a finger in the air and said,

"Not me, but never again, I'm going to stick with girls in future." The stunned silence that followed, took her out of her book. "What?"

"Did you mean that?" said Rosalind.

"Yes, I bloody do! For two days in the Summer I thought I was knocked up, I was scared shitless."

"And sticking with girls?"

"Yes, probably, I think so." Belatedly she must have realised that this might be a hard pill for friends who were girls and straight. "It's okay, don't panic, I have no designs on any of you, you're straight, not my type at all. But being shagged by a boy was a non event for me, so I'm looking for a nice gay girl; hopefully, sex with her will be at least as exciting as jilling off."

Predictably, it was Jennifer who replied, she leaned across to their little Mathematical genius, cuddled her head and clucked mother hen over her.

"Not virgin either," said Delia. "But, boys are my thing, haven't found the right one yet, but, like, I'm having fun looking."

Everyone chuckled at the older girl, as Jennifer continued,

"I hope you find her soon Sadie," then she kissed the shapely little blonde on the temple and added. "But that still leaves five to go, Virgin, only because I've never been asked."

"Virgin," said the Keener twins together,

"Virgin," said Jane, with Rosalind adding,

"Me too," at the end.

When she could, Delia asked Rosalind privately,

"Queen Bee, did Samantha, like, say anything?"

"Everything, burst into tears, but they rallied around, hugged her 'n that."

That other people had witnessed the incident became evident later.

Among the juicy titbits that came Delia's way in the toilets daily were:

"Did you know Harry the Humper's got the hots for the tall one of the First Year Toffs, the brilliant mountaineer."

"Laura? Plays volleyball?"

"Yes that one."

"Well, he's in for a nasty shock when she says, 'No! But, have you got a sister?'"

"Yes. I'm surprised he doesn't know; she makes no secret of it."

And;

"Talking of the First Year Toffs, I hear Samantha told them how she earns her money and they were okay about it," the voice of ex-classmate Gillian, drifting out of a cubicle, along with clouds of smoke.

"I knew they would be," replied the school's top hard case, Sara. "Shirley's a good kid and that Anna Monta's a wild child, all blonde and butter wouldn't melt, but you look carefully into her eyes; they made her a junior instructor at the fight club."

"Humph! They told Sam not to call herself a prostitute. She's a working girl."

"And you make sure you do as well, I don't ever want to hear you call yourself a hooker again."

"Yessumistress."

And the following day;

"We were talking of the toffs yesterday, I've just seen little Anna Monta break up a fight, well not a fight, Hopkins was stuffing little Jimmy Teale, she stopped him good."

"Can the evil jelly walk?"

"Limping, yes just."

"She must have held back then, I told you, they made her a junior instructor at the club, her and Shirley. Shirley's even tougher."

"Blood 'n sand! She just sorted him and she wasn't even looking at him, watching MacAuk instead, but MacAuk didn't interfere, just asked her to stop, told her she'd hurt him enough."

"Well, MacAuk knows not to take her on, he's a member of the club too."

Registration in Delia's Form Room was a chance to catch up on gossip or homework, provided that didn't mean just mindlessly copying it; or occasionally put the World to rights. As usual, the girls were arguing, but unusually, things were getting heated.

Mr Bryant had glanced up several times, apparently holding himself in check to keep out of it, the argument had been going on for several minutes, non the less raging in its intensity for it being conducted in whispers. Delia decided she needed another opinion.

"Sir which is worse, Sex or Stealing?"

"They are both wrong in the wrong place."

"Stealing is always, like, wrong. Surely." Her eyes were narrowed, her claws coming out, not least because her idol was showing clay feet.

"A brigand has stolen crops and children are going to die tomorrow if you do not feed them tonight. Would you steal those crops back from him, to feed those children?"

Delia didn't even bother to dilute with words, the answer in her eyes.

"Would you steal from me, today, to feed you now?"

"Of course not."

"So the line lies somewhere between. For the record, I believe you and **agree** with you; I might even agree that stealing is **always** wrong, but I might do it, under certain circumstances. I might choose to do wrong for good reason, but it is **still** wrong."

She should have known, no need to get her tits in a chaos, circumstances alter cases, specifically which way the rabbit jumps, but fundamentals remain.

"So which is worse, sex or stealing?"

"I can not say. You must decide and choose for yourself, I think all sex that is forced, or by deception, or the like is wrong. But, sex that is agreed, that is not hurting anyone, is basically okay--"

"It's fornication." Kim's interruption was spat at him.

"Possibly, it might involve betrayal, hurtful deception, treachery, but none of those have anything to do with the sex. It is the betrayal that is wrong, not the sex; the sex was just the mechanism by which someone was betrayed. I have heard people betrayed in this room, by words. There is nothing wrong with words, the wrong was using them to betray."

A few heads turned, looking at others in a pointed manner.

That day Robert discovered a cleaner's cupboard that was usually left unlocked.

With a secluded place to work on her every night, it wasn't long before he had worn down Kim's resistance. Delia would wheel herself through the School, until she found Mr. Bryant and then spend a lovely half hour talking with her Form Tutor, while waiting for her friend. There was, however, a worrying aspect about the whole affair. Her time with Mr. Bryant was uplifting, she went home thrilled, Kim quite the reverse. Delia couldn't understand it, half an hour with Ben riding her around the hayloft, left her feeling wonderful. Why was Kim so grumpy? It was so bad one night she decided to raise the matter.

"Are you shagging him?"

"Well --"

"Are you pregnant?"

"No, he always uses a condom."

"Well, what's the problem, are you feeling guilty? You know, like, Sex is Disgusting."

"No!--Yes--I don't know."

"I've been shagging Ben for months. I know I didn't tell you, but it's, like, true. But, it makes me feel good, not unhappy."

"I can't see what all the fuss is about. Painful! Grunting! Messy! Rubber duck does me better in the bath every night and I don't have to walk home wearing soaked knickers." The silence stretched out. "You've gone quiet."

"Sorry, I come with my boy every time, I just, like, assumed everybody did."

"You get the feeling, when you're shagging?"

"Every time--Sorry."

At home time the following day, 1AB came down from Chemistry, mingling with 1SB coming down from Physics. Kim and Robert set off for their cupboard. Delia retrieved her chair from under the stairs, but then held back to allow the crush to ease. When she pushed herself out through the doors she found Shirley Swyfte waiting to one side, idly watching Rosalind's little group of friends taking leave of each other.

"Goodbye," said Rosalind and set off towards the East gate.

"Why are you going that way?"

"I have to keep my clothes clean, the bottom path's too muddy."

"Oh. Yes, course."

"Goodbye."

Rosalind's friends, scattered towards their several destinations, while she set off home, obediently the long way round, avoiding the track that led to the field, to protect her new clothes. The School Minibus came by and squelched through a puddle, Rosalind jumped backwards in alarm.

Delia watched as the curving wave of mud changed its course in mid air, chasing the little brunette.

Desperately she dodged, to no avail.

The mud homed in and drenched her legs.

The brand-new knee socks weren't white any longer.

Ronnie Sakes laughed, hyena like, right in her face as he ran past.

The tears and anger, frustration and humiliation in Rosalind's eyes, were threatening to overwhelm her.

"Rosalind!" The call came from behind the mud-splattered girl. As Delia and Shirley watched, Rosalind pretended not to hear.

"Rosalind Schelle!" The second call was more insistent, she turned ready to scratch and bite; the boy stepped nearer. "Don't worry, they'll wash. I'm always falling in mud, they'll wash. They'll be as good as new tomorrow."

The watchers saw the kindness envelop Rosalind and the tension flow away as the thoughtfulness engulfed her.

He wasn't very tall. He had a round face with nice teeth and a caring smile, so unusual for a boy. All her anger and humiliation flowed away out of her body posture. The tears and frustration were safely bottled up.

A black-cloaked figure walked past between the pair, looking at Rosalind. Even with her oblique view, Delia caught the smirk on his face. Rosalind's eyes shortened focus to just past his right shoulder.

The healing effects of the care were wiped away, as if they had never been,

"I didn't fall!" she spat back.

The words had stung; Delia could see the hurt in the boy's eyes. Rosalind turned away, almost bumping into Shirley. Although Big Mamma had obviously heard the proffered, caring-support being savagely rejected, she said nothing, just regarded Rosalind steadily. Rosalind looked back at the boy, she half raised her hand and breathed in to call, but it was too late; he was walking disconsolately away, if anything she now looked even more wretched. Queen Bee walked off home, avoiding Shirley's eyes, her head down, wings drooped, the picture of dejection.

"Who was that? The boy, I, like, know who the Angel of Death was," asked Delia.

"Timmy Ebsenter, he's in my Form."

"Oh so that's him. He was in Kim's class at juniors, he's, like, quite bright, isn't he?"

"Especially at Science."

"Rosalind has a fan-club."

"Well, she did have. Probably still does. What's Pastor Benne doing here, I wonder?" Big Mamma was staring after the retreating figure in its sinister garb,

"Ogling young crumpet, he's always around if there's a chance of a glimpse of knickers," replied Delia, with narrowed eyes, also tracking the cloak clad figure. "The foot clinic's opposite Cathedral High. Their netball court front's onto Gosbury Main Street, I've often seen him loitering there when, like, there's a match on."

It was only later that Delia realised that Shirley had thought it unnecessary to introduce herself; she told the girl who lives in her mirror.

"She knew it wasn't needed, that I would know who she was. I don't know whether that shows, like, arrogance, or thoughtfulness."

Did you say who you are?

"--Er, no."

* * *

The First Years were taught dancing in PE after half term. Not the complicated, thinking on your feet driving, of the waltz or quickstep, but the stereotyped, more controlled, Barn Dances. The climax of the course was The Christmas Party, where the skills would be used in anger for the first time for most pupils.

Learning to dance, whilst publicly castigated and scorned, specifically by the more clumsy boys to maintain street cred, was revealed as being a secretly, sinfully, coveted skill, by the determination displayed in mastering it.

With Carol Services, Pantomimes and four other parties to fit into a limited number of nights, the First-Year Christmas Party was on the Friday, two weeks before the end of term. It was long anticipated and awaited with very mixed feelings by most pupils,

Classrooms had been set-aside near the main hall, to be used as cloakrooms. Mr. Baques was on duty at the time, he chatted Delia up as she titivated herself and checked the decorations on her chair.

"Have you any party tricks you can do in that?"

"Like, watch this space, man!"

He laughed as she manoeuvred the chair among the desks deliberately choosing a tortuous route to demonstrate her steering skills. She stopped among the girls from his form and curtseyed to him still in the chair. He grinned back at her and then watched utterly expressionless, as all Laura's friends took turns to snog the tall girl under a sprig of mistletoe.

"Laura!" Called Big Mamma, intercepting her on her way to join the queue for the mirror. "Here a minute." When she came close, Shirley produced the mistletoe and held it over her head, then used that arm around her neck and the other around her waist. Laura stood woodenly, until Shirley gently pushed her tongue into her, then she slid her arms around her, her body melting against her. When Shirley finished she said. "Merry Christmas Dear," softly straight into her friend's eyes. Most of the girls, like, Delia, watched with interest. Anna followed her friend and kissed Laura with gusto and the rest of their friends followed Anna's example, with Shirley holding the mistletoe above Laura's head. A few girls watched wide eyed, Sadie Parker watched avidly, wide eyed.

When Laura had calmed down from Sally's efforts, Shirley gave her the mistletoe, cuddled her head and whispered into her ear, whilst looking at Delia. That the disabled girl could hear the conversation obviously didn't bother her.

"When you get a chance, go to kiss Sadie under this, you just might get a surprise!" She tightened her grip. "No don't look around she's looking this way, pick your time carefully, little Sadie in AB, good at Maths." Laura nodded, as she took the proffered sprig with its pearlescent white berries and grey-green leaves.

Chapter 4
Ri{gh}t{e}s: December 1982 - March 1983
Delia

The First-Year Christmas Party was a mixture of games and dances. Mr Bryant and Mr Baques patrolled around, chivvying the boys to get the girls up for the dances. The third dance of the evening, when they began to walk around the hall, there was no-one left to chivvy. Their Year Tutor let the DJ play pop music and requests, after the interval. The entire floor was occupied with groups of dancers of mixed sexes. This was probably due mainly to the two teachers' earlier efforts. Delia had been dancing her wheelchair to the music, doing wheelies and showing off a bit and took a break to rest and take on liquid. From time to time, others did too.

Laura chose one of those times to make her move. She stood up, extricated herself from the ring of chairs around Big Mamma, walked straight over to little Sadie, who was sitting near Delia and bent down to speak with her; she had to shout because the music was loud.

"Would you care to dance with an old dyke?"

Sadie stood up, shaking her head and laughing,

"You're not old!" And she backed out from among Rosalind and company to join Laura, on the dance floor. They danced, talked and laughed for several minutes.

One of Sakes' mates saw them and headed across towards them.

"Anna, watch my back-," said Shirley.

"Right behind you!" she interrupted.

The low life was waving his arms in the air shouting,

"Lesie Alert."

Shirley crossed her arms, grabbed his wrists from behind and crucifixed, spinning him hard around.

Sakes ran at her from behind. Anna stepped in beside him, shook her hips and the obnoxious little creep flew over a chair upside down past Shirley's right shoulder, before she, in turn, whipped his mate over to land in a sprawled heap on top of him. She leaned over and told them to leave Laura and Sadie alone, or she would really hurt them. They heard; it was little more than their precious little egos that were sore, although a few muscles would complain on the morrow.

Delia had to smile, the rumours about little Anna Monta not being someone to cross with impunity and Big Mamma being arguably the best alley-style fighter in the year, were demonstrably true. By the time Shirley had turned around. Anna was standing behind her, balanced on the balls of her feet in a classic combat ready stance, one hand near her chin the other across her waist, facing the other two of Sakes' mates. She was half their individual size, but many times their combined fire-power and she and they all knew it. The fight died out of their eyes and body postures.

"Okay Anna, you can let them through. You! Bring those two straight to Mr. Baques."

The new couple disappeared and when Jennifer and Rosalind went looking for Sadie, Delia tagged along on her way to the toilet. Sadie had taken Laura down to the bottom stairwell to snog her and Anna and Shirley were watching out for them. They had a quick look through the door.

Laura had put Sadie up one step, to cancel some of their height difference and was dry grinding the shorter girl, who was loving it. Sadie's hands were caressing her lovers face and hair as she kissed her intensely. Laura's hands were on Sadie's bum, pulling her on, as they watched she slid her hands down to the hem of Sadie's dress and back up again under the dress, Sadie wriggled with pleasure and intensified her kisses. They withdrew from the fire doors and waved goodbye to Anna and Big Mamma,

"Well, at least somebody's getting theirs tonight," said Jennifer. Delia giggled and dived into the loo.

Just before the end of the party, Sadie caught Delia,

"I can't find everybody, can you tell them Laura's taking me home. We're going now, making an early start."

"Have you, like, found her then?"

"Oh man. Yes! With train whistles!"

A couple of minutes later Delia found Jennifer cleaning up some litter, which she was sure the redhead's group hadn't dropped,

"Laura's taken Sadie home, they've already gone, she said to tell you."

"Oh. Good."

"Can you, like, tell Queen Bee?"

"Yes, I'll tell her."

The following Monday when Laura and Sadie met, they kissed like lovers, right in front of everybody and although they then separated, to be with their own friends for much of the day, it quickly became understood that an arrangement with one, was understood to be with both.

They quizzed Sadie quite ruthlessly about Laura and she rightly told them to go and fuck a monkey and leave her to fuck her Angel. The stars in her eyes and the way she lit up when she saw Laura coming, completed the story.

The last afternoon of term was forms to Form Tutors and Mr. Baques agreed to 1SB bringing food and drink for an afternoon party, instead of a lunch. Shirley asked him whether Sadie and her mates could come also, which would also bring the sex split up nearer parity. His only demur was,

"What will the rest of 1AB think about only half a dozen

going?"

"No. All of them, I meant all of 1AB."

"No Problem then, I'll have a word with Mr. Bryant, but I think you can take it as arranged."

They had a combined PSE lesson to share out the food requirements. Anna Monta offered canapés, Sadie Real Ginger Beer. Delia nominated herself for Pigs in Blankets.

"Pigs in Blankets! And that's supposed to make you want to eat one is it?" Robert Davison's scornful snort, intended as always to humiliate and maim. But,

"That's okay Robert, we, like, wont force you to have one." Allowed their teachers to continue without remonstrating with the boy. They ended up with a reasonably balanced show because every time someone didn't know what to bring, Anna or Delia suggested something savoury. Morning School finished at 12.30 and the binge followed at 1.00 pm.

The teachers organised lots of games whose primary raison d'être seemed to be an excuse to jump and dash about, shout a lot, contort yourself like a boa constrictor, burst balloons, or avoid getting wet. The kids loved it and threw themselves into it with a level of gusto that ensured that whereas most objectives were a resounding success, the last was an abysmal failure. It was still going strong at 2.15 when Mr. Baques had to call a halt because the school was finishing early for the End of Term.

When Timmy Ebsenter, very bright, nice but silly, went over the top about Anna's canapés, comparing them to less spectacular offerings, she really went for him.

"You're Gross, do you know that, canapés are easy, all you need is money and I've got pots of the stuff, it's no effort," she held up her glass of ginger beer and ham buttie. "Have you any idea of the dedication required to make these?" She raised her glass. "This is a living plant, it has to be nurtured and cared for, for weeks, just for one glass and this," she stuck the buttie under his nose. "Is home baked bread, you can't buy this, you have to make it and it takes years of painfully acquired experience to get it right."

Tim spluttered desperate and obviously genuinely contrite

apologies, which Anna accepted, she turned to the whole class,
"Congratulations everyone, we done ourselves proud!"

No more was said about individual contributions, they were one class. Anna's canapés had taken four nights of skilled work, Delia knew; she had been consulted before three of them. Fred Waston was standing near Delia; Timmy crept over beside his friend,

"I thought the canapés were Rosalind's," he murmured.

"You're trying too hard, just be yourself, you're okay when you're being yourself."

"The butties are mine."

"I know that, you know it, but nobody else does, just be yourself."

"She doesn't know I exist."

"That's better than her thinking you're a prat!"

Delia's Pigs in Blankets had needed research and preparation too. She cooked a rasher of bacon, to test it for taste and then steeped the remainder overnight to reduce their salt content. She dried each rasher individually, before wrapping the chipolata sausages in them. Once cooked, she added quartered Silverskin onions on half cocktail sticks as legs and cranberries on more half cocktail sticks for snout and tail. She waited until Robert had eaten one and obviously enjoyed it, before speaking with him.

"Pigs in Blankets, should really be eaten hot, but, like, they're quite passable cold."

"I wouldn't know, wouldn't touch one with a clothes prop."

"Funny that," said Carly. "Didn't stop you from just eating one." Linked Delia and drew her away.

Sadie was interested, almost mildly shocked that Anna knew about Ginger Beer plants. She mentioned it quietly to Laura while Delia was standing beside them,

"It's odd, you don't think about millionaires as being 'ordinary people', but Anna Monta is 'ordinary people' first and a millionaire second."

Her lover agreed.

"You wouldn't guess, money is just something that everyone has some of, but some more than others, she hardly ever mentions it. I heard the rumours and looked her up, the rumours were understatements, she's a multimillionaire in her own right and her Dad is worth even more, but you'd never guess."

Sadie spent the party on Laura's lap, sometimes sitting primly across her knee, holding their plate, with Laura's arm around her waist, whilst they each ate with their free hand. At other times she lay back against her lover, her legs spread on either side of Laura's, her head leaning against Laura's shoulder, with her lover's hands linked just south of her tits and sometimes not quite just south! This did not mean they withdrew into their own world, quite the reverse, they joined in everything, sometimes on opposing teams, but during the lulls they coalesced again like a pair of oppositely charged pith balls.

Delia studied their teachers' reactions; they chose not to recognise that there was anything unusual going on, as if a twelve-year old pair of lesbian lovers, making love to each other in their every glance and word, was a common occurrence, at a party, in a classroom.

The other two pairs from AB lasted right through School until the Fifth form, but then parted company; things were quite fractured for a while.

Laura and Sadie were an item at every social event they ever attended together, yet in school, during the ordinary running of the school day, nobody would have guessed that there was anything between them, other than a close friendship.

After Christmas, the dark and cold, early nights meant there was a greater chance of finding Mr. Bryant in School. Delia sussed out where he was likely to be on any given night and seldom took long to find him.

* * *

Student teachers in Training Colleges are given the chance to show that they are either born, or will in time make it, or will never make it no matter what, at real chalk faces, in real Schools. This traumatic introduction to the reality of caring for between thirty and fifty of somebody else's children, goes by the utterly mundane title of Teaching Practice. During the Spring Term, several students were given placements in the West Novochester for Teaching Practice.

1AB were unlucky enough to get a never in Maths, but fate balanced the scales by supplying a deliciously pretty and athletic, born, in PE. The students observed for a week and then took over, being watched occasionally by the regular teacher.

The Mathematician disappeared after his first lesson alone and much to Miss Rogers' annoyance, he didn't reappear until the following week.

"Where were you last week?" asked Carly.

"In London. That new Education Initiative the Government is railroading through, that's designed to grind the Workers down. I had to go to lobby MPs. I'm on the Student's Union Committee." The kids looked blank, uncomprehending. "That's why they're getting away with it, because you don't see them doing it. Oh--Why bother?"

"Sir, I thought you were a Maths teacher?" Little Sadie, mature and confident, as well as an out of the closet lesbian, was also proving to be easily the finest mathematician in the School, staff included. Having been plucked from a siding and reset back on the main line, she wasn't going back.

"I need a teaching qualification to climb the ladder in the NUT and enter politics that way, somebody's got to stop them, I can't be bothered with this all my life." He waved about the classroom.

"Well, I for one don't think that's very commendable. I want to learn my subject."

"And so do the rest of us Sir," put in Jennifer. "So now that you are here, can we please have a lesson?"

Delia had to stifle a laugh at his thunderstruck expression, but Miss Rogers' lessons were fun and packed with good, solid meat; when you are used to the best, an empty poser quickly shows up for what he is.

A Second Barn: Warwickshire Spring 1983

Lovers

Because the Barn Conversion was being carried out under a sound roof, it continued, uninterrupted by bad weather, right through the winter. The only down side, from the lover's point of view, was that they no longer had a secure and private nest for their trysts.

"There's another barn come onto the market, would solve our problem, but you'd have to buy it, all my money's in the first one."

"How much? Just, I haven't got that much left."

"I'll put an offer in, test the water, but you'll need to see it, see if you want to buy. Tonight? Heater, air bed?"

"Pick me up at the usual place, eight o'clock."

"I brought some wine, it's in that bag there, bring it in would you? And I've been on to the vendor, they want eight, but I reckon, seven and a half, or even possibly seven, for a quick sale"

"Oh. Just, I could probably manage that."

Changes: Tyne-dale Spring 1983

Delia

Mr Baques' after school Maths Club was proving to be a welcome relaxation from the usual hard slog Mathematics of the normal curriculum. Delia had never regarded Maths as a strong tool in her box, but Sadie pleaded with her and encouraged her to go,

"You're really good, just, you're better at English, but you're still good enough for Mafematica." Sadie as usual, on things Mathematical, was right.

After a few PE lessons their student pulled Delia,

"I've noticed you've got very strong arms, what athletics do you do?"

"I don't like athletics Miss."

"Javelin, Shot, Discuss?"

"Don't know Miss, I've never, like, done them. I like netball, but I'm not supposed to be able to do anything, so I don't."

"She's good Miss Cape, got a netball brain, but she's not allowed."

Their friends were gathering behind Carly, murmuring their agreement, backing her assessment of Delia's ability.

"Doctors know best."

"Not doctor Miss. Like, lack of fit in the face."

"Come after School on Thursday, all of you, we'll have a netball practice, you can show me."

"Thursday Miss Cape. We'll be there," said Carly, as usual in anything to do with sport, assertively taking charge and led her group through into the changing room.

Delia wasn't sure,

"Caps-you-fits-you hates me so much she'll, like, turn on the rest of you even more!"

"We're going, we're doing this for us! What could she do to us that she hasn't already done?" asked Jeanette.

"We're going and she can boil her head. Full PE kit on Thursday everyone, we're having a proper PE lesson!"

Jeanette's and Carly's assertive trampling all over any demurs about attending, ensured that on Thursday night all six turned up to the gym and reported to Maureen Cape. They were taught to warm up correctly, practice moves and turns and throwing accuracy and then played a little match against imaginary opponents, performing moves worked out in advance.

"What positions do you like to play?"

"We've got a full team Miss, except for centre."

"Okay. I'll play centre. Goalkeeper?--Okay Marjorie, you have the ball, stand by your goal. Goal defence?--Kim on the edge of the D. Wing Defence?--Ingrid over here."

The girls were set out in their positions and practised getting the ball from goalkeeper to netted goal using one touch precision.

Miss Cape coached them constantly.

"Hard flat throws--Always aim for the head, never the feet."

And,

"That was brilliant," as for the third time in a row the ball flashed from the keeper to the shooter through all seven players and was perfectly netted. "Now, we will try some moving moves. Aiming wide of the receiver." The first dozen were understandably chaotic, but Miss Cape focussed the reaction,

"That's one nil to The Cathedral."

"Phwa!"

"No Way!"

"C'mon girls we're not having that!"

"Two nil."

"Zeech!"

"C'mon, get that ball!"

"That was better. But it's still two nil."

"Two one. Brilliant, another one straight away."

When Miss Cape called a halt it was four two, Carly grabbed the ball and stood directly in her way.

"How dare you invent a defeat for us, especially at the hands of The--The--**The Cathedral**."

Miss Cape laughed, cuddled the younger girl close and kissed her on the temple,

"Next time you'll try harder."

"I hate you."

"No, you don't, you love me really."

They walked off the court, with their arms around each other.

"D'y'want to try for your revenge tomorrow night?"

"Of course!"

Carly was shooed into the changing room, with a smack on her bottom and,

"Same time, same place, tomorrow night."

The following night they drew four all, with their cordially much-hated, imaginary opponents and by Easter, were beating them regularly, twice a week.

With half term came tests and setting in core subjects. Delia and her friends found themselves sharing a classroom with half of Stewart Baques registration form and a sprinkling of other people. A slightly built, very shy boy quickly showed himself to be a gifted Mathematician and, if Jeanette were his side of the horizon, a gormless, shaking, physical wreck. Sadie asked him why he didn't go to Mafematica.

"What's that?"

"The Maths club. Mr Baques' Maths Club. Jeanette goes."

"Oh. Right."

Jonathan turned up to Mafematica and obviously enjoyed it, but Jeanette reported back that they rarely spoke, except on Mathematical Topics. A situation she found very frustrating.

"He just looks and he's lovely, I wish he'd ask."

"Oh Jeanette, can I see your tits?" said Marjorie lasciviously.

"I'd peel. I'd peel to the buff. I'm going to write a notice on my belly, just in case, with an arrow, stick it in here!"

For a moment Jeanette's friends laughed, then

"It's not funny girls, she's, like, serious."

Discipline hadn't always been perfect in their lessons, although in response to Delia's ready use of her ruler, it was never bad, but with Shirley Swyfte to glare at miscreants as well now, it was usually perfect. They were told that a new policy had been implemented, because there were so many good students, the English Department decided that they had had to create two top sets.

Rosalind wasn't buying,

"But they're not proper top sets, because I'm a second set person, I'm not good like Delia or Big Mamma."

Fortunately, Mr Bryant overheard her,

"No Queen Bee you are selling yourself short again, you are not merely good, you are much better than that. I agree, you are not like Delia, she is brilliant, you are only very good, normal-top-set material. There are enough students of top set standard to fill nearly three sets, not one, and in Mathematics there is a super set."

"Sadie."

"Well, there is Sadie and a super set and a normal top set."

"Sir, what is it that makes Sadie so good at Maths?"

"Well, Jennifer what is the answer?"

The redhead looked astonished,

"It was my question!"

"But, you, of all people, must know the answer. It is the same answer to the question, what is it that makes Jennifer so good at Ecology?"

"I'm not, not like Sadie is at Maths!"

"My guess is, in your field, you're better than I am in mine," said Sadie.

"Which would be difficult, but might just about be true," said Mr Bryant.

The bell blotted out Jennifer's protests and terminated the conversation.

The English lessons in the library, with its less formal, although hushed tones ethos, was usually a chance for discussing important matters outside the immediate friends circle:

Like,

"What's with the crash hat Shirley, going on a motorbike later?"

"No, dangerous things bikes, go-kart."

"She's going to kill herself Fred, I mean I've just persuaded her to move in with us and now she will kill herself, by trying to win the Kart Club championship at Lowdown," broke in Anna, mildly annoyed.

"I've heard about that circuit, it's vicious!"

"No, it's not," argued Big Mamma. "It's just one nasty corner in a dip. Reverse camber job, nowhere near as dangerous as your canoeing." She waved at Anna and Jennifer. "It's not called West **Wild** Water for nothing, that's dangerous!"

The redhead barged in before the little blonde could reply.

"Yes, it is, we're all mad," she said. "Except me." She gurned at them, tongue up inside her top lip, cross eyed and tickling herself under the armpits. The explosion of laughter, was hurriedly muted as they remembered where they were.

And,

"He's looking at you again," whispered Carly.

Jeanette blushed.

"Don't, he's shy, you'll put him off."

"Why don't you, like, ask him then?"

"I couldn't."

"My boy, I just grabbed hold of him and kissed him. He, like, took it from there."

"I couldn't!"

"It's no use Delia, they'll never get together," said Carly, resigned. "Neither of them will ever ask the other out, Jonathan's shy, but he's got nothing on this one."

"Write him a note. Make it plain you'll say yes. I'm sure that's all he'll need."

"What note?" Delia pushed some paper in front of the taller blonde.

"Write--Jonathan-comma, new line, just ask me nicely-comma, new line and I'll answer nicely-full stop. New line, Jeanette."

"It looks stupid."

"Let me see. No, it doesn't," she eased out.

"What are you doing?"

"What you should have done, like, days ago, weeks ago."

"Delia--Don't!" Delia continued to struggle out of the alcove. "Don't! I'll do it." Delia finally got out and straightened up holding the paper,

79

"Come on then?"

"Well, when I'm--no don't."

Delia had set off, swinging wide between obstacles and doggedly planting the clump on clear floor and folding the paper over twice, as she went. Jeanette hurried to clamber out after her,

"Wait, I'm coming."

Delia didn't stop until she reached Jonathan's table, then she held the paper out sideways cocked back past her elbow. Jeanette took it, placed it on Jonathan's book and scurried back to her alcove, with the cloud of blonde hair, framing cheeks on fire. Jonathan looked up.

"I think she'd like a move soon, like, outside, at lesson change."

He opened the note and read it,

"Oh, right."

Outside, at lesson change, the shy boy blurted it out before his courage ran down.

"Can I have a date?"

"Yes."

Delia took over as the rubber-neckers quickly grew to six deep,

"She'll see you in Mafematica, tonight, without, like, the audience."

The new pair nodded to each other and slowly the group broke up.

Rôle Play: Spring 1983
Amelia

As spring approached and the evenings began to lengthen out, Amelia engineered one of her adventures,

"How's the fan getting on, in her wheelchair? Still as fervent?"

"She comes to see me on her way home every night."

"Would you fuck her for me, I'd like that. The randy teacher fucking his favourite pupil story?"

"Okay."

"You'll have to bring me a new tie home, I couldn't salvage the last one when we couldn't get the knots out and you had to cut me loose. Bring a tie home and give her a torrid time on Saturday and a badge, blazer badge."

On Saturday, Andrew arrived home from his match pleasantly tired, a little sore from a couple of late challenges and with several muddy scrapes under the track suit. Amelia met him at the door in her fluffy dressing gown.

"The shower's ready for you, I've just been out of it a couple of minutes," she said, kissed him and ushered him towards the bathroom. He made full use of the toilet facilities, had a wet shave and a leisurely shower and emerged some time later, wrapped in his matching fluffy dressing gown and feeling exultant.

"Amelia."

"In here," called her voice from their bedroom. He looked in. A schoolgirl was sitting on their bed. She was dressed in a white blouse, gym-slip, knee socks and tiny black shoes with a strap and buckle. The front of the school blazer stuck out like a pair of open cupboard doors. It was many years since those doors had been able to close on their contents, assuming they ever had. Her hair was done in bunches and several large dark freckles were sprinkled across her nose.

She was wearing a West Novochester school tie. The tie was tied very loosely, to match the open neck of the blouse, with the unfashionably large, triangular, Windsor knot, hanging low between the swell of her breasts. Round her neck, suspended from a leather thong, peeping out between the broad Vee of the blouse, was a small polished wooden plaque.

The plaque read,

Delia

"Could you please help me?" She shrugged off the blazer. "My back's all prickling with itchy little spots, could you get them out for me, Sir? You can loosen clothes if you want. The gym-slip has buttons on the shoulders."

Andrew unbuttoned the gym-slip and allowed it to fall rucked down around her waist. Then, he tenderly pushed Delia's blouse up her back. His large, calloused, but surprisingly gentle hands caressed, feeling with feather light strokes for the tiny itchy spots, that you can feel easily but have to look closely to see. Every time he found the tell tale little pimple, he neatly dealt with it and soothed the tiny crater with little dusting caresses. The titillated girl knelt square on in the middle of the bed, on all fours, head down, submissive, acquiescing, waiting, tingling, squealing softly with the erotic pictures created by the sexy story being murmured into her ear.

"--and I said to you,
'Your brassiere is in the way.' And you said,
'Take it off, I do not mind.' So I took it off."

Three little clicks, were followed by the obstruction parting, the caresses became slow intimate sweeps from waist to neck.

"Then you said,
'The rest of my back is itchy too.' And I said,
'I will have to take your gym-skirt down.' And you said,
'Okay. I do not mind' so I took that off too."

The fittings took a few moments to solve, she neither hinted nor helped. The gym-skirt slid off, down, around her knees.

"You were liking it so much you said,
'If they are in the way you can take my knickers down too, I do not mind.' I wanted to see you naked and feel your bare bottom and fanny, so I peeled your grey school-regulation knickers off

you."

A thumb gently eased in each side under the waistband of the knickers and they slid down over the plump round bottom, to halfway down the thighs.

The smell of hot girl, aroused girl, flooded everywhere.

"I enfolded you, caressed you all over and loved you, making love to your body, sensuously stroking you and feeling you everywhere, in all your secret places."

His arms were all around her.

Hands flowed all over her.

They were no longer feeling for blemishes, feeling for pleasure, the pleasure of her skin.

Together they swept up her back, pushing her blouse and bra up around her neck, down over outside her shoulders, tracing every curve, up inside her arms, around her breasts.

A blind artist was exploring every detail, to get a clear picture, in his mind.

Next the waist, still narrow and on, all around the exquisite reversing curves around hips and bottom, his hands now roved independently, separately enjoying her.

They came together again tracing down her back, onto her hips.

He snuggled closer, wrapping himself around her yielding bottom, kissing and licking her back.

His hands were at her hips, easing her back hard against his rampant cock.

"--I was getting so hot I said,

'I am sorry, I have just got to fuck you.' And you said,

'Okay. I do not mind. Have a fuck. I will give you a nice fuck.' And I gently took you." He matched his actions to his words,

"I had you right there, bent over the vaulting horse, in the middle of the empty gymnasium, with your friends waiting for you outside. And, you came with me hard up you and collapsed down--"

The schoolgirl fell face down, bum pouted, but otherwise flat on the bed, her grey, school-regulation knickers, stretched tight from thigh to thigh, restricting her spread. The randy teacher

83

had to hold her tightly to him and hump her firmly to maintain the close sensuous contact they were enjoying.

Andrew's whispered narrative, of a teacher seducing his favourite pupil reached its climax in her ears.

Delia's screams rose to full bore with her climax.

The orgasmic contractions bumped Amelia's latest egg, down the tube and into her uterus. Seconds later as he grunted with fulfilment gratified, the randy teacher spent into his schoolgirl and Andrew bathed the waiting egg with seed. The winner, a many millions to one long-shot, had persuaded the gate to open and carried its precious cargo home, before the couple enjoyed the second of several shared orgasms that day.

Caught, Twice: Early Summer 1983

Delia

Delia hadn't managed to resolve the dilemma of needing to eliminate one of the nicer activities in her life by the time she returned to her cousin's farm. The following morning he appeared at her bedside,

"They've all gone; time for wriggly kisses." Delia looked at the rampant pole just centimetres from her face,

"Do you know, like, what we're doing?" There was a short, silent pause, then,

"Yes."

With a sigh, she pulled the bedclothes back.

"Stroke me first."

"What?"

"Like this," she guided his fingers in to her clitty and showed him how, everything from sensuous circles to rapid vibrations, while she caressed him as Natasha had pleasured her boy. It didn't take long,

"Now--Do it now."

As usual, the wriggly kisses were accompanied by Delia squealing her appreciation of her cousin's efforts.

"Thank you, that was lovely."

"You're welcome but thank y--"

"What protection are you using?"

The young cousins stared at their elder relative, standing by the bed. The conflicting urges to hide, run, leap about, dive under the covers had them lying immobile and silent.

"Are you using any contraception, or are you just doing it?"

"Like, just doing it." Rachael turned her attention to her brother,

'Can you spunk." When he didn't reply, she shook him. "It's important, answer me, do you spurt when you come?"

"Yes."

"You stupid pair, are you trying to get into trouble. You go to

85

your room, you into the shower, thoroughly washed inside and out, dressed downstairs in ten minutes, we are going for help."

When Delia, gleaming clean, passed him on the landing on her way out, he apologised,

"Sorry, should have warned you, but I wanted to do it so much."

"It's okay. Like, if you hadn't, I would have, it's okay."

Rachael's doctor friend was bothered but realistic.

"What medication are you on for your condition?"

"Painkillers, like, sometimes, but not at the minute."

"This injection will bring you on, ensure you're clear. But, don't ever do it again unprotected. And we have never met, is that clear?"

"Yes."

"You were never here, is that **fully** understood?"

"Yes, like, I know what you're doing could get you into trouble, but you're still helping me. So yes, I was never here."

"Don't forget to take the cap out at the end of every month and always use the jelly."

"Yes, like, I understand."

* * *

On the first Thursday after Easter, with a resounding win against their Arch Rivals chalked up, five of the friends were nearly ready to go home after their Netball Practice, but Carly still hadn't returned from her call on Miss Cape.

"I'll go and get Carly," said Delia hobbling into the gym and hurrying, for her, to the gym office. Jeanette called after her, indistinctly. Delia ignored the call, she'd see to whatever it was, when she came back. She tapped on the open office door, it was deserted, but a through door, behind which lay the staff changing room, was open too. Little noises were coming from the changing room so Miss Cape would be in there, she stepped into the office and leaned around the door; the call of 'Miss?' already forming in her throat.

It was never said.

The noises were little, only because they were being heavily stifled.

"Delia!" Jeanette's urgent shout came from behind her, but the urgency was unnecessary, Delia was already back hopping fast. "Is Carly there?"

"Yes," said Delia, pale under her tan. "But she's, like, busy."

Jeanette closed up and put her hands on the taller girls elbows,

"It's not a State Secret, well it is with Miss Cape, but not that she's gay. Didn't you know?"

"No. No, I didn't."

"Are you okay? She's still the same girl she was yesterday."

"Oh yes. Gay's fine. It was just the shock; I didn't expect it. A good job it was me nebbing in not, like, Caps-you-fits-you."

"You go and finish up, I'll keep watch."

"Don't, like, say anything. I'll tell her when I'm ready," she looked into the blonde's eyes. "Promise."

"Okay. Carly's not a slut, they've know--"

"I never thought for a second she was. The shock was because Miss Cape's a teacher."

"They met before she came here, Maureen was her girlfriend all last summer. They didn't know they were ever going to meet again ..."

Delia gave Jeanette the eyes as she shrugged in understanding.

It wasn't until late the following day that Delia managed to get Carly alone.

"I've got something to tell you, it's, like, a warning too."

"What?"

"Last night, I came looking for you. I walked in on you, like, in mid orgasm, tribbing the luscious Maureen."

"Oh."

"I don't, like, mind. But, I could have been anybody, the Head even. For Goodness sake, lock the dodgy Dandelion-dip door next time."

"Sorry."

"So you should be, I jilled myself off three times straight last night and it was all your fault!"

"Why? You're not gay!"

"No, I'm not, but three-seconds of your orgasmic squealing took a lot of getting, like, out of my head, with the help of an imaginary certain person!"

* * *

Unusually, time was dragging for Delia.

Of Breaking Free: Warwickshire Summer 1983
Lovers

"Hello"

"It's me."

"Hello." The voice now soft and caring. "I've put it on for Seventy, we'll see what happens and we'll start your man on the new place in the meantime, now that we've got a brand-new bolt-hole to run to."

"Yes, please. Just, she's asked about the money. I told her what I did with my money was my business and walked out. I've never had the courage before to walk away from a beating. I feel really good, usual place ASAP, I've already got the wine to celebrate."

"Oh, my darling, I'm on my way."

The simple expedient of directing all purchasers to the converted barn first and extolling the virtues of instant vacant possession, produced a sale, for the asking price, within days.

With venture capital available and more to the point, subject to punitive levels of tax if someone found out about it, not to mention awkward questions, several more suitable barns were purchased, as quickly as could be accomplished.

Shocks: Tyne-dale July - December 1983

Delia

Spring came and the family holiday crept painfully nearer.

May seemed unusually long in arriving and even longer in departing.

The holiday had been two months away, for three months at least.

Then suddenly, warm days, annual examinations, Parents Evenings, Sports Days; the holiday was only two weeks away and the next morning it seemed,

School was out and it was only two days to go, before wriggly kisses --

* * *

"Come and meet my girlfriend."

Ben's bald announcement packed Delia completely in a box, but later she ruefully admitted to herself; she'd seen it coming from the moment they met at the farm gate. In the words of the song from Gigi, he was bright as spring, obviously not thinking of her.

She was chunky and busty and not very tall, tough farming stock from five miles up the valley. Delia painted on a smile, the war was already lost, her already victorious competition was 'the girl next door'.

"Hello. I've heard a lot about you, been dying to meet you. Please tell me, how do you get him to shut the toilet door and put the seat back down when he's finished."

"Try standing behind him with, like, an ash switch--"

"Ouch!" exclaimed Ben. "Do no such thing!"

"Nothing else works, not that I've, like, found anyway. Can he dive straight legged yet?"

"Can a pig sing? Still, never mind, you don't marry them because they can sing do you." She spun the chair around and pushed Delia away from the rest. "He does have other talents, but you know that already."

Delia was expecting a thorough grilling on her past relationship with Ben, but didn't get it, that was fish that swam away long since, apparently. What Betty did want was guidance on buying him a birthday present.

"I've got no brothers, girls are easy, rags or stink, but boys --"

"Big boy's toys. You can't, like, go wrong with boy's toys."

"Computer game?"

"Yes, good choice, or fishing reel, gyroscope, telescopic sight. Anything that he can get his fingers into, bolt onto something or something onto or, like, dismantle and improve."

"Or not, as the case --"

"No more bets please."

Delia finished up really liking the girl and happy for his besotted cousin.

"You don't mind do you?"

"Of course I don't, she's lovely, I'm, like, pleased for you."

Later alone in her bedroom Delia took a pencil from her case and snapped it and then the pieces, repeatedly until they were so short and she had to use so much force that she bruised her hands. She continued relentlessly until she couldn't snap them any more because they were too slippery, as well as too small. She sat before her mirror,

Satisfied?

Asked the girl who gave her the hardest time of all.

"Yes."

If Andrew had taken you into the PE stock cupboard and shoved his hand in your knickers what would you have done?

"Raped him."

So what right have you to be angry with Ben?

"Why do you think I'm dripping blood all over my pencil case? I'm not angry with Ben, or Betty for, like, that matter!"

Go and get cleaned up, she is lovely and you love someone else!

"Someone who doesn't even know I exist, not as, like, a sex

object anyway." Muttered Delia in retaliation as she made her way through to the bathroom whilst preventing drips onto the carpet.

* * *

One night at Mafematica in the Autumn Term, the Second Years were playing with the theorem of Pythagoras in three dimensions by doing two dimensions twice and Mr. Baques asked them to develop a single three-dimensional theorem. He gave them what vaguely resembled a box, but it was missing its front, right side and top. There was a dowel across the longest diagonal, it was labelled 'a'. The two shorter sides of the box were labelled 'b' and 'c'; but their diagonal was labelled 'x', and, oddly, the third, long, side was labelled 'y'.

"This cutaway box I've got, using the letters written on the box, can you just backtrack from your answer, to a general theorem?"

"Should be able to," said Delia.

Anna Monta and Big Mamma came in looking around for their Form Tutor,

"Yes, Shirley?"

"Would you sign some passport photographs for us, for Anna and me?"

"Yes, I'll just dig out my Ministry number," Mr Baques peeled off and headed for his filing cabinet.

Richard Keating, reading from the cutaway box, dictated,

"Pythagoras states that in a right angled triangle:$a^2 = x^2 + y^2$."

"They're strange letters," remarked his friend, Jim Teale.

"There will be a reason for it," said Sadie. "Stick with them. Let x be the diagonal of the rectangle b units long and c units wide. Then by Pythagoras,

$x^2 = b^2 + c^2$

$a^2 = b^2 + c^2 + y^2$,

Provided b, c & y are mutually at right angles a is the length of the longest diagonal of a cuboid box, b units long, c units wide and y units thick, like, the required three dimensional theorem!"

They sat back, smug as cats and smacked their pencils down,

but not for long.

"Very good," said Mr. Baques, looking up from his task, he gave some papers to Anna. "That's yours Anna." And then addressed the group. "Now what if y is the diagonal of a rectangle d units by e units?" He passed a rectangular piece of card over. It was marked d by e with the diagonal y drawn in, to demonstrate his question. He then turned his attention back to Big Mamma's Passport application.

Despite hardly being worth the effort of writing it down, the group all did so because they'd been there before. One innocent, little, easy, insult-to-the-intelligence, 'What if?' was usually followed by a mind blowing, second, innocent little, 'What if?'

$$a^2 = b^2 + c^2 + d^2 + e^2$$

but this time the pencils were waiting poised.

Mr Baques didn't disappoint.

"And what if b, c, d & e are mutually at right angles?" he said, turned back to the girls and flicked Shirley's papers, whilst looking at Anna. "I see you've co-opted your friend onto your board? What have you put her in charge of?"

In the group playing with Pythagoras, things got heated!

Anna replied to her teacher ruefully,

"Not me, I missed out; Dad got to her first."

"I sit in on interviews."

Across the classroom, voices were raised! Even Jonathan was murmuring dissent. Stewart Baques pointedly ignored the growing hubbub.

"She's in charge of Industrial Relations, Mr. Baques, and says who gets hired."

"That's more like it," replied the teacher.

Shirley produced her purse, with an enquiring look.

"Put something in the Cerebral Palsy girl."

"Okay and thanks."

In the middle of the growing row, Laura came in from her Volleyball training, joined the fiercely arguing group, sat beside Sadie and kissed her on the temple. Sadie responded by leaning against her lover, snuggling up. After a few minutes of careful appraisal, Laura spoke,

"I don't know what you're all arguing about, it's as plain as a snowflake."

Sadie turned to her astonished, Laura's scene was Geography, Mathematics merely a tool, not an obsession.

"What?"

"Two variables from two dimensions, three variables from three dimensions, ergo if four variables are used they must be from four dimensions. That equation gives you the diagonal of a four dimensional cuboid, you can calculate its length to as many decimal places as you like, but don't ask me which direction it's pointing, because I've no idea. Plain as a snowflake, beautifully simple, totally inexplicable!"

"Well-done, Laura," said Mr Baques, "I couldn't have put it better myself! Here's your problem for next week. It's in two parts,

1) What was that exercise all about?

2) 'Sigmund lives in a Four Dimensional Universe. The coordinates of his house are (5,6,7,8) how far does he live from my house which is at (17,21,0,0)?"

Outside afterwards,

"Why don't you come to the Mathematics club? We were nibbling at the edges of the answer, but you went straight for the kernel," asked Sadie.

"Because Mathematically I couldn't live with the rest of you, but I will come along to pick you up like tonight and who knows, once in a millennium I may spot another, 'don't reject it solely because you can't see it,' event." Laura dusted some specks off Sadie and held her bag, while the shorter girl shrugged into her coat. "After all, it isn't that long ago that you Mathematicians were telling us Geographers that 'Continental Drift' was horse feathers. Now there's a whole new science grown up out of the concept's acceptance."

"Part one of next weeks problem," replied Delia.

"Uh?"

"That's what the exercise was all about. Don't reject it, solely because you can't see it. He's always on at us to, like, keep an open mind."

"Neoteny, extension of childhood into adult life, particularly the inquiring mind of a child," agreed Laura.

"It also means the precocious sexual maturity of a larval stage, something of which we three are all guilty!"

Delia giggled at Sadie's comment, while Laura stuck her nose firmly into the air,

"I don't know what you mean."

"In that case I will be forced to remind you in bed tonight."

"Ooh!"

* * *

It was some weeks later before Delia managed to get Big Mamma alone.

"Shirley, can I be nebby?"

"Go on then."

"I take it from the snippet I overheard about your passport application that you're, like, on the Board at Monta Industries." Shirley just tipped her head. "I didn't understand Anna saying her Dad got to you first, if you ended up on the Board anyway."

"But not **her** Board. She owns Stybes; she's CEO of Stybes."

"Wobbly Wheelies! Since my Dad started his little weekend business, he sub contracts for them, some of his biggest jobs have, like, been for Stybes."

"For the last four years he's been working for Anna, him and several thousand others."

At home that night,

"Dad, you know your own jobs, the Weekend Workers Company?"

"Yes."

"Did you know that you work for someone who's twelve years old? Have done, like, since she was eight."

"What!"

* * *

Delia got herself ready for some serious Christmas Shopping,

"I'm off to Town Dad, I promise if I get tired I'll, like, get a

95

taxi back."

"Have you got enough money?"

"Yes, loads."

The bus driver knew her and waited patiently until she was seated before moving off. When she alighted, she made a point of letting him know she appreciated it.

"--and today it's more dodgy than usual, like, new clump," she pulled the trouser leg up, to show him.

"You take care now."

"I will, thanks again."

It was a lovely morning, warm for December and dry, with none of that brittle-brightness that warns of different to come. Eagerly Delia set off for the bookshop. When she rounded the corner, she could see her way ahead was obstructed by a large woman, with many bags,

She must have been shopping since dawn, thought Delia and increased her pace, being downwind of her was not pleasant.

A taxi drew up with a squeal of brakes.

The woman scooped up her bags, ran across the pavement, leaving a trail behind her and dived through the opening door. The youngster's warning shout only seemed to accelerate her scuttle. The taxi was moving before she was completely in and then it was gone.

"Nabcabs.

'Five take two,

'leaves three little furry bears,

'shouting slowcoach poo!" Delia chanted repeatedly, as she clumped sedately across to the fallen bag. It was capacious and full of new clothes, spilling out like a stream, but it was also old. The straps were frayed and decrepit and had recently parted. That was the most likely reason why it had fallen from the woman's grasp and spilled its contents as she ran for the taxi. She stuffed the designer gear back into the holdall and hefted it up. The first warning niggle was shunted aside by the weight that told her it contained more than just clothes.

"Nabcabs.

'Five take two,

'leaves three little furry bears,

'shouting slowcoach poo!" She looked around for a policeman. Never mind, although there was no packaging, she recognised the designer labels, the shop they came from was just a hundred metres or so back along the street; they could possibly trace her. She set off, concentrating on swinging and planting correctly the new and therefore, unaccustomed, built-up shoe.

The second warning niggle was stilled because her heart had turned over.

There he was.

That must be his wife, pregnant and consequently more stunningly beautiful than any girl has a right to be and people who have met her said she was lovely too.

Delia heaved a big sigh, squashed the pain safely back into its box, checked for traffic and crossed the street behind her Form Tutor and his breathtakingly comely and bloomingly-pregnant wife. A couple of minutes later she turned to enter the store.

Before she could even reach out for the door, she was jumped on.

The warning niggle exploded in her brain.

No packaging.

Chapter 5
Broader Horizons: December 1983

Andrew

Two young, officious and very eager security men, whose training had not included keeping rein on your jingoistic joy until the quarry was convicted, were climbing all over her. Delia; however, apparently did know the value of yelling at the top of her voice,

"Hey! Whatcha doin? Get off me! Leave off!"

The security men modified their approach, but remained undeterred in escorting her into the store and up to the offices. By the time they got there, however, the commotion had gained her an ally.

Andrew and Amelia Bryant were heading for Mothercare and buggys; when the Saturday morning peace of Novochester was shattered close behind them. They spun around,

"That is the fan."

"I think we both know what's happened."

"But she would not, I know from P.S.E. She is quite happy to shag her boyfriend, but not to steal; that is wrong."

"Either way, she needs assistance, I'll go for the buggy, you go and help out."

So only a few yards into the store, Andrew was blocking the Security men's way.

"She is a minor; you are not allowed to interrogate her on her own. I am her Form Tutor at School," then directly to Delia. "Do you want me to get your Dad?"

"No. I've done nothing. Tell them to let me go."

"The bag is full of stolen goods. Stolen this morning, twenty minutes ago. We've got her on tape."

"No you haven't; I've not been here for weeks."

"Is that true?"

"Honest Sir, I haven't been here since--since--for weeks. I've, like, never stolen nowt, you know I wouldn't."

"There is some mistake; I know this girl and she would not."

"I watched her myself and taped her." He waved at the dark sphere above their heads, "We've got her banged to rights."

"It--"

"Shut up Delia; if you were not here, they can not have you on tape." The girl visibly relaxed. "Would you like to see the tape and prove it was not you?"

The prospect of a safe house looming up over the horizon had Delia diving in, head first, through the door.

"Yes."

Andrew felt gutted. The tape was grainy, the picture indifferent quality, probably on its hundredth recording, but nevertheless there was no mistaking what was happening. Together the group watched as Delia selected jeans from a rack and sized them up against herself. A woman came into shot and dropped the holdall down, then slung the clothes on top of it. Delia stuffed the clothes into the bag and gave it back to the woman who walked out of shot. The date and time were the clearest things about the recording. He looked at his little tearaway of a fan club. She was sitting slumped in the chair,

"It wasn't me," she said dully.

Andrew glanced back at the screen; the camera was tracking Delia as she walked down the aisle. She paused to touch an elegant, scantily clad mannequin and his heart leapt with hope, by the time she had walked out of the store he was sure. The screen blanked.

"Turn it on again."

"That's all there is."

"Turn it on again." The scene was of the door with customers walking in and out.

"Now wind it back to the bag." The players jerked about backwards until the woman reversed into view. "Now play."

Again, Delia wandered through the aisles, touched the mannequin, feeling the texture of the bikini bottom it was wearing and left the store.

"Have you noticed anything?"

"What?"

"It is not she. It is a dark haired girl, wearing a pale top and dark jeans, but it is not she."

The revelation had no effect on anyone, least of all the person to whom it should have been the most welcome sounds.

"Put that camera live on that display. When we get there, track us through to touch the mannequin." A second screen, tracked across the store, the interesting bikini became, for a moment, centre shot, then the girl's walk was back tracked. "Be ready to run the tape when we are in position, Delia come with me." It was a dull zombie and a sceptical guard, which followed him down to the jeans.

"Okay Delia, walk to the mannequin," she obeyed him. "Now stand here, left foot here, right one here."

Delia took up her stance.

"Now reach out and touch the bikini like on the tape."

She bit, quite hard,

"I can't, you know I can't."

"Move to where you can do it."

"I'll have to turn around."

"Do it." Delia turned until she could take her weight on the left leg and reached out to the bikini,

"Again--Again--Again. Thank you, Delia. That is how she would have done it, if it had been she. And you can see that she is too tall." He turned to the dark opaque ball. "Well?" he said.

A few moments later the other Security man came down, with the rest of his team.

"It's not her, far too tall."

Fortunately, the police arrived before Security thought up something else to get wrong. They returned to the Security Office, and the lovely blonde WPC took Delia inside. Andrew was delayed outside.

"Right Sir. Thank you for your help, we'll take over now."

"No, you will not Constable, you can listen and make notes, but she will not talk to you, she will talk to me, but I assure you; she will **not** talk to you." He assertively insisted that he accompany them back into the room; the child's face lit up as she saw her anchor again. "Delia, do you want your Dad here, or will I do?"

"You please. Don't tell Dad."

"He--"

Andrew snapped at the policeman,

"Shut it. Not another word. Listen, in silence, make notes.-- Delia I know there is a lot going on, and some of it is private, but there are some things we have to be told. Trust me; I will keep off the private things until we have all had time to think, later."

There are times when you just have to trust somebody,

"Okay."

"Right," then formally. "Delia please tell me how you came about the bag."

"They won't believe me."

Andrew gently put his case,

"But, you will make them believe you, by being honest and truthful and explaining what happened." He paused, then spoke again very formally. "Delia, tell us about the bag."

With a defiant glare at the guards, Delia described the hurried embarkation of the woman into her getaway cab, her ignored warning shout and the camelling of the holdall back to the shop. She described both driver and fare in perceptive detail, finishing with,

"She had loads of bags; I'm sure she didn't know she'd dropped one."

"Which cab company?"

"Nabcabs, a proper black cab, not a minicab."

"Did you get the number?"

She looked at him scornfully,

"My Science teacher's Mr Baques."

"Ah. What was it then?"

"Five take two, leaves three little furry bears, shouting slowcoach poo!"

"What?"

"Five take two, leaves three little furry bears, shouting slowcoach poo!" She wrote the number down and handed it to Andrew. "It's a line from a poem, well the last bit is, so 5, 2--3 Little Furry Bears Shouting Slowcoach. Like, I was trying to return the stuff, I didn't know it was nicked. I chanted the number; it was my only lead; I had to remember it somehow."

"Oh, right," he turned his attentions to the police officers. "Well?"

"Seems pretty clear," said the lovely blonde. "Delia, is there--Can I just ask about a couple of details?"

"Yes."

"How do you know she has a little baby?"

"She smelled of milk, and she had sick down the back of her shoulder. That's where little babies are sick, older ones, like, throw up in your lap."

It was only a few minutes later, after arranging a time to make a formal statement that Delia was released into Andrews care and they left the store together.

"Thank you, Sir, I'll be going now."

"Not yet Delia, we both know who was on the screen."

The girl stopped, she had obviously been hoping that was not true.

"It has got to be sorted out. If you bring her and your Dad to see me on Monday, I will tell him what I saw and heard; then your Dad can decide what he will do."

"I--Well."

"Talk it over with your Dad, there might just be a simple explanation, do not jump to the same conclusions as Security."

"Thank you, Sir."

"Not me. Thank Amelia when you meet her, she sent me in to help; now I have to go shopping for buggies."

"Oh--Please thank her for me."

Delia

When Delia got home, she had come to terms with the difficult task ahead and realised that it had to be done. As her Dad would learn everything, she might as well tell him all, right at the start.

"Dad please sit down I've got something to tell you." The serious tone of his daughter's voice, had him sitting at once. "Like, this morning I was interviewed by the police."

Dave Summers' stone face suggested that he was steeling himself for further revelations.

"I hadn't done anything, but they thought I had stolen goods from a shop. Honest Dad I hadn't and now they, like, know I hadn't."

"So if there's no problem, why am I sitting down?"

"They caught somebody on camera; they thought it was me. It wasn't, it was somebody who looks like me. She looks very like me, only a bit smaller."

"You're telling me they've got Vicky on tape stealing from a shop?"

"She helps somebody to steal things. That's what it looks like anyway. But seeing they thought it was me, and it wasn't, it might not be her doing it either. Like, there may be a simple explanation. That she wasn't doing it. Mr Bryant is hoping so."

"What's Mr Bryant got to do with all this?"

"He saw the security men grab me; he jumped in to save me. He was the one that saw it wasn't me. But, he knows who it was as well Dad."

The Summers family went visiting their relatives that afternoon.

"I saw you in Bebopps, like, this morning Vicky."

"I never saw you, why didn't you say?"

"You were leaving, you'd gone by, like, the time I got there. That bikini's super."

"It was great, wasn't it, but far too expensive. It might get to the sale, with a bit of luck."

"Who was the woman?"

"What woman?"

"The one you put her shopping in, like, her bag for her."

"Oh her, the old bag woman. I don't know; she smelled, like, dirty-sweaty. I just shoved her stuff in the bag, like she asked me, to get rid of her, she smelled horrible."

Satisfied that, yet again, events had proved not to be what they first appeared, Dave and Delia explained and recounted the events of the morning. Later that day Vicky's Dad was on the telephone arranging an appointment with WPC Elaine Jacques. The arrangements were passed through Station Sergeant Deed and eventually to CID, as the first solid lead in combating an escalating Christmas shoplifting spree.

* * *

Monday morning and Delia was able to report to her Form Tutor,

"Everything is under control. Dad's, like, written you a note." She passed it over.

> Dear Mr Bryant,
>
> Thank you for looking after Delia so kindly on Saturday morning.
>
> Vicky too was an innocent bystander. We have spoken to the Police, and the girls have given their statements.
>
> Once again, thank you very much.
>
> D. D. Summers.

The need to notify meant the cat leapt from its bag and ran around scratching furniture all over the room.

"I'd sue for wrongful arrest. I'd--"

Delia let Kim rant on, easing the stress in her own life on a nice, safe, neutral, common-enemy. She just tuned her out; there was a more pressing difficulty.

"How are you ever going to thank him?" Jeanette was also ignoring the tirade.

"I don't know. Like, that's the next problem."

"I heard his wife is pregnant."

"She is. Stunningly good looking, nice, married to him and pregnant with his child. Is that a fair portion of life's goodies for, like, just one girl?"

Jeanette laughed at the grimace, knowing it to be sham,

"Buy something for the baby."
"Yes. His first Teddy."
"Or hers."
"I meant that."

Delia ran Andrew to ground that night, in the boy's gym.

Mary Smith: Warwickshire December 1983

Mary/Mr Beaker

In a hospital near Banbury, a woman was talking to her husband. Despite the ravages of terminal illness, it was still obvious that she was a generation younger than he.

"Don't spend any more money on private treatment for me Bill. I've lost the fight; I'm ready to go. I hurt all the time; I want to come home and go with dignity, with my loved ones around me." Silently her husband agreed to the request. "Send Mary in. I'd like to speak with her alone."

"Mum."

"I want you to be brave and grown up. Work with Bobby helping Daddy on the farm, take care of Mark and Little Will for me and look after Daddy, until he gets a new girl. I want him to marry again Mary, don't get upset if he finds someone new. Promise me."

"I won't."

"You remember I told you, when you were little, how Daddy isn't your real father don't you?"

"Yes."

"He took me in when my Dad threw me out because I was pregnant with you, I wasn't much older than you; he was struggling to run the farm and look after Bobby. Bobby was only ten. We got married when I turned sixteen; you were nearly two by then. And he's always loved us and cared for us, and I want him to be happy."

"Yes."

The dying girl pulled a cardboard box out from her case.

"This box has everything I know about your real father. We were young and daft. I was happy we'd made you, but he couldn't cope. One night, he kissed me Goodbye, and I never saw him again, he'd gone to sea. It's natural that you would want to know. But always remember that Bill took us in and loved you like his own."

"I will, I promise, he's my Dad."

Mother and daughter spent some time alone together saying goodbye, while they still could. The increasing doses of drugs to dull the pain would ensure that there was little time left for meaningful communication.

Later that night Mary hugged the only man she'd ever known as Daddy, while he pored worriedly over the books.

"We need some money quick Mary, and I don't know where from."

"Sell Stonecroft, not the farm, just the Farmhouse, Kayley's Dad got ten thousand for old Jenkins' Barn. We'd get at least that for Stonecroft. Sell it to Ternimal Investments; they'll renovate it, sell it to a local, they won't turn it into an incomer Colonel's Summer Home."

So Ternimal Investments gained their first property that was offered to them, instead of bought by them. The price was marginally on the low side of fair, but Bill Smith was happy enough to settle quickly for the cash he so desperately needed to keep the bank manager from being forced into bouncing the cheque for his wife's funeral.

* * *

Mary Smith returned to School the week after her mother's death, a child no longer. She still played with her friends, ran about, laughed occasionally, but with a gently detached air, as if merely waiting for her real life to restart, at home time.

Every lunchtime her father rolled up at five past twelve and delivered her back at twenty-five past one. Every evening he picked her up at four. When the car arrived, an eleven-year-old left her friends, donned young housewife mode and went home to look after her family. The Head Teacher, seriously worried how she was coping, monitored her test scores closely. The pretty, little, straight 'A's student, continued to deliver handsomely. He had only just begun to breathe more easily about her, when the girl herself knocked on his office door and entered without being asked to do so.

"Please help me, Sir. Mrs Patterson is going to beat me. I don't want her to."

"Whatever for?" He could hear his colleague approaching, shouting her fury down the corridor, he waved his secretary in too, closed the door behind them and locked it. "Sit down, tell me what the problem is." The girl remained standing.

"She asked me where I sleep. I said at home. She hit me with her stick." The girl pulled her blouse down off her shoulder. The mark was already clear enough, even the wider band of a node, with its accompanying pale stripe, could be made out. "Please don't let her beat me. I couldn't hide the marks and Daddy would see them and get upset."

The door was tried, discovered to be locked and pounded upon.

"Mr Beaker! Let me in at once! I have a most serious complaint to make." He turned to his secretary.

"Mrs Rogers, get the story written down, all of it, when Mary is happy that you have it all, she can sign it." He held a finger up to his lips, snapped the lock over, whipped the door open and forced his way through it, against something outside.

"Ah Mrs Patterson, let us return to your class while you tell me what happened." He stopped the shouted retort with his hand. "Tell me what happened, don't shout at me like a fishwife."

Mildred Patterson might never have been spoken to assertively before; the colour drained from her face, she opened her mouth a couple of times, but nothing came out.

"That's better, now just tell me, what is the matter?" He led them out onto the corridor.

"She's sleeping with her father. I asked her. She lied." The volume was leaping up,

"Keep it down; you're just talking to me. She can't be sleeping with her father; he ran off before she was born. She said she was sleeping at home."

"She knew fine well what I meant."

"What's your evidence?"

"They all do it, behind their mother's backs."

"So you've got no evidence."

"As soon as she's dead, they can't jump in fast enough. They all--"

"So with no evidence, you assumed incest, which isn't even incest and--"

"They all do it--"

"Assaulted a recently orphaned child with a stick," he continued louder, forcing her back down. "Leaving a huge, bruising-weal on her back."

Now he got silence, even the renowned School-ma'am Bully began to appreciate the trouble she might be in,

"The child isn't even in your class. You will leave her alone and never speak to her again, while I decide where we go from here."

Councillor Mrs Patterson left muttering, it was only an hour later, having agreed with Mary not to take the matter any further, particularly not to inform her father, that Carl Beaker realised what his irate member of staff had been saying and called a friend in Social Services.

"--She left muttering something about getting her another way."

"She's paranoid, we know it happens occasionally, but she insists it's every time and it isn't."

"Can you keep an eye out, tip me the wink if --"

"I couldn't possibly do that Carl. I'm surprised you asked."

"No silly of me. Bye."

Early afternoon, the expected return call came through.

"Would Mary Smith be in bed at home on Wednesday Morning at about Seven do you think?"

"It's a Dairy Farm, she'll have done a half shift by seven, more like four I would have thought."

"Thanks, Bye." He heard the message being relayed and the reply

"A certain person will love that; she's insisting on being on the raid." The telephone went dead. With a smile and a nod, he hung up,

"Bye and thank you," he said to the silent machine, researched a number and dialled out. "Can I speak with Bill Smith please?"

"It's Bobby; that's Mr Beaker isn't it, is Mary okay, the lads?"

"Yes, she's fine Bobby; they're all fine. Congratulations, to you and Doris, on the little one, doing your bit to keep me in a job. Mandy isn't it? She'll be scampering about on her hands and knees by now I should think."

"Into anything less than table top height."

"Is your Dad around?"

"He's in the byre, would I do?"

"I need to talk to your Dad first, but if Mary sometimes baby-sits Mandy --"

"She does."

"Then what I have to say will include you and Mandy."

"Oh right, I'll get him."

More Fan-Male: Tyne-dale December 1983

Delia

In the gym, Richard Keating and Jim Teale were being taught volleyball by Laura and Sadie, passing to space over the net, like Delia and her mates did, practising netball. Delia watched her Form Tutor listening to Laura coaching, he was there, but she was doing the teaching, presently he turned away, saw Delia and began talking to her.

Richard also saw her and changed from a competent, even talented, volleyball player, into a bumbling, inept Wally, instantly.

"Come into the office; you are putting Richard off." He pushed her inside and closed the door. "Did you know you had an admirer?"

"Sort of, like, that happens regularly and if he has a new toy he shows it to me first."

"He is a nice boy."

"I know. I didn't know he played volleyball."

"Neither did he. They both have half-decent hand-eye co-ordination, but are useless at any racquet or club sport, like tennis, or cricket. It has taken me four terms to find it, but they are good at volleyball. Best of the boys."

"But not as good as Laura."

"Be sensible! Nobody I know is that good, except Laura. How is the cooking going? Is it still your long-term aim?"

"Yes. The word's getting around, people don't buy me makeup, they buy me, like, kitchen utensils instead. Cookery books."

* * *

Late opening, the Wednesday of that week, Delia grabbed her younger, look-alike cousin and dragged the pair of them off to shop for a Teddy bear. She specifically chose the same department store; like getting straight back on your bike after falling off.

On Being Ready: Warwickshire December 1983

Mary/Mr Beaker

At four o'clock on Wednesday morning the Social raided the Smith's Farm, with the madwoman, illegally, spearheading the pounce. They found Bill Smith just getting out of bed, where he had been sleeping alone and Mary in a different room, curled up in a different warm bed, with a wet baby, her step-niece, specially loaned to her for the occasion by elder stepbrother, Bobby. The two younger half-brothers were still asleep in a third bedroom. It took all the Leader of the Council's political skills and an official letter of apology, not to mention several valuable markers called in, to keep the story under wraps.

Mildred Patterson was told unequivocally not to harass the Smiths again.

Not accepting that all her guns had been spiked, Bill Smith stored the official letter away safely and let it be known he wouldn't hesitate to use it if necessary.

No-one involved believed for a second that was the end of the matter.

Privately, Carl Beaker thought that there was a slender chance that Mary was sleeping with her stepfather, as their way of coping with the difficulties. Not having any proof, or a suitable alternative constructive strategy, he chose just to continue to monitor her progress, in an attempt to ensure that she came to no harm.

"And anyway," he murmured quietly to himself. "Even if she is, it's merely immoral and illegal; it's not as if it's incest."

The pretty little 'Straight As' student, after an understandable pause, recovered and resumed her 'Straight As' performance.

Wrapping Presents: Tyne-dale December 1983
Delia

Teddies came in all different sizes and prices; moreover, a hefty price tag didn't necessarily ensure a nice expression. Vicky pointed to a notice, several versions of which were displayed prominently around.

Ask about our
FREE
Gift Wrap Service

"That's something you won't need."
"It's an idea. I don't always do it that well."
"Bollocks."
At that moment a small sized Teddy said, 'Choose me,' so clearly to her that Delia heard it distinctly.
"Look."
"Oh yes. That's a nice one and under budget."
"And nice size for a baby."
The girls drifted over to the counter. Three, thirty-something assistants were discussing their levels of success while out clubbing the night before. Presently it became apparent that going out on the pull, with the clear intention of deceiving your spouse about doing so, was considered perfectly normal behaviour, a point of view that Delia totally rejected.

Not necessarily the extramarital sex, there's someone who I would be hard pushed to say no t--She killed the visions in her mind. *It's the deception.*

One of the assistants nudged another; she turned and moved over to the counter.

"Next please." The assistant was addressing the space above the girls' heads and a little behind them. Delia, mouth open ready to speak, turned to look.

"It's these young ladies," replied the tall executive suit, standing behind her. When she turned back she was being looked at inquiringly, she handed the teddy bear over and watched in horror as it was placed in a bag. She drew the money back, out of reach and waved at the notice.

"Can I have it gift-wrapped please?"

"We're busy."

Delia surveyed the queue of one behind her and the other two assistants still discussing their performance the previous night.

"I can see how busy you are and at what," she pointed to the notice "May have it gift-wrapped please?"

The assistant hauled a sheet of paper over towards her, grabbed a bow and some ties out of a jar, dumped the teddy back out of the bag and set about wrapping it. A second later Delia jumped in proffering the money and preventing her from creasing the paper.

"Don't bother if you just mean to spoil it. Like, I'll do it myself at home." She rolled the paper up into a tube and replaced the teddy in its bag adding the bow and ties to it. As she rang the money in, the assistant remonstrated with her,

"You shouldn't ask for things you don't really want--Madam."

Delia took her change and turned away on the good leg, her face burning with embarrassed annoyance.

"Now Sir. Sorry for the delay."

Delia could feel her body's response in the flames licking around her ears. She stopped.

One more, just one more.

"The apology should be directed at the young lady you've just served. Had you treated me like that, I would not have been as polite, or forgiving."

Delia turned again and addressed the man,

"Thank you." She limped away calm and cool, amazed at the speed at which soothing words douse fires and heal wounds.

* * *

Delia, Kimberley and their friends paused on the way out of the classroom,

"I wanted to say thank you, like, for your help 'n that, it's for Mrs Bryant, for the baby, I wrapped it myself," she was offering an artistically wrapped parcel, Christmas paper, bow, streamers painstakingly curled into springs. Vicky's expletive had been fully justified.

"That is very nice Delia thank you. Would you like to give it to her yourself as well?"

"I--Well--Erm--"

"Mrs Bryant has told me she would like to meet you."

"Oh. Okay then."

"Come for tea tomorrow, it is fish, you can have mine; I will have something decent."

"I like fish."

"Good, settled then, you are having mine." The girls laughed and left for their lesson.

Bryant House: December 1983

Amelia

"The fan is coming for tea tomorrow night."

"I only got fish for two."

"Good, I will have a steak then, she likes fish."

"Andrew I give you fish because it's good for you."

"Not tomorrow, you do not."

* * *

The following evening, Amelia watched her man turn into the darkening street, the deliciously pretty girl in the wheelchair, was talking to him over her shoulder, with animated gestures of her arms.

Well, Mrs Bryant, she thought as she turned away from the window and serenely waddled to the door. *She's pretty enough and no mistake! Now is she Nice-Wild enough?*

Andrew held the chair still; Delia eased herself out of it and climbed the steps sedately to the front door. It opened,

"Hello, you must be Delia."

"Hello, Mrs Bryant."

The elder girl leaned in and kissed the younger one on the mouth, Delia's intense pleasure showed in her eyes,

Good! Keep pushing!

"Call me Amelia, come on in."

The small flat was plainly furnished with the essentials, but bright with flowers. Delia noticed that many them were wild flowers, mainly gorse, sprinkled with a few Chrysanthemum sprays and said so, her surprise betrayed by her tone of voice,

"Oh! Wild flowers, lovely."

"And cheap, they didn't even cost a bus ride." Amelia picked up the telephone handset and placed it on its wall-mounted rest. The youngster followed her into the living room and rummaged the present out of her bag.

"I brought you this, a Thank You, Christmas Present like. For you and the Baby. I wrapped it myself."

Careful girl, give her a chance to explain!

"It's beautiful. Bebopps do wrapping paper very like that."

115

"It's Bebopps' paper, she wasn't taking enough care, so I did it myself."

There you are--no problem after all!

"It's really lovely. There's a box of presents over there, do you want to put it with them." Delia nodded and placed her contribution in the box.

Any initial nervousness that the schoolgirl may have had, was obviously vanishing fast, as Amelia's treatment of her as a much-loved friend took effect.

"How do you like your fish?"

"Can I help, like, help you do it?"

"If you want," she led the way to the kitchen, which, again, was small, neat and well equipped with the basics.

"I want to be a chef, have my--well I want to be a chef."

"You want your own restaurant, dripping with Michelin Stars."

"Something like that."

"Never be afraid of setting high targets for yourself kid, or making it obvious that you are working towards worthy goals. That's a whole lot different from boasting, or false claims. Now-- it's haddock. How do we handle haddock?"

"Like, don't overcook it. Bone it, warm it until it's just white, let it rest for a minute. Serve with hot waxy potatoes and parsley sauce. How much parsley have you got?"

Amelia pointed to a patch about the size of a tea tray, dimly visible in the light from the window spilling across the back garden,

"Several pounds weight."

Delia grinned broadly,

"That will do nicely. What potatoes have you got?"

"Potatoes? They're already boiling, nearly done."

Delia plucked the bag from the vegetable bin,

"Are they these?"

"Yes."

"Nadines. They're decent boiled, they make great chips, but baked with butter they are food of the Gods, they're my favourites, like, after a Jersey."

"Yes, a potato is an insipid thing after a Jersey. I'll get you the parsley, how many leaves?"

"A dozen or so, young, just going dark, with long succulent snappy stems."

"Stems as well?" Said the elder girl, amazed.

"That's where the taste is."

Despite her misgivings, Amelia followed her guest's instructions to the letter, managing the desirability of a third hand by jamming the torch between her left elbow and her bump. She returned with a large handful of greenery in one hand, scissors in the other and the torch still pinched in at her waist,

"Are you sure this is what you want?"

"Perfect," said Delia patting the fish dry. "Have you got a blender?" Amelia nodded wide eyed. "If you check that lot over for dirt and cat poo, rinse it off, then dry it and roughly chop it, we'll, like, run it through the blender, then--"

Amelia fetched pans and set trays and watched wide-eyed as two fish were gently cooked, whilst a oiled steak sizzled for seconds over a roaring heat. The piping hot Nadines were served with a fat knob of butter and the parsley sauce stood up alone, in soft peaks of brilliant emerald green. Andrew's dinner had a substantial heap of sultana and thinly grated carrot mix piled to one side.

"When did you do that?"

"While you were getting the parsley. He always has it at School, so -- like, I think we're ready."

Chapter 6
Friends for Life: December 1983
Amelia

Andrew laid his knife and fork down, regretfully staring at the empty plate.

"Wow, thank you, that was something else. Would you like to come for tea every Friday?"

"Or just move in?" Added Amelia, folding her knife and fork together on a matching platter.

Delia giggled,

"I'm glad you liked it, I did too."

Andrew marked some English books, while the girls did the dishes. Amelia wallowed in the unaccustomed treat of some girl talk, as she handed down the crocks to her young guest in her chair. Delia dried them and stacked them on the bench.

"Seventeenth of February. So I'm on the last few weeks countdown, beginning to get really excited."

"The last few weeks always seem the longest, like, you're itching to get going, but you can't, not until the little boss decides to let you, by arriving."

"Would you like to see the stuff?"

"Yes, please."

Delia cooed over the baby clothes and general accoutrements. It was obvious where any spare cash in the Bryant household went.

"What do you want?"

"Andrew wants a girl, but I don't care."

"You just want the right number of fingers and toes and only forty-six chromosomes and, like, not one of these." She was indicating her right leg.

"Exactly! But, it will be nice to be able to go out and buy pink dresses, or blue trousers someday."

"Pink dresses are, like, scarce in our house, with clothes being recycled through two younger brothers."

"How long since your Mum? If you don't want to talk about it, that's okay."

"I was nine. I miss her, but it doesn't hurt anymore. But, like, the anger hasn't gone. On the great day of reckoning, somebody had better have some answers ready."

"Do you feel the same about your leg?"

"No. My leg's part of me, I, like, have to take more care of it than I do the other one. But given the choice, I'd not change it."

"So you're not going to get anything done about it?"

"Not anything more. I never want to see the inside of another orthopaedic ward ever. That's where I lost all the schooling, in hospital, while my body obstinately refused to cooperate, to grow new bone and that. The one thing that did improve was the pain, I only hurt when I get tired now, instead of, like, continually. Which is good, because Dad gets upset when I hurt, and it's not his fault; it's not anyone's fault."

"How's he doing?"

"Better, there's something going on, like, at work. For a couple of months, it's been Madeline was a good worker and Madeline's little one had an upset stomach and Madeline was going to the Works Party. Then nothing since Tuesday, the Works Party night, but he's not moping, or sad, or angry, so no more bets please."

"You think decisions might be being made; consequences thought through."

"Mmm."

"Would that help you, do you think? A girl around to talk to."

"It would help Dad. Personally and as Dad. He does his best, but he solves problems better with, like, boys."

"So I bet you've got no girly underwear."

"No. Not so that you'd, like, notice anyway."

"How about sanitary towels and that kind of stuff?"

"I usually use press-on, but I'd like to use tampons. I bought some to have in, like, in case."

"They are more comfortable; it's just that --"

"I'm not virgin Amelia, not for, like, a long time."

"No problem then. Would you like me to take you shopping, show you what your Mum would have shown you, tell you what she would have told you."

"Yes, please."

"Tomorrow?"

"Yes, please."

When Dave Summers called to take his daughter home, Amelia held him back and spoke with him in private, while Andrew loaded the chair into the boot.

"So I'm not trying to usurp your place Mr Summers, just give Delia the girly low down on bras and things."

"That's fine Mrs Bryant, I'm grateful. Not the sort of thing I even thought about. Too busy papering over the cracks and I know that's no excuse--Erm, will twenty pounds cover it?" Then seeing her face. "Thirty?"

"Thirty down and about fifteen a month. Girls are more expensive to keep than boys I'm afraid."

"Here." Amelia found a substantial wad of notes being thrust into her hand. "Stock her up and while she's not looking get me some things she'd really like for Christmas if that's okay?"

"Fine."

* * *

In Novochester, the following day, Amelia and Delia met for coffee in Jennifer's café, before going shopping. The redhead, still only thirteen, was working for love and 'tips' and like the café, because of its popularity with her friends, doing rather well.

Amelia was advising Delia on underwear,

"It depends on what nature bequeaths you, if you're busty like me, and kid, you're gonna be, believe me," said Amelia, nodding significantly at the youngster's already impressive mammaries. "It's easy to misread the signs and go for a cup that's too small on a bra that's too big. You can always tell. The big girl who looks as if she has four boobs."

"Two little ones, like, above the proper ones."

"Yes, she'll be wearing a 36 B, when it should be a 32 D."

"How will I know?" asked the younger girl.

"We're going to get you properly measured at J.L.P. or M&S, and we'll get you measured again every time you buy a new bra; until you settle into what you're going to get." Amelia selected some stockings and suspender belt, as well as tights, checking the colours for Delia's preference,

"The tights are for school, but the stockings for dances and parties and you wear the belt under your knickers."

"Yes. Trips to the loo would be--"

"Complicated otherwise, yes. Now the other thing. Contraception. What have you been using so far?"

"Cap and jelly."

"Oh--Oh well that's fine. Forgive me Delia I assumed that you wouldn't have, sorry I--"

"My cousin Rachael found out, dragged me off to the clinic by my ear and bending it too. My Mum wouldn't have given me as a hard time as Rachael did. Not for doing it, for, like, doing it unprotected."

"Quite right too. You remember that when you're facing the same problem with your own daughter."

"Yessum. Nosum. Three bags fulsum."

The two girls laughed easily together.

"How did it happen so young, the first time, if that's not too personal?"

"I wasn't that young, fourteen, young enough I suppose. It was by accident. Like, my cousin, Rachael's brother, they live out at Loblom. We were very good friends, best friends. We grew up together, played together, got bathed together. So when we went swimming in the lake, it was skinny-dipping, no big deal, we'd be in the bath together later anyway. We were splashing each other, chasing each other, then one time when he caught me, I'd tripped and fallen. He pounced on me, but I was hurt, there was, like, grit and stuff to see to. He eased the small stones out, gently, it turned sore into excitement. We ended up close together, face to face. It felt so nice, I took his face in my hands and kissed him like the film stars. I only meant to, like, kiss him the once, then run away and splash him some more, but he pushed me down, with him on top of me and kissed me back. It was much more exciting than splashing. We wriggled against each other and Boomf. We didn't know what we'd done, just that we wanted to do it again in five minutes and after lunch and tomorrow and next week and next year's holiday. Rachael walked in on us last year, by then I knew what it was of course, like, what we were doing. Then, this summer he met someone else, but we're still friends."

Amelia reached out and gently caressed Delia's cheek. The younger girl covered the comforting hand, turned into it and softly kissed the palm. Amelia's heart thumped, only one other person had touched her so deeply. She breathed in deeply, and spoke,

"Changing the subject completely, can I ask you about the spelling of your name?"

"Why it's a 'U' and not an 'O'. I don't know, but I suspect it's because when the ancestors came over from wherever black haired, brown eyed people came over from, none of them was literate and, like, the name got written down by someone else phonetically."

"That's as good a reason as any," replied the elder girl, smiling.

By the end of the Saturday shopping trip, Delia and Amelia were firm friends. Best friends.

"Would you like to come over for Boxing Day lunch? We could have a Bran Tub; I could open your present with you beside me."

"Yes, I'd like that. What does Mr Bryant like?"

"Scroggin. You could make some up yourself. Get a little jar, some hazelnut kernels, not mixed nuts, just Hazels or Cobnuts and a handful of raisins or sultanas. Dice up a plain chocolate bar, not milk, plain. Mix them all up, into the jar, wrap it in Christmas paper. Not much money, lots of pleasure."

"I'll do that."

Delia

Dave Summers picked the pair up from town and dropped Amelia off at home; he later reminded his daughter about the boys' arrangements.

"When you're planning Christmas, remember the boys will be at the Pantomime trip with the Youth Club on Boxing day, they won't be here to eat, so don't do a shipload."

"I've got an invite out for Boxing Day lunch as well, so we'll, like, all be not here."

"What am I going to do with a big turkey to eat? And no family to eat it."

"Invite Madeline over." Delia had to struggle not to laugh at her Dad's face as it revealed his brain racing through the options of denial, interrogation, acquiescence. She took pity on him. "The Madeline who has just come to work at your place, a couple of months ago, who was, like, the only topic of conversation when you came home at night, until the works party last Tuesday, since when she has not been mentioned. Madeline Falconer?"

"Oh, that Madeline. Okay."

* * *

The end of term tests produced few surprises, Delia and Big Mamma came top of the year in English; Sadie in Maths; {And also on the third-year paper.} Jennifer in Biology; and Rosalind took the top spot in 2AB in Chemistry and second overall to Timothy Ebsenter. At break, the results were being discussed outside,

"Timmy beat me again; he's obviously the best in the year at Chemistry."

"But not by much," said Big Mamma.

Rosalind shrugged, obviously not much put out, Timothy Ebsenter was apparently a suitable brain to come second to, in Chemistry Examinations. At that moment the boy himself came running around the corner, saw the girls, took evasive action clumsily. He slipped and fell in some mud, splashing it on Rosalind's shoes.

"Sorry. I'm so sorry."

Queen Bee turned and walked away in silence, her hands

123

pumping up and down as if she were, Khrushchev style, banging on a table. While rounding the corner almost out of sight, she let go a short, fierce left hook into the wall. There was a soft BOK, and mortar and brick dust fell out. The rest of the girls winced, but Rosalind merely walked on, banging her table.

"Who's she really mad at?" asked Big Mamma while looking at Anna.

Her friend stared at the retreating back,
"--You're right; it's Rosalind Schelle!"

Bryant House: December 1983

Delia

Dave Summers dropped his daughter at the Bryant house on Boxing Day morning.

"You can give Madeline some turkey to take home if you want, but, like, don't just give it away to get rid of it, I've got plans for the rest. Some new recipes to try."

"Okay."

"So she is coming. Good! You never said. Like, it would have been nice to be told, I don't mind, and I'd like to meet her."

"Sorry."

Amelia already had the door open for her.

"Bye," she waved her Dad off and joined her friend. As the door shut behind Delia, Amelia produced a sprig of mistletoe, held it up and comprehensively smooched the astonished youngster under it, sensuously squishing her bottom with her other hand. After a moment Delia surrendered, wriggling up against the older girl, as much as the bump would allow. When they came up for air, she pressed the sprig into Delia's hand,

"Andrew's miffed because the toy his Mum bought him came without batteries. Go and give him a right snogging, cheer him up. Cuddle him close for me; he can't get near me now."

Delia edged towards the living room.

"You can wriggle up against him if you would like to."

Astonishment gave way to pleasure in Delia's eyes,

"Yes, please."

"Get him all hard and flustered, give me something seriously deprived to take care of later."

The girl limped away to the living room, a grin spreading across her face. The telephone fell off the wall mounting as Delia passed, she deftly caught it before it hit the ground and replaced it.

"Sorry. Like, I didn't know I'd knocked it."

"You probably didn't. It's always falling off for nowt! I think it likes attention." Amelia waved her on into the room with both hands. "Go and get snogged," she whispered.

Andrew was sitting, slumped, on the settee,

"Merry Christmas."

125

"Merry Christmas," he replied and began to get up.

"Stay there," she replied, hoisted her skirt up and swarmed onto his lap, straddling him. "Amelia said I had to, like, cheer you up." She held the mistletoe aloft, then leaned in and with her heart thumping, kissed her secret love as best she could. They came up for air. "She said to give you a good snogging, make up for no batteries," and enthusiastically dived back in. His penis responded at once to the renewed wriggling against him, when she felt it, Delia intensified the wriggles and snuggled firmly up against it. His hands roamed over her back, intensifying her pleasure.

The heavily pregnant girl waited several minutes before calling through,

"Delia, can you come and help me dish up?" When the youngster appeared, smiling nervously, she asked her quietly. "Was that nice? A nice surprise present?"

"Yes. Lovely. Like, thank you."

"Would you like to do it again, before you go home? Say Goodnight with kisses and snuggles?"

Delia's eyes shone, lighting up the room,

"Yes, please."

"And me? Could I have a good snogging off you too?"

"Yes; of course, like, I'd enjoy that."

"How good? Can I really snog you--Would you mind if I **really** meant it?"

Belatedly Delia caught on and simultaneously realised that far from minding, she found the prospect exciting.

"Like a lover? A lesbian lover?"

Amelia nodded.

"If, like, that's what you want. Why not?" She watched some of the apprehension ease out of the elder girl's eyes.

You need me to meet you halfway on this don't you? She moved in and slid an arm protectively around her friend's waist and her other hand up her top. Amelia stood quite still and acquiescent, looking at her fondly as Delia confirmed that, as she had suspected, the other girl was wearing nothing under the top. She intimately caressed her, fondling and soothing.

All the rest of the tension flowed away out of Amelia's body, as her eyes softened losing their fear,

"Oh--Oh," she murmured.

Delia leaned in and softly, sensuously kissed Amelia's jaw

126

line, neck and earlobe with plump, moist lips, after several seconds, gently, she disengaged,

"Now--What do you want me to do?"

After lunch they collected around the bran tub, Amelia plucked out the presents, expressing surprise when a second with her name on appeared,

"I take it from the Bebopp's paper that this is from you?"

"I bought one for myself, but then I got one in my stocking as well, like, we can twin it, if that's okay."

Amelia hugged and kissed the other girl,

"Of course, we can." She opened the present; it was a neat little appointments diary, and address book, casebound in Royal Purple tooled leather, half-hidden under a gift tag reading,

To Amelia,

with love from Delia,

Christmas 1983

"Thank you," she kissed her young friend again. "And thank you for writing Christmas out in full, properly. I hate the four letter shortening."

"I put me in as your first friend and you in as mine, I hope you don't mind?"

"I'd be upset if you hadn't."

"Dad put in for a telephone last week; I'll let you know the number, like, when we get it."

"Okay. This is ours, but keep it to yourself, Delia."

"Don't, like, scrawl it all over the School Bog."

"Exactly don't like."

"Plain Chocolate," said Andrew peering into his scroggin. "Somebody has been doing her homework, thank you, Somebody."

Delia watched nervously as Amelia unwrapped the bear, but relaxed when the lights went on in the other girl's eyes.

"It's lovely, thank you! Y'baby thanks you as well."

Delia began clearing up the strafed wrapping papers, her eyes glowing with deep pleasure in the firelight.

"You look really happy," said Amelia.

"I am. I can't wait for baby to see his teddy, like, for the first time."

"Where are you going?"

"To get rid of this lot." She held up the ball of paper.

"We're not finished yet, look in the tub."

In the bottom of the tub lay a large rectangular block, wrapped in Christmas paper, with bows and streamers, to a level of style to rival one of Delia's own creations.

The gift tag read,

To Delia, Christmas 1983.

With love from

Andrew, Amelia and Bump.

Delia reached it out; it was obviously a book. She tore the wrapper open as ladylike as her trembling fingers would allow. It was a mighty tome on Basic Restaurant Management.

"If you've already got it, or don't want it, they'll change it."

"No, it's fine. It's lovely. Thank you so much."

With tears in her eyes, Delia kissed the other two again.

Andrew

Andrew and Amelia waved Delia off until the car was out of sight. She waited beside him as he locked up,

"Did you come?"

"No. No thanks to you. Encouraging me to frot her was bad enough. Are you trying to get me the sack?"

"No darling I was testing the water, seeing what it would be like."

"Besides being my pupil, she is only fifteen; she does not know her own mind yet."

"Oh I think she does and when she leaves, she will be nineteen. Besides, it won't be long before she will need to move out, yon Madeline is already measuring her Dad for curtains."

The couple drifted through to the bedroom while they discussed the project.

"I'm going to invite her to be this one's Godparent," She caressed the bump. "And we will give her another good snogging at New Year."

"And you will follow up on your throwaway line to move in."

"I already have. She's prepared to baby-sit and stay overnight. Weekends. I'll let her know the offer of a ménage à trois is there; she can choose. You promised me I could have a wife if ever I found the girl I wanted."

"It is different when it is a reality."

"And the bonus is she loves you too. It would be a three-way ménage; you would have two wives, and we would each have a wife and a husband."

"I'm fully aware of the bonus; I just do not want to lose any of what I have already got."

"That's all right darling; we'll make sure you don't. She's a mature, level-headed, sensible, wild-child. The identical twin I never had. Together, we'll take the very best care of you. Now then, have I got a deprived man to take care of?"

"Seriously deprived and seriously aroused, woman!" Andrew lay back demonstrating the truth of his claim. "What are you going to do about it?"

Bryant House: 1 January 1984

Amelia

On New Year's Day morning, Andrew Bryant kissed his wife goodbye and left for his match,

"Don't start the year by being sent off."

"I am never sent off, cheeky baggage."

"Only because you're so good at disguising fouls, one day some wide awake referee will see them."

"I love you too! Bye."

"Bye. Love you. See you at the restaurant, one o'clock on the dot, or before of course."

He waved and walked away grinning; his playing dirty was a standing joke between them. The main reason he had failed to make the grade as a minor league centre-half was that he wasn't a big enough bastard, not prepared to boot the opposition halfway up the terraces. That was until some un-clued-up centre striker came over the top at him, of course. Then, the gloves came off; Andrew couldn't remember ever conceding a goal in a match once he'd been hurt.

Amelia leisurely had a shower and put on her face. She put on the other new dress Andrew had bought her for Christmas and settled down with her magazine to wait for her parents. Baby Bryant woke up and began marching about. Amelia had only just returned from the consequent urgent trip to the toilet when her father's top toy crept serenely around the corner and moments later glided to a halt at her door.

She grabbed her coat smiling; the lad next door was leaning over the fence calling to her Dad. She knew that he would be offering to buy the car, which, because of the care lavished on it, showed no sign of its twenty and change, years of age, 'to take it off your hands,' she could hear his patter in her head. As she shut the door, she heard her Dad replying,

"You offered me twice that at Easter."

"Depreciation, I tell you what-"

"Shut up you, you're not getting it, and that's final," broke in Amelia, kissed he neighbour, wished him a Happy New Year and waddled on out to greet her parents and wish them a Happy New Year also. Her Dad settled her into the car, and they set off sedately for the restaurant. His grandchild wasn't due for over a month, but that was no reason to take chances.

The roundabout over the bypass was busy,

But at least they've removed the slip-road-on priority, on the exit, mused Amelia, sizing up the traffic, while her Dad waited for a suitable gap. *That left-turn into the car park, a hundred metres or so past the roundabout, isn't any longer a dangerous dice game, with traffic with right of way, charging up your nearside.*

When the gap in the traffic appeared, it was wide and clear, Amelia's Dad drew smoothly away around the huge circle, changing up for the second time as he lined up for the exit. The other side of the bypass was equally busy, an apparently solid phalanx of cars was paused, engines revving, waiting to join the roundabout.

Chapter 7
Of Starting Again: January 1984
Sales Rep.

It was already after midday. The salesman taking his new client out for New Years lunch was later than he meant to be, but with a clear run, he might still get there before the appointed time. He signalled left and took the slip road exit between slower moving cars, accelerating hard up the slope, away from the bypass.

Thank goodness there's a priority left off this slip-road, he thought as he cut across to the left-hand lane in front of a lorry and accelerated smoothly away from it up the hill.

The road ahead broadened. The lane to his right divided and divided again as it approached the crest of the hill. The other exits were jamming up with cars waiting for breaks in the traffic; he smiled as he dived left along his clear lane.

The hill crested out.
The Give-Way markings
flashed under his car
at over fifty miles per hour.
The road ahead was full
of a lovingly cared for,
ancient, Austin Cambridge.
Realisation hit.
The madman in charge of

Novochester's road markings
had changed them again.
But not warned anyone.
Again.
The modern rep-mobile wrapped the vintage car around its
bonnet, like a stamped on lager can.

Fighting: January 1984

Delia

Madeline opened the door; her eyes narrowed when she saw the uniforms,

"Dave!" she called.

The lovely blonde patiently waited until Dave Summers appeared and Madeline had stood aside to let him through.

"Good afternoon Mr Summers, sorry to bother you, it's Elaine Jacques again and this is PC Jones." She flashed a small Royal Purple tooled leather book at him. "I'm looking for Delia, is she around please?"

"You'd better come in."

The blonde Officer stepped elegantly over the threshold, her huge minder followed, ducking his head.

"Delia, it's the Police."

The youngster hobbled through from the kitchen, apron and foam-covered, rubber-gloves explained what she was doing.

"Hello again Delia, sorry to interrupt." Again, she held up the diary. "But I think you know Mrs Amelia Bryant?"

"Yes."

"Could you tell us where we might find her husband, Andrew Bryant?"

"They're having New Year's Dinner at the Panniers, with Amelia's Mum and Dad. I'm going over for tea later. Like, not to the Panniers, to the house. What's happened?"

* * *

Delia sat in her chair watching through a gap in the curtains. The wait in the hospital corridor had seemed much longer than its true duration of several hours. The vibes were if anything even worse now, in Intensive Care, sorrowfully weeping. Delia feared that she already knew. Her friend lay still and pale, several tubes sprouted from her, her face, her hand, more vanished under the single sheet draped over the still form. How small a head was, swathed in bandages, instead of a cloud of luxuriant hair.

"Who are you?" Despite the high rank on her nameplate, the doctor was young; she was also pretty, tired and too thin.

"Delia Summers, Amelia's friend."

The other girl nodded, parted the curtains and moved in to join Andrew, after a moment she drew him outside.

"I have bad news I'm afraid." Delia reached out and held his hand in both of hers; the young doctor glanced at her.

"Like, just tell us, doctor."

"It's very bad news; Amelia is severely brain damaged. Her body is fighting, but the straight lines showing on that screen there, indicate that there is hardly any brain activity. Well, none at all. Do you understand what I'm saying?"

"Amelia is dead?"

"Her brain is dead."

"Are the machines keeping her alive?"

"Ordinarily they should be, but they are not. I think that Amelia is fighting for her child, Mr Bryant. Your baby survived the crash, as you know, and Amelia didn't miscarry. That level of trauma often induces a miscarriage. I think she's fighting for her unborn child, as her dying gift to you. Every day she lives will improve the baby's chances of survival. It's my opinion that she will give up the fight when she gives birth."

"What should we do?"

"While she's stable, let's wait. If there is a sudden deterioration, particularly if the baby becomes stressed, we should perform a caesarean section at once."

"Do I have to give permission?"

"If you give permission now, we could act swiftly, not need to contact you if things get a bit hasty."

"I am definitely going to lose Amelia?"

"I'm afraid so, yes. In my opinion, you've already lost her; her body has shut down, concentrating on one thing."

"No chance you are wrong?"

"There's always a chance. Would you like a second opinion?"

Delia butted in; Mr Bryant might not have read his labels, but she had. She waved at the nameplate hanging from the girl's hip.

"You're the Senior Registrar, aren't you? Like, there's only Mr Dale above you, isn't there?"

"Yes. He did what he could, but it's his opinion too."

Andrew Bryant looked from Delia back to the Registrar and faced reality,

"I'm in your hands doctor, where do I sign."

135

"There's one other thing; Amelia was carrying a donor card."

"When the baby does not need them, you can have anything still useful. We feel--felt very strongly about that. I will sign anything there too."

* * *

It was late when Dave retrieved his daughter from the hospital and returned her to their home. Madeline's little one was in a shaky-down on Delia's bedroom floor.

"With it being so late and everything, we thought--"

"It's okay Dad." She took the supper that the other girl was offering. "Thanks, Madeline, you two get off to bed; I need to blubber for a while. I'll try not to wake Jane. I'll see you, like, in the morning. You will be still here in the morning won't you?"

Madeline looked at Dave,

"Well--"

"Good, not everything that happened today is a tragedy then. Goodnight."

* * *

Delia awoke to the touch of someone creeping into bed beside her and gathered the little bare body to her.

"Where's my Mummy?"

"In the next room, she's quite safe. I tell you what, we'll give her, like, a nice surprise, make her breakfast in bed and take it into her and Dave, shall we?"

"What will we make?"

"Something very plain. We've all had much rich food recently; we need a plain meal for a change."

"Wet egg on toast?"

"We'll have wet egg on toast, but we'll, like, hold the egg and add some marmalade instead."

"That's silly; you can't have wet egg on toast and hold the egg."

"Yes, you can, come on, quietly, I'll, like, show you."

"It's just toast."

"It's wet egg on toast with, like, the secret ingredient, no egg."

Giggle.

"Now have we got everything? Hot toast, butter, marmalade, tea, cups, spoons, sugar, milk and the secret ingredient, yes, like, that's everything. Can you carry that little tray and I'll bring the big one."

"Yes."

"One second, I'll open the doors ready." Delia slipped through to her Dad's bedroom, ostensibly to open the door, but in reality to make sure that certain activities were not being interrupted. The couple was still asleep, but the covers were down a bit and Madeline, lying prone, was naked to the waist, if only then. Delia looked at the bare back for a moment, then slipped her own nightie off and returned to pick up the tray.

"Ready?" She whispered to Jane. The youngster nodded. "We go in talking, but not loudly, we haven't made the boy's breakfast, so, like, don't wake them."

"Right."

As expected, Madeline's first reaction to being woken up naked, was to reach for the covers, but the sight of their respective daughters, nipples rampant, allowed her to sit up and enjoy the meal, apparently without embarrassment. Later when the general conversation and laughter woke the boys, and they joined the group, she didn't cover up then either.

* * *

As she had done every day since the accident, Delia called into the hospital to visit Amelia. The bed contained a be-tubed middle-aged man sleeping peacefully. On seeing her, a nurse hurried to her side.

"Where's Amelia?"

"It happened early this morning, the baby's fine, in Intensive Care, but it's just precautionary, she's fine."

"How's Mr Bryant?"

"His telephone's out of order we could not contact him."

"Oh--Oh--It'll have dropped off. It keeps dropping off the hook, like, if you just look at it. I know somebody lives in his street, could knock on his door, he hasn't slept much since--"

"What's the number?"

"They're in the book."

The girl guided Delia over to the ward office and slid a directory out.

"Louise--Er Kent Blyths, like, 48 The Dale."

A few seconds later, the nurse dialled out, carefully tracking the number in the book with her finger.

"Hello, It's Sister Susan Joyce at the Royal who am I speaking with please?--Hello Louise can I speak with your Dad-"

"Mum, Kent," interrupted Delia.

"Sorry, your--Yes please."

Delia waited as the arrangements were completed.

In a World of modern communications, where you could watch a war from your armchair, it was reassuring to know there was still room for a messenger with a note in her forked stick.

"Can I see Amelia? Say goodbye."

"No, she's in theatre; she donated herself to save others."

"Oh--Yes."

"You can see the baby."

"Yes, please."

Sister Joyce spun the chair around and pushed the schoolgirl towards the baby unit,

"Have you seen newborn babies before?"

"Like, all blue and bloody."

"We've cleaned her up, and she's a nice pink colour now, but she's still a few weeks premature so don't get a shock, she looks very strange, with tubes and things, but they're just precautionary, she's fine, we're very hopeful, confident even. Amelia did a grand job this last fortnight."

"She's so little."

"Just under three kilogrammes, some full term babies are only that weight. She's breathing by herself, big gong of a heart banging away, we're so confident we haven't baptised her."

"Can I touch her?"

"Wash your hands in that special douche--Dry them in the hot air blower--Don't touch anything else other than baby. Don't move her. Put your little fingers in her palms."

"Oh, what a strong grip."

"Strong enough to support her own weight."

"Like, she can swim too, can't she?"

"Yes, no fear of water at that age. You have to learn to fear it."

"Our Science Teacher believes we came down from the trees and went straight into lakes or even, like, the sea."

"That'll be Stewart Baques then?"

"Yes."

"He told me the same thing. It's only a minority view."

"Yes, he said."

"But I think he's right. Remember, don't move anything."

"I won't."

Delia sat quietly beside the tiny, almost naked person in the incubator; from time to time she scanned the screens. The baby did seem to be doing fine; if consistent, regular-repeating, wavy lines were anything to go by.

Movement over to her right drew her attention; Andrew Bryant was being guided towards her. She waited until he was close,

"She's beautiful."

"Oh." He stood, indecisively looking into the cot.

"If you wash your hands, like, sterilise them, over there, you can touch her." Sister Joyce watched from the background as Delia led her Form Tutor through the procedure and encouraged him to sit beside her. He hadn't been sitting for more than a minute when the tears began to course off his chin. The girl cuddled his face to the 32D cup breasts, as the sobs racked him. The nurse mouthed,

"You okay," at her and she nodded as she hugged and caressed her distraught friend.

A Fateful Decision: Warwickshire Spring 1984
Mildred

The local elections looming up in only a few months time, made it imperative that the leader of the party rein in his loose cannon, before she lost them any more votes. After consultation with senior colleagues, it was agreed that the safest place for her destructive actions was in planning. There, at least, decisions were made at leisure, with time to redirect their aim. He didn't call her in; he specifically caught her on her way out to an important meeting off site.

"Ah Mildred, we're having a reshuffle, and I propose to promote you out of Social Welfare into Planning, I know it's more work and greater responsibility, but I'm sure you're up to it. Any questions?fine. It's effective from now. I know you're in a hurry, so I won't detain you, the new files will be on your desk later today. Thank you so much." His attention switched away from her, "Ah Rex, can I have a word?" and he'd gone.

Councillor Mildred Patterson bought the pup and all its fleas, her mind blinded by the word promotion.

She eagerly tackled the new responsibility of refusing planning permission, whether desirable or not, with a level of zeal worthy of any convert.

Plagiarism And Adapting: Tyne-dale Jan-Mar 1984

Delia

That the accident and loss of a girl she had been expecting to love for the rest of her life, affected Delia deeply, was apparent almost immediately. Never again would fate, with impunity, deal her a losing hand.

Their Newly-Qualified-Teacher in their English class had given them an essay assignment,

A Narrow Escape

Delia did Georgiana Darcy and George Whickham, creating the scene that Austen only tells readers about, where Fitzwilliam Darcy discovers the deception and puts a stop to it.[4]

She wrote it in the first person from Georgiana's viewpoint and told the story through dialogue.

Rosalind did Jim Hawkins in the apple barrel.[5] She put a humorous twist on the story as Jim, sick of dodging the plunging knife, stuck an apple on it.

Several students read personal stories out, from their own life. Delia thought them very plain and was eager to read hers, then came Rosalind's turn. The protests began within a minute of her starting and before she reached the end, she was being howled down. Far from Mr Charlton doing anything about the howling, he joined in. Then he grabbed her book and crossed out her work in slashing strokes of his red pen.

Rosalind was devastated, curled over in her seat fighting the tears, the hard shell she habitually hid behind was lying shattered in fragments around her feet. Jennifer was crouched over her, shielding her, as best she could.

Delia looked around the room; she hadn't expected Big Mamma to be howling with the rest, and she wasn't. She was staring intently at Mr Charlton's antics. Delia caught her eye,

4   Pride And Prejudice: Jane Austen.
5   Treasure Island: Robert Louis Stevenson.

"Me first?"

"Okay." Came the reply. Delia struggled to her feet.

"Sir! Like, what's so wrong with that?" The howling had a new target; she imperiously held her hand fending it away, palm out, but otherwise ignored it. The howling diminished.

"It's unoriginal; she has plagiarised someone else's work."

"Un-orange-anal!"

"Play-jarised!"

"Someonelse's werk!" The shouts, from the boys, rang around the room.

"You can hear the problem, Sir. I did Georgiana Darcy and Mr Whickham, so I'll be wrong too," she waved at the baying horde. "They don't understand a word you're saying and nor do I. I'm, like, a thick little fifteen-year-old, with no qualifications."

"And I'm just twelve!" Shirley too had stood up. "You have a degree in English; perhaps you can tell us what she did wrong. I was going to do Marjorie Baldwin, dealing with Mel Dickey when he pulled his gun on Janet,[6] but I couldn't get the cadence right; Heinlein did it better. Perhaps you can explain, so we get it right next time."

With Big Mamma on her feet too, there was now silence, the class got an explanation of sorts, mainly repeating the words already used, but the bell for the end of the lesson rang, before honour, or even knowledge, had been satisfied.

Outside the classroom,

"Thanks." Rosalind hurried away with a bent head.

"Telemarks!" Exclaimed Jennifer, threw her hands up and hurried after her.

"I'll check with SB," called Shirley.

Delia looked at her,

"I'll see what Mr Bryant thinks of it all."

The upshot of that was that 2SB and 2AB had a joint meeting in PSE and the difference between plagiarism, quoting and adapting and the necessity to acknowledge sources, was explained to them. Whereas they all now understood that their work was not what was required from the brief, they also understood that

6   Friday: Robert A. Heinlein.

nor had their Form Tutors endorsed its wholesale castigation. Nothing was said, but it was the very fact that nothing was said, that revealed their teacher's attitude.

Mr Charlton never referred to it again either. Stewart Baques and Andrew Bryant had spoken with him in the English office. No-one was supposed to know, but Jeanette's younger brother had been thrown out of his lesson and eavesdropped and told her. When he heard the teachers refer to, 'a serious complaint from Senior Pupils,' he crept up to the door.

"Is it correct that two of the girls stood up in your lesson and defended her?"

"Well, yes --"

"Took on the job that you should have been doing."

"And it was only then that the class stopped baying at her like a pack of dogs?"

"Well, yes --"

"I cannot tell you how to run your classroom during your career, but I can tell you that neither Stewart nor I would allow that sort of mass bullying to occur."

"And, we don't know of a single teacher that we respect that would--"

At that moment Mr Bryant whipped the door open, revealing the listening boy and sent him away. His wildly embellished account contained enough truth for Jeanette to identify the incident and report back.

At night, when Delia patrolled the School, she sometimes ran Andrew to ground in the Materials Technology Room,

"I wish they'd just call it Woodwork, I mean, like, that's what it is."

"They used to, they used to teach kids grammar in English, so I am told."

"Don't start me off--that's, like, beautiful wood."

"Oak. It will be a desk companion when it is finished, at the minute it is mind control--"

"I know. I know exactly what it is. How's Amy?"

"She is fine, we have worked out a routine, she bosses me about, I obey her to the letter, and we get on fine."

"How are you going to manage the School Activities Show next week?"

"I do not know."

"I could baby sit. If, like, that's the problem."

"Would you? If it is not too--"

"Visiting your house was the best part of my life. It would be a pleasure and, like, I'd love to see Amy again."

Baby-sitting Amy Bryant settled into a regular occupation, with Delia moving the boundaries of her relationship with Andrew, steadily through friendship, to something more intimate. She kissed him goodbye from the very first one. Later she hugged him as well.

As Easter approached, with her sixteenth birthday looming, she was ready significantly to raise the stakes.

Chapter 8
Political Manoeuvres: April - May 1984
Delia

The view down the street was nearly the same as the last time she had looked, just a bit darker. It was nearly nine; he'd vaguely hoped to be home from the Parents' Evening before now, and he'd be trashed. Delia switched the TV off; she hadn't paid much attention to it for an hour anyway, between watching for him and deciding to cook the meal that he'd planned for himself in readiness for his arrival. She'd found it in the freezer, all neatly labelled by the home help who came in four days a week to 'Do', defrosted it and warmed it through in the microwave. It was still there, ready on the plate, sealed against drying out by a tight glass cover. All it needed now was a few minutes blast on high power to--he had turned into the bottom of the street. She limped through, checked the settings and began the final blast.

The view through the glass panel in the front door was restricted, but good enough in April to see him turn into his gate; she opened the door for him as he climbed the steps,

"Sorry, I --"

"Shh. It's okay, like, I know what's up. Your tea's nearly ready. You look trashed, do you need a hug? Come on, have a hug until your food's ready."

He leaned against the kitchen units, as he had done the last time Delia babysat and had given him a hug before she went home. She stepped right into him, an arm around his neck and the other around his waist, she was plastered up his front from knees to neck, slowly wriggling sensuously against him. His penis reacted exactly as it had done every time before, from Boxing Day onwards. She wondered if he could feel her breasts pressing into him as he was pressing at her. She hoped so.

The microwave pinged. Delia disengaged, rotated the food a quarter turn, reset the cooker and climbed back onto her man. His hand slid onto her bum. She turned her face up slightly; the lips that brushed across her forehead had bristles around them. She tilted up even more, when his lips met hers the hand on her bottom gripped firmly, squishing her. She snuggled and wriggled, acquiescing, compliant. She rubbed up and down.

The microwave pinged again. She ignored it and rubbed him again, up and down. He returned the rub, dry shagging her, squishing her bottom, but then after a few brief seconds disengaged,

"Thank you, Delia, that was nice. What have you made for me?"

"The Chinese. You were going to have yourself. I knew you wouldn't bother this late. You would just have a sandwich. Or cereal. You should have, like, a meal."

"I have School lunch." He allowed her to settle him down and serve the meal, while they argued.

"Huh!"

"It is good nutritious food; it has to be, by law."

"Once maybe, a long time ago, now it's rubbish. All the taste is chemically added. Has it got any vitamins? Any variation? Is there enough to fill, like, a man's belly? Don't bother answering, Andrew. We both know the answers."[7]

She rarely used his name, preferring to call him nothing at all, although she was perfectly happy to call him Sir at school, in front of her friends and other staff, it came naturally. She picked up the telephone and dialled her brand-new home number. "Mr Bryant's finally made it Dad, can you come and get me?--Thanks--Bye."

Madeline knocked on the Bryant's door while Dave turned the car around.

"Thank you so much, I'm really sorry for it being so late."

7   1984: Jamie Oliver's crusade is still two decades away. P.C.

"It's okay we knew you would be, we were going to offer you a lift, but you still had a queue when we left."

"I should have just stayed. Much easier. Next time I'll bring my Pyjama Blag." Delia hobbled down the path.

"Pyjama Blag?"

"It's a talking pyjama bag, like a doll, Delia got it for her first Christmas. You pull a string, and it speaks random phrases, in an American accent, like 'Can I have your pyjamas now?" and "It's time for bed." one of them is "I'm a pyjama blag." Dave's new, young girlfriend shrugged at Andrew, before following Delia to the car. Her man drove the family away smiling. Delia relaxed with satisfaction; the arrangement was that next time she would stay, in Delia's World, no argument was agreement.

* * *

The next scheduled babysit was the following weekend, and it clashed with a Wedding Invitation. The upside, from Delia's point of view, was that the invitation was for all of them, Dave, Madeline, all four children and Grandma and the car should only take five and a squeeze at that.

"The best idea is if I babysit and just stay over. I'll stay until Sunday. Friday-night the do. Saturday morning he's got a Volleyball match. In the afternoon, he's playing Cricket himself. Come and get me when you bring Gran home at teatime on Sunday."

"Delia--"

"Look I'll ring him. If it's okay by him and okay by me, make it okay by you. Right?"

"Delia it's not a question of being okay by--"

"Madeline, I don't meddle between you and Dad. Like, I really hope you two make a go of it, but you're not my Mum, don't meddle--Please."

"Okay. I'm not meddling."

"I'll ring him, without your input young lady; go to your room for five minutes."

Delia left sedately and calmly without a backwards glance, climbed the stairs, one at a time, on the left leg lead. Once in her room, however, she let the grin surface as she finished her packing for two days and nights, confident in the knowledge of where she would be.

* * *

Andrew Bryant met them at the gate to heft Delia's case into the house. Dave followed with her chair.

"Are you sure this is all right Mr Bryant?"

"It is fine."

"It simplifies our arrangements dramatically. It's still not exactly the right number of seats, but enough space."

"And it solves all my problems for this weekend. It is really fine."

They waved Delia's Dad, step Mother to be and the rest of their children, off to pick up Grandma and depart for his cousin's Wedding. The forty-four-hour round trip, would be with a car jammed full.

Delia checked over the baby gear for that night while Andrew would be out and unavailable for advice.

"I think it is all there."

"Yes, so do I. Lift your trouser legs up--You've got odd socks on. I bet you've got another pair in your wardrobe exactly the same."

"No, they are not."

"You can't see, lift higher. Same colour, different SPORTY around the top."

"Oh--Bonk." He trekked through to the bedroom and changed one, so that they matched.

"That's better. Have you got a clean hanky? Money?"

"You are worse than my mother."

"Of course I am. I'm a friend," she slid her arms around his neck and gave him a smoochy kiss. "Go and have a nice meal, I'll wait up for you. Bye."

* * *

The taxi discharged her tired and slightly wobbly Form Tutor to his front door. Delia guided him through into his bedroom, with Andrew obeying her instructions in silence.

"Stand there. Stand!" she turned the bed down quickly.

"Can you take your top off?"

Laboriously he proved that he could, while she loosened his shoes. She undid his belt and flies zip and pulled his trousers down.

"Stand! Andrew! Stand Up!" Despite her instructions he was

buckling, she heaved him so that he collapsed onto the bed. It took her several minutes to strip him down to his boxers and tidy the rest of his clothes away. His breathing deepened and became regular. She did her rounds checking on the baby and making sure the house was secure. With barely a glance at the camp-bed made up for her in Amy's room, Delia returned to the master bedroom carrying the pyjama blag.

"May I sleep here?" she whispered and a moment later. "I asked, and you didn't say no." After a moment of thought, she laid the doll down, stripped to her own knickers and sat in beside him. He grunted turned over, reached out for her and cuddled her back into him, holding her firm young tits, as he snuggled into her back. His breathing resumed its regular rhythm. Delia slid a finger into herself; almost as if he knew, Andrew squeezed the plump breasts and not long after she was stifling orgasmic squeals. The squeals subsided as she too slid down to blissful sleep.

Hands were squishing her breasts, nice; a big, rigid cock was thrusting against her bum, lovely.

No, Andrew! You mustn't!

"Andrew stop," she wriggled away from him, turning, looking at him over her shoulder. "You mustn't, you're playing a match, like, this afternoon."

His eyes were open, full of shock.

"You mustn't shag me, like, before the match."

He blinked, even now not fully awake.

"You can do it after, if you still want to, but don't do it before; you won't play well. Get up, it's, like, time anyway," she rolled him over away from her and gave him a firm although gentle push in the back with hands and left foot.

"Go and get your shower, leave the boxers out for the wash." She piled out of bed after him, her proudly erect teats still tingling with remembered caresses.

"Give me them now; I'll put new out for you."

Obediently but also on autopilot, Andrew dropped his boxers; his erection was slowly wilting. Delia glanced at it, then smiled up at him,

"Shower."

After his shower Andrew discovered his clothes lying in a neat pile on the bathroom floor, he'd not heard her do it. His breakfast was laid for him, cereal and boiled egg and soldiers.

The baby was in her high chair, with Delia sitting next to her, plastic spoon in hand, stolidly pushing baby rice into the little one's face; scooping up the spillages and making them form the basis of the next mouthful. She was still dressed only in her knickers. She was coping with the distractions of Daddy moving about, by anticipating the moves; an unenlightened observer might think the mouth was following the laden spoon. Baby Amy was working steadily down the little pot of food.

"I don't know where your cricket gear is; I haven't got it out for you."

Andrew tore his eyes away from the pert naked teats,

"It is okay, I will get it later, it is all ready."

"Soup and bacon butties for lunch, steak and chips for tea, like, after the match?"

"Sounds fine, I will need lunch at eleven; the match starts at noon. Twelve until six."

"Lunch at eleven, dinner at seven, unless you're, like, going on to the pub."

"No, I am coming straight home thanks, Delia. I had my ration for the year yesterday."

"How many was that?"

"Four Vodkas, maybe a couple of wines too."

"Just four. That's why they get to you if you only have four a year, but all on one night. Is that more or less right, like, only four a year?"

"Much more than less. I am just not keen on the taste of ethanol, hardly at all."

"I'm glad, I've seen the damage it can do to people. I'll need some money, possibly a fair bit, the larder's a tad bare, like, empty, tins, makings, baby food, nappies 'n that."

"Do you want to go shopping?"

"Need."

Andrew pulled a Styx face,

"Are we looking at a lot of money and a big load?"

"Yes, I'm afraid so."

He pulled a drawer open in the dresser and pointed to a large rectangular purse,

"Housekeeping, I will just check--Bonk, is there anything in the larder?"

"Not a lot. No."

"Because it is all in here. Sorry Delia, I have had things on my mind, skipped mere details like food and stuff. Don't fill the freezer, nor long term, buy one get six free bargains, but you can lay in plenty fresh and everything for Amy; of course."

"No alcohol. No tobacco?"

"Absolutely not. I used to smoke, but managed to kick the habit last year, but it is like alcohol, once an alcoholic, always an alcoholic, I am a nicotinic, a non-smoking-smoker. Get a taxi, there and back." He glanced at her nodding. "From the supermarket."

After breakfast, with Andrew off to his match; Delia cleansed and prepared Amy for her day and settled the little one into her buggy.

Half an hour later, showered and dressed, she tackled the shopping list.

She searched for paper on Andrew's desk, and her eye caught the letter, it was among pens and drawing instruments, the only document on the desk -- impossible to miss.

--- offer you the position of House Master of Prior House, as from September 1st, 1984. Please complete the enclosed acceptance and return ---

She tore her eyes away, closed them and rested, leaning forward on the desk breathing heavily. No, it was no good, she had read too much, she had to read the rest. She had to know if her plans, to court and later marry her Form Tutor; plans of which he had no knowledge: were about to be diverted by plans of his; about which she had no knowledge.

The letter was from a Private Sector School in Warwickshire, and there was no reply slip, her ship wasn't being diverted, more like sunk.

She opened her eyes; somehow she'd slumped down into his chair. She sat up straight, speaking out loud,

"Okay, it's a setback, but that's all. It wasn't ever going to be easy, but if it adds one extra problem, it also takes one away. You write every week Delia Summers, and you go for the holidays and make sure that he enjoys your company as much as you enjoy his. If he's eagerly awaiting your visits intensely enough, he'll, like, do the necessary."

She filed the letter in an empty docket, cleared his drawing instruments up and stowed them neatly away in the drawer under the desktop. The top drawer on the right was proud; she nudged it shut; it wouldn't move. She tried to open it; it wouldn't move; something was jamming it. She bounced and bumped the drawer; it freed and popped open in mid bounce. It was the corner of the hem of a gym-skirt that had been jamming it. As she straightened off the grey tunic, Amelia's heady, musky scent enveloped her, her friend had worn it at some time. She lifted the gym-skirt out and hugged it. Underneath was a white blouse, although folded for storage, it was slightly creased and grubby and heavy with Amelia's perfume. Beneath the blouse were some School ties. She recognised those of West and East Novochester; others were unfamiliar. Nestling alongside the ties were some elegant wooden nameplates on leather thongs.

Among *Susan* and *Maria* and *Sandra* and *Audrey*, lay *Delia*.

Chapter 9
Of Living Dangerously: May 1984
Delia

"Go and say Goodnight, if you're quick, she'll still be awake." The baby was gurgling sleepily at her mobile, Andrew kissed his beautiful daughter Goodnight and rejoined her sitter in the kitchen. She was obviously tired.

"Can I help?"

"Get the trays and stuff. It's not chips, like, I didn't realise that the Jerseys were in, so I got some and butter. It's a high cholesterol tea I'm afraid."

The potatoes were the softest wax, bursting with flavour, the steaks rare and succulent and the root, fruit and leaf salad, crisp and juicy. Andrew carried their meals through to the front room on trays, and they sat side-by-side listening to soft background music, their silence doing justice to the youngster's, seriously better than average, culinary skills. After washing up together,

"No don't throw the fat out, I've, like, got plans for that."

Delia dried the draining boards down while Andrew, apparently unwilling to get in her way again, stood indecisively to one side. She smiled her softest, friendliest-smile at him, trying to reduce the rising tension gently,

"I've had a lovely day with Amy, and I'm, like, eagerly

expecting a lovely evening relaxing with you. You don't have to sparkle and scintillate. Gently, quietly, growing together is what I have in mind."

"I am not, not talking, because I do not know how to handle this situation, but because I can not talk easily."

"It's okay; I prattle on enough for two--"

"No, Delia you do not understand, I am not apologising; I am explaining. I really can not talk easily. Not the best talent to lack if you want to teach, I know, but I am improving. When I was thirteen, I lost the ability to speak. It took a long time and a lot of speech therapy to get it back as a whisper and then as talk. But, even now I lose it sometimes and have to go back to the basic mechanics."

"You'd never guess."

"Yes, you would. No-one talks as I do naturally. Only someone who has to think, how do I say, 'See Spot run,'? Then form the words like moulding them out of Plasticine."

"You're quite wrong; you'd never guess. It's a little slow and precise at times, but you'd never guess that it was, like, hard work. Honest."

"You are nice, do you know that?"

With the tension easing dramatically, Delia moved smoothly into her plan for the evening,

"Thank you, kind Sir, can I, like, make you a drink?" She said taking the tea cloth away from him.

"Just a can."

"Go and sit down, I'll bring it through." Then a minute later. "There's only the Pepsi."

"That is right."

"Oh. Can I have one?"

"Of course."

She gave him his can and opened her own.

"While you are in charge of my house, do not ask whether you can have something unless it is the last one. If we are in danger of running short, put it on the shopping list."

"Okay--Thanks--I know it's still early, but can I close the

blinds?"

"Yes, if you want to."

She crossed to the window and began closing them off one by one,

"Well, I'd like a really good snog and petting. Pick up from where we had to leave off this morning. Might be better with the blinds shut. Like, I don't mind you seeing everything I've got, but not the local riff-raff." She sat down beside him and swung around, across him. "And it might be prudent to keep it our secret." She lay back along the sofa and rested her head in his lap, expecting to have to cajole and persuade. To her surprise,

"What do you want?"

"Kisses and petting. Like, snog me silly, everywhere. Then, you can take me to bed and fill me up."

"I am leaving in the summer."

"I know."

"Permanently. I am not coming back."

"I know, I went looking for paper for the shopping list this morning, I didn't mean to pry, but the letter was open on your desk. Twenty words are easier to, like, scan than avoid. I'm sorry for accidentally reading it. The reply slip is missing, so I knew you'd accepted."

"It is a big promotion, House Master to the day boys, those who live off site, so I can too. I am going house hunting at Whit."

"I thought you might be."

"We will not see each other after the end of July."

"Not necessarily, I could come down and help you settle into your new place, like, look after Amy while you're house hunting. Visit during the holidays, until you find a new girl. Once that happens, I wouldn't want to intrude anyway."

"If you came with me, I would end up shagging you."

"So! I'm sixteen, it's not, like, illegal. Malfeasance-- Unprofessional conduct--Instant dismissal conduct--But only if someone complains and nobody will, because no-one will ever know."

"I do not know how I did not do it last night. Did you fight

155

me off?"

"Of course not, you were too tired, you fell asleep, but you can do it tonight, and when I visit you, like, I don't mind you doing it. You can make me squeal--I squeal a lot when I'm coming--"

"Delia, I would love to, but I have not got any condoms."

"All taken care of, Andrew dear. Dutch cap in place, full to the lips with spermicidal jelly, a troupe of Cossacks couldn't impregnate me tonight. Now, no more bets, please, stop moulding your Plasticine and, like, start making love to me."

Andrew went to speak, but changed his mind, mirroring her gentle smile instead. He curled forward and down and kissed her, as he found that, under the tight top, she was braless. A few minutes later he discovered that she was naked under her skirt too.

Presently as the need became imperative, she got up and led him through to the bedroom, walking hand in hand.

Inside the bedroom it was Delia, already in control, that took the initiative, assertively undressing him and voluptuously caressing erogenous zones. It wasn't long before she was urging him to mount her and squealing her appreciation of his efforts.

He lifted himself off her and looked at her naked form. She was smiling at him.

"Was that nice?" She asked.

"It was lovely." He picked up the limp, twisted and tiny, right foot and kissed it, licked it, sucked each toe in turn and then kissed up the inside of the shorter leg. He stopped, glanced up at her, his lips still in contact with her inner thigh. "It was lovely, thank you."

"Thank you too."

He resumed his lovemaking, homing in on the glistening lips.

"Careful. Spermicidal Jelly, I don't know whether you can, like, eat it."

He burst out laughing and moved up to lie down beside her.

"My first boy did that, made love, like, to my bad foot. Thank you, it helps."

A couple of replays, with variations, followed, before the satiated couple drifted off to languorous sleep.

Delia awoke, although it was light, Andrew was still asleep; she slid out of bed and went to check on Amy. The baby too, was still asleep, as the youngster watched her, her arms reared up in astonishment and then sank down again.

The girl hobbled through to the kitchen, fired up the grill and turned it up high. She mixed up two desert-spoons-full of raw cane sugar with about the same volume of Balsamic vinegar and a generous pinch of salt.

From a bag full of tomatoes, she selected a dozen evenly sized ones. She cut each end of the core free from the rest of the fruit, by sliding a knife under the skin, but leaving everything in place and halved them as evenly as she could. Next, she scooped out the pulp from each half and folded it into the sugar-vinegar-salt mix. She replaced the pulp mixture into the tomato halves, in turn, adding a pip of steak dripping to each. The roll of kitchen foil, which she had bought the previous day, had been selected because it was wide enough to line the grill pan in one sheet.

When Delia placed the tomatoes in the neatly lined grill pan, she took great care to ensure that they were horizontal. The grill she slid them under was roaring, it was only several minutes later when the tomatoes had firmly skinned over, that she turned the heat down.

Using only the thinnest smear of the carefully conserved steak dripping, she prepared several doorsteps of wholemeal bread for grilling. When the tomatoes were cooked she grilled the doorsteps.

The pair ate their breakfast of caramelised-top tomatoes served on golden-brown grilled bread, with optional Tomato sauce and lightly sweetened tea, in silence.

Vainly, Andrew searched among the tomato skins, for something else to eat,

"That was fantastic, thank you. It is strange, sometimes the skins come off easily, sometimes they stick tenaciously."

"Mine always come off, I help them along a bit, like, with a sharp knife."

"Ah. Another cup?"

"Yes, please."

Andrew put the steaming second cup of tea down on the bedside cabinet, took his own around to the other side of the bed and climbed back in beside her. Delia humped up to a sitting position again.

"Thanks," she said and began sipping her tea. "There's something else, like, about yesterday. I found something else in your desk. A drawer was stuck, it was Amelia's gym-skirt that was jamming it. It's not now."

"Where have you put it? You did not wash it did you?"

"Of course not, like, what do you take me for? Holding her clothes with her scent is like holding Amelia again. I held them, for comfort."

"What else did you find?"

"The name tags."

"They were for playing games."

"I guessed. Did you play games too, like, for Amelia?"

"They were Amelia's games; she got a buzz from being other people. Last night was not the first time I made you squeal."

"Oh -- Right --"

"The first time I made you squeal, Amelia got pregnant. We used to say it was Delia's baby. Your baby. Amy."

The lump in Delia's throat took some swallowing, eventually,

"Oh -- Y'baby, I remember. That's nice." There was another long silence while they sipped tea. "What do you like doing?"

"I might tell you someday. What do you like?"

Delia nodded and sipped her tea,

"Different, like dressing up and pretending, I don't know, I'll think about that, ask me again in a few months. When are you going house hunting?"

"Whit week."

"Okay. Suggestion. We go during Whit week, I look after Amy while you set up your short list, then we girls visit the properties with you and, like, tell you which one to put an offer in for."

"You can not come with me."

"You're not going alone, Andrew, and that's final. It's going to be Amy's house too, and it won't be long before you will be expecting her to pull her weight about the place, tidy up, wash and clean and stuff. Like, it's only fair she sees it before you buy it, at least express her opinion."

"Your Dad will not allow it."

"Dad will do whatever I say. Leave him to me. Just don't you mess it up, by telling him you don't want me. Plan on going down there accompanied, because that's what's going to happen. Unless you, like, really don't want me beside you, in which case I don't want to be there either--Well?"

He shifted about uncomfortably.

"Andrew -- Andrew!"

He turned and looked at her.

"Like, tell me straight to my face that you don't want me beside you."

"I do want you beside me."

"Fine. I'll be there whenever I, like, can be."

He turned over away from her, reaching into the bedside cabinet, she thought for a moment that there might be another problem, but when he turned back, he was holding a sheaf of papers.

"I've already got the short list."

Chapter 10
Choices: May - June 1984
Delia

ogether they scanned the sheets.

There was a terraced town house whose front door opened directly off the street and a ranch style bungalow, apparently surrounded by an unkempt ranch. A suburban semi with neither garage, nor room to build one, contrasted with another, cheaper semi, spacious and welcoming, with garage, carport and patio at the rear. Included among the sheets were some for a pair of flats with vacant possession of the lower one and a brochure advertising a narrow boat. The brochure was open and folded at a middle of the range one.

"Why the boat?"

"I love boats; it was just an idea."

"Can you, like, afford all of these?"

"No, well, yes, Amelia's Insurances come through soon, and there is her parent's Estate, half of which goes to Amelia because she outlived them and hence to me, Amy inherits the other half; it goes in trust for her until she is eighteen. That brings them all within reach. Some even have a bit over."

Delia sorted through and pulled out the bungalow.

"Why is this one cheaper than the town house and the semis?

Yet it's got loads of land."

"The land will be farmland price, possibly poor farmland price, peanuts. Only the bungalow land will be building land price. Besides, it says something about finishing touches required."

"I thought that meant, like, decorating."

"More like half the roof, the half you cannot see? Do you like it?" Delia flipped through the attached sheets and pointed to some small print near the bottom of one of them.

The Property has 200-metre Frontage on the Oxford Canal

"Even with the boat on top, it's barely more expensive than the town house. Boats are like horses, the main problem's not buying her, it's the provision of a mooring for her. Like, if we got this one, that problem vanishes. House first--That boat, or a different one to follow, there's some really nice ones in the brochure, for not much more money, as soon as we can afford her."

"We?"

"I would like it to be we."

"Delia you are-"

"I'm three years older than Juliet of the House of Capulet. But I'm not a fan of the Grande Gesture, so, like, if it isn't we, I'll be disappointed, but I won't be trying to drill a hole in the quayside by taking a header off the Tyne Bridge."

"Can I think about it? Not the Love and Care aspect, I do love you, pet, it is just the problems and consequences."

"You can have up to thirty months. If I haven't convinced you by then, I never will. I'm going to get Amy up and seen to. When I've got her settled, I'd like another very sexy session please, before I, like, go home."

"Okay."

* * *

Delia grasped the nettle, when she arrived home, before her courage sublimed, or mundane activities swamped her,

"Dad I want to talk about Andrew and our future."

"Yes."

161

"He's applied, well got the job of House Master in a school down south--house hunting in Warwickshire at Whit--So I want to go and help him choose the house and go down every holiday to look after Amy. Make sure she doesn't forget me. See, like, how it works out."

"And what does Mr Bryant have to say about all this."

"He's terrified. I'm too young. You won't allow it. It's just a phase I'm passing through; I'll peel off and scurry after the first cute butt that walks past. But, he'd, like, settle for me at the minute."

"At the minute?"

"I think he sees me as Miss-Right, but if I'm up here, like, three hundred miles away, for three years without seeing him, Miss-Nearly-Right-But-Available-Now might become a better bet."

"If he really loves you, he'd wait."

"I think he does and he would. But there are other things besides love, losing Amelia was a tragedy, but good can come out of it, like, I already think of Amy as my daughter; I'd rather not risk it."

"Leave it with me, Delia; I need to think about this one."

"I promised not to meddle, but can I say something?"

Delia looked steadily at the girl only a few years older than herself who shared her Dad's bed almost every weekend. She got the strong impression that if she said No, she would be obeyed.

"Yes."

"How long have you loved him?"

"Ever since I first saw him, nearly two years, but Amelia was my friend. Like, until she died, it was a none option, well, not even a thought."

"You've got no choice Dave; she **needs** to go."

"Whit week is a week on Friday; I'll start my packing."

The following week, 2AB and 2SB found themselves dumped in the library, during Languages' Oral Examinations. Delia's friends were making plans for the Half Term Holiday.

"Nowhere on the Monday, we'll never get on the buses, and if we do manage the buses, we'll never get space.

"Tuesday then?"

"St Mary's Island on the Tuesday?"

"Yes, miss the crowds."

"Not me, like, I'm babysitting Amy all week."

"That what they call it now is it, spelt S-C-R-E-W-I-N-G pronounced Babysitting?"

"I promise you Hopkins if I ever do manage to lure a teacher into bed, you'll be the first I lie to about it. You still got the silver chains you stole from The Goldsmiths Truck?" Gerald Hopkins turned on his heel and found something very interesting to do on a shelf full of dictionaries. Delia's intense stare tracked him away; Big Mamma regarded her with amusement,

"Nice one." The tall brunette mouthed silently at her, with a smile. That was okay; Shirley was secure. A Big Bull-Dyke if all the rumours were true, but she was definitely secure.

The plans for Whit week required meetings with Andrew at School as well as elsewhere. Occasionally Delia's friends were present, but often, partly because of the subjects of the conversations she needed to have with him, speaking with him alone.

"How are we going to get down?"

"I was thinking of hiring a car."

Delia just looked at him.

"I enrolled for some refresher sessions at the driving school and counselling. The counsellor thought it a good idea."

"Oh right, good on yer."

He walked over and shut the door.

"I also told her about you, the counsellor that is."

"And?"

"She mentioned the word rebound."

"I'm, like, on the rebound too. Not quite as dramatically tragic as you but."

"It does not worry you?"

"No. It was the one word my Dad never mentioned; he was

163

on the rebound when Mum scooped him up and put him back together. It took about half a decade, but he suddenly woke up to the fact that he'd fallen in love with her, while scraping a home together and fathering a squad of kids. Madeline's on the rebound, like, I don't rate it as a factor."

"What have you told your friends?"

"I'm the babysitter. Up front, no secret about it."

"And they believe you?"

"What they believe doesn't matter. I say 'the babysitter' and look them straight in the eye. Queen Bee and Big Mamma talk about it as if it's kosher and most everybody else follows. Those that don't." Delia shrugged, "I know where too many bodies are buried in this Burgh for most people to, like, risk it."

"Does your Dad know the truth?"

"I've never told him, but neither has he asked, so yes, like, he'll know. Can we go on the Friday, spend the entire holiday together?"

"I have only just plucked up the courage to book us into The Nine Isles for the eight nights."

"I bet they never turned a hair, did you do what I said, A double room with a cot, for myself and my baby and the babysitter?"

"Yes."

"See I told you. Good hotels like the Isles provide a service and don't ask boat-rocking questions. All they ask in return is that we don't crap on their front step. I'll come around tonight and sort it."

"Delia," but he was talking to a closing door, she'd already gone-- "Oh, Okay."

* * *

"The Running Pheasant Hotel, Prior's Torvilke. Selena speaking, how can I help you?"

"You can extend our booking one night to a linked hotel a couple-o'-hundred miles north of you, like, Yorkshire way. We'd like to break our journey on our way to stay with you. We need a similar room for the Friday, June 1. What do you need first? My name's Miss Delia Summers; my employer booked it."

"The booking code number please Miss Summers."

"5/84/Streamside/3."

"And the name?"

"Andrew Bryant."

"And who are you please, Miss Summers?"

"I'm the babysitter."

"One moment please." Delia waited, Andrew bounced Amy on his knee, talking to the gurgling child,

"It is all right Amy, we are in safe hands, we will have to fight like buggery to be allowed to stir our tea widdershins, but we will never want for toilet paper."

"You should, like, be so lucky."

"Pardon?"

"Oh! Sorry, I was talking to Mr Bryant, he's, like, sitting here being stroppy."

"Oh -- The booking is for a double room Miss Summers, is that correct?"

"And a cot for Amy."

"Yes, there's a similar room to the one you've booked here, available at the Abbeyford, on the ground floor?"

"Yes, I'm in a wheelchair, some of the time, it's no big deal, just makes things, like, easier. What's the Abbeyford?"

"It's a Nine Isles Hotel, in Leeds. Is it just the Friday?"

"Yes, please, what about discount? That'll take us to, like, nine days."

Andrew looked up sharply.

"The nine-day discount is 5%."

"I was hoping for ten."

"There's a sliding scale up to ten depending on how often you patronise the restaurant."

"Is it any good?"

"I had my hen night and my Wedding here, I was more than satisfied, pleased, Leeds is similar."

"That sounds fine Selena, would you book it for us and, like, if Leeds send us the details we'll confirm in writing if required."

"Hold please -- That's done Miss Summers, the details should be with you -- it'll be the day after tomorrow now, if you--"
Presently Delia disconnected and went through to the bedroom.

"Have you packed yet?"

"What was that about discount?"

"If we eat in the restaurant we qualify for 10%, have you, like, packed yet?"

"We could not eat anywhere else, not with Amy, It woul--"

"We're only getting what we're entitled to, like, it's silly to pay for something if you don't need to, if it's so called free, which means we've already paid for it, don't pay for it again. Have you packed yet?"

"I was going to do it next Friday night."

"Not anymore, we won't be here. Pack anything you don't need before we go, use your blue flight bag for the important papers, the hotel bookings, like, houses 'n that. May I borrow Amelia's?"

"Of course. Her case too if you want to match."

"Yes, please. You get busy here; I'll pack for, like, Amy."

Packing, seeing to Amy's needs and getting her settled had Delia's lift home arriving while they were still flying about and long before they had any space even to squeeze in a quickie. Although her Dad had not asked awkward questions, that proprieties were being observed, overtly at least, was obvious by their reaction.

On their way home Dave described the deal clearly,

"Delia, I deliberately came early tonight, not exactly spying on you but seeing how things might look to outsiders. If what the World always sees, is what I saw tonight, I will let you run your life as you wish. But, it has got to be always."

"Okay."

* * *

The Abbeyford turned out to be a small, family hotel, situated on a gentle south-facing slope overlooking one of Leeds' green spaces, of which it has many.

"Are we really in Leeds?"

"Yes, I think so; the Welcome notice was miles back."

"I expected smoke and grime and industry."

"So did I, but this is a lovely place."

"I know we've got many parks, but, like, this wins hands down! And I don't feel great admitting that. We're here, wow this is some place."

The large welcoming notice invited guests to park their car and report to reception, where all their Worldly needs would be met.

"If you get everything out, I'll, like, get some help." Delia punted her way around to the front, where her way was blocked by a huge revolving door. Already; however, a porter was beckoning her into one of the sectors. She pushed in, and he revolved it slowly, allowing her through,

"Good Evening Miss Summers and welcome to the Abbeyford," he said. "If you report to reception, I will see to your bags."

"Oh," said Delia. "Like, thank you. Mr Bryant's getting them out."

"Yes, Miss." He was already departing to his task.

Again as she approached the desk, she was addressed by name,

"Good Evening Miss Summers, I hope you had a good trip?"

"Yes, thank you. I take it you're only expecting one wheelchair tonight."

"As it happens, we are expecting three, but only one with a Tyne-dale number plate, only one with a baby." The girl nodded at her side of the high desk between them. "We picked you up on the car park camera. You were a very short odds favourite."

"Like, nine to one on?"

The room and evening meal merely enhanced the feel-good factor that Delia's welcome had inspired. By the following morning, she was almost loath to leave.

"Are all Nine Isles Hotels, like, as lovely to stay at as this one?"

"We all claim we're the best Miss Summers, so yes, probably."

So it was no surprise to roll into the car park of the Running Pheasant and be greeted by another porter at the door,

"Good Evening Miss Summers and welcome to the Running Pheasant. If you report to reception, I will see to your bags."

And at the desk,

"Good Evening Miss Summers, I hope you had a good trip?"

"Yes, we did, is it Selena?"

"Yes, Miss."

"The Abbeyford lived up to every expectation; I'm confident the Running Pheasant will be at least as good." The girl's professional smile was replaced by a softened, more personal one.

"If you come this way, I'll show you the room."

* * *

The town house and semis in Prior's Richmount had been possibilities, but all suffered from the same obvious drawback.

Despite being in the middle of a rural area, the one with most land attached was cramped up against its neighbour, the others weren't merely cramped up, they were in their neighbours' knickers and fronting onto a busy street.

When viewed, however, further drawbacks became apparent, one of which was much more sinister.

Chapter 11
Big Decisions: Warwickshire 10 - 12 June 1984
Delia

Juliet Means, Manageress of John Means Ltd. Estate Agents of Prior's Richmount, lit up and sparkled when she saw them come into her shop. At first, Delia thought business must be slack, the girl had volunteered to be available over the Whit Bank Holiday, but when the tall gaunt figure emerged from behind her desk and spoke with them, a much baser and utterly personal motive was instantly evident.

"Good afternoon, Sir, I am Juliet Means," she said pointing to her nameplate on her lapel. "How may I help you?"

"Good afternoon, I'm Andrew Bryant, this is my friend Delia Summers and my daughter, Amy."

"Hello." Delia readjusted Amy on her hip and looked behind Andrew to see who was being addressed. The protest had no visible effect.

"You sent me the details on some properties Miss Means," he proffered the sheets. "We would like to have a closer look at the town house, the semis and the unfinished bungalow."

"Certainly, Mr Bryant, but please call me Juliet. The town house is just around the corner, walking distance; the semis are on the estate, a short drive. We can go now if that's convenient."

Andrew looked at Delia who nodded to him, when they

looked back to Miss Means she was still gazing star-struck into Andrew's eyes.

"Yes, that would be fine."

The town house was stone built and impressive; the front door opened straight from the high street into the living room. Stairs ran up to the upper floors from directly in front of them, and the dining room and kitchen were reached by a through door at the back of the living room on the left. Andrew looked at Delia who shook her head minutely.

"It's nice Juliet, but straight off the high street with children is not an option, can we see the semis?"

"Certainly."

The first semi also faced a busy street, through a tiny garden, but it did have another slightly larger garden at the back, which sloped upwards away from the house. It was a straight forward, if significantly expensive, estate-built semi and unless faults appeared, would be acceptable, with more pros than cons. The builder's daughter, however, was looking with educated eyes at the DIY patio along the rear wall of the house, where the garden sloped upwards away from it most steeply. Tiny green, fingernail-sized plates, each with a tiny parasol rising out of it, were growing in every crevice. The gleaming fresh paint on the woodwork was also a source of interest; she reached out and thrust her thumbnail upwards into the underside of a window frame.

"Can we see the other one?" She said.

No reaction.

"Where's the other one?" asked Andrew.

"Just around the corner Mr Bryant, if you would come this way."

The second semi had a larger garden; green shrubs stood shoulder to shoulder across it, almost concealing an ornate lychgate type porch to the front door. The brown painted woodwork, gave an overall sombre aura, accentuating the impression of heavy eaves drooping across the windows, half closed lids obscuring sad eyes. Delia stopped abruptly, grabbing her man's arm with her free hand.

"Don't! Don't go in, not even the garden," she dragged him away. "Come on, back to the hotel; we'll talk about this. We'll, like, look at the others on Monday."

* * *

"The town house was never an option, but what was so wrong with that semi?"

"It's a weeping house. There was a tragedy there, or more likely there is going to be a tragedy there and soon. I got the impression that it, like, hadn't happened yet."

"Are you serious?"

"I've never been more serious in my life. Don't ever go there."

"Okay, I will not. What about the first semi?"

"Water damage, damp and rot. Whoever built the patio, built it too high, like, above the damp proof course."

"I noticed the greenery."

"Liverworts, totally and completely harmless, but they only grow in, like, damp conditions and the woodwork is rotten; I could push my thumb nail into it."

On Monday afternoon, Miss Means collected them from the Running Pheasant and took them out to see the unfinished bungalow. The road out of Prior's Eastwicke ran towards the Oxford Canal, with the view opening up by the second before them. Just when it seemed that the road continued straight down to the canal, it passed over a cattle-grid through a gateway and forked. Miss Means turned right onto a track and drove along the bottom edge of the low scarp slope to the East for several hundred metres.

"We've been on the land for this property since the road," she said to Andrew conspiratorially, as the bungalow came into view over the top of a small rise. "So there is no lurking financial penalty of a ransom strip."

"That is good," he replied.

To the east, a sheltering fir plantation rose up the slope. "The plantation belongs to the property, as does the land down to the canal."

Delia could see a building nearer the water.

171

"What's that Barn?" She'd spoken loudly, to ensure a reply,

"It's currently being used as a feed store by your neighbour, Mr Blake, but it was a café originally, so it's a good sound building--"

Delia wasted no time in cropping accidental potential bonus points,

"But too far from the house to be any use as, like, an extension."

"Er--Yes I suppose so."

Andrew too wielded the shears.

"It's a long way from a road."

"It's less than a kilometre."

"Humph," called Delia from the back. "I'll need a powered chair."

The quartet disembarked, one really interested in the utterly new; one unsuccessfully trying to hide her apathy, while making no attempt to disguise her enthusiasm for her other agenda; while the remaining two successfully put on almost the exact opposite performance.

The stone built bungalow looked really forlorn; a drift of leaves curled up against the front door like a breaking wave. The land around was choked with fat hen and thick stalked, dense drifts of chickweed. Taller stands of stinging nettles punctuated the wider area. Near the door, a few dwarf Rhododendrons were bravely swelling seed pods, and new young shoots were emerging. The year's growth since planting was a similar dark green to the year before. Delia surreptitiously squeezed her man's hand. Instead of waiting to be shown around inside, the couple made their way over and peered into windows.

"That's what a house looks like when the workers just walk out," said Delia to the little one perched on her hip, pointing in through the window. Amy peered into the room, empty but for a lidless pot of paint, a few sad brushes and a newspaper splashing last September's headlines. Although there was no evidence of fittings in the room, at knee level, waste pipes emerged from the wall and led off along to the right, disappearing several metres away, around the corner of the house.

Delia followed them along the footpath between the house and garage. Around the corner, they plunged into the ground alongside a grate, under a window into what could be a generous sized, second bedroom.

The view from her new vantage point, across rich farmland, was devoid of mountains, but full of interest. The track from Prior's Eastwicke, the continuation of their front drive, ran, past the Café, down to the canal, becoming a bridleway on the other side of the ornate stone bridge.

From where she was standing Delia could see several furlongs of canal in the foreground and isolated farms across the broad valley to the west and north. She continued right around the building, eventually rejoining the other two on the track. The glint of running water drew the eye to a spring bubbling from the base of a small rocky outcrop a few metres down the slope to the west. If she listened hard, she imagined that she could just hear the sound of traffic from the intermittently visible Welsh Road to the North or the A 423 several miles to the West, but in reality, the only sounds were the gurgle of the spring and the constant high-pitched zing of insect wings. She resurveyed the field down to the canal, it was definitely one field, to all intents the bungalow's back garden. She assumed that the impression of size must be an optical illusion brought on by the concave slope.

Andrew listened impassively to the agent's loquacious spiel, extolling the very obvious merits of view and price while glossing over the serious deficiencies, like lack of access to anything short of 4 x 4 performance, unkempt estate, no neighbours within sight, not to mention--

When she paused for breath, the counterpunches slammed in,

"I know it says unfinished; I did not expect this level of unfinished."

"Just a few touches, Sir."

"Like, the entire Kitchen?"

"It's all in the garage Mr Bryant, ready to be fitted."

"And of course it will be flooded every six or seven years so that we will need serious flood defences, I tell you what, we will look around the inside. You get on to the vendors and tell them that their first live buyer for over nine months is offering forty-five thousand, cash, for quick closure." The agent began to bluster and protest.

"There has been steady interest in the property--"

"We both know the interest has been steady at zero. Or that tree shed its leaves last week. Do it," interrupted Andrew pointing to the girl's Landrover and built in car phone. Reluctantly she left them, and Andrew steered Delia around to the front, out of view, with Amy drinking in the scene round-eyed, on her hip. He brushed the leaves away and unlocked the door; Delia hooked her free arm around his neck, he plucked her up, carried his girls across the thresh and kissed them. They said nothing, just walked through the reverberating empty rooms, looking at the views from the windows. When the agent joined them, she began to negotiate; Delia chopped her off.

"I'm not happy with the kitchen, that's where I'll spend most of my time, but it has the stupidest view, mostly garage. Like, I'm not prepared to pay good money for a stupid view. Forty-five's all a stupid view's worth."

It was only a few minutes later that Juliet Means gave up and sold them the bungalow, subject to contract.

* * *

After their baths and while waiting for dinner, with such a crowded and successful day behind them, Andrew and Delia just had to reprise events.

"And 'of course it will be flooded every six or seven years', and you said it with a straight face too. In a pig's eye. Like, Amy could have told her the house was safe. Maybe not the far reaches of the garden, but the house definitely."

"What about you, I am not prepared to pay good money for a stupid view, little Miss Spoilt-brat stamping her foot. You had moved the kitchen around the corner into that bedroom, before you even got into the house."

"Well, she should have known, done her homework, prepared for the obvious criticisms. And anyway, it really does annoy

174

me, builders ripping Joe Public off; building crap to evade the building regulations and expecting me not to spot it. So, I play by their rules. They don't expect a tits and bum to be able to, like, out-think them. Makes it so easy sometimes."

"Which builders?"

"Nearly all of them. Fitting Georgian windows with tiny panes to evade the double-glazing standards, leaving show houses with the doors off to disguise the fact that the rooms are too small to live in properly. I even saw one where if you walked into the bathroom and if the door cleared the basin, which wasn't certain, you'd side-swipe anyone getting washed there and it wasn't even under the window. So--"

"So tall people, like me, bang their head every time they get washed." He lay back on the bed. "Are you happy? About the house?"

"I can see all my plans, like, sprouting. And the garden, over ten acres, that'll probably include the trees 'n track 'n that, but still--"

"No darling, ten acres does not include the trees and the track. I have been on to the land registry, because it looked to be too much land."

"I thought that too, like, Ben has a seven-acre field, but our land looks much more than half as big again. I thought it must be the odd shape."

"The odd shape may bear some responsibility, but it is not half as big again as seven acres. Try three and a half times as big. It is ten hectares, not ten acres."

"How come?"

"There is a printing error on the sheet. I have pointed it out once, when I first got the sheets, now it is up to the vendor. I have offered our price for the plot as listed in the Land Registry and I made sure she wrote those words down."

"Oh--Oh! We have cut the deal to end all deals."

"Subject to contract, but the solicitor seems very positive."

"While not, like, counting chickens, I am going ahead with my plans. I've already picked the spot where we're putting Amelia's garden, and I could feel you slobbering."

"Well, do you blame me? Rhododendrons growing slowly but dark green, because the soil is only just acid and the weeds were a dead giveaway. Fat hen and lush stands of quality nettles, telling us the soil is rich."

"The last time I saw chickweed like that, it was, like, growing on a prize-winning compost heap."

"I might not be able to feed us out of that garden, but I will get bloody close. You need fresh, clean water for ducks. Did you notice the spring?"

"I've already got it filling the pond. We could, like, keep chickens and pigs."

"There are pure breed pigs, slow growing but producing quality pork. They would plough the land, grubbing up the weed roots, hoovering up runt crops and leftovers."

"Are you serious, that we could keep chickens and pigs?"

"Yes, why ever not?"

"Vorwerks and Buff Orpingtons for eggs, Dorkings for the oven, Silkies to brood our own stock."

"I take it from Buff Orpington that they are chickens?"

"Mmm and we could have Tamworths, Durocs, Gloucestershire Old Spot--"

"Pigs?"

"Yes, Large Blacks."

"And do not forget the ducks. I like duck eggs."

Delia hurled herself onto him, snuggling him,

"Indian Runners and Khaki Campbells! Although these days, they're not necessarily khaki! Oh, Andrew! I always wanted a mixed farm, I never, like, thought I'd ever have one."

Amy looked up from her blanket on the floor at the flurry of activity, gurgled and resumed posting blocks through holes into a box.

"You have obviously done your homework. Are you really serious about this? Holidays down here. Moving in--As in knickers, wooden spoon and bottom drawer, at the end of the Fifth Year?"

"Yes. Hearth, slippers and kids. Yes."

Andrew held her to him, while he reached for his bag,

"In that case, I had better give you this. I know she would want you to have it." He slid Amelia's engagement ring onto the third finger of Delia's left hand.

The telephone rang, It was their solicitor, Mike Stillwell,

"Hello--It is me speaking--And it will definitely be listed as the plot in the Land Registry, not as described in the flyer--We will call in to sign tomorrow--Fine. Oh, I meant to ask you before, what is a ransom strip? -- I see, and it's ongoing? -- I'm very pleased to hear that, thank you, goodbye." Andrew replaced the receiver and looked at Delia. "It is as I thought, the vendors are desperate to get rid of it, all ten hectares of it. Mike suspects that it may be the difference between tax breaks or some similar iffy financial chicanery. We sign on the deal tomorrow, and exchange contracts on Friday."

For the second time in just a few minutes, he had to field a flying girl, squealing joyously.

"And, like, 'ransom strip'?"

"If you don't own an access track to a property you buy, you might have to buy the access, and the cost is usually about a third of the **value** of your property. Not the **price**, the **value**. And if you add value to it with improvements, you have to pay again."

"A thousand years ago there was something similar, we, like, call it Danegeld now."

"Indeed, but it was the first thing he checked for us, and we do own the entire access, all the way from the road."

* * *

After visiting the solicitors, Andrew decided to go shopping for a 4 x 4, before negotiating the return of the family hatch to the hire Company's local agent.

"Take me with you, in my chair."

"You are coming with me."

"In my chair, trust me darling, I'm in devious, calculating-bitch mode."

The County Concessionaire had a low mileage demonstrator that didn't rattle and had several thousand missing from the list price.

"When can I take delivery? I need it tomorrow."

"Hmm, that might be--"

Delia jumped in hard, indicating her wheelchair,

"We need it tomorrow; the reasons should be, like, very obvious."

"Just a minute Madam, I'll have a word with my boss."

The following day, jesting fate brought the despot to meet her nemesis.

Chapter 12
War and Peace: Wednesday 13 June 1984

Delia

In the Post Office Delia finished her purchases and proffered the money.

"Why are you not in School?"

The arrogantly imperious question was so divorced from relevant in Delia's current world that she was unaware it was aimed at her and ignored it. She slid the change into her purse and went to put the purse in her pocket, while the assistant slipped her purchases into a bag and placed the handles together ready to give to her.

A lot happened in the next few seconds.

A hand grabbed her by the shoulder,
and spun her around.
Amy swung dangerously
away from her.
Her bonnet caught
on the chocolate bar display,
and pulled it over.
The tot was yanked
even further out of Delia's grasp.
Her discarded purse skidded across the floor.
With her brain,

body and both hands
concentrating on saving the baby
that she thought of as her daughter
from falling,
Delia dealt with the arm
that had spun her around
and was now across her mouth
cutting off the air, on autopilot.
Her teeth would have met together,
with the ferocity of her bite,
but for the ulna between them.
The scream of a cacodemon ripped her World.
The vicious swipe of the walking stick,
aimed to shatter her face,
shattered the clip, holding Delia's pineapple tuft,
as she ducked under it.
There were loud shouts from behind her.
The stick was raised high.
She was cornered, between counter and displays.
With Amy to protect.
She crouched covering the baby.
Triumphantly the stick crashed down for the kill.
To the accompaniment of even louder shouts,
it smashed through the glass top of the display counter,
burying itself into racks of chocolate bars.
showering Delia with debris.
Amy was squealing.
With an oath,
the stick was wrested out from
the bomb site of shattered glass,
and raised again for a second try,
with better aim.
Delia leaped for the tiny gap
between the legs of her attacker,
and a display cabinet.
A piece of plate glass she stood on for the lunge,
shot backwards.

With all thrust lost,
as her left leg shot out behind her,
the weak, right-leg, crumpled.
She fell down, not forward.
This time there was no escape.
She braced herself,
like a cowl over the screaming child.
"Stop!"
There was the authoritative ring of command in the shout.
The stick fell harmlessly, clattering to the floor beside her.

The legs blocking her escape leant backwards, their attached feet scuffling on the vicious shards, vainly scrabbling for purchase.

"You can get up now Miss; you won't be assaulted again."

A large, grey, middle-aged woman was screeching. Froth and spittle were spurting from her mouth as she struggled in the arms of a tall, young, police constable. The shopkeeper had hurried around from behind the counter and helped Delia to her feet, solicitously picking shards of glass off her back and out of her hair, while glancing warily at the pair still struggling and endangering another of his display stands. Although Delia was aware that her attacker had been arrested, she was concentrating all her resources on calming her distressed daughter.

"--and I'll add resisting arrest to that list if you struggle anymore."

"She bit me."

"Okay, resisting arrest as well." The handcuffs snapped slickly into place; the screeching woman was now cuddling a pillar, although still lashing out with her feet. Two other customers as well as those tending to Delia, kept well out of the way. It was several minutes before the shopkeeper was satisfied that Delia was free from large shards, but he warned her, again, about the smaller pieces that were still in her hair. Meanwhile, the policeman, ignoring the relentless rant, raining from his captive, had quickly noted down the memories of himself and the other witness who had seen everything and got the names and addresses of those who hadn't seen the initial altercation, but had seen some of the later events.

"She's truanting from School. She bit me! She's a wicked truant. She's evil--"

Sensibly getting his facts straight, before going for Delia's throat, the Police Officer asked,

"Why aren't you in School, Miss?"

"It's half term."

"Monday and Tuesday, today's Wednesday."

"I'm not from around here. It's half term where I come from. Can't you, like, recognise the accent?"

A panda car drew up outside, and a burly police sergeant and huge, young and pretty, mountain of a WPC leisurely climbed out of it. Their entry to the shop produced a renewed surge of screeching from the captured woman.

"Good day Councillor Patterson, please wait a moment while I talk to my officer. Then, I'll be with you." The screeching stopped. The sergeant moved over to the group who were gingerly separating chocolate from glass and murmured to the young constable. "I hope your evidence is fireproof--"

"Look out!" interrupted WPC Enermouse, but too late; a pointed court shoe whipped across the front of his legs and buried itself in the sergeant's gonads.

"And that's assaulting a police officer I think," added Delia, as the big man grunted and doubled over onto his knees among the shards.

* * *

Only two statements by the doctor who examined the various injured raised much interest in the police.

"Oh yes, Mrs Patterson was definitely bitten, but you see these deep gouges here, and here, they were made by canines being forced apart by the arm being thrust between them. The flesh would have been ripped differently if they were a withdrawal wound. The wrist was thrust into the mouth, deep enough to gag, the bite is a defensive wound, probably an attempt to rid the mouth of the obstruction, rather than an attacking wound, it was an attempt to force disengagement, rather than to disable."

And, "Miss Summers has cuts to her ear from something

very sharp. A bunch of her hair on the top of her head has been severely tugged; a good portion of it has been pulled out by the roots and some of the shattered remains of a plastic clip are sticking into her scalp on the side of the bunch of hair, opposite the uprooted fibres. I think she might have been wearing a plastic hair adornment and if so, the injuries are consistent with her being hit a glancing blow, across the top of the head, with something hard and heavy. She was definitely showered with broken glass from somewhere, because her hair is full of small splinters. Some of them are in the among the broken hair roots, but none, however, are in, or under the tugged bunch of hair. So the glass shards showered on her after she was hit.

Elsewhere full advantage was taken of the day's events.

Gift Horse: Wednesday 13 June 1984

Lovers

With Councillor Patterson safely answering questions at the police station, the planning sub committee quickly endorsed all the recommendation of their officers on the nod. In addition, they passed all the applications from the previous three meetings, that would have been passed but for her objections. Somewhere in the final list were the lovers' next two barn conversions. When the Councillor found out she was livid, she gave the impression that salt had been rubbed in.

Blissfully unaware of the developments at County Hall, the lovers continued to acquire new properties, managing to maintain a minimum tax liability, while accruing maximum assets.

"We're making a lot of money, I know it's tied up, but it won't always be, had you thought about what we might do with it?"

"No. Just, run away together."

"That's exactly what I had in mind too."

"Really. Just, do it?"

"Yes darling, really just do it, when we've got enough."

Devious And Calculating Again:
June - July 1984

Delia

On Thursday Delia overruled her man; prepared a letter of authorisation; met with her solicitor and took Amy on a tour of their new home village of Prior's-Eastwicke. Intentionally she finished at The Three Turnpikes Public House.

She met the solicitor by arrangement on the Welsh Road, on his way through to the Boddingtons and gave him his authorisation.

"The barn Mr Blake's using as a feed store, I plan to reopen it as a café. It is a café, and I'm, like, going to restore it, as soon as it's ours, I need you to do the necessary."

"Will you be selling food?"

"The works, a full restaurant, eventually, like, options for expansion."

"That's quite a big task, permits, approved contractors, there's bound to be some reserved matters."

"Permits and reserved matters 'n stuff, I'm expecting that, like, planned for it. Whatever it takes to satisfy the legalities. Don't agree to anything that's merely fashionable, or somebody's pet thing. I want it fireproof, completely legally unassailable."

"Fine. I can manage that."

"Write to me when you know what's required so that I can cost it. That's me, not, like, Mr Bryant. Inform him of course, but write to me."

"Very good Miss Summers."

Again in calculating, devious-bitch mode, Delia walked Amy around the village, sometimes in her pushchair but mostly on her own hip. Presently the wayward foot, as expected, began to ache and Delia limped into the bar of the pub, for a packet of crisps and a pint of Pepsi. The Olde Worlde pub carried a sign outside showing a spiked barrier across a road as header and a similar one across a cattle dip for a footer, with, between them, a detailed and vibrantly coloured picture of an angler, into a big fish and guiding it away from reeds. Delia couldn't help it, she giggled every time she saw it, or even when she heard it as it creaked, swinging gently even on almost calm days.

She took the snack out into the sunlit garden and settled Amy down with a rusk, at a table next to some locals. The locals were looking at her.

"Morning," she said brightly and dropped her crisps down, before reaching out a pack of Paracetamol. She broke the pack open as she sat down herself. A rugged individual in tweeds and big boots leant back in his chair,

"Morning Miss Summers-"

"Delia."

"Delia, I'm Peter, how are you today, bit sore I would guess?"

Delia stretched the right leg out and lifted her trouser up far enough to reveal the clump.

"Was I, like, limping? It'll be okay, it often doesn't hurt for weeks, then I forget to take care, and it reminds me. It'll be okay, the painkillers'll kick in soon." She waved the packet she was opening. "It'll be okay." The reaction was entirely as she had intended.

"What?"

"How?"

"When?"

"It's just a foot. I'm lucky; I see how lucky I am. Young kids with no legs at all, flying around in their wheelchairs, racing each other around the corridors, laughing their heads off," she readjusted Amy and recovered the fallen rusk. "And how not to behave, grumpy oldies, with, like, just corns, complaining because their ambulance is a few minutes late. Give me the wild kids any day. I will never be a grumpy oldie." The Vicar recovered first,

"You have to attend a clinic?"

"It's nothing and Colin's great, the man, like, on the desk. At Christmas, he buys the kids little presents and stuff, most of us look forward to going."

"Sorry. No, er, Delia. We didn't know about the foot," said the young woman, she leaned over, reached out and touched

186

Delia's hair. "We meant your head. Yesterday?"

Delia winced and pulled away,

"Ow!"

"Steady on Freda."

"Oh, sorry."

Amy's face crumpled,

"It's all right chick, look, Mummy's smiling, she didn't mean it, she said sorry, she didn't know, suck your rusk, there that's better, Mummy's fine." She spoke over her shoulder while looking at the child. "The head's fine, like, until someone hits it. But, as you said, that's yesterday's news, dead and finished with." Finally satisfied that Amy no longer thought she was under attack again and heavily buttressing the finished-with stance, before anyone could challenge it, she pulled out her notebook. "Perhaps you could help me; I need to know about livestock. Ducks, hens, pigs. Permits, restrictions, reliable sources, like, disease free stock 'n that. Certified stock."

Tweeds and boots waved at the vacant seats,

"Come and sit here, bring the little one over."

Delia complied.

The Vicar also piled in alongside with reinforcements,

"You'll not be buying from the market then?"

"Absolutely not, I wouldn't know a point of lay from a 404 with 500 eggs behind her, and until I do, I'll be buying from a reliable source, with a reputation to uphold and sustain."

"A little knowledge is a dangerous thing, but a little more is a springboard to higher things."

Delia responded to Peter's eyes with a twinkle of her own; he nodded in complicity.

"It could be expensive." he added.

"It'll cost me a few quid more, but I won't be, like, the one importing Foul Pest into the region. Likewise, though, I won't pay over the odds merely for a name; I never was into designer gear. I want quality, disease-free stock, at a fair price."

The interest at the table sharpened up and focussed in,

"The NFU might help--"

"Peter!"

"Not the Chair, not Winston Scuffer, don't bother him, his secretary Mrs Plenny. She'll help, especially when she learns your reason for avoiding dodgy animals. But don't be surprised if they refer you to somewhere local."

The girl called Freda pointed to the speaker and said,

"Him for instance."

"Local's no problem, quality, certification, reputation, guarantees, are."

"Start with the NFU, take it from there."

"What's your daughter's name?" asked the Vicar.

"Stepdaughter. To be, Amy. Now then. Restaurants. Where would you go for a good meal in Prior's Eastwicke, or, like, Prior's Torvilke?"

After a lengthy discussion, it was agreed that there was no high-class restaurant this side of Banbury and there probably never would be.

"Who's going to drive a thirty-mile round trip, on our roads, just for a meal?" asked the Postmaster rhetorically.

"It would have to be, like, a rather special meal?"

"As you say."

"That's fine too. Now, where I come from, even though we're only ten miles from the sea, it's cold, even now, in a normal year. Our last frost is often late May. Media gardeners reckon we're a fortnight behind; local gardeners know better; it's more like a month. So, like, when's your last frost, usually?"

The discussion blossomed, occasionally getting quite warm as pet topics were aired. By the end of the morning, the notebook was bulging with scribbled-on pages, and Delia had put the names of Peter Fortress, the old Squire's grandson, to tweeds and boots. Freda was the clumsy girl who had touched her head, the Postmaster was Sid, but the vicar was still Vicar.

Delia was just preparing to leave, to meet Andrew, when a thick set man, good looking, in a distinguished, greying-at-the-temples way, scurried into the garden and came straight up to her. She sensed the vibes instantly; Freda was friendly but anxious, the others watchful, apprehensive almost, she knew at once who had arrived.

"I'm so sorry about yesterday."

Delia blanked him.

"Mildred--Just, I'm Cade, Mildred's husband."

The blank look intensified.

"Cade Patterson, Mildred Patterson, yesterday."

"Oh. Not my problem, yesterday. Yesterday's gone, like, finished with." She began to collect her and Amy together.

"No, I want to make it up to you. I know a good builder. Kitchen, flood defences, he'd do a good job."

"That's okay, I'll bear it in mind, but we're probably okay, my Dad's a builder, in a small way, but, like, he's good. But thanks anyway."

The tension flowed away and Freda made space for Cade next to her; Peter smiled minutely at Delia with a hint of an appreciative nod. A moment later, she took her leave of the group and went out front to meet Andrew who took her back to the hotel to write up her notes into her log; this took most of the rest of the day.

Friday was spent exploring their newly purchased home and unkempt ranch of a garden and especially the café-cum byre down the slope near the canal.

From a distance, the building was unimpressive, shabby to the point of being unkempt and leaning drunkenly into it and through the roof was a partly fallen tree. Closer inspection, however, showed the initial impression to be misleading. The Café was a large rectangular stone built and beautifully proportioned Georgian style building.

"The stonework is smooth and tough, with no greenery and I like the windows."

Delia moved over and tested the wood,

"They are elegant hardwood window frames, and they are, like, hard, as hard as the day they were fitted."

"The fallen bit of the tree is just a branch; it is split from the main stem. Yes, it has punched through a couple of slates, but obviously, someone has been up and weatherproofed the resultant hole."

"But sadly not removed the, like, branch!"

"Delia, have you seen this foundation stone?"
The stone proudly announced that:

Lady Harriet Wallace laid this
Foundation Stone
7 August 1788
And officially opened
The Café On The Canal
5 June 1790

"The Café On The Canal"
"Yes, that's the first thing I'm, like, going to change."
"What to?"
"Dunno, yet, we'll see."

The big ornate key turned sweetly in the lock of the huge, probably original, front door, which fitted flush with the frame and although it could do with a coat of varnish, obviously still had a century or two left in its lifespan. Inside, the ceiling and walls, although heavily shrouded in dust, were very obviously original Georgian. Ahead hay had been neatly stacked in rectangular bales filling half the space. To the right, separated off by a narrow walkway, most of the remaining floor was covered by tightly packed straw bales. There was a space to the left, behind the hay. Delia saw something sticking out and went to investigate. Andrew moved over to the right to examine the ceiling beneath the hole in the roof.

"There has been no water leakage that I can see." When he got no reply, he turned to look for Delia to call her over. His girl was standing staring dumbstruck at something behind the hay out of his sight. "What is it?" He called. Again there was no reply. He walked over to join her and see the problem for himself.

Behind the end of the neatly stacked bales of hay were equally neatly stacked items of furniture, covered in straw and dust. Mainly tables and chairs, but further back against the wall he could see sideboards and other more bulky items.

"Did we buy the contents, like, the furniture as well?" Delia

190

asked.

"Yes, furniture, fixtures and fittings."

"So from noon today, these chairs and stuff are, like, ours too?"

"Yes, from ten minutes ago these dusty brown sticks are yours, why? Is there a problem?"

"Well, yes there is. Have you any idea how much this, like, collection of dusty brown sticks is worth?"

"No."

"Try for, like, one chair."

"One, perhaps a couple of quid, say £100 to £150 for the whole lot."

"Assuming that most of them are broken, or damaged in some way. And I cannot see any damage at all, but, like, being pessimistic, try adding two zeros."

"What!"

"If they are largely okay and they, like, look it, try adding your two zeros, and then multiplying the answer by five, or maybe even more!"

"Delia you can not be serious."

"I'm, like, deadly serious. We need these insured for half a million quid **now!** And we need them out of here to a French Polisher and restorer **today**. There's between one and two-hundred chairs alone here, they are Chippendale designs, or maybe Hepplewhite, classic Ladder back and Shield back carver chairs; the earlier, more ornately carved and inlaid style and the tables match them."

"They could be modern copies, worth nothing."

"The Oxford canal was in it's heyday between 1790 and 1805, after that it declined, this, like, section of it anyway. Although the Canal Company stayed in profit until it was Nationalised, much of the revenue came from other sources. This Café would not have made much money after 1805, not enough to refurnish. Certainly, not enough to refurnish with such high-quality items. I mean, look at these, like, wonderful inlaid veneers, swags, urns, trees, these can only be original George III. And -- **and** after two hundred years you'd expect the seat covers to be in ribbons, but they're not, I'm guessing they are linen. Ultra top-quality Irish Linen!"

It took much frantic telephoning and rapid fancy footwork by their solicitor, not to mention several seriously fat cheques being written, but by the time the couple set out for home their windfall was insured and being transferred and securely locked away from harm.

Behind the main hall and difficult to get to through a narrow channel between the bales, was the original kitchen. Delia was entranced. Five huge Jellies wood burning stoves occupied one side. Down the centre was a series of food preparation areas and the other side was in effect several marble walk-in-larders, in a row.

"I'd need gas stoves, instead of these, but if we can get them out safely, I reckon that they could, like, largely fund their replacements. And these walk in larders are a real find."

Behind the kitchen was a large hard standing where lorries could turn and park up to unload.

"It's brilliant. Can I, like, go ahead and make plans, investigate costs and such?"

"If all money decisions are joint, yes."

"All money decisions are joint, agreed."

The large pillared portico on the front of the building, which should have been one and a half coach and sixes wide, was barely half that, demonstrating that the original owner had run out of money at a critical moment and decided to economise on guest arrival instead of anything else. Delia took photographs, intending to show them to Shelley later,

"I'd like to make the front entrance as it should have been, but I'm not sure that I can, bearing in mind, like, proportions, but the Artist will know."

Later, in the Three Turnpikes,

"Who do you entrust with, like, building repairs, Peter?"

"That café of yours?"

"Yes, well my kitchen first, but the, like, café as well, later."

"Mission and Bagette, they're not cheap, but they are excellent and reliable."

"That's the guys I, like, need. No more bets please."

On the Saturday, James Bagette Junior inspected the kitchen and bedroom at the rear of the bungalow,

"Yes, it's not a problem, the internal piping and electrics are minor changes; the external piping can largely be recycled. Can I ask, Miss Summers, are you quite set on using the kitchen in the garage?"

"That was my next question, because I wasn't, like, entirely happy with the quality."

"Your bungalow is built and finished to a good standard, we oversaw the build, but the kitchen is decidedly budget by comparison. If you could stretch to another two thousand, we could part exchange that kitchen for a far superior one, designed and built for the new room."

"Do it," interrupted Andrew, "The kitchen is the hub of the house, do it now, rather than economise and regret for the next twenty years."

When it turned out that Mission and Bagette were local concessionaires for Delia's favourite kitchen manufacturer, the revised plan was agreed on a handshake.

On the advice of her solicitor, Councillor Patterson pleaded guilty, but also for leniency on the grounds of stress induced by seeing a truant from School.

As the case was undefended, the prosecution was denied the opportunity to ask several questions they were itching to put.

Other locals asked the questions of Cade Patterson in the Pub, though.

"How come a teacher was out of School chasing truants, when there was no-one absent that day, except the teacher that is?"

* * *

"Shelley, can I, like, speak to the Artist?"

"It's me listening."

"Oh! Erm, I have bought a Café. This is, like, it."

"Very nice," said the Artist, "Georgian, lovely happy windows."

193

"I was wondering if I could make the Entrance Porch bigger, I mean, like, wider, not bigger, to let cars through."

"The Café would be sad." It was Shelley had replied.

"Oh, how?"

"The whole frontage was designed around that Entrance. Change it, and you would have to change the proportions of everything else." This time it was the Artist giving a comprehensive appraisal.

"Oh. Okay."

That night, Delia told Andrew,

"So I was, like, quite wrong. The owner didn't run out of money at the end, but at the beginning and cut his cloth accordingly."

"Well, nothing else was skimped upon, so I guess you are correct."

Madeline and Jane moved in for good, shortly after Whit. Only then did the young mother's very full life become completely revealed. Cubs, Brownies and junior football team, each occupied one evening a week. The Parish Committee complicated matters on an as-needed basis. Other commitments wiped out at least one weekend in four.

"We saw more of you, before you, like, moved in."

"No, it just seemed that way, but it's nice to be missed."

"What's a Parish Committee?"

"It decides how certain Church based events are run, you have to be careful, there's always one who thinks it's his own personal; rubber-stamp permit."

"Like, Pastor Benne?"

"Exactly, like."

"I'd like to see one in action sometime."

Andrew wasn't the only West Novochester teacher to be promoted to a new job that summer. 2SB lost Mr Baques, but everyone got him back, because he became their new Year Tutor. SB's new name was CC because their new Form Tutor was Mrs Cumpbell, a change of fortune for the worse, of Galactic proportions.

2AB waited to hear whom their new Form Tutor was to be with trepidation; Andrew Bryant would be impossible to replace. The year ended, and the pupils still didn't know.

Chapter 13
Foundations--Foundations: Summer 1984

Delia

Their separate Summer Holidays didn't quite match, but five of the weeks overlapped, Delia commuted down with Andrew and stayed for all five.

Arriving at the bungalow was strange, seeing it appear from behind the trees, tuning into its vibes, locking on to its emotions. Everything clicked snugly into place; it felt like Home. Delia crept nervously into her kitchen. The stout worktops locked together seamlessly around the room. The splash-backs, that frequently, in budget, and sometimes, not so budget kitchens, fit only where they touch, were integrated with the tops. The cupboard doors closed with a dampened thud, and the drawers, given only a firm nudge, closed by themselves.

"Oh, Andrew! What do you think?"

"I like it, but the important thing is what do you think?"

"It's lovely, really, like, really lovely."

On the first Tuesday Morning, she loaded up the 4x4 and drove herself along the track to Prior's Eastwicke, then, using Amy in her pushchair for support, she went shopping.

In the Post Office,

"Good Morning everyone," she called brightly and continued to speak in an animated, friendly manner to Sid, while she made

195

her purchases. The silence inside could have been served on cones. Delia checked her change and smiled at the shopkeeper,

"Thank you, Sid. Come on Amy; we've got a garden to make. Good Day Mrs Patterson. Oh, Vicar, I liked the sermon. One of my teachers does ones like that. Interesting, with a point relevant to, like, today."

"Oh, thank you."

"The ones I hate are those where the Vicar analyses a word that Jesus is supposed to have said. Considering that he spoke, like, Aramaic, not English and his words were written down decades later, with the benefit of hindsight. Bit pointless those ones, don't you think. Bye everyone."

She couldn't help it, once out of the village; the grin broadened widely. As she completed a neat three-point turn, at the end of their track and headed back home, it took every ounce of control not to laugh out loud.

Delia took Amy with her when she went to lay out Amelia's garden, with canes and string and stones as markers and explained what she was doing to the tot, as she worked. She altered the pencil drawing she was working from, as realities on the ground interfered with it. Specifically, she moved the whole garden around clockwise, to take account of the westward slope of the land. Her final position was almost straight up and down the slope, rather than the skewed, neither down nor across, first idea.

She planned the main shelter as being provided by their fir plantation.

A triangular segment, comprising about a third of the patio could be let into the slope; the rest would be jutting out from it, step-like into the lawn.

"We'll have to build a retaining wall," she said to Amy. "I reckon about three Bradstone Blocks high, with a Bradstone Rumbled Stone Edging top, it will look like a dressed dry stone wall, with, like, a bit of luck."

Amy, sitting in her chair, gurgled her agreement and pointed out improvements in the design.

"And as if it had been here for centuries, when the lichens

and mosses get to it." She measured out the length, yet again and moved a string a few centimetres, stood back and looked at it critically. "It's just like icing a cake," she told the little one, as she worked. "You have to get the balance right. It can be deceptively simple, like, Japanese minimalist, or it can be a voluptuously, extravagantly rampant, cottage-garden, but if the balance is right it will look good."

Presently Delia called Andrew away from his tasks, to give his opinion on her plan.

"It will front to the west and south, but mainly west. If we have windbreaks to the north and northeast, here and here. Pergola type things with clematis growing up them, with this large patio area for sitting out, with Amelia here, like, under the table. There'll be a flight of steps up from the West and a ramp continuing around along the North side here," she clumped up the slope swinging her arms in unison, graphically illustrating where the ramp would lie. "I reckon about three steps at the front, for good leg days, but if the ramp goes towards the back curling around onto the patio; I'll get up easily enough. There will be a low wall to the front and the South side. What do you think?"

"The table is more central than I realised, I had pictured it more at one end."

"That's so that when we have meals out here, we don't sit with our back to Amelia. I know she's gone, I know she'll never come back, but I remember her alive, her love, her care, her sexy kisses. So her garden will be, like, a place of love and laughter, centred around her, not mourning."

"What plants and things?"

"Permanent beds on the East side here and here, they're far enough away from the trees, I've checked. With bulbs and shrubs 'n stuff, to link it to the plantation. I thought maybe, even a herb border." Delia limped back to the western edge. "But then I thought we'd have some summer bedding across the front here and, like, some ethnic pots on the South side, a riot of colour."

"It is already looking good in my head, will the Vicar do the business do you think?"

197

"I'm working on it."

"So when are you thinking of making a start?"

"The digger arrives tomorrow."

"What?"

The visit to the Monumental Mason's premises was both rewarding and, to Delia, frightening.

The trio patrolled his yard looking at what was available; the girl knew roughly what she wanted. A few possibilities were noted, then suddenly she saw the tabletop. It was a rough piece of black granite, shaped like a slice from the side of a huge pear, with large and colourful, pearlescent-flecks embedded in it. The slab measured a little over three metres long and half that wide for most of its length. The cut surface was highly polished. Trembling with anticipation, Delia hobbled in beside the block and measured up.

"This block," she asked the proprietor. "Could you cut the bulge off, so that it finishes about, 300 mm thick, like, most of the way down?"

He was obviously reluctant,

"We could do it Miss, but you'd have to buy the block first. Just, it's a question of waste; we'd have no use for the off-cut sliver."

"Oh, I want the rest. I want to use the rest for, like, an inscription. Well, a crypt stone, with approximately these dimensions, I'll give you the exact size when we've measured up properly."

"No problem Miss."

"The cut surface on the sliver would need to be polished, but not the one left on the block, that'll be, like, underneath," she quickly sketched an outline of the table for him, and pointed at two more granite lumps propped up nearby. "We'd need two pillars for legs, something like those, rough, unpolished."

"They'd do."

"With this wording on the sliver?"

"Anything, you get the first hundred letters free."

"Can you do it?"

"You're looking at several tons weight. Just, It would need a substantial concrete base on good undisturbed subsoil."

"It's grey clay under about half a metre of topsoil. It, like, looks undisturbed."

"Come into the office; we'll look at some figures--"

It was the figures that Delia found frightening.

"Oh. As much as that?"

"That includes a free survey, to see whether the job's feasible. Just, excavation of founds, concrete base, delivery, erection and make good."

"It is nearly a mile from the nearest metalled road. There is a farm track, rough metalling."

"Yes, Mr Bryant, that's been taken into account in the estimate."

"We are building a patio around the monument, would that be best done before or after this work?"

"After, please, we would be sure to smash it up. Just, with the heavy plant needed for this job."

"Can we, like, think about it--"

"It is Amelia's money, and it is what you want for her."

Delia took a deep breath,

"We've thought about it, when can you, like, do the survey?"

"This afternoon, Miss, two o'clock?"

"Fine, we'll see you then."

"What are you facing your patio with?"

"Reconstituted stone slabs. The dyed ones with a York Stone finish."

"May I ask, was your choice mainly on cost, or some other consideration?"

"Like, wholly on cost."

"Our other yard, next door, is an Architectural Salvage Yard. Just, we have much reclaimed genuine York Stone. If you could stretch to the extra cost, your patio would have the facing that this monument deserves."

Delia looked pensively at her man.

"Do not forget the chairs you have at the restorers. You said yourself that you would rather have new ones. There will be money left over from the sale of the antique ones, even after buying the new."

"I'm prepared to do a deal on delivery if you would be prepared to take everything in one load. Just, if you had somewhere to stack it all."

The only significant difference the afternoon's meeting produced, was an extension of the planned concrete base, to form the foundation of the patio, which would allow Andrew to lay the flags himself on a pre-prepared base.

"This hard shoulder, beside your track here. Just, There is enough room for you to store your stone for your patio. I could deliver everything for one charge."

"That could be the tipping point. What do you think?"

Delia breathed in deeply,

"I think that was a dreadful pun, but, yes, we'll have the genuine stone too. It's what I really wanted."

Now that the order was going ahead, Delia described what she wanted for the memorial,

"We'll have a stepped hole, with these dimensions," she said. "So the memorial plaque needs to be this size. And this is what we want for, like, the wording. Will it fit?"

"That's fine; we adjust the size to fit."

"And space, like for when --"

"Yes and as it will need to be removable, but not by thieves. Just, you'd be amazed what people will steal Miss; we will insert special left-hand-thread nuts and bolts, to secure a lifting frame."

"Where on Earth will you get left-hand-thread bolts?"

"Any truckers garage. Nearside truck wheels have, like, left-hand-threads."

Andrew just gawped at his girl.

* * *

The site was excavated and the concrete run in onto steel mesh reinforcement. There was a rectangular block of earth left just off-centre. Around it, Delia had erected precisely constructed, polythene-lined shuttering. As the concrete was run in, Andrew inserted corner strengthening around the edge of the rectangle. A further, larger, polythene-lined, precisely aligned, shuttering box was laid on top. There were two satellite boxes equally positioned either side leaving shallow mortices in the concrete. He placed, even more, corner strengthening around all three holes. All this caused raised eyebrows among the ready-mixed-concrete lorry crews who were tamping the concrete level, square and free from air bubbles, but no-one asked, so no-one got told. At the last moment, just before it became out of reach, Andrew neatly skimmed the edge of the centre block with a float.

The following day, Andrew put slippers on and walked gingerly across the firm, but not set concrete, to the block. He removed some earth from behind the shuttering, eased the wood out in rotation and brushed down the edges, leaving a well-engineered, smooth-sided, strongly reinforced, stepped, rectangular hole. The satellite shuttering got similar treatment. Three days later he could dig out the rest of the earth block and line the little crypt with gravel.

The Vicar blessed the plot and said a prayer over Amelia's ashes, after Delia lowered their little casket into the crypt. There was still room for several more beside her. Several stout onlookers were co-opted to help lower the memorial stone into place and the left-hand-thread bolts and lifting frame, were removed and stored away safely.

* * *

Two weeks later, a second crew assembled the table, cementing the legs into the prepared satellite holes, but only after double checking that the table was sitting securely on its glued in pins and that the fixing was mostly cosmetic; short of a major earthquake, Amelia's table wasn't going anywhere fast.

Andrew, Delia and Amy entertained their friends to an inaugural al fresco buffet in Amelia's Garden. Although Cade Patterson called in, it was only to apologise that he and his wife would be unable to make it, Council business was just too pressing.

"Just, At least have a look at the spread," said Freda, clutching his arm and trying to steer him across. Cade gently disengaged, caressing her arm down.

"No. I have got to go, Mildred's waiting back at the road. Bye." His friends watched him go sadly.

"Well, it's a shame, but I'm afraid I'm not going to let it spoil my day." The Vicar waved a piece of crisp toast carrying a small whole fish in a nest of leaves and sauce. "This food deserves reverence and respectful consumption." With that, he ate it, smiling.

"What are those?"

"Pigs in blankets."

Peter's wife, Abigail, looked up at her hostess,

"I know that, I can read." Delia giggled and told her, then pointed out some others displayed set upright, with a baby beetroot as a 'head' instead of the cranberry.

"Have you tried the variation, Caped Redhead Teddies?"

Councillor Mildred Patterson's naked animosity towards an in-comer that everyone else thought a really nice person, had polarised opinion. The main public outcry against Delia came from Colonel Winston Scuffer {retired}. Fortunately, this counted close to zero on the scale, as he was covertly disliked by all who knew him. The outcry was because he was Mildred's equally bigoted brother. This was also the reason her friends had directed Delia's research away from him. There was also a pale shrewish girl called Lea whom Delia had never seen, but whose opinion counted even less as she was Councillor Patterson's PPS at County Hall and needed the job. Few in the pro-Delia camp attempted to argue with words that wouldn't be listened to anyway, but chose to demonstrate their feelings, in a similar manner to Cade. They would pointedly turn away if Delia's name were mentioned with intent to slight, or broadcast the depth of their welcome when she appeared, or choose to accompany her, or sit beside her if she were already around.

Back home in September, the question on everyone's lips for most of the summer was answered with various levels of disbelief—and joy.

Another New Beginning:
Tyne-dale Autumn Term 1984
Delia

The Third Year reassembled in the main hall, situated in West Novochester's East Wing. This was larger than the one in South Block and had a stage at one end and a raised area at the other, both of which, incongruously, were reached by steps. The stage was purpose built for Gang Show type performances, but pretty useless for any kind requiring footlights. At the other end, the steps were wide enough to accommodate a line of chairs each. There was a certain amount of gossip and news to catch up on, although the fact that Robert wasn't speaking to Kim at the moment didn't quite qualify as either.

Carly was entranced,

"Who's the scrumptious bit of crumpet talking to Stewart Baques?"

"Dunno, like, never seen her before."

"She'll be a new girl."

"So where's her uniform?"

Sadie half-turned in her chair, to address the group behind her,

"Her name is Jean Ripson, but it's good news, bad news time, Carly. First the good news and why she's not in uniform, Miss Ripson is our new Form Tutor."

"She can't be! She must be younger than me!" said Jeanette, among a chorus of similar minded comments.

Sadie continued,

"And she's terrific; she'll do fine." She was nodding sagely.

When she could speak, Carly muttered,

"Wow hold me back girls."

Sadie completed her message.

"The bad news is, she's straight, we've got no chance."

"You're married to Laura, and there's always a chance for a fling, even with straight girls."

"Not when she's talking to the competition. She's Stewart

203

Baques' very own."

"Oh shit!"

"And every Straight Boy and Big Bull-Dyke in the place is, like, saying the same."

There was an explosion of invective from behind them; Mrs Cumpbell was castigating Timmy Ebsenter,

"Stupid donkey, leaving your bag in the way, get rid of it immediately!" She turned and stormed off, still shouting the odds.

Tim heaved a big sigh and picked the bag up. It wasn't his, it was Shelley's, but The Artist was furiously sketching the new assembly location, her pencil flicking from detail to detail like a blur. Setting fire to her hair might have got her attention, but not much else. It was several minutes later that the pencil slowed down and he could reunite the bag and its owner.

Sadie's assessment of their new young Form Tutor proved to be pin-sharp accurate. Jean Ripson grasped 3JR firmly by the scruff of the neck and the seat of the pants and had them away down the road she wanted them to tread before the tongues dragging on the floor could even be re-mouthed. They also quickly learned where the line was and that if you crossed it, you did so at your peril.

"Miss, have you got a boyfriend?"

"What's that gotta dee wi ye?" From lips that normally spoke only posh, Home Counties speech;

and,

"That's a lovely dress Miss, if you turn a bit the sun will shine right through it."

"I told you, John, I'm not going to lend it to you. You'll have to buy your own."

During that day, football and hockey goal posts grew out of the school field. The tennis nets, which had provided free facilities for the entire locality since Easter, were removed from the yard and a clump of netball posts appeared in their place. Delia and her friends nudged each other and gave each other thumbs up signs, Ingrid tapped her bulging bag, grinning. At the end of school, they met in the girl's toilet and exchanged a selection of sensible shoes, not so sensible shoes, court shoes and clump, for trainers. The six moved outside onto the yard and piled their gear up in a corner. They retrieved two netball posts and set them up. Ingrid produced the ball from her bag, and the girls arranged themselves at the corners of an imaginary hexagon.

The complicated exercise routine that followed would have filled the heart of Miss Cape with pride had she known about it. After the opening loosening and stretching sequence, all six were glowing pink. Then, they took the ball and began lobbing it to each other randomly from corner to corner. On Carly's command the lobs became throws and on the next command, hard fast hurling. When they finished, the ball hadn't been dropped during the last hundred throws.

"Okay." Carly held onto the ball. "Five down the right, five left then Jeanette chooses and calls. Right?" The others agreed and spread themselves down the court.

Carly missed her first shot, but the following nine went in mostly without touching the ring.

"Random now," she called as the ball was passed back.

Marjorie to Kim, running left to right, Kim to Ingrid also running left to right, Delia held her right hand out and had to hobble quickly and jump, to collect the fast ball.

"Yes!" The call had come from behind her left ear. Delia turned, ducked under an imaginary marker and launched the netball. She was aiming for the top of the ash tree at the edge of the yard. Jeannette running fast from centre court, collected the ball at the height of her jump, landed, spun around and hurled it in a hard flat trajectory at the empty space close to the 'opponents' net. By the time it got there, Carly was waiting for it, and a moment later the ball was dropping softly through the netting hanging from the ring.

That's one of the things I love about West Novochester, Delia thought. *Not only do the team have nets for matches, but we renegades also have them for practice.*

She took Ingrid's pass and curled the ball high out to the right again and again Jeanette and Carly had it in the net with surgical precision. Carly passed close to her goal provider,

205

"I see your shadow's here." Jonathan's sister's blue bicycle could be clearly seen behind the little group of watchers on the touchline. Jeanette snorted,

"Not my shadow, it's you she watches, crush like pack ice on you she has."

Carly winced,

"Just my luck, a girl fancies me; and she's too young."

"Why's she too young?" Asked Delia astonished. "There's no age of consent, like, for lesbians."

"Well, she's younger than me; I'm not into corrupting minors." Jeanette stood square on to her blocking her way, arms akimbo.

"She's the same age as I was when Jonathan and I started and even older than when you got to me."

"Yeah, but you're straight!"

"And ages on from when Sadie, like, lost her cherry."

"Carly, she is either straight, or she is gay, your having an affair with her won't change that one jot, you didn't convert me into a lesbian, but you did give me some fun filled nights. I tell you what, on Saturdays when I go around, Emma is there and we sometimes can't even snog because Jonathan is scared she comes in. You know what he's like. Come with me on Saturday and spend some time with Emma, you will either get on and get laid or you won't, either way, you will both know where you stand afterwards."

Miss Ripson asked about the training session the following day.

"I saw the moves you were practising last night. Is it as slick when there's an opposition?"

The girls looked stunned, silent.

"You know, in matches. Against other Schools."

"We're not in the School team Miss."

"Oh."

"We're naughty girls Miss. We aren't allowed to do anything. And I, like, can't anyway."

"Please don't tell Cap-you I mean Mrs Stonker Miss. She'll stop our using the court."

"Mrs Stonker? Who's she."

"Head of PE Miss."

"Nope." Their new Form Tutor reached for the Staff Handbook and began flicking through it. "The Head of PE is a Miss--Miss J'Enson."

"Well, where's Mrs Stonker?"

"Not here. Unless she got married again during the holiday."

"No. Like, Miss J'Enson was a student here, then a teacher, now Head of Department. It fits." Delia turned and called across the room. "Sadie, has Mrs Stonker left?"

"Yes, gone abroad, it's Miss J'Enson now."

"Ladies we have a proper teacher in charge. We'll have, like, proper PE now." Delia was grinning inanely and nodding her head.

The lesson change bell terminated the conversation, but not the topic. At her first opportunity, Jean Ripson went to see Margaret J'Enson.

"I knew they were good; it was just that Grace wouldn't hear of it. She had her team, all girls together, Jolly Hockey Sticks; she wouldn't have it disrupted by naughty girls."

"Are they naughty?"

"Red-blooded, yes. Naughty? Who cares? I wasn't a Saint."

"Would you like to watch, from my room, judge for yourself."

Margaret nodded.

"I'll let you know the next time I see them."

* * *

Margaret J'Enson watched as the well-oiled net-balling machine popped goal after goal into the net. Presently the players had a discussion, and the next few moves were down the left wing. At the end of the session, the girls packed away, straightened off the court and left their several ways. Carly Helendale was given a lift on the seat of a blue bicycle, while holding the hips of the younger girl doing the pedalling.

In PE a little league was formed to play competitive matches in netball, with twelve teams from the girls in Population One. Despite only having six players and one of them released from her wheelchair to play, 3JR Red Team won the league handsomely, winning every match, although occasionally by a tight margin. After turning up for trials, Carly and Jeanette became first choice attack for the school team and Ingrid first choice defence; the other three were incorporated into the squad.

Delia relayed the news to Andrew down the telephone,

"--Julie was off, so Miss J'Enson wanted to play me and she couldn't, because I'm too old. Your schoolgirl mistress can't play for her School because she's, like, old and past it!"

She got a peal of laughter in reply.

Chapter 14
Options: December 1984 - Easter 1985
Delia

When Delia propelled herself into the Library to research some homework; she found Big Mamma there, with unusually, no-one with her. She greeted the Company Director, slid in beside her and settled to her work. After a few minutes, Shirley checked that the locality was lacking listeners, then asked quietly,

"Everything still all Sweetness and Light with life?"

"If you're asking if the goose is, like, flying south for the winter, the answer's yes. It'll be our first Christmas together." She reached into her neckline, withdrew the locket and snapped it open. "Andrew's asked me to go and live with him. I'm going. I love them Shirley; he asks Amy, 'Where's Mummy?' And she points to my picture." Shirley admired the ring lying in the locket.

"Snap," she said and flashed her own locket complete with an engagement ring.

"Am I allowed to know to whom?"

"It's not somebody you know, heard of probably, but you don't know the person. I do trust you, Delia; it's just--"

"It's okay."

"Several people know, have done the sums and got the right answer, but I've told nobody. There's somebody I need to tell first, somebody who deserves to be told before anyone else and at the moment, I can't tell them. I'll tell you when that changes."

"I think you've just, like, told me too much."

"Well, if I have, as I said, I trust you."

She discussed it with Andrew, down the telephone that night.

"What do you think, have I, like, guessed right?"

"I am sure you have, she moved into Goldrill, with Anna, in the First Year and Anna's Mum died years ago."

"The only thing is the rumours, she's supposed to be seeing her mechanic, at the racetrack, her mechanic's, like, called Sylvia."

"How do you wrap a giraffe, so that nobody knows it is a giraffe?"

"Put it in an elephant-shaped box and, like, wrap that."

* * *

At Banbury station, Delia alighted from the Birmingham train, oriented herself and headed for the exit. Andrew saw her coming and pointed her out to Amy,

"Go to Mummy," he said and set her down. The tot took two slow steps then ran straight at her; Delia just had time to drop her bag down before catching her and swinging her up,

"Amy walking."

"Yes, darling you're walking, aren't you a clever girl?" A moment later she was melting into her lover's arms. "You didn't, like, tell me."

"We have been rehearsing the surprise for a week; of course, we did not tell you."

* * *

The Wednesday assemblies were given over to Options-Advertising during the Spring Term. Naturally, every Head of Department was anxious that the maximum number of students took their courses. Student numbers affected timetabling, staff allotment and kudos, but most of all they affected money!

So Options were publicised in diverse styles of hard sell, by the Heads of Departments, touting their wares like Barrow-boys

210

and like Barrow-boys, with varying levels of success.

Mr Baques warned them all not to be blinded by the luscious deals on offer. Especially not to be swayed by their own liking for the teaching style of a particular teacher, because there was no guarantee that teacher would be available, but to choose instead their options with an eye to what they were good at and what they wanted to be, when they left School.

The Head of Craft was extolling the virtues of doing his subject and filling the heart of the School's best cook with despair.

"--theory of cooking and the chemistry of cooking, leading towards a City and Guilds qualification --"

She grumbled to Kim about it afterwards,

"City and Guilds! Great!"

"Sounds good to me."

"That's the point; it sounds good. Have you ever, like read a City and Guilds syllabus?" Kim looked blank. "They teach you where to find the knowledge, which is great; if that's what you want. I don't want to know where to **find** it; I want the knowledge! To know, like, the nitty gritty, now!"

One break-time, just after Half Term, Delia free-wheeled into a gossiping group. The girls were clustered around Samantha whom, although silent now, was obviously the centre of the conversation.

"Will you get a chance to slope off to see Paris?" Someone asked.

"Even if you did, I think you'd be disappointed," said Anna. "London, Bath, even Novochester, all have architecture as striking as most of Paris."

"Oh."

"Paris has a lot of it and the top places; Notre Dame and such are stunning. But, when you've been and had a good look, come back and take another look at London and our own Nineteenth Century Streets. Look past the smoke damage; they're beautiful."

"The thing I remember about Paris," said Jo. "Was looking everywhere for the Eiffel Tower and I couldn't see it."

"Because you were standing underneath it?"

"Yeah!"

"I wouldn't see Paris anyway," said Samantha. "Even if I find a way to slope off, I'll only see the south of France, maybe a bit of the Pyrenees."

"Slope off? From where?" asked Delia.

"School, then Work, my regular German client's asked me to go on her yacht for a month, after Easter. Touring, Barcelona around to Naples, it's just I don't need the wagger man chasing me up."

"And uncovering all sorts of bureaucratic anomalies the LEA are, like, better off not knowing about?"

"Like how I pay the mortgage? Exactly."

"Get Mr Baques to grant you, like, leave of absence."

"That's it! You're going on a course, to practice your German. He'll have a way to wangle it," said Shirley. "Come on; we'll go and see him now. What about your kids?"

"I'll take them with me; Janice said I could."

"Come on, let's find out how to do it officially." Big Mamma grabbed their little linguistic-genius, working girl and dragged her off to the school building.

"The South of France in spring must be wonderful," said Jennifer. "That's when all the alpines and meadow orchids flower."

"It is, I've seen them so thickly grouped on the ground, you couldn't walk across the field without treading on some, every step," agreed Anna. "Bee orchids, Spider, all sorts."

The conversation became general about the friendliness of the country folk of the foothills of the Pyrenees, but the ironical inadvisability of romping through the woods at any time, but most of all during the winter.

"Yeah, wild boar."

"I've heard they're, like, pretty ferocious."

"It's not the boar," said Jennifer. "It's the trigger-happy French who hunt them. Something moving's likely to get shot at."

"Fatal shooting accidents every year."

"The natives are friendly, but, like, their guns aren't."

A few minutes later Shirley and Samantha returned,

"Job done, well it will be when we produce letters from Samantha's Mum."

"How will you manage that?"

"Buy them. My Mum's addiction is tragic, but it means that given the choice between the pleasure of being vindictively spiteful and getting paid, the money wins every time."

* * *

When Samantha returned home, thinking in German instead of English, she was nut brown {all over, as Delia discovered later in the showers,} and had added 'Schooner' to her list of 'Goodies of this World', that someday she would possess.

During a Library lesson:

"I can tell the Sun shone."

"Even where the Sun, like, don't--" in a murmur before Samantha interrupted her,

"Shut up you. Yes, Fred, the Sun shone, and I fell in love with sailing and I got a job offer from a client of Janice's, Munich-based businessman which I'm seriously considering."

"By the light in your eyes, I take it that it would mean a basic change of career."

"The job description includes humping the boss, but except for that, yes. PPA, very Private, very Personal and very trusted Assistant. And he's young, good-looking, rich and single and I like him a bunch!"

Fred rolled his eyes,

"I think you've seriously considered, instead of considering. What about your brother and sister?"

"My kids have said they'll come with me and go to School in Germany."

"Best of luck Sam."

Mrs Cumpbell entered, killing the gentle murmur of voices like a plague virus and spoke to the librarian,

"I'll come back some other time; you'll have your hands full coping with these donkeys, especially that one!" She flounced back out of the room.

Tim looked up from his research into the life of the daughter of 'Mad, bad and dangerous to know,' Lord Byron, Augusta Ada King, Countess Lovelace, the World's first computer programmer,[8] and surveyed the ring of concerned and shocked faces regarding him.

"Is it me?" He said precipitating a round of tension releasing giggles.

Options Choices continued to be under severe fire from Delia, frustrated to the level of seriously annoyed. Fortunately, by sheer chance one of her outbursts was said in the correct company.

"I want to learn how to cook. Theory's fine. The Chemistry of cooking's fine, but, like, I want to be a chef, a stunningly good cook."

"You'll be a better cook with the background knowledge."

"Only if I have the cooking knowledge too, we all know a History teacher who is a spectacularly brilliant Historian, but who can't teach bubbles to float. Like, definite article pits guys."

Jeanette nodded changing her stand from foot to foot.

"You're already pretty good," she said.

"That's not good enough."

"Night classes?" Asked Shirley.

"Yes, if I were eighteen no problem, like, embarrassment of choice. I don't want to do it next year; I want to do it now."

"The minimum age is sixteen, but there's always a way around any age restriction, I did Engine Bay Service last year, I think I might have accidentally written my age backwards or something." Shirley glanced at the girl twitching beside her, then back to Delia--Really!" She was reacting, most probably, to the elder girl's double take, then she continued. "I'm doing the Advanced course this year; I had to remember that I'm twenty-two. Look, I know that there is a Chinese Cookery Course on this term, get yourself along to Stewart Baques and ask him, I bet he can get you on it." The blonde's obvious discomfort claimed her

8   In Countess Lovelace's time, 'computers' were Clerks in finance houses that did Arithmetic. She wrote programs for Babbage's Difference Engine, the world's First {Mechanical} Programmable Computer.

attention. "What's the matter, Jeanette?"

"Friction burns," said Carly.

"Don't you juice up enough?"

"Not where she prefers to take it, no."

"Carly!" Exclaimed Jeanette, blushing hotly.

"KY Jelly," said Big Mamma. "But make sure you've got lots of tissues for wiping down afterwards." That conversation stopper worked perfectly.

"Mr Baques, Big Mamma's sent me to ask if you can get me on the Chinese Cookery Course that's running this term at night classes?"

"Well, yes, but it starts tonight Delia. Seven o'clock!"

"Oh--Oh--Okay."

Virginal Status: Summer 1985

Les-Girls

The last day of the School year was warm and sunny. Several girls were together on the grass at break.

Rosalind leaned back on her arms, spread her legs and looked down at the inviting V pointing the way to the goodies.

"Third year over and still nobody has lain there and changed my status and Yes Anna, like you I'm prepared to add 'Dammit!'"

"Things are improving--actually been asked," replied Anna. "By the wrong boy, of course, so still virgin dammit!"

"Would you, if the right boy had asked?"

Shirley answered for her,

"Yes, Ingrid, she would."

"I'm waiting for the Wedding Night."

"Good for you, but like most of you, for Anna there's more than one right boy, eh Jennifer?"

"Too right, easier to list those I'd say 'No!' to--and still virgin dammit!"

"Virgin," said Kerry.

"Not me," from Delia.

Various combinations of 'Virgin' followed, with Samantha's 'No change' and Laura and Sadie's 'Same Status' slid in somewhere. Shelley was looking at Laura,

"Do I say, 'Me'?"

"Yes."

Shelley went from being wound up like a cat about to pounce to a relaxed English Rose in June and held her hand up,

"Me, not virgin." She sat back and calmly resumed eating her lunch.

"It's been worrying her dreadfully," said Laura generally to the group. "Since the scrupulist found out that she was saying things that were not true. She painted Unhappiness at the weekend, it's very unpleasant to look at, now she's put it right in her head; she'll be okay."

After lunch, Shelley slipped her drawing pad out, and The

216

Artist began sketching, there were a dozen or so small sketches on the page, she flitted randomly from one to another, adding details. As if in the middle of a conversation The Artist suddenly said,

"It's William as well now."

Jennifer was first to twig,

"You're not virgin with William too?"

"Yes." The flying pencil had neither paused nor wavered.

"But you've wanted that for a while haven't you," said Sadie

"Yes. But just William, nobody else, Dad said." The Artist enlarged, the last seven words filling in loads of detail for her friends.

"Ah, yes, that's good," said Laura. "Shelley are you okay?" The pencil stopped dead, mid stroke.

"My thoughts are happy."

"Good."

The pencil resumed, flying fast again.

Chapter 15
Small Steps: Warwickshire July 1985
Delia

When Delia drove herself into the Turnpikes' car park, she did so with a poorly concealed smirk, for which the pun, creaking as it swung in the wind above her head, was only partly responsible. She and Amy bought their drinks and crisps and moved through into the sunny garden at the back of the Pub. A large pair of boots clumped to a stop at her side.

"May I join you?"

"Yes. Like, why not?"

"I saw you drive in, so congratulations must be in order?"

"Yep."

"Mummy, can I go and play?"

"If you've, like, finished your crisps." The little one nodded and slid down off her seat,

"I'll finish my drink when I come back." Delia watched her daughter fondly, then glanced at her companion as he said,

"Can I ask, how you manage the pedals?"

"I passed my test on a standard car to, like, get the full licence, but it makes the foot ache, so we've had a second throttle inserted on the column, like a tractor. I use the brake. When Andrew drives, he uses whichever one he feels like at the time."

"Neat. Cost you a bit I imagine?"

"It wasn't cheap." Together they watched Amy creeping up on a rabbit and smiled at her obvious disgust when it scurried away.

"So when am I going to get the chance of unloading some 404s, with Foul Pest and 500 eggs behind them, onto an unsuspecting neighbour then?"

"Not before next summer, but, like, we'll have to be ready to react to circumstances, depending on how things go. I'm going to run trials, three or four of each of several breeds. See who does best."

"Hens and pigs?"

"Mmm."

"I'd like to be in on them too."

"Okay. Yes, darling, you can play on the swings. There's also a few small changes planned. Marriages. Restaurants. The odd Kid or six, like, depends on how busy I am."

"Nothing important then," said Peter and,

"Six kids!" said two voices simultaneously from behind her.

"Oh. Hello, Freda, like, join the gathering Cade, there are spare chairs."

When Sid and the Vicar joined them, they filled the table.

The conversation ranged over several topics, while Delia, although contributing to it, watched Amy almost constantly, as she swung on the swings, rode the rocking horse and leaped on and off the slowly rotating teapot lid.

"I got nothing for those calves, don't know why I bothered to send them to the market."

"I'd have given you, like, nothing for them Peter; you could have sent them to me, saved the cost of the market." The belly laugh at the Squire's grandson's expense was enjoyed by them all, himself included.

And:

"Auntie Betty's left me that little cottage of hers, can I interest any of you in a sale."

"No thanks Freda, not with worm in the joists and water in the cellar, no thank you."

"I'll have to get an estate agent to sell it as seen, I mean, I'll

219

tell him about the problems, and that's only two of them, but I don't know any. Any other than my competitors, of course."

"I know plenty I wouldn't let sell a rabbit hutch. Anyone know an Estate Agent? A good honest one?" Asked Peter.

"Oxymoron, surely. Present company excepted, of course," said Sid.

"Don't look at me. Just, I don't know any."

"With Mildred on the planning committee?"

"Especially with that. The less I know about that, the better."

"I know one. Juliet Means from Prior's Richmount, but I wouldn't recommend her, I wouldn't advise against her either, I don't know her well enough to, like, pass an opinion."

"You've dealt with her Peter, haven't you?"

The squire's grandson looked at Freda,

"Hmm!"

"Oh!"

He turned back to Delia,

"Will you need one. Just, for your restaurant?"

"Don't think so, we're not buying or selling and, like, it's not even change of use. Old Mr Blake just used it as a hayloft, which he really shouldn't have. It carries a fresh food certificate; we're renewing it."

"You'll never get that place certificated."

"Wrong Freda--"

"It's perfectly structurally sound, no rising damp, it was just one bit of roof where the tree had dropped a branch on it. It looked awful, but, like, was really okay, just one new rafter and three new slates, we salvaged all the rest."

"She's already got her certificate," continued Peter. "Subject to final inspection of course, but approved contractors have been hired for the job, there should be no problem."

"You're really going to open it as a restaurant?" Asked Sid. "Where are you going to buy your produce?"

"Anywhere that guarantees the prompt delivery of quality stuff, for fair money, if that means the Post Office, so be it."

"Can't say fairer than that," said Peter. "But I'll be quoting too."

"You'll never run that place at a profit. Just, there isn't the custom."

"If you'd accepted one of the invites to garden parties, you wouldn't have said that Cade. You'd know differently. You'll have heard of the better mousetrap?" Sid just opened his hands in Delia's direction. "You'll need a good booking system if you don't want to be serving at midnight and regularly running out of food."

"We're going computerised from square one. Anybody know a decent piece of software to, like, run a business on?"

"Hate computers," interjected Freda, with feeling. "Invention of the devil."

"I wish they'd bring one out for sub-Post Offices," argued Sid. "It's exactly the sort of job a computer would do well."

"I'm like you, looking," said Cade.

"I've got one, could be adapted to do what you want I suppose, but they're expensive."

"That's, like, the big problem. I thought as they came more into common use, the price would fall, but it's not."

"It will. It's just that, at the minute, demand outstrips supply," commented Sid, with his retailer's hat on. "When that tips the other way, watch those prices fall."

"Or they'll hold the price, but increase the value; if you're still looking when you're ready to open, tell me. I'm sure I could rent you time on mine, something like the operator's hourly rate," put in Peter. "A day's work for the operator day's pay, plus markup, of course. There are days when I pay him for nothing because he's waiting around for work."

"That would be great. Thanks."

"You've set me thinking, on slack days he could do work for other people." He turned to Freda. "Would you like to hire time, seeing you hate computers so much?"

"I might. It would depend on the rate."

"I'm sure our accountants will suggest two different figures and Delia's probably a third. On a more personal note kid, are you going to be able to manage?"

"I'm, like, determined to manage."

"Ah, well. No contest then."

Then later:

"I have many rabbits on my land, I presume, like, the rabbits are mine."

"And you're welcome to the critters."

"I get a lot of your pheasants too."

"You can't shoot 'em before October 1." Peter reminded her.

"But they're, like, yours."

"Not on your land they're not, just don't let me catch you hiring beaters to do a bit of assisting."

"I won't, like, let you catch me." Produced another guffaw.

"I need a gun and, like, to learn how to shoot."

"Gun Club up at the Lodge, they'll teach you all you need to know." Put in Freda. "What did you have in mind?"

"Small bore, 0.22 or something."

"Deadly at half a mile, to anything it hits, it's hitting the right target that's the problem."

"At that distance, I would be lucky to see the barn, never mind the rabbit, like, sitting in front of it. I want to be able to drop a rabbit at twenty metres without filling it full of shot."

"At twenty metres there wouldn't be much left of the rabbit," said the Vicar. "Unless--"

"I got, like, the neck. Hence the club, I want to learn how to do it properly."

"At twenty metres there would be nothing left of the rabbit, the hen behind it, or the duck behind that. How about a pump-up air rifle? You could adjust it to the power you need, and it wouldn't devastate the area," argued Peter. "Besides which the bullets are cheaper."

Later at home, she regaled Andrew with the events of the day.

"And a puzzle. Why would a decent person, like, tell a pointless lie?"

"Did they?"

"Yes," she explained. "I even teed up an opportunity to retract, never took it."

"I do not know. It is strange."

Membership of the rifle club was by invitation, but with Peter and Sid endorsing her membership, Delia got in with minimum fuss. It was when her instructor watched her sign in and selected a rifle for her that things began to develop a southerly slip. Out on the range, she put it to her left shoulder.

"No, Delia, you're right handed, that's a right handed rifle. Your cheek rest's on the other side; you won't be able to snuggle it, to see through the sight correctly, left-handed."

"I am right-handed, but I'm left eyed, anything that needs good sight, I, like, do left eyed. The right eye just balances the face up; I don't see with it."

"Sorry, my mistake I just assumed. You need an ambidextrous rifle; we'll have to go back in and change it."

Delia quickly achieved the status of a first-class shot, but the fasciated cloverleaf group that she smashed into target after target stubbornly refused to leave the eight and move over to the bull, no matter what she did. So the coveted description of marksman eluded her.

"Would you get there with your own gun?" Asked Andrew one night, before bed.

"No. I don't think so, the fault's mine because I get my group. Sometimes three through the same hole, but it's never the same place twice, that's what they call me at the club. Entee-espeetee."

Andrew laughed.

"But I'd like my own rifle, even so. We'll have to, like, warn the shop in advance that I'm a lefty, or they might not be able to supply."

"I'll telephone them tomorrow."

The gunsmith advised that they usually got a wider selection of guns, including ambidextrous or even left handed ones, in stock for the start of the shooting season and especially Christmas. If Delia could give them a general idea of what she wanted, and what she was prepared to pay, they could have a selection available for her in December.

* * *

At the end of the Summer Holidays, a small group of teenagers, took advantage of a hot afternoon and, totally illegally, went skinny dipping in Prior's Richmount reservoir, some nice kids interpretation of being really wild and naughty.

Then, one of the girls stepped on a piece of broken glass, which sliced up, straight through the trainer, into her foot.

This put a sharp end to the pleasures of the day before the youngsters had a chance to pair off for the planned climax activities. The resulting infected cut needed powerful antibiotic treatment before her body won the battle with the germs. The girl was Mary Smith.

* * *

With the success of her Chinese Cookery course and planning permission for her restaurant well on the way to being granted, Delia's first act on returning to School was to enrol for an Indian Cookery Night Class. She asked Mr Baques about an English Cookery Course.

"We could put one on if enough people enrolled."

"How many, like, do you need?"

"Ten, minimum."

"Is there an age qualification?"

"Oh yes! All students must be at least sixteen. So that means that Anna cannot come, but her elder sister A. Monta can of course."

"Anna, you're the best cook I know, would you go to an English Cookery Night-class, if I could, like, get one organised?"

"Of course."

"You have to be sixteen. But the way Mr Baques told me that you couldn't come, he was virtually telling me to tell you to lie about your age."

"Second nature, I've been doing it for years! You'd be amazed how devious the World of Business is--no on second thoughts; you probably wouldn't be."

Delia giggled,

"Ask about for others, like, I need ten."

"Madeline, would you go to an English Cookery Night-class, if I could, like, get one organised?"

"With you? Yes, if you wanted me to."

"How about your Mum?"

* * *

It was only a few days later that Delia was knocking tentatively on her Year Tutor's office door,

"Erm, Mr Baques, I've got twenty-seven, could you, like, put two classes on?"

Chapter 16

A Chance Meeting: London September 1985

Carole Friendly/Rupert Henchmow

The visit to Party HQ was officially to bring everyone up-to-date with the new look of the policies that would run the country locally for the next ten years.

The Councillors took heed of the changes, in so much as they could be profitably incorporated into their own little Empire at home. The major attractions, however, were the various junkets organised by interested parties. At some future time, these interested parties would expect and not always to the benefit of the taxpayer, usually receive, a return on their investment.

Councillor Mildred Patterson was incensed at the understanding and broadcast her fury to anyone who would listen. A girl in her late teens/early twenties, and a businesslike suit, homed in on the source of the complaints.

"So--What would you be prepared to do for the organisers of this meal?" The questioner unsuccessfully took evasive action as a sizeable chunk of half-masticated lobster tail burst from her interviewee's mouth.

"Nothing! It's immoral. It's on a level with the sluts that sleep with their fathers."

The youngster pounced while retrieving lobster from her cleavage.

"What sluts that sleep with their fathers?"

"The poor little motherless ones," Mrs Patterson sneered. "That are sluts under the respectable skin and all the rest." She waved her glass about gathering the entire human race into the equation while losing half the champagne across unsuspecting backs nearby. "The rest who do it as soon as their mothers are looking away."

"So--I take it that's a problem locally is it."

"Rampant! They're all at it--"

Another delegate stepped between the pair and almost aggressively broke the contact,

"Come on Councillor we need to be somewhere else--"

"Er--Can I have your name please--"

"No, you may not and--" The Council leader paused assertively to turn his colleague's back. "I'd be careful what you print; she rarely gets anything right and nothing at all when she's angry." He hustled her away.

"Bugger--How the hell did he know?" murmured the girl, examining herself and dusting specks of lobster away.

"A professional politician knows, I smelled you coming in the door," said a man standing nearby, while he reached over and gently brushed her shoulders clean with his large, stylishly monogrammed handkerchief. He stopped tidying her up but moved closer to her personal space to murmur. "Now just how accommodating would a young cub reporter be, to get the information she's after?"

That sort of invitation usually came from drunken middle-aged hacks, with three hands to paw you with at Christmas Parties and was repulsed accordingly. She looked him up and down. He was tall, elegant and distinguished and immaculately groomed in a dark suit; his short dark hair was greying at the temples. He had an attractive open face, and sweet breath was drifting her way from a nice smile. He was exactly the sort of partner where accommodating might fall well short of hardship. She couldn't help it; the return smile welled up spontaneously,

"Dunno--Possibly accommodating."

"Good. I have a room upstairs. If you're accommodating

enough, you can have what you want."

She sat at his dressing table notebook open, pencil poised, smiling, excited, eager,

"Right--I'm ready." She glanced at him lounging back on the bed.

"No, you're not, you've still got your clothes on, they're very nice clothes, but they're not where I want them. Accommodating first, information later."

"Oh."

He simply waited. She took her jacket off and hung it up, then turned her back and removed her blouse. She managed to peel her knickers from under her skirt, without showing any more bare skin. They waited in silence; presently she half-turned to look at him; he just slowly shook his head.

"Not everything--Please."

"I'm not going to hurt you gratuitously, or even make you do something you really don't want to do. You are a very attractive girl-"

Her eyes narrowed.

"And I want you naked because, in the common vernacular, I want to fuck the arse off you. How badly do you want to know what I know? Badly enough to ask me to do it repeatedly, until I can't get hard any more? Or not badly enough to stop you picking up your clothes and walking out of here? If that's what you want to do, I'll be disappointed, but I won't stop you."

She was staring at him intently,

"Attractive--Very attractive--You said I was very attractive."

"I said a lot more after that, which I suspect you never heard. Of course you're very attractive. You're beautiful. You're bright, with a lovely smile, your skin glows with luminescence, your figure is wonderful--"

"My tits are too small; they're ugly! Misshapen! Wrong!" She'd jumped in hard, a jagged edge to her voice.

He continued the praise in the same gentle, encouraging tone as if she hadn't spoken.

"They are beautiful, just like the rest of you."

Now, slowly, gazing intently at him, she turned to face him,

"Who told you different? Why do you think I want you? Want to have you and do you and fuck you, until I cannot stand? Eh? Because your tits are too small, or, because you're lovely? Which?"

In the silence that followed, they looked steadily at each other; gradually determination replaced fire in the girl's eyes. Slowly her hands went up her back; the man watched the elastic slip. The straps slid down her arms until the brassiere came to rest. She discarded it carelessly with a slow open lift of her hand; her eyes fixed on his. He looked and then looked back to her eyes,

"There, as I said, they are beautiful; you are beautiful. Come here."

While continuing to watch him intently, she closed the gap between them. He sat up onto the edge of the bed, reached out and drew the zip down and slipped the hook and eye on her skirt. It slid over her hips, down around her ankles and elegantly, she stepped out of it. Now revealed were the lacy tops of stockings, held up by hope and a gauzy gesture in the general direction of a suspender belt, he leaned in and kissed her pubic hair,

"Beautiful."

She stood quite still watching his actions, as he stood up and circled around her, until he moved out of view behind her. Then, her eyes slowly closed, as he toured her body caressing, kissing and squishy-licking erogenous zones. When he drew her down onto the bed, he too was naked, and she was aroused to a level where she was prepared to welcome, perhaps even, given the chance, invite further intimacies.

He caressed her and suckled her, and when he slid his hand down to her cunny, she spread to allow access. He tried several styles while noting her reaction closely. Fingers sliding in and out, while pressing her clit hard with the heel of his hand seemed her thing. He kissed her with lots of moisture, licking her lips squishy. Her moans became squeals, and the involuntary jerks began to join up into constant vibration. When the man finally relaxed and allowed himself the luxury of mounting the squealing, orgasmic girl, thrashing about on the bed; he realised that although probably not a virgin, she had rarely used her cunny for the purpose for which it had been designed. It was small and dainty and like its owner, luscious. A few moments later he joined her in the union of souls, softly grunting, while she dug her nails into his hips, pulling him tightly to her and squealing with each thrust.

He lifted himself off her and hauled her over onto him, caressing her back and bottom as sensuously as he could, trying to keep her simmering gently, ready at any moment for a second round. The loving nature of the tender caresses, unexpectedly, also released the floodgates, she was lying across him, tucked under his arm, one leg between his, her face on his breast when the tears spilled over, and the huge racking sobs erupted. He held her and cuddled her and caressed her and kissed her on the forehead, as she slowly won the battle for control. The sobs diminished and finally stopped.

"If you need to talk, I'm a good listener. If it's too heavy, that's all right too."

"I never thought--That was so lovely--I never thought something so lovely would ever happen to me--But --"

"But what?"

"You--You said I'm beautiful."

"And you are. Would you like to tell me why you thought differently?"

"It--It was the man who raped me. I was thirteen. He said I was ugly and the only way I'd ever get fucked was if somebody raped the ugly little slut--and then he raped me."

"So you've never had sex until today."

Her neck snapped back, her face intense, eyes blazing,

"He raped me! I was lured to a house, knocked out, bound and gagged and blindfolded--and raped."

"Rape is about power, not sex. He picked a child and lied to her on a topic where she would be bound to feel tentative and unsure; you were thirteen for floppy bunnies, your body just a jangling mess of conflicting hormones. And he hit you where it would hurt most and did it in a frightening way. Not Sex, Power. You've lived through and survived one of life's nastier experiences, but it was all about him demonstrating his power over you. Today was about sex, and between us, it was loving sex."

"Tell me more--I need more."

"He chose someone he could dominate, someone who had no chance of winning because he had to win the encounter. Had he been thirteen too, he would have run from you like a scared rabbit, because the outcome would not have been certain. Today, I asked you whether I could have you, asked you to give yourself to me. Yes, I offered you a trade, but it was your choice. I gave you the power, the authority to decide. But, then you were nervous, didn't want me to see you. I could do anything I liked to your body, to my heart's content apparently, but not look upon your nakedness, not do you. That was when I realised you needed more and anyway, I wanted much more, I needed you to want me, as much as I wanted you."

"Oh--I thought it was just a business deal."

"It was never just a business deal, not from the moment I first saw you down in the lobby. Oh, I'll honour our deal of course, but I want you. I wanted you straight away. But then I realised you needed something more, better, more profound. I think we got it and you contributed to that, so thank you."

"Thank you--Do you mean we could have done it differently and still enjoyed it?"

"In a different way yes. Provided you were aroused, hot, up for it, we could have rutted like animals, and you would have still probably enjoyed it. I would have enjoyed you anyway, but you might have too, but as I say, we: **we** needed something different. Of course, that means that we still have a rutting session to investigate, to see whether we enjoy it."

There was a long pause, her beautiful eyes, now dry, were getting bigger,

"Now?--Would you like to rut me now? Do it. Now. Do it." He wriggled out from under her and stopped her from lying down, hauling her up onto hands and knees.

"Oh."

He forced her knees apart.

"Oh."

231

His manhood stood up between her cheeks proudly rigid. He reached around and caressed a breast and vibrated her clitty. "Oh--Ooh!" She gushed over his fingers, and he gently eased himself in, only when he had bottomed out up her, did he settle into a steady thrusting rhythm. Again, she began to squeal; he reached forward for her breasts, and she collapsed unable to support their weight. He kissed and licked her neck and shoulders and moulded against her, as sensuously as he could, as he held himself hard up her trying to push deeper with minimal withdrawal as he came, grunting in harmony with her squeals.

He awoke, with a sweaty hot-water bottle lying prone under his front, his back was cool and dry. The hot-water bottle turned her face half over her shoulder, opened her eyes and smiled at him.

"Hello, Kitten, Rupert Henchmow at your service."

"Oh--Hello, Carole Friendly."

"Am I squashing you?"

She wriggled sensuously,

"Yes--But it's nice too."

Their breath was warm on their faces; he moved in to kiss, as again his body betrayed its arousal. She spread and pouted, responding eagerly.

"I'd like to do something else. It's illegal and very naughty, and it will hurt you at first, but you might like it later."

Carole's mind was suddenly full of a wonderful description of a sexual adventure told to her by her best friend on a sleepover, while they masturbated each other,

'I was in the shower and cousin John jumped me and began feeling me. I squealed and tried to fight him off, but the feels were too nice. I just gave in and let him, his cock was rubbing my bum, and his hands were on my boobies, but nice you know, feeling, not yanking at them.'

Carole had reached out to caress the silky orbs,

'Like this?

'Yes, then he frigged me. I was spread wide and willing, but he didn't fuck me, I'd have risked it and let him, but he didn't even try, He soaped my bum and shoved it up my bum.'

232

'Really?'

'Yes, I was shocked and squealing, but then I was coming like a Ten Shot Roman Candle bang after bang, and I didn't mind or care any more.'

She made her decision,

"Okay."

"Just 'Okay.' No questions? Shocked reaction? Nothing? You are full of surprises."

"Well--I think I know what you want. A friend of mine told me what her cousin did to her once. She was shocked, but after she had got over the initial pain, she loved it. If I'm wrong we can try what I have in mind some other time; meanwhile, going by what we've done so far, I'm quite sure that I'll get something out of what's about to happen."

"Let's transfer to the shower; it will be best in the shower."

They climbed off the bed and, without pausing even to remove her suspenders and stockings, she drew him through to the shower hand in hand. While he hunted out the soap, she adjusted the spray for temperature and force and then grasping the rail firmly, spread her legs and pouted her butt. It took several minutes of soaping her up and, while stimulating her clitty, sliding first one,

"Oh!'

Then two,

"Ooh!

And eventually three fingers into her bottom,

"Oohee!"

Before he was satisfied that she was sufficiently open and he thought it safe to attempt to push his rampant member into her cute little rear. Throughout she stood compliant, spread legged, squealing softly and waiting patiently to be debauched.

"If you bear down as if, yes--that's it, we're there. The pain eases soon, are you okay?"

"Yes--It's hurting, but sort of naughty-nice, I can stand it." Despite their conversation, she still needed reassurance. "Is it nice? Am I nice?"

"You are the most lovely, sexy little Kitten." He began a gentle thrusting rhythm. "You are gorgeous, beautiful and sexy and. Ugh, the most. Most incredible. Ugh, most incredibly lovely fuck."

"Oh--Ooh."

She collapsed again, and he had to hang on tightly to avoid dropping her, suddenly he realised her squeals were words,

"Oh--I like this, I love this. I love you, I love you, I love you."

He rhythmically poked her jerking body, until the little cries ceased and she lay still in his arms.

He looked up from his writing; she was nearly dressed,

"Her name is Councillor Mildred Patterson, and all the rest of the details are on this paper."

"Oh--Thank you."

"Do you know how I know?"

"Well--You'll be an off--"

"I'm a hack, just like you, but older. I bunged one of the porters a twenty and got all the details, on everyone, not just her. And that, my beautiful, noisy mistress is what you should have done. I'm glad you didn't, but don't ever buy information with your body again and never pay, **never** pay before you take delivery. Now then, about us, when is our next date?"

"Oh--Oh--"

"Stop dithering girl, when is our next date?"

"Oh. What about your--Wife?"

"Situation vacant. Are you applying Kitten? If so I will interview you again on Saturday, have you got a card?"

She gave him one while looking at him saucer-eyed.

"Right, Saturday, five o'clock, I'll pick you up here." He waved the card. "Meanwhile let's scarper before they let this room."

Her mouth dropped open.

"That was another twenty to the maid. Much cheaper than through the official channels."

The life of cub reporter, Carole Friendly, became quite full and she and Rupert quickly agreed it would be more sensible if she moved in with him and she could borrow his car for her investigative trips to Warwickshire. Under his care and tutelage, it wasn't long before her skills were polished and shining and she was following a trail of unproven rumour. A trail that would, eventually, lead to Mary Smith.

Chapter 17
Themes: Tyne-dale Autumn Term 1985
Delia

"Have you realised, with Options and that, Timmy and Queen Bee are on identical courses, except for registration they're in the same room all week? Will be for the next two years," said Anna to Shirley.

"Even PE," replied the other. "Swimming, tennis and basketball."

"It will give him a chance to show her the true him, if he relaxes and, like, stops trying too hard."

They looked at Delia, eyebrows raised.

"He's quite nice when he's just being Tim, and he's very bright at Science."

"Together they're the best in the year, except for Jennifer in Biology," said Shirley. "Rosalind really likes Timmy you know; all that castigation isn't because she's mad at him."

"No, she's, like, mad at Rosalind. I don't know why, there's not an easy answer, like there is with Kim."

The other two gave her the eyes, and together they drifted off to their next lesson.

Early in the Fourth Year, Mrs d'Silva interviewed each pupil in her Art Class individually.

"Right Jennifer, what is your main study theme, paint or

sculpture, pottery, what?"

"I think it should be sculpture; I like making daft Heath Robinson devices that work in a complicated way to do a simple task."

"Have you got anything in mind?"

"Many things, here's my no splash tea stirrer."

Jennifer unrolled a scroll, on it was an exquisite drawing of herself on a bike, mounted on a training stand. Wires led from a dynamo on the rear wheel to a tower that carried an endless belt from which were suspended weights on strings. More wires led from a box at the bottom of the tower to another box under a steaming cup. Neat little rounded rectangular bubbles carried explanations of each stage's materials, construction and purpose.

"When you pedal, the dynamo on the back wheel induces an electric current in the wire. This powers the electric motor to wind the weight up to the top of the tower. The weight goes over the top and falls under gravity onto a piezo crystal, which sends a charge of electricity through to the motor in the box and hence to the remote stirrer in the bottom of the cup."

There was a silence; then Mrs d'Silva turned to look at her pupil.

"It works. I've built it and it works."

"There are three or four stages in your contraption where you could have short-circuited straight to the tea."

"Exactly!"

"I'm trying to decide whether you are just mad or certifiably insane."

"Oh, the latter Miss. Definitely the latter."

Rosalind and Tim both, independently, chose Sculpture, neither was aware of the other's choice initially, but nor were they or anyone else surprised.

"They were sure to end up together, except for Shelley and Jennifer, who are in a league of their own, there's nobody in the School to touch them," said Shirley. Shelley stood quiet, listening as usual, but the redhead was shocked,

"What do you mean me?"

"Shut up you, we're, like, talking about you, not to you. Cavy!

237

Queen Bee's coming."

* * *

"You know what," said Jeanette. "We've had the same decorations every year at the party, and they are getting a little tired."

"At my brother's College they have a theme for the Christmas Ball, last year it was Dickens' Christmas. Everyone in his group of friends made it fancy dress, came as a character from Dickens," replied Tim.

"That would be great; we could have a wild party, a West Christmas, Christmas in West Novochester."

Delia surfaced into the remark, plucking out the words important to her and rearranging them. Jim beat her to it,

"How abou' Christmas In The Wild Wes', Jeanette?"

"Yes! That would be great."

The end of break bell went, and the group began to break up in readiness to go their separate ways. Delia's aggressive exclamation had them all stopped in their tracks,

"Is that it?"

"Is what it?" Asked Anna.

"Jim has just come up with the best idea since some genius spilled mint sauce on a Yorkshire pudding and nobody's going to, like, take it on?"

Everyone stood looking at her in silence.

"Three twenty tonight, JR's classroom, meeting to, like, thrash an outline plan?"

"Okay," said Carly. "There's usually not much on, on a Monday. Can everyone make it?"

"Yes," said Kim. "Tonight three twenty."

Delia glanced at her as she slid around to push the chair.

"Robert will be going straight home tonight; I'm on."

"Oh, right!"

* * *

"Miss, can we have your room for a meeting tonight?"

"I take it that's without me?"

"No, not necessarily, in fact, can you be there, like, as a

238

reference?"

"Okay."

The word quickly got around, most of the Fourth-Year contingent from the various School Clubs like Mafematica and West Wild Water came, whole sports teams turned up; JR's room was packed to the doors. Delia surveyed the orderly but noisy crush with some apprehension.

"Do you know what you will say?" Shirley murmured.

"Yes, I've, like, written some notes down."

"But you didn't expect this response, how about if I chair it for you, then you can concentrate on the content."

"Yes! Yes, please."

"Anna, secretary?"

"Okay," said the little blonde producing a writing pad.

Shirley moved over behind JR's desk and addressed the meeting,

"Thank you for coming everyone." Her voice cut through the hubbub with the need for neither effort nor shout. "To begin with I will be chairing this meeting and Anna will be recording the minutes. The events planned for this term came up in conversation this morning, and several people came up with suggestions. Jim and Delia put the suggestions together, and Delia would like to put an idea before you, to see what you think. Delia?"

"It's, like, the party. The staff have taught us to dance, laid on music and given us pupils a good night for many years. We would like to give something back. The suggestion is that we make our party a Fancy Dress Ball, with a theme of Christmas In The Wild West. We decorate the hall with Wild West icons and come dressed as Ranchers; Native Americans; Cavalry; Trappers; Gamblers; Prospectors; Bar Girls. I know Jennifer has already designed a possible Pocahontas costume if we decide to go ahead and I'm working on how to convert my chair into a stagecoach. What we need to know tonight is how does that grab you? Who would, like, join in unconditionally?"

Shirley jumped in quickly before any possible reply

"Right, The idea is we decorate the hall in a Wild West theme and make the party a Fancy Dress Ball. Anyone can wear ordinary party clothes if they so wish. So well, who likes the idea and would like us to put it to Mr Baques for consideration and endorsement? It will require some contributions from us pupils, drawing scenes in Art and building a corral in the hall after School."

"Does it have to be Christmas in the Wild West?"

"Yes. There is not enough time to discuss which theme or what dress. If it's a success, we can think about next year's theme for longer, give ourselves time to plan it properly. Tonight, the idea on the table is to make the Fourth-Year Party a Fancy Dress Ball, with a Christmas In The Wild West Theme. It's a no choice package for this year I'm afraid. Who would like to go ahead with it?" She raised her hand. "O-kay, best count those against?--Against?" Shirley repeated, peering between bodies "--I count none--Abstentions?--Again none. So carried unanimously. Right, tomorrow we formally approach Mr Baques; meanwhile, if we have triggered any ideas would you jot them down on paper and give them to Anna, or if you can't find her, one of us by Friday. Don't forget your Name and Form on the paper, as well as your idea."

Within a couple of days, Anna had a great wad of papers. Among the many, possibly facetious, suggestions for a 'Real Saloon,' were, A Chuck Wagon Tuck-shop; a Miss Indian Nations beauty contest and a Gunfight At The OK Corral.

Anna listed and correlated them, then passed them over to Delia without comment.

One of the notes brought the disabled girl up very short.

I will do some

Bandit Wanted Posters

with the Teachers' Names And Faces.

Michelle

1985

She looked up sharply,

"How much is a Shelley, like, going for in the Stevens Gallery?"

"Thousands."

Delia thrust the note under Anna's nose.

"If she was prepared to part with them, we could, like, auction them off during the ball."

The Company CEO was nodding,

"I've already had a word with William, provided we give the proceeds to charity, we can do it. And don't lose that note, even that's worth money!"

Not only did Stewart Baques endorse the idea unconditionally and have it cleared by Management within an hour of being informed of the kid's desires, but he also piled in with suggestions,

"We will have a Saloon bar, but it will be selling fruit juice and crisps, sweets and the like. I'll give you £50 worth of stock; I'll have £50 back. Any profit is to be shared out among the bar-girls."

"Will there be, like, a significant profit?"

Anna chipped straight in,

"Oh yes! Only thirty percent or so on the sweets, but the mark-up on crisps and drink has to be seen to be believed."

"And keep the Wanted Posters secret from everyone else. I want them to appear on the night as a surprise. I'll get some display boards ready, with heavy-duty plastic covers as protection."

"Yes. We don't, like--" Delia shut her mouth quickly. "Sorry."

"As everyone uses the same hall for their party, all years are having Christmas In The Wild West, with whatever little variations they can come up with, in time. With that in mind, can I have a word with Jennifer please."

* * *

The site manager excused himself into Mr Baques lesson and handed him an envelope.

"Ah, yes. Delia," called the teacher waiving it. "William's writing, it could be about -- you know."

Delia took the letter, in Shelley's Business Manager's handwriting, that was being proffered to her and opened it,

"Yes, Sir, they're ready apparently, would you like to see them with me tonight, I think you'd better."

"So do I, I've heard rumours."

Delia and Mr Baques examined the work.

The posters were stunning and erotic to the very finest edge of good taste. Every member of staff was represented, and a few of Shelley's pupil friends. Shirley is a female Doc Holiday, Anna a heavily armed Painted Lady. Delia is drawn wearing her twin six-guns with their butts facing forward, the way Belle Starr is reputed to have worn hers. Mr Baques is a Hangin' Judge and Miss Ripson, Calamity Jane.

People who in real life were ordinary folk, are alive and well and stunningly good looking, staring out over their Reward Prices. Their characters are also laid bare for examination. Although Shelley had soft-pedalled on vices somewhat, she had still hinted strongly enough for them be clearly recognised in many posters.

That is she had soft-pedalled in all but one:

In the largest landscape poster, a small donkey stands centre stage among a class of pupils, braying loudly. Tendons and blood vessels stand out from the animal's neck, emphasising the decibel level to the edge of pain, it is frothing at the mouth. Among the seated pupils withdrawing from around her, while wincing at the noise, are Galileo, Newton, Darwin and Faraday. Watson and Crick are glancing over towards Franklin's desk. Archimedes is wrestling with Meccano bits. Every one of the two dozen or so faces is recognisable to knowledgeable members of the scientific community. Tim, Rosalind and Jennifer with Laura kissing Sadie on her temple are scattered among them.

The personality whom it represents is unmistakable, despite the animal being all donkey. It is Mrs Cumpbell screaming with apoplexy in her classroom.

Mr Baques made sure that Shelly was looking at him,

"Thank you, Shelley, they are lovely."

"My hands are happy," said Shelley smiling, but then The Artist took over. "There is one more. I have been working on the idea for a while, but Christmas In The Wild West made it possible." She pulled the drape off a nearby canvas. "Hang this over the bar, then sell it for charity."

'This' is a large oil-painting of the bar in a western saloon; Rikki Tikki Tavi is pouring a drink for Bullseye, while Nag and Nagina watch for a chance to strike. Various other famous animal characters are sitting at tables. Stetsons, chaps and revolvers are prominent personal accoutrements. A chorus of voluptuously endowed, dancing-girl mice scantily dressed as Santas are on the stage, and a poker game is in progress at the central table. Mole, Ratty, Badger, Toad and Weasel are gambling with hundreds of chips, some of which are cascading onto the floor from wobbly piles. The inspiration has most probably come from the various famous humorous paintings and ceramics of gambling urchins, but Shelley has added her own touches. The cheating card being passed from one extended leg to another is being exchanged for chips pinched between the available toes. More pneumatic bunny-girl mice around the table are surreptitiously sliding chips from one player's piles to another; one is holding a mirror up behind Toad. On the floor, urchin mice are painting extra zeros onto chips to raise their value. A tankard being drunk from has a card stuck to its base, Mr Bun the Baker. Only then do you look more closely at the visible cards and realise that the group is playing, not poker, but high stakes Happy Families.

On the left, a box of Gold Strike Claims Forms is resting against the bar. One of them has fallen out of the box and rolled away slightly. The writing on the scroll can be seen through the thin paper, faintly, but, naturally, it is upside down and laterally inverted.

1985

Worldwide

Christmas In The Wild West

* * *

Delia had got used to the fact she had an admirer.

Richard Keating could hardly take his eyes off her, from

243

the moment she appeared on the skyline. Then, several times, during the work parties drawing the Wild West Scenes in the Art room, she thought he was going to pick her out to speak with her. He finally managed to raise the courage to corner her in a West Wing stairwell.

"Delia, can I take you to the Ball?"

So that was what he had been working up to, obvious with hindsight.

"Push me into the stairwell, let's, like, talk about it," she turned and reversed into seclusion. Jim Teale stopped at the end of the stairwell, overtly not listening, but waiting for his friend. "Come closer, this is private--Are you asking me out on a date, with snogging goodnight and, like, plans for the future?"

"Well--Yes that was the idea."

"I'm sorry. I can't, not ever. I've got a boyfriend. If I were free Richard, I'd say yes, straight away. But, I found my man a while back, I'm, like, not available."

"Oh."

"I know that's a disappointment; I know how you feel, but please don't feel hurt. Your asking me out made me feel really good, thank you, I'm only sorry I have to say No."

"It's okay."

"I know it's not okay, but I do really like you, I would love to say yes, but, like, I can't. Thank you for the lovely invite." She grabbed his head and pecked him on the cheek. "If you are prepared to take me, just as a friend, I'll come with you. But, you might find that harder than me not being there at all."

"Oh! No. I'd like to take you."

"Fine, thank you for the invite. Can you come for me at six? At night, I'm in my chair mostly."

"Yes. No problem. What are you going as?"

"Well, before you asked, it was Belle Starr as a Stagecoach Guard, the, like, incongruity appealed to me."

"And me; I like it. I plan to go as Hiawatha, but with a difference." He bent down and whispered in her ear.

Delia's face lit up,

"Oh yes!"

"Could you possibly lend me an old--" He waved across his front.

"Of course. I've got a very short, dark brown suede skirt that Madeline gave me from her wild-child youth. You can borrow if you want. You might, like, need it taken in a bit."

So on Fourth Year Party night, Delia would get taken to the Fancy Dress Ball by a boy. In due course, it transpired that not only would she have a lovely time, but she would also take a bouquet of flowers home with her.

They smiled at each other; he obviously didn't know what to do now.

"Come on; we'll be late. Can you, like, push me?"

A coarse yell peeled out,

"Yes! There's the Firehose, thinks it's for pissing with!" Hopkins was shouting at Jim's unresponsive back and laughing as he ran off down the corridor.

Jim locked eyes with Delia,

"Don't hear it," he silently mouthed, then as Richard pushed her level, he murmured to her. "If I haven't heard it, it was never said."

Delia tipped her head in understanding and led off down the corridor.

With the best will in the World, the word got out as these things do and the fact that ballet dancer and closet exhibitionist, Richard Keating, was planning to enter the Miss Indian Nations beauty contest reached the ears of the teachers. The School Management promptly split the competition and created two prizes, Miss Indian Nations {Female} and Miss Indian Nations {Male}.

Interestingly it also reached the ears of Mrs Cumpbell outside the school office. Her reaction, voiced on full power, was immediate and impressive, several dozen pupils passing by, stopped and gawped in silence.

"What! That's disgusting! It's bad enough that there's a party! Putting a cattle market in it as well! I've never heard of such wantoness! Such lewdness! We are not having that atrocity!"

"Mrs Cumpbell, you are being overheard by pupils."

"I'm off to see the head about it now! Right now!"

"Mrs Cumpbell, please come this way." Stewart Baques, took her by the arm and led the still screeching woman into the head's outer office. Several times he tried to speak with her, but eventually gave up and knocked on the head's door. A moment later they had vanished inside.

"I thought Management had, like, okayed it, Shirley?"

"They have!" Miss Ripson's assertive interruption was followed by, "Off to lessons now please everyone, there's nothing to see here."

* * *

The produce end of the saloon bar had besides its sweets and crisps behind it, a bushel box of apples and a sack of carrots, on it. The reason for the unusual fare at a Ball became apparent when Pocahontas rode her pony into the Ballroom and secured him and a couple of others, in the corral that had been deeply lined with sawdust and wheat straw.

"I didn't think even Jennifer could get away with riding a pony into school!" exclaimed Kim, astonished, rather than her usual annoyed.

"She didn't, it was Mr Baques, he asked her to, like, do it, and bring the others too."

"What on earth will Mrs Cumpbell say?"

"What indeed? But I'm dying to, like, hear it."

"Sadly, you never will. She never comes to the parties."

"Parties; concerts; fairs; in fact, but for the lash marks on several backs, you'd never realise that she was a teacher here," murmured Shirley, triggering a round of everything from suppressed snorts to outright whoops from those nearby.

During the evening, the ponies made a significant dent in both apples and carrots by eating those bought for them by the populace. {And the following day a delighted Mr Carpenter gathered up the tarpaulin floor of the corral and bore its contents away to his allotment.}

Hiawatha shed his trousers and donned a dark brown wig

to strut and sway down the Miss Indian Nations catwalk, as his alter-ego Minnehaha. Behind a dab of makeup, he was as pretty as almost any girl in the room and very few indeed could match his stunning dancer's legs, which were being shown off to perfection by the lack of length in Madeline's 70's suede miniskirt. An old bra of Delia's packed with foam added the only physical attribute where he fell a little short. Consequently, no-one was surprised when he scooped Miss Indian Nations {Male}.

And few, when he also picked up the Miss Indian Nations {Female} award, before being disqualified on a secret Height qualification that Mr Baques thought up in response.

"But Sir, that means I win it, and I'm taller than Richard; I must be disqualified too."

"No, Laura, I'm just not telling you which bit of Richard fails the Height qualification!"

There were giggles and delighted laughter, from all within earshot.

One of the bar-girls pulled Delia,

"Are you sure Mr Baques said this about the money?"

"He wants £50 back, or money and leftover stock."

"We've sold out."

"What's the problem then?" Anna asked.

The girl indicated the cash box she was holding,

"Even after taking out the £50 and the float, we--" She waved at the pile of loot still on the bar, a significant portion of which was paper and silver. "Our purses are full. He gave us the fruit juice cordial; the drinks were all profit, and we've made too much money."

Delia took the cash box,

"Leave it with me," she said. "I'll, like, check."

"Mr Baques, the girls are a little concerned at how much money they've made. They, like, can't close their purses."

"Good! They worked for it."

Before the last waltz, 'Hangin' Judge Baques', resplendent in robes and wig complete with the black cap, sat at a desk on the stage and auctioned off the Wanted Posters, most of them were bought in by the criminal depicted, for between £5 and £10. If it looked as if an unpopular member of staff was to be unsold, the school bought it, with Mr Baques pretending he had a £3 bid on the books already. The sale raised over £800 pounds for charity and gave dozens of people an original portrait signed and dated by Shelley, in any Art Auction worth thousands and counting, that they could never have hoped to own otherwise.

That is, all except the Donkey. The Head bought that one, had it framed and hung it in his office.

'Christmas In The Wild West' was sold in Shelley's usual Art Gallery outlet for a Shelley's usual price, which swelled the charity donation several-fold.

Investigations: Warwickshire December 1985

Carole

It had taken a considerable amount of library research; several preparatory visits and much waiting around to see porters and cleaners in private, but several twenties lighter, Carole Friendly had finally run her quarry to earth.

"Er--Councillor Patterson?"

"Who are you?" The reply was barked at her. The greying face, with its angry hair fighting its way out from under a bush hat, was aggressively thrust deep into Carole's personal space. The level of confrontation, barely one rung down from attack, normally cowed people, but the young reporter was ready for it having been on the receiving end once already, at the conference junket. She whipped her press card between them; just not brushing the councilor's nose and forcing her to withdraw, minimally, in order to read it.

"I'm--Carole Friendly." The girl had her fingers over PRESS and anyway the photograph on the card, in its neat little leather case, got only the merest glance.

"What do you want? I'm busy."

"Social Services--Children in moral danger, I wo--"

"Useless bunch, the lot of you. Lily Liberals, I told you all about them; you did nothing."

Thinking fast, she could almost hear Rupert whispering in her ear,

'Never lie, but it's perfectly fair to take advantage of unwarranted assumptions other people may make.' Carole changed course and dived through the proffered opening,

"Er--I'm from a different department. You're right they did nothing, suppressed the evidence and nailed the covers down on the contacts. I need your help to chase them up again. You could get me the lists. Better than anyone else I would have thought, the lists, contacts, case-notes. Allow us to reopen the files and nail the little sluts."

Councillor Mildred Patterson donned the garb of the Avenging Angel and stole papers and occasionally complete files for copying. The latter were meticulously sifted and the lies, that the officials had inserted into the files that indicated everything was kosher, edited out before being passed on.

Particularly, the one on Mary Smith that was passed on to the journalist bore no reference to the raid; or its aftermath.

Fame Spreading: December 1985

Lovers

"Hello."

"It's me."

"Oh hello, darling. I've got news; Ternimal Investments has been offered Jenkins' Stables. It's a huge project, big commitment, it would take everything we've got, but I think it's what we've been waiting for. We could make twenty starter homes, thirty-thousand on each would bring in the half million we need and a bit spare; we could go."

"Do you really think so?"

"I really do."

"Test the water then. Just, subject to contract of course. The usual place at eight?"

"I'll be there."

"I'll bring the wine."

Between wine and loving sex the project was agreed, twenty starter homes, liquidise and flee.

Chapter 18
Surprises and Homophones: Christmas 1985 - Easter 1986
Delia

"Wake up, sleepy head," said Andrew, setting down the morning cuppa on her bedside table. "You have got a big day ahead; we are going to get your Christmas Present."

Delia half sat up and looked out over their garden towards the canal. She could barely see the waterway,

"I've got a wet day ahead of me, and I'd rather have my Christmas present in four days time as a surprise, if you don't mind."

"We have got your surprise present hidden away, this is another one, wake up, get that inside you and get up!"

The big day was a visit to the gunsmith, to select her target rifle.

As with many people, totally misreading the wheelchair, the assistant handed her the rifle tentatively and dropped it.

"Please," said Delia patiently. "Please assume I'm strong, it's just the right foot that's crocked, like, the brain and hands work fine."

They bought the rifle and ordered a pump-up air rifle, which, as it was the top of the top of the range, was not a stock item.

Also, it was left handed, with a left-hand bolt, a second, and the definitive reason for the well-stocked shop not having one on the premises. Along with the air rifle, Delia ordered telescopic sights, silencer and a 7 litre, 300bar Cylinder & Air Gun Charging Kit, all to be picked up when the air rifle was ready. Andrew was, not unreasonably, a bit shocked,

"300 Bar! That is--"

"Nearly two tons per square inch, yes Darling, a lot, and that is why it will be stored in that special armoured cupboard that I had built in the garage. The cylinders are rigorously tested before they leave the factory, but we'll not be taking any chances."

They took the target rifle straight to the club to get it signed in and, after a quick practice;

five fasciated clover-leaves;

at different places on the clock face;

8,

got it locked away safely.

In the back room when she didn't immediately stack it with the rest,

"Do tell me, for what reason are you taking it to pieces, instead of us to lunch?"

"I'm not."

"Yes, you are Mummy!"

Andrew didn't bother to reply, just counted them with his eyes.

"I'm cleaning it."

"It can not be dirty already surely?"

"I've fired it, so, chemically, it's filthy and, like, so am I. If I left those chemicals on it, I wouldn't have a good gun for very long."

"Oh, right."

"You're still taking it to pieces!"

"Yes, darling, but only far enough to clean it. If I took it, like, completely to pieces--"

"Which she could do," interjected Andrew.

Delia glared at him in mock annoyance at the interruption,

"Completely to pieces, I'd need the whole dining table at

home, not just this little table here."

It was a couple of days later that Delia noticed the tiny piece of glass deeply embedded in the stock. She had had another practice session and cleaned her rifle in the service room in the back and was about to hand it to Cade to lock away.

"Hang on a sec." She examined the stock closely. "Look at that. I thought I heard a scrunch when he dropped it. That's, like, glass!"

"You'll never get that out," he replied after examining the hole. "Not without further damage, a gunsmith might, or a French-polisher."

"Huh, I suppose I could always cherish its individuality, like a wart on the end of my nose!"

Cade laughed, slid the gun into the rack and snapped the huge, ancient padlock shut; he plucked the keys out of the cylinder lock base of it and drew her away. The large bunch of keys was totally dwarfed by his enormous ham of a hand clutching them. He surrendered them carefully into Peter's care.

"All locked away safe Captain," he said. "Including those with blemishes." He grinned at his Captain's puzzled expression and left Delia to explain how her rifle now had a lifelong souvenir of the assistant's clumsiness when he sold it to her.

* * *

On Christmas morning Delia unwrapped what proved to be a shoebox, but inside that were several other, gift wrapped, smaller boxes, that she would have identified instantly from their shape.

"How do you, like, wrap a giraffe?" She said. "Thank you so much."

"You have not opened them yet."

"That's a quality telescopic sight for my air rifle, when it comes, two boxes of pellets and the book-shaped parcel is the comprehensive cleaning and maintenance kit, thank you." She unwrapped and opened the tooled leather case and cooed over the contents. "It's not only a telescopic sight, but it's also the really good one that I secretly wanted, it's lovely, thank you so much."

For another half hour or so they fondly watched Amy open her presents and play with the favourite one.

"Did you check up on the turkey, when you, like, came through?"

"Well, the timer kicked in properly, I could smell it before I opened the kitchen door. I peeped in; it seems okay, but I have not checked it as such."

"I'd better take a look, like, in case." With another fond look at her daughter and grin at her man, Delia left to check up on the main ingredient of the day's feast. She hobbled into the kitchen and read the settings on the oven. Satisfied, she turned to retrieve her oven gloves and stopped, mouth open in shock. Goldfishing, she tore her stare away from the bench, the other two were standing in the kitchen doorway. Amy, perched on Andrew's hip, grinned as she said,

"Merry Christmas, Mummy."

"How? When there's, like.--They told me--You told me, three weeks delivery."

"Twenty-one days exactly, I took a chance and ordered it in November, it was the one I liked best, and I thought you would too."

Delia looked back at her workbench. Lying on it, centre stage, with a single red ribbon around it, was her top of the top of the range, left handed air rifle.

After lunch, while Amy was having her nap,

"Andrew come and sit; I've got something to show you." Obediently he sat beside his girl on the settee and, responding to her snuggles, cuddled her into him.

"I've bought this book for Amy." Delia placed the book before him, open at a full-colour drawing of a young adult couple having sexual intercourse. The drawing had overlays which when folded back, revealed a series of sequential cutaways eventually showing the relative positions of the sexual organs in explicit detail. Andrew stared. She quickly riffled through the next pages showing a sequence of further overlay-cutaway drawings showing fertilisation and the development of the foetus inside its mother's womb. He caught a glimpse of a no holds barred drawing of a birth as the book closed.

"I want her to know the details before she is old enough to understand them, then, like, later, when boys are trying to get into her knickers, she'll know the score and be able to make properly thought out decisions." A few deep breaths and some serious thinking later,

"Okay. But one of us-"

"I'll read it with her, like, it'll be a good way to tell her about Amelia."

"Oh. I have been thinking about that; I did not know what to do."

"We tell her before she's old enough to understand, then, like, when some trouble-making gossip tells her, she already knows."

Later the same day Delia took her daughter through the book, encouraging her to ask questions and replying as truthfully as she could. Eventually,

"So now you know all about babies."

The child nodded,

"When you have a tickle fight with Daddy."

"Yes, that's how you make babies, but you don't know all about you. You are very special. I have to tell you why your Mummy's still at School, like, why I come to visit, instead of living here all the time. You're very special, to Daddy and Mummy and your natural Mother." Delia slid Amelia's photograph onto the book. "You know who this is?"

"Of course I do, it's Amelia. Amelia's Garden."

Unshed tears stung the backs of Delia's eyes; she clamped down hard to control them. "She's with Jesus, in Heaven."

"She was my best friend before you were born."

The sudden stinging pain was almost unbearable. She reopened the book at the sexual intercourse picture and hurried on,

"Amelia is your natural Mother. Daddy put you into Amelia's tummy, just like the book says, and you grew there, just like in the book here. But Amelia had an accident. She was out with her Mummy and Daddy in their car, and they crashed. Her Mummy and Daddy were killed and your Mother, Amelia, was so badly injured that she died too, thirteen days later. She should have died in the crash, and if she had, you would have too, but she refused to let go. She fought on, stayed alive, for another thirteen days to give you the best chance she could. You were her dying gift to Daddy and me. Amelia was a very special lady, very brave, very strong, very determined. You are her life's work, and Mummy and Daddy love her very much for giving us a lovely daughter. For giving us you."

"Can I love her too?"

"Yes, Chick. Like, that's why I told you, most people only have a Mummy and Daddy to love, but you have Amelia as well, she was your Natural Mother, you carry her memory inside you, it's called Genes. Walk tall, be proud of her, worthy of her. She was wonderful."

"These jeans?" Amy was pointing to her trousers.

"No, same sound, different meaning, like in Amelia's Garden when we change the flowers on the table?"

"Yes."

"Well, you could call that table an altar because it's religious."

"Like in Church?"

Delia nodded,

"And if you change something, you alter it. So we alter the flowers on Amelia's altar. Same sound, different spelling, different meaning. Your genes are, like, what make you, you," Delia held a mirror up to the child's face. "What colour is your hair?"

"Yellowish-white."

"It's called blonde and Amelia's?"

"It's the same."

"You both have the genes for blonde hair. Anything else?"

"Her eyes are blue, like mine," she turned suddenly, peering into Delia's. "Yours are brown, and so's your hair."

"That's right, your mother's genes give you blonde hair and blue eyes and many other things too."

"What have I got from you?"

"You have my love, Darling."

"Oh. Right," she snuggled in. "Do you have to go away after

257

Christmas again?"

"Yes, Chick, I have to go back to School, but at Easter and in the summer, I'll come home again for the holidays. Next Christmas is the last Christmas when I'll go away from you afterwards. The summer after that I, like, come home for good."

Amy nodded, turning her attention back to the book. After a moment,

"When Ivan jumps on the hens is he making babies? Is that what he's doing?"

"Yes."

"He's rough. Does it hurt?"

"It doesn't hurt, done properly; it's lovely. Ivan's rough because he's a rooster, all noise and show. The hens don't mind; they're used to it. We humans prefer our men to, like, have more to them than just a loud shout and fine feathers."

"Like Daddy?"

"No more bets, please. As you say, 'Like Daddy!'"

* * *

When they met in school, on the first day back in Tynedale,

"Richard, can I, like, have a word?"

Jim and Kim began to edge away from the happenstance meet.

"It's not private, in fact, you're, like, welcome to come. I want to visit a few local restaurants, check out the standards."

"Oh well in that case, yes please," said Jim and,

"Sounds good," and

"If you are asking for an arm to lean on, I'm in," said Kim and Richard together.

"Oh--Oh right then. Erm, like, a couple to start with, the Tiger and the Swan, then we'll have a discussion and take it from there."

Andrew

Down in Warwickshire, Andrew too had been called to a meeting, job appraisal, general analysis of how things were progressing and the new contract. After an accurate and satisfying analysis of his progress, but more precisely the progress of the pupils in his care,

"--so what did you have in mind for your new contract?"

"Broadly what I have now, extended to a ten-year contract, with an annual salary incremental increase of a thousand a year, to be reviewed upwards if inflation rises above five percent."

The Chair of Governors gasped,

"That is a seriously big hike for a young teacher."

"I think that I am worth it. Make me a counter offer."

"Five years and five hundred."

"That is a reduction on both, how about reducing one increases the other pro rata. Five years at two thousand." The head waved his Chair down,

"We can't go for that Andrew, but there is something which could be a problem in the future, which if you meet us half way on it, we might be able to meet you half way on your requirements. You know that we are going co-ed in Eighty-seven?"

Andrew nodded,

"Yes, it was one of the main factors influencing my decision to apply for this job."

It was the Head's turn to nod,

"It's been brought forward a year; it's this September. We have a very conservative board, as you know and a Councillor who is actively looking for trouble to stir up, particularly for you. You personally, she hasn't forgiven Delia for being agile enough to escape a beating for long enough for help to arrive. Now I do not agree with this; the Governors know my feelings well, but I have been instructed to ask the three members of staff in stable but unmarried relationships if they could see their way to a more formal status. So basically --"

Delia

The opportunities for West Novochester Students to go on Work Experience occurred in the Fourth Year. As far as everyone was concerned, it was a win, win, win situation.

A bad placement alerted pupils to the reality of work sometimes being tough. A good placement showed them how it should be; and a significant number resulted in a job offer, particularly for those students to whom School was not to their liking, but the more self-reliant World of Work was. Employers frequently chose to take on a known good worker, in preference to a more highly qualified unknown.

The pupils were off site for a week, yet receiving good education and giving Staff a breather from seeing them in a classroom. This was always welcome, and Stewart Baques and his Tutor Team plugged Work Experience strongly, although as it also entailed visiting the pupils on site, the staff often ended up scurrying about like demented chickens, in their own cars, using their own petrol.

Typically in Assembly;

"Our School ran the pilot for this years ago, and it was a resounding success. I want you all to take advantage of the opportunity and don't just go for what you want. Go for anything. You want to be a nurse, you can't do that on Work Experience, so work in a shoe shop or an engineering works. Learn about Work! If you can get a placement yourself, for your chosen career, fine. Give us the details, and we will process it, and if it turns out to be nursing, we'll know not to get sick that week."

West Novochester itself provided several students with placements, in the laboratories, the office and the gym.

"Carly," asked Miss J'Enson. "Where are you going on Work Experience?"

"I don't know Miss; we haven't got the placements yet. We're doing it in next week's PSE lesson."

"I'd take you as a Student Teacher, in the gym, for a week--"

"Would you, that would be lovely."

"I could take three, Jeanette?"

"Yes, please Miss."

"Do you think Laura would want to?"

"No Miss," said Jennifer. "She wants to be a weather girl, we've got Own-Placements at the local TV station."

"Oh. Do you want to be a weather girl too?"

"No Miss." This was said with the polite finality of Subject-Closed, that only Jennifer could get away with. "But Jo wants to be a PE teacher, Jo Keener."

"Of course she does. I'll hold the third placement for her if she wants. Let her know will you?"

"Yes, Miss."

Stewart And Jean

Jean stared at the dining table, covered with piles of paper and memos scattered over the outline shapes of the Main Hall and the big Gym in North Block.

"Stewart--"

"Don't say anything; it's only for a few days. It's my first Fourth Year Exams, and they are going to tick like a Swiss Watch. Go and get freshened up."

Jean's expression said it all. Stewart reached out and caressed her while he spoke,

"I'm taking you out for dinner, so get showered and changed and put some sexy glad-rags on and be ready to leave at twenty to seven."

"Who's driving?" She asked him suspiciously.

"Me, both ways."

"Oh, well in that case, when we come to bed you can saddle me up and ride me off into the sunset."

"Don't I always?"

"Tonight it's my choice. I happen to choose our normal night. Two off!"

"What?"

"Or possibly three off. We'll have to see; it depends on how good the wine is.

* * *

Stewart found a space in the car park of The Crouching Tiger and made a show of getting Jean out of the car and escorting her into the pub.

"Stewart Baques, I have a table in the restaurant booked for seven o'clock."

"Yes, Mr Baques, it's ready, can I get you some drinks?"

"Pepsi for me and a bottle of that good house white, the more expensive one, for my friend."

"If you come with me sir," said a young waitress. "I'll bring your drinks through."

Again, discretely but significantly, Stewart pulled out Jean's chair for her and settled her into it.

"That settles it," she said. "It's definitely three off."

When he had sat down and composed himself, she added, "Did you see who's in the end alcove?"

"No, who?"

"Delia Summers, Richard Keating and Kim Hart. My guess is Jim Teale is probably in the corner, out of sight."

"Delia?"

"Yes!"

"Mmm. What are you having?"

"Garlic mushrooms, the lamb and something really naughty to finish with."

Stewart didn't even bother to open the menus, just held them up. The waitress materialised at his side.

"Can we have garlic mushrooms and the lamb, twice please?"

"Certainly, Sir."

When the girl departed, with the best will in the World their conversation sporadically returned to the slightly worrying aspects of Stewart's friend's young fiancée, being out to dinner with a boy who fancied her. The culinary wonders that arrived shortly after however drove all else from their minds.

The wheelchair rolled to a halt beside their table.

"Dodgy dandelion-dips!" Said Delia. "Can't I sneak off anywhere without ending up under your nose?"

"Think how I feel," replied Jean, "I can't even turn over in bed, but he knows about it."

Stewart laid his irons down in pretend high dudgeon, while the other five laughed at his discomfort.

"What are you doing here?" Asked Jean. "Celebrating Friday?"

"I'm casing the joint; these three are, like, my cover." Said Delia in a conspiratorial stage whisper.

"For a possible work experience placement," explained Richard glancing around at other diners taking an unhealthy interest in the disabled girl's comments. "Honestly, you can't take her anywhere."

"Tell me about it. I'm her Form Tutor remember!"

263

"It's between here and the Swan at Devington," clarified Jim.

"The Swan's carpet and trays, the Tiger's more sawdust and smiles," said Kim. "No contest."

"Oh by the way, at the last Pastoral meeting it was decided that the theme for the School Parties is to be decided each year by the Fourth Year, who will then take on the responsibility of decorating the hall," said Stewart. "It was a management led decision; but I happen to agree with it."

"That's okay sir, we had our go at i', that's fine," said Jim, precipitating general agreement all around.

Decisions and Reasons: Spring 1986
Mildred

The planning committee's April meeting was in uproar, with, possibly, fortunately, no member of the public there to witness it. Although there were more than a dozen people in the room, the vast majority were there only as experts, or observers; only the Councillors had a vote on any proceedings. The item under discussion was the reopening of a Canal Side Restaurant under the name The Prior's Secret. Even by her standards, Mildred was being the most strident person present, shouting the others down, gesticulating, gurning and shaking her stick. When she had beaten them down,

"Refused. Next item."

"I'm sorry Councillor," interjected the Council's Solicitor into the seething silence. "But there are absolutely no grounds for your action. Provisional permission was given a year ago, all reserved matters have been agreed, and you **must** pass it."

Spittle and froth spurted from Mrs Patterson's mouth,

"Never. Refused."

"You **must** pass it. If you don't, you will be sued for malfeasance, and if personal feelings become known, which they will, it will cost you your life Councillor, you will be lucky to walk out of court with clothes on."

"It's Change of Use; it was a feed store."

"It was using it as a feed store that was illegal, it is a café, Miss Summers is reopening it as a café." He spoke significantly to the Chair. "You **must** pass it."

Quickly the Chair put it to the vote,

"All those in Favour--three--Against--one. So that means abstentions none. Approved, next item, twenty starter homes."

Having been frustrated in her sworn intention to sink Delia's Café, Mildred was not going to let anything else get away. The blatantly palpable merits of the scheme for twenty starter homes had convinced her that there had to be a catch hidden away somewhere. That, coupled with the assumption by the rest of the personnel present that even she would be in favour, made her objections even more fiercely vehement and unyielding.

"But it's twenty starter homes; we need starter homes."

"For riff-raff incomers! Never! Refused."

"They're for our local people." Bleated the Planning Officer desperately.

"Refused! Next item."

"If you're going to refuse, you must give a reason." The Council's Solicitor, was again, interjecting a note of sanity.

"I don't see why. Developers get away with murder; we have our hands tied!" Her voice rose in triumph. "It's change of use! That's how the trollop got hers through, on a technicality. If Change of Use is an issue, that'll do. They are Stables and Stables they have to remain. Refused on grounds of Change of Use. Next item."

More Preparations: Tyne-dale Spring 1986

Delia

Unaware of the storm raging around her restaurant and the first tragic consequences of having, unknowingly, bested a paranoid opponent, simply by following procedures and doing it correctly, Delia too set about getting her Work Experience placement.

"Dad, could you take me driving, like, this afternoon please?"

"This is costing me a fortune and anyway you could go yourself."

"I know, but there's something I want to do, and I might need you available."

When his daughter headed firmly out Westwards, Dave was perplexed,

"Where are we going?"

"The Tiger."

"What are you going to a pub for?"

"I'm not, like, wait and see."

When they arrived at The Crouching Tiger, Delia parked the car and waited for Dave to alight before locking it up.

"Right, I want you to watch and listen, but if I, like, get it wrong, let me, don't interfere, tell me later, but not now. Right?"

"Okay."

Delia clumped across the car park, into the bar, picked out the slightly built man behind the bar and politely declined to be served by other staff, until she could speak to him directly.

"Mr Brown, I'm Delia Summers, I'm in the Fourth Year at West Novochester, and I'm a good cook."

"I'm not hiring at the moment."

"I'm not applying, not for a job anyway. I've come to ask permission to do a week's Work Experience in your Restaurant. I came specifically here to ask you; because I have eaten here in the past and was impressed with the food and the service. I would like to work the lunchtime shift. It would cost you nothing; you would get an extra hand who, like, wouldn't let you down and I would see how a successful restaurant is run."

It was only a few minutes later that Mr Brown and Delia were filling in the details on her Work Experience, Own Placement Form.

A letter arrived from Stillwell and Passer, their solicitors in Warwickshire; Mike Stillwell needed to see her. Delia rang him and made an appointment during her Easter Holidays.

Chapter 19
Meetings: Warwickshire March - April 1986
Delia

The doctor's waiting room was busy, but not crammed; flu viruses and other cyclic maladies must be on holiday.

As well as the baby clinic that Delia and Amy were attending, there was an antenatal clinic on, with several women waiting. Among the plump young-matrons proudly sporting bumps sat a nervous couple, obviously in love, but barely into their teens.

"Hello Amy," said the girl. "Baby's awake."

The toddler walked over.

"Would you like to feel him kicking?"

"Please." The girl pulled her top up and her stretch-pants down, Amy reached over and placed her hand flat on the girl's tummy, about ten o'clock of her belly button. Almost at once the kick lifted it. She turned to Delia. "He's really strong Mummy."

The three teenagers, one toddler and a bump, chatted amiably for a few minutes, until the time for Amy's appointment for her check-up.

* * *

The problem that the solicitor wanted to discuss was a pleasant one.

"Just, How much of the Georgian furniture do you want to retain?"

"All the sideboards and, like, the best of the table and chairs sets, a twelve seater."

"Just one?"

"Yes, for, like, the top table at Weddings and stuff. I'd love to keep them all, but needs must and I'd not feel easy with furniture worth a fortune just lying about."

"Well, in that case. There is a big specialist Antique Furniture Sale booked for a few weeks time in Banbury. Just, I've heard that there are already many rare and valuable items listed. Hence the critters will be cascading out of the kindling. If we could get yours that you want to dispose of into it, I reckon you'd get top prices."

"Well, in that case, go ahead, the restorers know which set I want, I, like, cable-tied the labels on myself."

"And Jellies are eager to swap their old wood-burners for the modern gas equivalents, Just, they offered 25% discount, which was on the low side of reasonable."

"Yes, I was hoping for a little more, well a lot more. Those old ones are, like, really good stuff, just obsolete, they are valuable, provided you've got a buyer."

"Just, I got them to agree to 25% discount provided they stripped out the old and fitted the new."

"Ah, now that's a deal, like, I'll go for that. Is that, like, everything?"

"Yes."

"Right, I want a hundred new chairs, Hepplewhite reproductions to match the chairs I'm keeping, but Chairs, not Carvers and twenty-five, four place square tables to go with them. Proper wooden tables, traditionally jointed, ones that will last. We got some new desks at school, donkey's breakfast, all you have to do to destroy them, is knock them over a couple of times, the tops come off. I've got quotes from several firms, two of them in Banbury, but they are, like, too high. Retail quotes. I'd like a real hard-nosed negotiator brought in to get those prices down to nearer Factory Gate, after all, they are going straight from the factory to the Restaurant!"

"Just, What will you settle for?"

"Wait until you see what the Banbury sale realises, bottom line, after fees 'n that. Then feel comfortable if you can bring everything in for less than half. That's, like, Price and all Costs, Professional Fees, VAT and such, everything, bottom line. Let me know, because Andrew has to agree too, but if you are under my limit, you can feel confident it will go ahead."

Mildred

Councillor Mildred Patterson made no secret of her conviction that The Prior's Secret was on borrowed time. Her withering rant was aimed at anyone in view, but especially at the Council Employees responsible for analysing Planning Applications and assessing their merits.

"I want it reviewed at every planning meeting! It has got to be stopped; we'll be the laughing stock of the World! Trumped up trollop getting Planning Permission when it's change of use!"

"It's legally--"

"You've been bribed as well! You have, haven't you! Admit it!" The Senior Planning Officer managed not to hit her, but only with difficulty,

"I--"

"Yes! You have! You're all the same, the lot of you! Corruption personified, I'd have you all shot, and then you'd do your job correctly next time."

Her party leader, in desperation, hauled her in and roasted her over it, although he received at least an equal roasting in return and merely succeeded in adding his own name, to her Money Has Obviously Passed list.

"You as well? How much? Go on how much did she pay you?"

"Councillor Patt--"

"Phwa! I'm not staying here to be lectured by a corrupt little pip-squeak!" She banged the door ferociously on her way out.

Delia

A few days later her solicitor rang Delia with the news. Had she overheard the conversation, it would have given Mrs Patterson no comfort at all.

"Just, in case you're worried about the planning permission."

"I wasn't, is there, like, any reason why I should be?"

"Mrs Patterson's trying to get it revoked."

"Can she?"

"No, that's why I've rung you, to tell you not to worry. It's as you instructed, absolutely to the letter and spirit of the law, fireproof. She can't touch it, Delia. Just, you are reopening a local amenity, a Historic and Valued local amenity and providing business to local firms and in due course, employment to local youngsters. I've dropped a few hints where things are discussed, the Round Table and so on. Don't worry, not only is it fireproof, it's wanted, by big bums on important seats."

"Oh, like, thanks."

* * *

It was the last Saturday in June when Delia was coming downstairs and heard Madeline talking and realised it was about herself.

Lovers

The lovers sat in a beautifully converted barn, overlooking the Oxford Canal, holding each other, desolated. All their hopes, plans and dreams were now mockingly hollow. The evening paper sticking out of a briefcase was folded at a small filler mentioning an accident at some place in the Soviet Union called Chernobyl.

As yet the name meant little to most people in Britain, the lovers' misery was caused by a small local entry, on the same page, about planning permission.

"I'm sorry. Just, she doesn't know it was us of course."

"Do you think that would have made any difference? Sorry. I'm not mad at you."

"I know. Just, where do we go from here?"

"She has to go."

"What responsibilities she's given's not down to us. Just, they moved her from Social because she was causing so much grief."

"I didn't mean that, she has to go, you know. Go!"

"We can't."

"We have to. You've told me often enough you'd thought about it before we met."

"Couldn't she--Just, have an accident?"

"Get a grip. She doesn't drive, do DIY, any dangerous sport. What accident might occur, choke on some unpalatable news in the paper? I'll see to it. We've even got a sponsor now. Somebody who will be suspected."

"We can't. Just blame someone else."

"She won't have done it; so she won't be convicted."

"Would you like to tell that to Timothy Evans?"

"That unfortunate man was simple. She is not, she will not be convicted. But neither will we be suspected. The matter has been decided. Only the details remain. So firstly --"

Chapter 20
Of Work, Experience and Salary:
June - July 1986

Delia

"You've got to lend her the car Dave; she can't get there otherwise."

"I know! But what am I going to do?"

Delia sat down on the top step, waiting while Madeline argued her corner for her.

"Buy a van. You've been on for weeks about needing a van; now your business is picking up."

"I was going to do it when I branched out on my own."

"So how about now? I'll run the office for you, the lads are poised, just waiting to come in with you. Panting for the nod."

"I know, I'm just scared to make the jump. It's the cash, at the minute somebody else pays their food and rent, I just add the bonuses. If I--"

"You're not going to anything, except succeed that is. Your order book's bulging and Stybes pay on the nail. It's now, the time, besides --"

"What's this?"

"The cushion, cash flow cushion."

"This is your money, from your house sale, I --"

"Which I'm investing in us, because I believe in us --"

Delia withdrew into her bedroom and settled down to read a few chapters of her book.

When she returned to the stair-head the conversation was about lunch; she went down.

"How were you going to get to the Tiger?"

"I had hoped --"

"Well, thank Madeline, she's persuaded me to lend you the car."

Delia hugged her,

"Thanks," she said.

"And in September, I start the business, full time."

"Well done," Delia whispered into the other girl's ear, before releasing her. "And, like, about time too."

The following Monday she turned up at the Tiger early, eager and fully equipped to cook and take copious notes on how to run a restaurant. Mr Brown introduced her to the chef,

"This is my son Reg, he's the lunchtime chef, you'll be working under him." Mr Brown left them to it and Reg, in turn, introduced her to the rest of the staff.

"Do they make you do homework on Work Experience?" He asked indicating her notebook.

"There's a sort of log thing you have to write, but this is, like, for me. I want to be a chef. You know, in the fullness."

Reg smiled thinly and set her to work,

"Batter for the Yorkshires, one hundred and thirty patrons and twelve staff?"

Delia realised with a start he was expecting an analysis,

"You do big puddings here; I'd be looking at more than two dozen eggs, like, thirty, forty perhaps?" He nodded.

"Mmm! Three-dozen. That bench there, the ingredients and the timings and settings are on a laminated list. I'll let you get on."

Delia was well aware that her progress was being closely watched, every time Reg passed close he looked, thrusting his nose deeply into her workspace and occasionally asked about something. He also nosily turned the pages of her notebook, reading the hurried entries:

Watch everyone all the time.

Check things are being done.

Assume nothing.

Everything gas fired.

Adequate Space.

One hundred and Fifty means three waitresses and

one chef pro rata.

Cleanliness is Paramount, even more, important

than food.

"What does one hundred and thirty means three waitresses and one chef pro rata, mean?"

"My restaurant seats fifty, well, I'm starting at fifty, if you have two chefs and half a dozen staff, I presume the twelve staff includes the bar staff?"

"Yes."

"Well, I'll need about four, possibly three, but more likely four, like, there'll be the same overheads with fifty as there is with a hundred and odd. Greeting people, answering questions, solving problems."

On Tuesday Delia was moved to vegetables and on Wednesday meats.

Thursday and Reg asked her to look after the store for an hour; but didn't reappear for nearly two and at the end of the shift called her into the office, where his Dad was waiting.

"What did you mean by, 'My restaurant that seats fifty'?"

"It seats fifty. Well, that is it could seat a hundred, it used to seat well over a hundred, but I'm starting with fifty, I've got trials planned, but we open for, like, serious business not next Easter, but the one after."

"Why so long?"

"I don't finish school for a year, and it needs a lot of work. I've had to have the roof fixed and part of it has been a hay loft for a while, furniture to buy. Thankfully most of the capital hardware is intact, it's, like, old, but quality stuff. I'm replacing the stoves with modern industrial equivalents."

"How would you feel about an early trial?" Asked Mr Brown.

"Next week and the week after?" Clarified his son.

"Here in the Tiger. We're a chef short, Raymond is going to America for two weeks, and we need a senior chef to do the lunchtime shift, let Reg move over to the evening slot. Fancy running a kitchen for two weeks?"

Delia sat silent for a moment, took a deep breath and,

"Yes, I could do that."

"School won't cause trouble?"

"No, they wouldn't. I'm pretty sure Mr Baques would give me leave of absence, but I'm, like, eighteen anyway."

"Just because your restaurant seats fifty, doesn't say that's how many patrons you'll have daily. On a good day, it may reach over twice that, more if you have occasional seating." He waved in the general direction of the pub garden and well-filled patio. "Where's your restaurant going to be?"

"East Warwickshire, but it's just is, not going, there are men working on it, like, right now, should be."

"Oh. Tell me more. Whereabouts in east --"

On her way home Delia called into School to see Mr Baques,

"I've been asked to stay on and run the restaurant for a fortnight, so would it be possible to have, like, two weeks leave of absence."

"Easy! I'll just extend your Work Experience from one to three weeks, that way you get your attendance mark as well."

"Can you, like, do that?"

"I haven't the faintest idea. Let's see who squeals and why, shall we? If you were in the Sixth Form with the other eighteen-year-olds, you wouldn't even be in the building. And anyway it's fun pushing the boundaries, you don't stop wanting to be naughty occasionally, just because you've grown up."

"No, you just get better at, like, not getting caught!"

* * *

After Work Experience, on her return to School Stewart Baques met Delia at the door,

"Welcome back Kid, was it worth it?"

"Yes. I found out loads that I would never have known unless I was in charge, about produce of dubious quality and staff thefts and how they can bugger up--Sorry--"

"It's okay, how they can bugger up what?"

"Long term plans. You go to get twenty trays of prawns out, to defrost for starters, for a big lunch the following day and, like, there's only eighteen. And a bushel box of Bramley's has ten bad ones, and that's a lot of apple!"

"Did you cope?"

"Yeah! Loved every minute of it, especially when I had to, like, think on my feet."

"Just like teaching."

"Did anyone squeal?"

"Yes. But it's all taken care of, if anyone says anything, you say Mr Baques said to ask him. Okay?"

"Okay."

"Welcome back Delia," said Miss Ripson as the chair glided into her form room. "I hear that the extra two weeks were full of rewarding incidents."

"Very rewarding Miss, like, wouldn't have missed it for anything."

"And it'll help you this time next summer?"

"Priceless. I've already redesigned part of the kitchen, in my head. Putting wash-up areas away from, like, food service areas."

"You don't want soap in the soufflé."

"It's more physical obstruction, a waitress with six dinners up her arms can't see the floor too well. Someone burrowing into a dishwasher could get hot soup down their neck, do it too often and you have to take the soup off, you've, like, got none left."

Jean Ripson looked hard at her pupil, caught the twinkle and snorted in a most unladylike manner.

In the crowded corridor after registration, Delia's form was slowly drifting along in the flow when,

"I see it's safe to go back to the Tiger for a meal," said Bill Carpenter to the Head as Delia passed him.

"I'd wait a while; she's probably left a time bomb."

"I, like, love you too!" Called with a half-glance over her shoulder, waving.

There were grins from staff and 4JR, puzzled looks from younger pupils all around.

"I thought you'd come back swelled up like a Santa Suit, but if anything you've lost weight." Miss J'Enson's familiar voice had floated into the changing room, from behind Delia.

"Hello Miss," she replied, without turning around. "It was all the stress and worry. Nervous energy, like, roars up the calorie consumption."

The teacher put her arm around the pupil's shoulder and hugged her.

"Did you enjoy it?"

"It was terrific."

The troll was spitting venom and pulled Delia as she walked past,

"Where were you last week Miss Summers?"

"Mr Baques said I was to refer--"

"I'm asking you, not him!"

"That's fine Miss, you can risk disobeying the head of your Tutor Team if you want to, I cannot; anyway, you probably know already, everyone else does. Will that, like, be all?" She clomped away. Around the corner, she walked straight past Stewart Baques,

"Mrs Cumpbell will probably want to report me, Sir," she said while flicking a thumb over her shoulder.

* * *

A week before the end of the Summer Term, with Delia already half packed, Andrew telephoned Dave at his office.

"Something's come up. Can I come to stay for a couple of nights and take Delia back with me?"

"Sure."

On the Thursday night, Delia arrived home from School, to find her lover and his daughter, waiting for her in the Summers' family lounge.

"What are you doing here?"

"I have not come to see you, I have come to see your Dad." Andrew smiled at her bemused expression. "But it is about you."

When Dave and Madeline arrived home, the whole family collected in the living room and Andrew related the gist of his appraisal meeting with his bosses.

"Ten years at a thousand? You didn't seriously expect them to go for that did you?"

"Nothing like it and I think the head could see it, so he butted in. They have brought forward the co-ed switch to September. I am one of the few staff experienced in a co-ed School, so they desperately want me, but not at any price. If they were going to pay me, somewhere near what I think I am worth, they needed something to take back to the Board, to trade with." He turned to Delia. "They want us to get married before September, and they will put a better deal than I could reasonably expect on the table in return. So Dave, may I please have the hand of your daughter in marriage, civil ceremony, next week, we will still have the proper one in Church, as planned next Year."

"Don't I have, like, any say in this?"

"Yes, on the proper one, when we really get married, in the sight of God. That one is all yours to do with as you like, this one is mine, just a piece of paper, but legal and just so no-one is in any doubt, I'm marrying you for your money. Well, the money you will be worth as a married woman."

"Does everybody understand that I won't consider that I'm married, other than it being, like, legal?"

Madeline, hugged her,

"Yes, dear, we do."

"Oh. Well, that's, like, okay then. So nobody will be surprised when I turn up to the Registry Office in grubby Tee shirt and Originals."

"If I ever find your Originals, I will personally burn them, woman!"

"I haven't got any, not real ones, but you, like, know what I mean!"

"Delia, you can't!"

"I can wear what I like for a piece of paper of less worth than the Munich agreement."

With permission granted and the ceremony, virtually worthless in the eyes of everyone but Andrew's employers, agreed upon, Delia returned to the important matters,

"So what am I worth as, like, a legal hot water bottle?"

"Five years at fifteen hundred."

Dave gasped,

"When you'd asked for ten at one, they never went for that?"

"They did. I actually heard someone say; it is seven and a half instead of ten. The Head could not believe it either."

"Who does their accounting? The caretaker's dog?"

"More like his chickens," said Madeline.

"But it gets better, I offered to take some of it in shares; I reckon that in about seventeen years, I will have a controlling interest, as good as own the place."

The following day, Andrew obtained the Special Licence.

"So when can we get Married?"

"Not today or tomorrow, but any time after that. There has to be one midnight to midnight day, between issuing the licence and the wedding."[9]

"So a week on Saturday will be fine?"

"Absolutely fine."

* * *

9   These requirements change frequently and erratically! If you are thinking of getting married, please check them. *D.C.*

"I was rather hoping that you would, like, have gone for it by now."

Madeline stopped scraping potatoes and turned to face her common-law stepdaughter,

"Dave wanted to, but I want to wait, not because I'm not sure, I'm absolutely sure. It's because I want more babies. We'll get the business on its feet, I reckon about three years, then I want to get pregnant on honeymoon, with twins if the prayers get answered. September '89ish. Meanwhile--how would you feel about being adopted?"

Chapter 21
Of Shocks, Dresses And Letters: Warwickshire: April 1986
Carole

The heavily pregnant girl answered the door to Carole's knock,
"Yes?"

Utterly taken aback by the bump, Carole could only bumble, "Er--Mary Smith?"

"For now, yes."

"Oh--I'm doing a survey on--on antenatal care, could I come in and talk to you for a while."

"If you dry the dishes and fold my ironing, yes."

She called her questions through from the kitchen and later over tea, face to face, with her little dictation recorder softly whirring away.

"--it was a shock at first of course--but Bill pleaded with the Social and they decided to take no action--like Mother like Daughter. Mum fell with me at thirteen, but her Dad threw her out, Bill took her in off the streets and looked after her, he's treating me better than a real father."

"Have I got this right? Your Dad--I mean, Bill Smith isn't your Dad, not your real Father. Or is he?"

"No, he's everybody else's, Bobby's and my younger brothers, but not mine, it just shows what a good man he is--could have slung me out when Mum died--I expected him to go loopy when he found out about this." She was gently patting the bump. "But he just loved me the same as always and pleaded with the Social."

The story was taking shape in Carole's mind, 'Serial Incest' had neither alliteration nor truth to recommend it, but neither had most headlines her paper printed, what it did have was Attention Grabbing, by the lorry load. Need she chase up whom Mary's true father was? If it really were the Dad who had thrown her out, that would be brilliant. Conversely, there were plenty ways to write the story which would leave the necessary question marks, without bothering too much about the rigorous research required.

By sheer chance, just before she left and telephoned in her article about moral turpitude in the sticks, she asked the right question,

"So--What did your boyfriend say?"

and watched her story disintegrating before her eyes.

"He was thrilled. Not at first obviously, at first it was a shock, I mean I was on the pill, it wasn't supposed to happen. But do you know to take other precautions when you take antibiotics?"

"What?"

"I thought not. Some antibiotics mess with the pill. Don't rely on it, use a condom. But then he was thrilled, he's doing papers and working on Saturdays, all for things for baby."

"So--Your boyfriend is the father of your baby."

"Of course, we've been sweethearts forever, who did you think it was?"

"But--You said Bill had to plead with the Social."

"I'm under age, somebody had to intercede for Steven, all the locals signed a petition; even the Social takes notice when an entire district asks them to forgive a mistake. All we did was get caught, almost everyone I know is at it, were you virgin at my age?"

"As it happens I wasn't, but I was taken against my will, I was raped."

"I wasn't. The boy I love, loves me in return, we planned our family, lack of knowledge interfered. You didn't answer my question. Who did you think it was?"

Carole decided the hole was already too deep and to stop digging, but the pause had been a dead give-away; Mary Smith had already made the connection and went for the jugular.

"Do you know Councillor Patterson?"

The reporter's face gave the answer. Mary raised her voice, "Dad!"

"I'm right here."

Carole jumped; the voice had come from directly behind her.

"I think we have an undercover reporter here Dad, would you be so kind as to show her your letter from the Social, no don't turn your recorder off, you'll need it on, to dictate yourself a copy of the letter, before you leave. Mind, if I were you, I'd have a word with the Social before you head back to the Smoke, get your explanation in first, before we file our complaint. Against Councillor Patterson, not you."

"Meanwhile I'll see how far up the Councillor's tender arse I can shove my twelve bore, before I squeeze the trigger that is!"

* * *

Back home, Rupert needed all his consummate skill to keep Carole sub orbital.

"She used me--Cynically used me to extract revenge on a child that had done her no harm. Who she had harmed! That kid still carries the imprint of the stick on her back, even now, years later."

While providing hugs and tissues for his sobbing girl,

"Don't fret Kitten, you're not the first reporter to be sold a pup for a hidden agenda, and you won't be the last. Learn from it, check your information, from as many viewpoints as possible."

"I don't know which has infuriated me more? That Mary-- She was furious and yet she still treated me nicely, she's so nice."

"Some people are, surprisingly."

"I don't know which is worse? Bloody Councillor setting me up--She'd doctored the file, taken out all the proof everything was okay, or doing it to try to harm somebody who's so nice. I would have sold her into slavery, and she knew it and still treated me nicely."

"Pay her back, learn from it. Think how you would have felt if you'd filed the story and then found out how nice she was and innocent, wronged. Write your story, but the real one, about Elected Officials, with no training for the job, being able to overrule the professionals who occasionally at least have some idea of what they are doing."

"I'll pay her back all right--I'm going to kill the bitch!"

"No Kitten, the consequences would be bad for you, which in turn means me! Instead of wielding a sword, do her some real harm, wield a pen, write the story."

"Huh!"

Thinking It Through: July 1986
Amelia

Delia knelt next to the table in Amelia's garden,

"I promise I'll take care of them. I'll bring Amy up as I think you will have wanted her brought up."

I know you will, you usually get it right, when you've thought it through.

"There's, like, a but in there."

There are girls who can't afford a Church Wedding, or are not allowed one for some reason. Have you thought how she is going to feel when you turn up in your originals and a grubby tee shirt?

"No, I hadn't." There was a long silent pause. "But I have now, thanks for, like, pointing it out."

Preparation And Planning: July 1986
.../Lea/Lovers

In an otherwise quiet office, late at night, a daisy-wheel printer rattled off a test piece. Close examination, by the only person present, showed no obvious deformation of the letters.

This decidedly unwanted perfection was quickly rectified with a craft knife and another test piece printed. Lower case e, upper case B and P now all showed clear uniquely identifying nicks.

The worker printed some correspondence and then four addresses, two on labels and two on plain paper. The letters were slid into two separate envelopes and addressed with the self-adhesive labels. Transparent tape stuck over each of the labels with a large overlap, not only protected them but also provided a firm base for the plain paper addresses which were fixed over the top of the self-adhesive labels, with yet more transparent tape.

The worker was about to leave when the daisy-wheel was remembered and swapped for a new one.

The letters, carefully separated from the genuine post, were slid into a different pillar-box many streets from the office. Three mornings later, they arrived at their tranship destination among other mail. When the transparent tape carrying the plain paper addresses was removed, the letters appeared to have been delivered to the wrong address.

Coincidentally on the same day that the letters arrived at their tranship destination, Councillor Patterson's PPS was collating her boss' papers for the planning meeting. There were many items on the agenda, and she had been working late thinking up ways to delay or refuse them. She was apprehensive because the few pseudo-genuine reasons she'd been able to come up with were finicky and unrealistic, but for most of them, she had been unable to find any premise and had had to resort to fantasy. The telephone rang,

"Councillor Patter--"

"I've got to go to see my specialist." Her boss interrupted

peremptorily. "Tell Councillor Beets to postpone the planning meeting and have those objections ready for me when I get in."

"Yes, but --" she stopped and replaced the receiver, it had gone dead half way through her reply. "And exactly how long have you known you had an appointment?" She said to the silent machine. "Oh, just found out. Not!" She cuddled the papers to her wanting bosom and went to the office three along.

"Yes, Lea?"

"Councillor Patterson has had to go to hospital; she says to postpone the planning meeting."

"Has she got many objections?"

"Yes."

"Show me."

"Oh I couldn't poss--"

"Show me." He held out his hand.

She gave them up.

"Thank you, Lea, that will be all."

When Councillor Beets thrust them under his nose, the solicitor's assessment was succinct,

"Do you really want to be charged with malfeasance?"

"No and I'm not looking gift horses over too closely either, the meeting goes ahead as planned."

The Planning Meeting was called to order promptly at ten; and the planning officers asked to submit their reports and recommendations.

The resubmission for Jenkins' stables was typical.

"The developer has pointed out that the grooms and some of their families lived in the stables in the past, so that 'Change of Use' doesn't apply."

"Mr Sanders?" said the chair turning to the legal representative.

"Nice legal point. If this went to court; I would not be confident that we would win."

The Chairman looked around the table as he spoke with feeling,

"A derelict, rat-infested building is planned to be cleansed and converted into twenty economical starter homes for purchase by local people. Our solicitor is of the opinion that we cannot prevent it legally. All those in favour to pass? Three, so that means against none, abstentions none. Passed. Next item."

One by one, with all dispatch, the chair put the applications to the vote, according to the planning officers recommendations, most of which were to pass, three of which were to refuse for good planning reasons and one to pass subject to reserved matters.

Mostly reference to the solicitor was not required.

Sixteen public servants, who had been expecting a trashing day of infighting and woeful miscarriages, found themselves out in the sunshine, before lunch, with a morning filled with solid, worthwhile achievements behind them.

When she arrived back from her appointment, to discover the note left for her by Lea, Mildred Patterson threw herself on her office floor and bit holes in the carpet. Lea had wisely decided to take the rest of the day off.

Later that night, in a converted barn,

"We can go ahead. Just we don't need to--you know."

"You were doing next to nothing anyway, just do it, as planned."

"But--"

"No buts. Do your bit as planned, and I will keep doing this!"

"Ugh!"

"You want me to keep doing this, don't you?--Don't you?"

"Ugh!"

"Then do your bit as planned!"

But Otherwise Legal: July 1986
Delia

On the morning of Friday 25 July 1986, before breakfast, the telephone rang.

It was Peter's voice, urgently needy,

"Delia, we need another shooter, can you shoot for the village team tonight, against Prior's Richmount?"

"Well, not re--"

"Please, we'll get possed, we always do, but that means it's even more important for village morale that we field a full team, not show fear in the face of the enemy, even if they are the best in the county.

"Just a minute Peter," she placed the receiver against her breast. "Peter wants me to shoot, like, for the village tonight."

Andrew gave her the eyes,

"Cast your bread --"

"All right Peter, your timing's crap, but I'll do it. Six o'clock?"

"At the range yes. Thanks, Delia, I owe you."

"You do man and, like, you don't know how much."

The Prior's Richmount team, as usual, kept themselves apart. Other than a professional 'Hello,' when they met, her solicitor hadn't exchanged another word with Delia.

She suspected it might have to do with Winston Scuffer being their Team Captain and like sister like brother, exercised rigid control over his team and, if anything, treated Cade more coldly than Delia, although he made his dislike for her obvious.

She didn't come last, or even last of the Prior's Eastwicke team, she beat both Cade and Freda and the lowest scoring member of the opposition. Her joy was heavily tempered by the fact that although she had shot straighter, it wasn't by much. The other two had performed poorly and consequently, the match had been lost by a bigger margin than usual, so it was easy to hide her personal delight as she slotted her cleaned rifle into the rack.

"Well done." Cade was feeding the chain through to secure

292

the guns. "Just, you shot well tonight."

"No, I didn't, you're being generous, I, like, did my usual, just about."

"Better than me anyway." He tugged at the padlock and held it up encased in his huge hand, indicating to her. "There, all done." He lobbed the keys across into her grasp and pushed the padlocked chain out of sight among the guns.

"You did shoot well." He drew her through out of the back, into the range. "Just, Freda and I shot badly too, but that doesn't detract from your performance, without you we would have done much worse."

The Prior's Richmount team were still keeping themselves apart. Juliet Means hadn't even acknowledged her existence. Delia felt like a bumbling amateur in the presence of a haughty World Champion.

I wonder if she even knows I'm here? The other girl slung her capacious rifle case over a shoulder and left the room, heading into the back.

Why tote a truck to carry the contents of a van? Her thoughts were interrupted,

"Would you let her sell a rabbit hutch?" Murmured Peter.

"Not after the way she performed selling, like, our bungalow to us." The pair exchanged meaningful glances, as Delia passed the keys over to him. A couple of minutes later the subject of their conversation returned, picked up her handbag and holdall and shucking the rifle case into an easier position on her shoulder, left with neither parting to friends, opponents, nor backward glance.

"Where's she, like, been?"

"Loo?"

"Without her handbag?"

"She's weird, so manly, but she comes on strong to every man that gets close."

"I had, like, noticed."

"That butch, you'd expect her to be giving the girls the once over, does she?"

"Standing beside Andrew, I'm, like, invisible."

He nodded,

"Thanks again for stepping in kid." The pair kissed cheeks. "Bye."

"Bye."

Her solicitor came out from the back and touched her on her arm,

"Sorry," he murmured while watching the rest of his team depart to various parts of the car park. "Just, it's easier on everyone if--"

"It's okay Mike, like, I understand."

"Well done, you shot consistently well. Just, you're getting better; you'll get marksman yet."

"Thanks, but sadly not as good as you, so, like, well done yourself."

He depreciatingly shrugged his rifle case further onto his shoulder,

"Breaking News; Just as I left the office I got a call from Clarice Chairs, they are prepared to do a deal on a multi-order. Not got the final details yet, but, just, even worst case I think we are coming in several thousand under your ceiling. I'll know early next week, and I've got some other papers for you at the office, about the work on your restaurant, can you drop in sometime?"

"Later next week then, after, like, final details?"

"Fine. Just, I'll ring you. Bye then."

"Bye."

The telephone rang again early on the following morning. Amy answered it and held out the receiver to Delia,

"Madeline."

"Hello."

"Best wishes for this morning. You're not really going to do it in filthy jeans and grubby top are you?"

"No. I've been persuaded to put a dress on, mainly for the other girls. Those that it's, like, all their getting."

"Oh good. Have a lovely day."

"Thanks."

"Here's your Dad. Bye."

"Bye."

"Hello."

"Hello, Dad. No, I'm, like, wearing a dress."

"Oh--Oh--Right then, er--Have a lovely day."

"I will --"

During the day, at suitable moments when the recipients were occupied with other matters, the apparent mistake of two letters being delivered to the wrong addresses, earlier in the week, was corrected and the doctored daisy-wheel disposed of into the refuse.

Down in Banbury, a few minutes after ten,

"--pronounce you husband and wife. Congratulations Mrs Bryant. You may kiss --"

Andrew stowed their purchases into the car,

"What do you want to do now, Mrs Bryant?"

"Get laid, please. Could you organise a suitable stud that might take on, like, an old married woman?"

He looked around the car park,

"Can you wait until we get home?"

"Only if I decide later it was, like, worth it."

"It will be worth it."

* * *

Andrew opened the door and pushed it wide; the happy couple had to wait while Amy picked a letter up off the mat, then the bridegroom scooped up his bride and carried her over the threshold.

"Amy, Mummy and Daddy are going to have a tickle fight, we're going to squeal a lot, because we are enjoying it. Can you, like, play with Pippa?"

"In Amelia's garden?"

"We'll go out to Amelia's garden after. Play in your bedroom, until I come for you." Obediently the child took her dolls through into her room.

Delia's squeals, at first inhibited and soft, grew louder and carefree. Amy went through into the kitchen to get her juice, barely glancing into the room where her Dad was consummating his marriage to her stepmother.

There was a knock on the door.

The Appointment: 26 July 1986
Mildred

The first letter filled Mildred Patterson with excitement

"Dear Councillor Patterson," she read out loud. "Please meet me at Berryhill plantation, at noon on Saturday 26 July 1986." the voice got quieter, the words became an indecipherable mumble. "I have information about the immoral practi--eral of--constituents. You will--interested in what--bout Delia Sommers." The last two words were shouted at the top of her voice. "Now I'll get somewhere." The stentorian tones reverberated through the house; Councillor Patterson was shouting again and, as usual, seemed completely unaware of it.

"What, dear?"

"This is what I've been waiting for!"

Cade may as well not have spoken, it was most unlikely that Mildred had heard him. Certainly, she gave no sign.

"I knew there was somebody out there who has a conscience."

"What are you talking about, dear?"

"Now I'll sort that trollop, make a café out of a feed store will she?"

"Who, dear?"

"Well, not any more she won't."

"Sorry dear, I don--"

"What time is it? Yes, plenty of time I'll --"

The pair of disjoint conversations continued as Councillor Patterson, got herself ready, checked her notebook and abruptly left the house, without a word to her husband. The fact that her behaviour was absolutely normal for her made it hurt not one pinprick the less.

In the public call box in the nearby village of Wormleighton, the telephone rang,

"Hello?"

"She's left. Just left."

"Understood, I'm onto it."

Councillor Patterson followed the bridleway up to Fox

Covet and along the ridge to Lodge Spinney. The entire walk was accompanied by a tirade of character assassination aimed primarily at Delia, with occasional excursions towards the rest of the younger generation generally and Mary Smith in particular. The animated waving of her stick, included most sentences being punctuated by a vigorous swipe at innocent vegetation. The path behind her was strewn with decapitated umbels, foxglove spikes and rose bay willow herb tops. She saw her appointment wave to her and retreat before her, beckoning her in and down through the trees into Berryhill plantation. The hooded figure was darkly clad in clothes designed to disappear into the background. She followed, calling instructions to the unknown person ahead, to stop, to wait, to tell her the information. The figure disappeared among the trees. Mildred Patterson pursued it, calling even more loudly. She stopped, the ground dropped off quite steeply ahead.

"Where are you? Come out, tell me what you know! I'll get that troll--"

"Councillor!"

The call had come from some distance behind her; she'd walked past her meet.

Mildred Patterson turned, her mouth opened, but possibly for only the second and certainly the last time in her life, nothing came out.

A few seconds after Mildred left for her meet, Cade made his way to the pub for some lunch and stayed there well beyond end-of-lunch time, telling anyone who would listen that Mildred had gone to see Miss Summers and he hoped there wouldn't be any more trouble. His friends, to a man, thought there was no chance of anything else, but in deference to his feelings refrained from saying so. Peter helped Sid load and despatch some heavy post for one of Peter's important clients, but afterwards, when he was free,

"I'm off to see Delia, make sure everything went okay."

"Good idea, give me a bell, let me know."

"Okay."

298

Chapter 22
Of Meeting Old Enemy: 26 July 1986
Maisie

Sergeant Enermouse knocked on the door and crouched down to talk to the mite that opened it,

"I've come to talk to Daddy."

The little girl picked the letters up from the mat and waved her through towards the living room,

"Having a tickle fight."

After carefully ducking through the doors, just in case; the big girl straightened up and froze. The man she had decided to court was kneeling on the floor between the spread thighs of a young girl who was lying back on the settee. The couple were naked, and he was energetically spending into her. The jerking girl was watching her, but unfocussed, also deep in orgasm. The girl's left hand, digging hard into her lover's back in her passion, was sporting both Engagement and Wedding rings.

Her secret love was either Adulterer or Married.

Maisie Enermouse turned sharply, cutting her head on the doorframe in her haste and shot out of the house like a greased ferret. Amy closed the door after her, returned to the living room and placed the letters on the table,

"New Letters," she said to the panting, but otherwise relaxing, couple, collected her juice and returned to her dolls.

Delia

Some time later,

"I've just remembered, sort of realised. Someone walked in on us, just when we couldn't,like, do anything about it."

"Who?"

"Maisie Enermouse."

"Oh dear. She has been really friendly since she came back. I was beginning to wonder."

"As you said, like, oh dear."

"Well, at least she will know the score now, I am sorry she has been let down with a bump, but it saves me from having to do it gently. She got her Sergeant's stripes while she was in Bunburt."

"That's good; she deserves them."

Delia opened the mail and Amy reminded her of the one that had arrived earlier.

"First Letter."

"Thank you, darling," Delia replied, smiling, as she opened it, "I didn't know we, like, got a second post."

"We do not--"

"We did today, well we got a first letter, an invitation for me to meet Councillor Mrs Patterson at Berryhill Plantation. Where she will explain the problem and make sure there's no more in future, then we got the rest, the rest's the usual."

"What are you talking about?"

"It's a good job I've had another shower, I have to, like, go out after lunch."

"Delia, just because you are now my wife does not give you the freedom to talk in riddles."

"Oh, yes it does; but today I am not. It's this letter, I have to go out to meet Mrs Patterson."

"Delia?"

Delia showed him the letter. It was completely typewritten, even to the name on the bottom.

Dear Delia Sommers,

Please meet me at

Berryhill plantation at 15.30 hrs on Saturday 26 July.

I have something to show you, which will explain everything, and stop all problems in future.

Yours faithfully,

Councillor Mrs M. Patterson.

Apart from its very existence; the only other unusual aspect of the envelope was how long it had taken to travel from the nearby village.

Delia had quite a hard time preventing Andrew from forbidding her to go, or insisting that he come with her.

"I'm off to see Councillor Patterson."

"I am still not happy about this."

"I know. I'll come straight home after, like, tell you what's up." She reassured her man and continued to insist that he stayed at home, despite being nervous herself about the meet.

However, by the time she had driven to the road, Andrew's disquiet and her own misgivings were winning; Delia was having second thoughts, and in addition, she was convinced she had missed something. She had almost persuaded herself to turn back; when she found Peter waiting for her at the end of their track.

"What's all this about you meeting Mildred Patterson? You okay?"

"Yes. Why shouldn't I be?"

"So everything went okay?"

"I'm not meeting her until three thirty and anyway, like, how do you know?"

"Cade's been telling everyone in the pub that she's gone to meet you. You're not going alone are you?"

"Yes, like, why shouldn't I?"

"This is the country, Delia. There are places in your hometown

I wouldn't go in daylight, places where you'd feel happy in the dark because you know. In the country it's people. There are certain people I sup with a long spoon, Mildred Patterson's one of them, I want to come with you."

"It's people in the town too Peter. Okay, like, I accept. Hop in."

The road to Stoneton Crossing followed the base of the concave slope for most of the way,

"There she is," said Peter, pointing at the figure striding along at the top of the slope. The bush hat and vigorously waving stick were in clashing contrast with the new flower-pattern dress.

"Yes, I've seen her."

Mrs Patterson strode out of sight, higher up, over the top of the slope, towards Berryhill plantation.

"She's having, like, a good leg day."

"Ugh?--Oh, yes, sort of thing you'd notice, I hadn't, but you're right."

Delia swung the 4x4 off the road close by the trees and parked. The pair surveyed the plantation, which, now they had arrived, was looking less and less like a sensible meeting place.

"So what do you want to see her for?"

"She wants to see me, she, like, sent for me."

"I'm glad I came with you, this is smelling stranger by the minute. That's not the impression Cade was giving in the pub."

"Thanks, I'm not arguing. She sent me a letter, but I knew there was something, like, wrong with it. I've just realised what's wrong; she didn't write it."

"How do you know?" Delia reached the letter out and gave it to him.

"She's an old-fashioned Schoolma'am pedant, with many faults, but, like, inaccurate letter writing won't be one of them, my guess.

"Oh. Yes. I see what you mean,"

They alighted from the car and Delia froze.

"What's up?"

"The copse is weeping. There's something bad and, like, it's very near."

"Do you want to go back?"

"Yes, but I mustn't, I have to press on, I have to meet her, I can't explain."

Peter waited, but when his young friend determinedly squeezed through the fence, he followed her. Together they pushed into the wood, Delia taking the steep slope with difficulty, left leg lead, one step at a time.

"Wouldn't you be better off zigzagging?"

"I'd be better off not being here, but going up's not as bad as coming down will be. I'll have to, like, zigzag down, no choice."

A shot rang out, unmistakable and quite close; Peter crouched down and pulled her down with him.

"That's it; we're going back. The next time somebody accidentally stops a bullet just because nobody knew they were there, won't be the first. Come on."

Still crouched down low, they turned, Peter towing a silently acquiescing Delia with him, heading away from the sound of the shot and more diagonally down the slope than the direct route they had come up.

And stopped aghast. Councillor Patterson was blocking their way. Although it would be the last time she blocked anyone's way, because Mildred Patterson was dead.

She was sprawled backwards, star-fished, head down on the slope, her huge shock of wild hair framing her face, her eyes wide open, mouth gaping in disbelief and with a substantial, although no longer flowing, trail of blood from a small dark smudge near the centre of her forehead. For Delia, reality became something passing her by, on the other side of a window,

"Is that what I think it is?" She murmured.

"Yes, I think so. Keep back, keep down. We can't do anything for her now; you're going to have to take the direct route."

Peter helped, supported and occasionally almost carried Delia down to the road. He bundled her into her car and drove the short distance himself to Wormleighton and a telephone and immediately summoned the cavalry.

* * *

Sergeant Enermouse was jotting notes down in her pocket book, while a colleague spoke to Peter in another room.

"We'll need a formal statement later, but it's essential to get your immediate reaction."

"Yeah, things get, like, distorted, bent around to fit, later."

"Quite. Okay, Delia Summers--"

"It's Delia Bryant, since ten o'clock this morning, for, like, official documents. They don't come much more official than this."

"Oh--Oh, I see, congratulations, you're having an unusual Wedding Day."

Delia nodded,

"I'm glad to hear that, wouldn't want to think it was, like, normal practice around here."

"When did you first see Mrs Patterson?"

"It must have been about three-fifteen, three-twenty. She was walking along the top of the slope towards the plantation. We only, like, saw her for a few seconds, we saw a person, but we knew who it was. Then she disappeared behind the trees."

"You recognised her?"

"Twitcher's jizz. Hat, dress, the flowered dress, that new one. Right place, right time and, like, she was waving her stick at someone."

"Ah, right! Then?"

"We pulled in and climbed up through the trees. I, like, found it hard going."

"What time did you hear the shot?"

"Three-thirty-two. Well, like, we found her at three-thirty-two, and that was just a few seconds after the shot.

"So you'll have heard her fall, possibly cry out?"

"No, nothing after the shot. Nothing before it either."

"But she broke a dry branch when she fell."

"I know, well at least I could see the snapped off stump. But I heard nothing after the shot. Like, when a Barn Owl flies by, what you hear is silence. You're not aware that normally you hear animal noises, rustlings and squeaks and stuff; then it flies by, and everything goes silent. That's what I heard, silence."

"You seem very sure of the time."

"Yes, three-thirty-two on my watch, but it's usually not far out."

"People don't usually give us the time so exactly."

"Mr Baques, he was my Science teacher, and now he's my Year Tutor, he stages happenings, to keep us on our toes, then asks us about them. He'll say, 'When did the fire engine go past yesterday?'And then, like, complain if you don't know. We sometimes ask him, try to catch him out, we hardly ever do."

"So now, when you trip over a dead body, you look at your watch?"

"Second nature to look at the watch, not, like, trip over the body."

"How near did you go?"

"We didn't. You'll be able to see, we churned up leaves and such, scooting out of there. We knew Mildred was dead. I'd had bad vibes since I left home, but they were really bad in the copse. Peter dragged me away, but I didn't take much dragging, like, there was nothing we could do and if somebody was shooting rabbits and couldn't tell the difference, we didn't want to be next."

"Why were you going to see her?"

"I wasn't, like, I was, but it was because she had sent to see me," she pulled the letter from her bag. "On my way there, I realised she didn't write it; she would have written 'Yours sincerely', after addressing me by name, not 'Yours faithfully'. Andrew wanted to come with me, but I wanted to sort it out myself and anyway somebody had to look after Amy. But I thought it was strange. It came by itself in the first post."

"This is the sticks, Delia; there isn't a first post, just the post."

"That's what we thought too. But it definitely was alone in the first post because Amy picked it up when we got back from Banbury. I checked, she hadn't, like, missed any. She picked the rest up later; when you called."

Maisie nodded, but declined the invitation,

"It's postmarked the 19th."

"I know, seven days to go a few kilometres. By the time I got to the end of the track, I'd had time to think it through, and I was

305

regretting being alone, so when Peter offered to come with me, I, like, accepted."

"Thanks, Delia, that's all for now I think."

"Where's her hat?"

"What?"

"Her hat, like, she was wearing her hat that she always wore and then she wasn't, where was it and her stick?"

"On her tummy, more like her lap, about here, with the stick under it." The police officer graphically illustrated on herself.

"No, it wasn't. And she didn't have her stick either."

"What!"

"They weren't there. Ask Peter. Somewhere between the top of the slope and where we found her, she lost them both. If they were there when you got to her, somebody else put them there, like, after we left." Sergeant Enermouse stood shaking her head, then brightened as a less complicated task became possible.

"Ah. Here's Joe, I need you to do a paraffin test."

"You will remember I was, like, shooting in the match last night, won't you?"

"Oh! Shit!"

"So was Peter."

* * *

The newly-weds were considering bed when headlights played on their window, with a rueful smile Andrew got up to answer the door. It was Sergeant Enermouse, mob handed. The welcome cooled dramatically as she spoke,

"Mrs Bryant."

Delia glanced apprehensively at her spouse who was doing the same.

"Do you own a two-two rifle?"

Chapter 23
Of Being Fitted Up: July - August 1986
Delia

"You know I do. I own two. A target rifle and, like, an air rifle."

"May I see them?"

"The target rifle's at the gun club, the air rifle's, like, through here."

She led the way to the secure cabinet and opened it. The powerful pump-up air rifle was securely double locked into place.

"And the target rifle?"

"It's at the club; I've never brought it home, like, never. It's always at the club."

"It is not at the club, and the club records show you signed it out yesterday, after the match. So where is the target rifle please?"

"Andrew, Peter said it smelled wrong, like, I need a solicitor fast!"

An hour later, with legal protection, Delia was ready to talk further about her guns.

"My client says she did not sign her rifle out. May we please see the evidence that says she did?"

The Rifle Club Official Record Book, open at the correct page, was placed in front of them.

The signature was very clear.

D. Sommers.

The solicitor relaxed back and looked enquiringly at Delia, but it was Andrew that replied to his unspoken invitation,

"Delia did not write that, that is more like my writing and I did not write it either."

"Had either of you written that, you would at least have made some effort with the spelling," Mike Stillwell finished.

"What's wrong with it?" asked the startled CID Inspector.

"That's how the local paper spelled it, two years ago, when, like, Mildred assaulted me."

"That is how it is spelled on the letter too."

"What's wrong with it?"

Several minutes of assertive defending by Mike had the police Inspector grinding to a halt in his questioning. Andrew pointedly drew attention to the fact,

"Are we free to go now, Sergeant? It is our Wedding Night."

The Inspector, no doubt nettled at being bypassed, answered,

"I have your assurance that neither you nor Mrs Bryant will leave the district without telling me."

"Yes," again Delia addressed the uniformed officer. "But why the suspicion, like, the attitude."

"I'm sorry Mrs Bryant, it's not always easy dealing with villains, but it's much worse questioning friends, but I have to be professional, remain detached. When you saw Mrs Patterson, walking along the hill?"

"Yes."

"She had already been dead several hours, as yet, we're not sure quite how many."

"Peter saw her too!"

"So you are either lying, or you are mistaken. As Mr Fortress is as sure as you are that you saw her, we are assuming that you are mistaken, rather than anything more sinister, for the moment."

"We're not lying. We saw her. But, like, that explains the good leg day."

"What good leg day?"

"She was striding along the ridge, making time, not limping at all. The dicky leg wasn't hurting her. But if she were already dead, it, like, wouldn't be, would it?"

When they put Amy to bed for the second time that night,

"I'm not sleepy, can I stay up for a bit?"

"No darling, you may not be sleepy, but you are tired. Lie still and make up an adventure for Pippa to have tomorrow. If it's a good adventure, complicated and interesting, you'll, like, wake up before you finish it."

To trip over a dead body on your big day was not the best of the Wedding Presents. To be in the frame as the principal suspect for the murder before you had reached your marriage bed was decidedly the worst. Delia had put on a good show when it was required.

As she got undressed, however, the cracks showed through, widened and her hard shell collapsed. Andrew hugged her and caressed her and let her get it all out. Not until the huge racking sobs had ceased did he set about making the tenderest, most passionate love to her that he could manage.

The searching police officers found Delia's rifle the following day, about fifty metres from the murder site.

On her way to report to her superiors, Sergeant Enermouse called at the Bryant's to have it positively identified. Her attitude, while still most professional, had moved back almost to the level of friendship they had enjoyed previously and she had a small bus-full of helpers.

"The serial numbers match, but can I look at it?"

"You can't touch it, sorry."

"No, just, like, look at it. Then I'll be able to tell you if it's really mine."

Although the Sergeant wouldn't let her lift it out of the evidence bag, Delia could see enough.

"Yes, it's mine. See that little hole in the stock? It's got glass in it; I couldn't get it out. I would have spoilt the finish getting it out, so I, like, just left it. Is it?--I mean, was it? --"

"We won't know for a while, but for now--"

"No more bets please!"

"Quite. Do you wear much makeup at the range?"

"I hardly ever wear makeup, bit of eye shadow, lip care, not, like, makeup. You'll know yourself I don't."

"Do you own any?"

"A bit, people give you it, like, by mistake."

"May I see it?"

In the bedroom,

"Is this all? There's not much."

"I don't use it, that's, like, why most of it's still sealed--Maisie, you're not suspicious and hostile any more." They drifted back outside, while they talked,

"Sorry, didn't mean to be either, but in my mind things have changed. The last person to use your rifle did three things that I'm sure you wouldn't have. They didn't clean it, and they were heavily made up, which as you say, I know myself you don't do. The third thing I also happen to know myself you wouldn't do."

"What?" Andrew asked.

Sergeant Enermouse, still concentrating on Delia's reactions, didn't answer, but was obligingly twisting the rifle from side to side to assist her examination. While the right side of the stock was clear, there were makeup traces on the left side.

"Oh!" said the girl.

"Oh indeed."

"What?" Said Andrew. "What is it?"

Sergeant Enermouse again didn't answer the question, her Inspector's car had rolled up behind the minibus, he had jumped out of it and was bearing down upon them. Without preamble he addressed Delia,

"We have the post mortem report. Councillor Patterson died at noon, give or take a few minutes, so where were you at midday yesterday?"

"Here. At home."

"Who with?"

"Andrew and Amy, we were, like, all at home together."

"What were you doing?"

The questions had been delivered with an increasingly

pugnacious attitude; Delia replied in kind,

"At midday, I was lying back on my sofa, like, consummating my marriage." Her eyes softened as she looked at her husband. "And very nice it was too." Almost as if it hadn't registered, the DI continued,

"Can anyone confirm that?"

"Oh Yes." Delia's eyes had reverted to flint-like intensity.

"Apart from your husband."

"Oh Yes. Someone came visiting; we weren't expecting her, and, like, we were too busy to greet her properly. Amy let her in; I'm afraid she walked in on us. I think she'll remember exactly where she was at noon yesterday. I think she probably fully understood, because she didn't wait around, probably decided to call back later. As it happens, I had to call her, well Peter did."

Pugnacious had been augmented by anger,

"What are you talking about?"

Delia endorsed the finish of her explanation with folded arms and weight back on her heels stance; the trace of a smile crept up.

"I came here yesterday, Sir, at noon," said Maisie Enermouse. "It was a personal call. It was exactly as Mrs Bryant says. She was here with her husband and daughter, at noon yesterday and for at least fifteen minutes either side. Mr Blake was leading hay along the track; he held me up both ways."

The knowledge that his prime suspect had an unforeseen, and solid, alibi; and that he had charged straight off the cliff to crash and burn ignominiously on the rocks below, unaided, turned the inspector's pugnacious anger to fury,

"Why was I not informed?"

"We didn't know married couples had to tell the police when they are having a shag, and we're not telling you, like, when we have our next one, either."

"You were not informed, Sir, because it has only just become relevant. You are being informed now. At the time of death, the Bryant family were all here, nearly two miles from the scene."

The Inspector hummed, hahed and fumed for a further few minutes, with the faces of his silent audience becoming increasingly bland, as the irony of the situation deepened. Suddenly, he seemed to realise the circumstances and departed as abruptly as he had arrived.

Maisie Enermouse watched him go, without comment or sign, commendably professional, then turned back to Andrew and Delia,

"Mrs Bryant, someone has killed Councillor Patterson and gone to a great deal of trouble to set you up as the culprit. It's a quite detailed stitch-up, with some errors of deep fact. So the situation is; either you killed her and are leaving obvious clues that can be discredited later; or you are being seriously framed for the crime, by someone who doesn't know you that well. I'm staking my career on the second option. My guess is that--"

"There are more clues to find, and you want to search the place, like, to find them?" Delia waved at the waiting officers in their truck.

"Yes."

"Okay."

Maisie pulled on some latex gloves and waved her colleagues in from the bus.

The search of the house produced nothing: that of the grounds and garden, on the other hand, something interesting.

"Have you just changed the daisy-wheel on your typewriter, computer printer?"

"Haven't got one, like, not yet; it's on the list, for my menus 'n that."

"School?"

"I really could not say. The girls in the office use golf ball typewriters, but there may be a daisy-wheel somewhere."

"Oh, there is Mr Bryant." She held up a daisy-wheel for a printer. "It was in your rubbish bin." Reverently she placed it in an evidence bag. "We will have to wait for the lab report, but I've had a quick look and I'd bet serious money now, that it's the right one, the one that wrote your letter, there are slight errors in the print, and matching blemishes on this wheel. I've had a good look, and I also believe that we can fit it to a precise printer."

"Not just a model?"

"The hub of the wheel is slightly damaged, it wouldn't affect the printing, but the printer will damage all it's wheels the same way, my guess. All we have to do is examine every daisy-wheel printer in Warwickshire, the one that inflicts this damage on its wheels, printed your letter."

"Oh, like, that's all?"

The search squad completed their task to a Teutonic level of thoroughness after finding the daisy-wheel, but then finished up and left, having found nothing more of interest.

* * *

Delia took Amy to the village as usual on the following Saturday morning. She bought her crisps and Pepsi and sauntered through to the garden at the rear with as much insouciance as she could manage and far more than she felt. They were all there, but judging from the levels of their drinks, hadn't been for long. Amy peeled off to the swings, while Delia took the chair pushed out for her by Peter's foot.

"How are you, Cade? I know you won't be, like, fine, but are you coping?"

"I'm not fine; I think I'm coping. Just, it's a week--We were all here, all my friends around me except you, when it happened, and you were finding her."

"Not exactly, I was busy getting married, Peter and I found her, like, later."

"Married?"

"Just legally, Vicar. The proper Wedding, in the Sight of God, is next year. You're all invited. I need to see you about a free day, August-ish. So who was here, last Saturday?"

"Apart from your chair, exactly as you see us now, Sid and I had a big loading job to do, but the wagon hadn't arrived, so we came here to wait. Cade picked Freda and the Vicar up and virtually followed us in."

"So we are, like, all your friends Cade, are we, there's no-one else?"

He nodded his reply.

Freda enlarged upon the analysis,

"Most people wrongly lump partners together, treat them both the same."

"Just, look I need to see the Undertaker, thanks for the pint Vicar, but I've got to go." He left his friends and his barely tasted pint and didn't glance back.

"Did I, like, mess that up?"

"No," said Freda. "Not any more than me anyway, I shouldn't have said that about treat--"

"Enough." Interrupted Peter. "Let's try to behave normally; if anyone can think of something good to say about Mildred, say it. Otherwise, we behave normally. Which is never to mention her. Right?"

"Right."

"Now then young Delia. What's all this about married? I had long term plans, which you've now scupper--"

"You, like, have a wife already, Squire."

"Details, mere details."

"And I have no interest in, like, reviving Droits de Seigneur thank you very much."

"Spoil sport!"

* * *

At home, Delia had a long think about what she knew and wrote it all down. After a relatively short further think, she drew out a new exercise book and began to write much more down.

Following a lengthy discussion with Andrew, the pair collected their solicitor and reported to the small country Police station.

"We need to inform you of our plans because they include leaving the county, which, make no mistake, we are going to do. We have a holiday planned, and Delia must return to Novochester to finish her GCEs. But we are fully prepared to give you our itinerary; we are not running away."

The Station Inspector was more than mildly put out and began insisting that they stay, report in every day and generally give themselves up for interrogation by rubber hose. Delia's flat refusal to be cowed had him goldfishing.

"No! No! And No! Again! I didn't do it. I wasn't there, and I can prove that. I am going about my business. Either let me, or arrest me and charge me and, like, put me before a court. I will be acquitted, and no matter what other frame-up evidence you find, Double Jeopardy will apply."

The goldfish remained silent.

"Fine. There's, like, our itinerary. Good day."

Chapter 24
First Try: August 1986
Richard

The canal was bathed in sunshine. Irregular dimples on the otherwise mirror-like surface marked where rudd and other surface feeders were feasting on the morning rise.

Richard Keating stepped out of the narrowboat's cabin and into the sunshine, closing the aft door quietly behind him. His parents were still asleep. He wouldn't wait much longer before waking them; today they would do the Hatton Flight, they had intentionally moored just short of the start; and Warwick and Royal Leamington Spa as well. He had a private target of Newbold Comyn Park in mind, but there were sure to be berths available in the towns if they got delayed, maybe even a marina. He climbed the steps to the rear deck; there was a softness about the light that forecast high temperatures later. He was aware that they were double moored by another and very long narrowboat, it overlapped their boat by a considerable margin. He took in the name, Amelia, unconsciously.

"A lovely day, in a lovely place and you beside me," he said out loud.

"I didn't know you, like, knew I was here," replied Delia. He spun around, his eyes frantically searching the landscape, looking from Delia, climbing the companionway up onto the stern of Amelia, to somewhere else and back to Delia, repeatedly.

"I didn't--I didn't--I--What are you doing here?"

The girl tapped the deck beneath her, as she readjusted the weight of the child on her hip.

"Same as you I would imagine, having a holiday on a narrow boat." She referred to the little one. "Amy, this is Richard, he's very nice. He's a very good friend of mine from School, say Hello."

"Hello."

"Hello, Amy."

"Mummy, can I pick my flowers now."

"Yes, darling. If Richard would lift you across. Will you please?"

Nodding on autopilot, as the shocks piled in on him too fast to assimilate, he reached out and took Amy from her and set her down on the jetty.

"Thank you," she said, moved away from the edge and then along to the towpath and began to collect wild flowers from the side of the path. He turned back to Delia,

"Mummy? Congratulations, I didn't know."

"Step-mum. Well, I will be when Andrew makes, like, an honest woman of me, in Church, next year sometime."

"Hello, Richard. It has been a while, you have grown, but a way to go yet, judging by the size of those Reeboks. How is the volleyball coming along?"

Richard stood gawping at the teacher, who had steadfastly refused to accept that he was useless at sport and successfully introduced him to volleyball. His mouth was dry, the more he tried, the less sound came out.

"Andrew. Call me Andrew, all the rest of my friends do."

At last, some semblance of control returned,

"Er--Hello, it was just the surprise. Volleyball's fine--I, we--Jim and me, we play for the county."

"Well done," said Andrew and ostentatiously breathed on his fingernails and polished them on his top.

"We double berthed you, when we saw the hitches. We expected to be away by now, didn't know it was you, but we're, like, triple berthed, we'll have to wait on for the outside boat."

Delia waved at the sawn off cruiser, tied up to their starboard side. "May I come across you?"

"Oh sure."

Delia clumped softly across the stern.

"Do not wander far; breakfast will not be long."

"I won't," she smiled at Richard. "Coming?" He followed her onto the towpath, and together they drifted after Amy.

"This is why I turned you down; I'd already found my man. Had I been still looking, I'd have, like, said yes." They talked filling in the gaps. "--then Amelia was in that car crash, and I lost the girl I loved, but the man I loved became available. No darling, not that one." She gently obstructed the little ones reaching hand. "That one's poisonous, I know it's pretty, but it could make you very ill, just by touching it. I had visited them several times while Amelia was alive. Andrew needed a babysitter, I, like, offered-- Who else is on board?"

"My parents, just the three of us."

"Same here."

"It's a huge boat, couldn't you hire a little one, or do you like big boats."

"She's not a hire boat, she's ours, we live on the Oxford canal, we like narrow boats, we're planning on more kids, the answer was, like, obvious."

He reappraised 'Amelia',

"Oh, Amelia! She's lovely, a fitting tribute."

Delia smiled and nodded.

"You said, 'honest woman, next year.' Why are you wearing a wedding ring? Or is it just camouflage?"

"Legally, I'm Mrs Andrew Bryant--"

The thump in his guts nearly made Richard cry out. Instead he painted on a smile and forced it up to his eyes.

"Since, like, the 26 July. But the Church Wedding's planned for next year."

"Oh."

"Facts I'd, like, kept to yourself, please Richard, you'll be getting an invitation in due course."

"Oh! Yes--Okay, of course."

The call to breakfast came shortly after. On their way back,
"Where are you headed?"

"Down to Napton Junction, then, off down to Banbury."

"So are we, not quite to Banbury, but, only a few miles short.
You'll go right past our back door. We could, like, tandem it?"

"I'll see what the folks say."

The folks were perfectly amenable.

For much of the remaining time, Richard travelled on
Amelia, as much as on his boat.

* * *

On their last night together, Andrew and Delia entertained
the Keating Family on board Amelia.

"I want to try out a new recipe, spread the culinary wings a
bit, would you come for dinner, make like guinea pigs?"

"It won't be egg and chips, Dad, unless, that is, they're
sturgeons eggs--"

"Foul things," interrupted Delia. "The only use I'd ever have
for sturgeons eggs is, like, to raise sturgeon. I was thinking more
along the lines of leg of lamb. I know it's August, but it's cool
enough. Roast Lamb, a few other bits, to fill up the corners."

When their guests arrived, Andrew presented them with
drinks and a menu.

First Special Dinner Aboard Amelia

August 1986

Menu

Fruit Juice

Hot and Cold Sea Food Toasties

Slow Roast Leg of Lamb

Choice of Vegetables from

Sweet Baby Beetroot: Mixed Beans

Cabbage: Fresh Peas

Sweet Green Grapes: Cauliflower in Cheese Sauce

Roasted Onions: Roasted Sweet Baby Carrots

Roasted Tomatoes: White Turnip

Root, Fruit and Leaf Side Salad

New Potatoes

Roasted Potatoes

Creamed Potatoes

Toad In The Hole

Choice of sweet from

Fruit

Ice Cream

Sorbet

Each place was laid with wine glasses, napkin in a ring, finger bowl and an extensive assortment of matching cutlery.

"Delia's training to be a chef." Explained Richard to his astonished parents. "Don't take a big helping of anything, try it all, come back for seconds later. Trust me; I've tasted her bits before."

"What's in the toasties?"

"Shellfish and crustaceans in the cold ones, oily fish mainly in the hot ones."

"These are scrumptious, my dear." Richard's Dad was waving a toastie over his small plate.

"Leave room Dad; you'll need it."

When the main course plates appeared, each was half filled by a huge cloud of crisp batter, with a large sausage resting in the middle of it. The portion of plate that wasn't Yorkshire Pudding was largely covered by succulent slices of lamb, each held in place by the crisp, crunchy skin. The adults served themselves from tureens, and Richard helped Amy.

"Please, I need some vegetables. Mummy says I must eat vegetables."

"Mummy's quite right. Would you like a bit of everything?"

"Yes, please."

"Try some mint sauce on the Yorkshire, like, just a touch, see what you think."

"Phwa! That is so good it must be illegal my dear."

"I've never served mint sauce specifically with Yorkshire Pudding; I'll never serve it without again." Richard's Mum tapped the crisp shell. "How do you get them this high?"

"Eggs. If your Yorkshires don't rise, stir the batter, don't beat it, sling, like, another egg into the mix and turn the oven up of course."

In a repast, any part of which would have earned a specialist restaurant praise, the item that had everyone gasping with pleasure was:

"My dear, this sauce--It's--"

"I've never tasted --" Interrupted Richard then turned his

hands up in defeat.

"You must give me the recipe," continued his Mum. "I've never made a sauce like this, ever."

"It's just a gravy; it's even got corn flour in it, not much mind, just to give it, like, a touch of body. But it's got all the meat juices, diced onion, handful of herbs, all the vegetable water, a bottle of wine and the secret ingredient, a beef stock cube,"

They all laughed at her moon face.

"So when do you open your restaurant?" asked Jacob Keating patting his paunch.

"Christmas next year. Christmas Day, Boxing Day and New Year's Day. Provisionally the name is The Prior's Secret, but we will see."

"I was joking."

"Can we come?" asked his wife. "And I'm not."

"I am afraid not," replied Andrew.

"We're, like, booked up. I've been entertaining the important locals to dinner, the ghillie, the farrier, you know, those with influence, the poacher. When I let it be known that the restaurant would be open for trials next Christmas, we were booked up overnight. All fifty seats are gone, for all three meals, and they've all paid, sixteen months in advance."

"Do you know what my dear, I am not surprised. How many on the waiting list?"

"Twenty-seven, that's for Christmas, but there's an even longer list for New Year, and we've got several thousand pounds in long-term savings, like, growing interest nicely."

Richard detected the complicated undercurrents,

"But that's not what it's all about, is it?"

"Yes and No. I want to be a chef, because I want to be a chef. I love cooking; I'm good at it, and I think I can be, like, great at it. That's, like, the yes, but my restaurant has to make a profit. Otherwise, it goes under and I fail, no matter how good a cook I am. That's the no. I am not going to fail, today good, tomorrow better, eventually some stars."

* * *

Just like the Fourth Year Party, occasionally Delia would hear someone make a throwaway remark, realise the implications and burst through it to a spectacular conclusion. Back home in September, Jeanette teed another one up for her.

Chapter 25
Operation Rock It Up: Tyne-dale Autumn 1986
Delia

"I've been thinking about the Carol Service," said Jeanette into a pause in the lunchtime conversation. "D'y'know what I would love to do?"

"Apart from having Jonathan drag you up onto the platform and sodomise you in public? No." Carly replied, moon-faced, to everyone's amusement.

"Not in the Carol Service, in the Troll's assembly, apart from that--I'd love to--Ooh, I've gone all squishy I'd love to--You know the light hearted Christmas Numbers, at the end of the Service, Rudolph, Jingle Bells?" The others nodded, now paying attention. "I'd love to Rock Them Up--You know, give it that." She held her Toon scarf up two handed and swayed seductively. Several of the group smiled and supported the wild desire with encouraging comments.

Buried in the comments was the axiomatic assumption that the project was a non-starter from its inception. It was this universal acceptance of inevitable disappointment, above all, that produced a totally unexpected reaction in Delia's mind.

* * *

Since the summer on the canal, Richard was able increasingly to be close to Delia merely as a friend. Only then did she truly become aware of how many times a week Jim had to be deaf. The friends were chatting with her in a stairwell when MacAuk approached,

"Teale, 've got a problem. Think y'could help. If y'would.

"What?"

"Army entrance exams. Queen Bee's telling m'about Chemistry. But there's Maths--"

"Yeah, there's the Firehose thinks it's--"

"Shut it, Hopkins," snarled MacAuk. "W'are discussing business, don't need owt from y'."

The loudmouth shut it and slunk away, mildly to Delia's amusement. What was causing her serious joy was the subject of the business.

"'ve got to master quadratics for the entrance exam, to be a technician, don't mind fixing the tanks under fire, that's expected, but 'll not settle for being merely expendable tank fodder. So can y'help m'?"

"Where and when?"

While the coaching appointment was made, Delia mused on the change of heart of a typical idle boy. The reason would irrefutably be a pale skinned waif, with a will of steel, in the Year below, whose father was a serving soldier, currently based on the firing range, north-west of Novochester.

* * *

Sadly being forced to live in each other's knickers for a year hadn't done anything for the Ebsenter-Schelle relationship, quite to the contrary. The worst time was in an Art lesson in November, when Tim accidentally spilt some blue dye on the workbench. How such a usually clumsy boy produced the exquisite work that he did was a mystery, but his figurines in Art and his miniature furniture in Design Technology were wonderful. The spillage was nothing, barely half a cupful and contained in innocuous space by Delia, while the clumsy boy fetched cloths to mop and clean. The lesson ended, and everyone packed up.

Then Rosalind went ballistic; her work folder was full of blue dye.

The subsequent interview with Mr Baques, however, was an experience Tim did not want to repeat. Delia, hurrying to the meet, to give him an alibi, nearly barged into the pair, had to brake hard and withdraw, before Tim saw her, and then wait around a corner until Mr Baques released him.

"There was nothing anywhere near it Sir, there really wasn't, I went to get a cloth and came back and began to mop it up and Rosalind blew up, her work was ruined! Somebody had wiped it in the dye while I was getting the cloth."

"Taylor says it was you." Tim could only bluster and whinge, "It wasn't --He's lying!"

"Everyone thinks it was you, getting back at her for treating you badly."

"I don't like the way she treats me sometimes Sir. But, I like her, I'd never hurt her."

"You fancy her?"

"Yes."

"This your way of getting her to notice you?"

"Sir, every time I do anything wrong, I do it right under Rosalind's nose. I don't need to spoil her work to get her to notice me. She sees me being a Pratt a hundred times a day."

"Mrs Cumpbell was complaining about you today as well, why was that?"

"Last week she said my essay was too short, so this week I gave her two thousand words. That was too long apparently."

"Ah--Go back to your lesson now."

When Mr Baques dismissed Tim, Delia collared her Year Tutor.

"It wasn't Timmy, Sir. I don't know who it was, but I saw him spill it, and he went straight for the cloth, to wipe it up. I helped him, I don't even think it was the blue that he spilled that got onto Rosalind's work, well, I know it wasn't! Somebody else, like, just used the chance."

"Who?"

"If I knew, I'd tell you, but I don't. But my list of suspects is,

326

like, no more bets please."

"If I believed it was Tim I'd have suspended him. But I need help on this Delia; I need to know for certain who it was."

Delia nodded, and half turned away,

"If someone who isn't half as good in her field, as I am in mine, ever calls me a donkey, you'll, like, hear about it fast."

"What?"

"Just a straw in the wind of complaint you mentioned to Tim. See you Sir, Bye."

Timmy told her later,

"Mr Baques must believe it wasn't me because he would have slung me out for ruining another student's work. He's given me until the end of term to come up with an explanation. I got that stony stare. I'd heard about it and been amazed that genuine hard lads like MacAuk feared it. Now I understand."

* * *

Delia pondered the situation, getting increasingly irate for the rapidly growing and consequently even more gawky boy, that hardly anyone disliked, but found irritating, most of all when he tried to please.

"Fred, would you help me find out who did the blue dye on Rosalind's Art?"

"It wasn't Tim."

"I know, like, I saw him not do it. But I don't know who did. Can you help me squeeze the truth out of Taylor, he says it was Tim, we know it wasn't; I wonder who told him to say it was?"

"What do you want, me to hold him down while you run him over?"

"Why not?"

Walter Taylor was heading for home without a care, when he found himself grabbed from behind and slammed, tailbone first, down onto the concrete. He squealed in pain and squealed again as Fred twisted his ears around the wrong way and then again as Delia reversed between his legs until her power wheel used his crotch as a wheel chock.

"Have you any idea what I could do to your chances of, like, being a father?"

"Don't--You wouldn't Agh!"

Fred released an ear only sufficiently to speak into it,

"Who told you to blame Timmy about the blue dye?" He re-twisted it.

Delia nudged Taylor's gonads again.

"Hopkins! Agh! It was Hopkins, it's always Hopkins, he did all of it; then he made me blame Tim."

Delia pulled her chair away,

"Get up you weasel."

Fred helpfully lifted him up by the ears,

"Thank your lucky stars I had your head. Had I been in the chair, I'd have reversed over you," and flung him away.

"Thanks, Fred."

"I'll let him know."

"Will he--Do I need to, like, call the undertaker?"

"Not immediately anyway, he'll work it out carefully, pick his place."

"Lookout Hopkins!"

"Mmm."

"Fred--Can you tell me, like, why the troll hates Tim so much, I mean every other thing she says to him, she calls him a donkey, but his English is fine, I mean it's--it's, like, good."

"I don't know, but I suspect that it's because he's so good at Science."

"I'm glad that she doesn't treat me like that, I'd not be able to keep my cool like he does."

"I think he's getting close to responding; he's working on something."

From time to time Operation Rock It Up was discussed. The opinion of little Kerry, who had been the first choice pianist for the School orchestra since the First Year, was that Mrs Macey probably wouldn't object. From just an idle desire voiced by a friend, the project began to grow into a fierce need in Delia's breast. She analysed it and thought it through; there were two people who had to join in, Big Mamma and Queen Bee. Without them, it would be a squib in a thunderstorm and a cheap one at that.

One evening, in early December, Kim pulled her friend,

"Our usual cupboard's locked, will you watch for us, the PE store's open."

"It's, like, on the corridor!"

"I know, but things haven't been too good between us lately --." Kim dried, but then came clean. "He hasn't shagged me for two weeks, and I need to know."

"And you need a shag?"

"--Yes--Even a naff one's better than none at all."

"Okay."

Delia waited out of sight for a moment, then checked along the corridor. It was empty, and the PE store door was shut. She patrolled the corridor, limping slowly from the main hall to the first stairwell and back again. On her third traverse, the door clicked open, but no-one appeared, and the sounds needed no explanation. Important pair-bonding activity was obviously still in progress. She waited and waited, unwilling to pass the open door and witness the soundtrack again. Presently a check on the other stairwell became imperative, she hobbled back, to check it. As she passed the cupboard, Robert's voice, suddenly and loud,

"Oh--What a shag Big Mamma! What a lovely shag!"

"What?" Cried Kim, shocked and angry.

"What?"

Delia hurried on blotting it out.

"What did you call me? You called me Big Mamma again, you bastard."

The raised voices pursued her down the corridor.

"Stupid bitch, of course, I didn't--"

The sharp crack of an open handed slap stopped her and had her spinning around. Kim appeared, skirt around her waist, knickers clumped around one knee,

Like sister, like sister, thought Delia and had to suppress a grin, as Kim hopped towards her struggling to get the other leg back into her knickers. Robert came after her, holding his gaping, sagging trousers with one hand and his face with the other, stopped dead when he saw Delia and vanished back into

329

the cupboard. Kim, failing, yet again, to find the knicker leg hole whipped them off completely and stuffed them into her bag.

The walk home was quite an ordeal. Delia chatted to her friend on shallow topics that largely needed no reply and managed to eke them out until they were nearly home.

"Thanks," said Kim as she turned into her path, Delia carefully didn't ask, 'For what?'

Relations between the couple became frosty, but polite, quite different from their usual bust-ups.

The following morning at start of school, Delia and Kim were waiting for Carly and the rest of their friends at the bottom door; Fred and Tim walked into School together.

MacAuk, Talleston and Wheadley were also waiting at the bottom door. The two friends very obviously tensed up at the sight, but Hopkins' gang didn't attack, they didn't even speak first, so Tim did.

"It was a fair fight MacAuk, one on one."

"What fight?"

"Hopkins. My argument was with Hopkins. For the blue dye."

"When?"

"Last night. I've got no argument with you."

MacAuk tipped his head back to look straight into Tim's eyes. An action he had only recently needed to begin doing. He then looked up and down the still rapidly growing angular frame; there were no signs of recent combat showing.

"H' not be coming then, did y'call an ambulance?"

"I left him with his brother."

MacAuk nodded,

"'Did warn h'." He turned away with the other two and walked into School. "But h' never listens. One day it'll be the death --" The closing door cut off the rest of the observation. The gang passed into the school, across the corridor and out the rear door, heading for their own form-room, they didn't even look back. Apparently, the showdown had been foreseen, the outcome anticipated and the incident was now regarded as closed.

Hopkins did not return to School until after Christmas, but it was not until some time after that even, that he allowed himself the luxury of laughter.

Last lesson, the troll, yet again, managed to avoid teaching them and Mr Baggott was also off. Mr Carpenter and another craft teacher were pressed in to relieve. When he saw which fifth-year classes were involved, Mr Carpenter sent his colleague away and took both classes into the library.

Delia's six settled themselves around an alcove table and dashed off the scratch work left for them, then relaxed and talked about other things. Presently Operation Rock It Up surfaced and with it the need to co-opt Queen Bee and, especially, Big Mamma. Not everyone was in agreement.

"We will have to get her on board," argued Jeanette.

Kim was, as usual, spitting spleen,

"Oh Yeah. We can't do anything without the great Shirley."

"If Big Mamma doesn't go along with it, like, no one else will."

"Why can't we just do it, it's nowt to do with her anyway."

"Why does everything have to be a fight with you?" Delia stopped, everyone knew why everything had to be a fight with Kim, she more than most, she had regretted the outburst as she was saying it. "It's just sense, we want to do something off the wall, let's, like, do our homework first."

Kim folded her arms and grumped her head forward; the other five watched her in silence.

There was conversation from the next alcove, punctuated by movement as someone eased out,

"Ah, awake at last I see, are you all right, Shirley?" Mr Carpenter's kindly voice.

"Yes, sorry Sir, been burning it at both ends recently I'm afraid, it--"

"She's been burning it at both ends and the middle Mr Carpenter, doing too much, I tell her, she doesn't listen!" said Anna.

"You take care now, get to bed the same day you get up occasionally."

"Sir."

A moment later Shirley joined them, leaning in among them, making the conversation private. The group watched her warily. She looked straight at Delia,

"What am I required to 'go along with'?"

Kim snarled something under her breath; Shirley ignored it looking intently at Delia.

"The End of Term Carol Concert? The light numbers, Rudolph, Jingle Bells?"

"Yes."

"We want to, like, Rock It Up."

"Sounds like fun. Why don't you get it officially sanctioned, have a quiet word with JR or even SB?"

"And when we fail, the great Shirley can persuade them."

"Kim I really don't know what I've done wrong in your eyes, but whatever it is. Sorry." She turned back to Delia. "Have a word with Stewart Baques, at the very worst he will negotiate; my guess is he will be all for it."

"Will you speak to him?"

"No, it's your idea, and it's your scene, not mine. I'll willingly join in anything you arrange with him, but **you** speak to him."

Stewart

Stewart Baques had been nervously looking forward to the Carol Concert. He liked singing Traditional Carols and Mrs Macey, the Head of Music, had for some years now finished off the concert with some more light-hearted ones, White Christmas and the like. The concert had been potentially the high spot of the week, getting there, through the other four days, was the problem.

When Delia came to see him about treating the Carol Concert as a Gig, he grabbed the opportunity with both hands.

He wheeled her into his office and thrashed out the deal.

"Okay, but I want something in return."

Delia, astonished and reeling could only answer,

"What?"

"I want Full School Uniform and correct behaviour Monday to Thursday."

"Right."

"Full School Uniform on Friday, underneath; on top, you can deck yourselves out like Christmas Trees, but if any Teacher requires you to take the decorations off, they are obeyed, without comment."

"Right."

"No Eggs, No Flour, No Crugg of any kind. Anyone trying it on, to be jumped on by you, Big Mamma, Queen Bee and Uncle Tom Cobley as well as the Staff."

"Fine."

"Sing your hearts out during the Carols."

"We will. Will you help, like, gee up from the front?" He nodded,

"Oh, I'll help. Then you can rock the School to its foundations for the last, light-hearted, numbers."

"Yes, Sir!"

"Come on, Mrs Macey's been down in the hall a lot recently, she might still be here."

The Head of Music was in the hall, putting the finishing touches to several months of hard work.

"Enid, you know those songs you finish off with?"

333

"Yes."

"We're going to Rock 'em Up, you know give it that." Stewart held his hands over his head and swung from side to side from the hips. Enid Macey smiled,

"The full works?"

"If we can manage it, can you cope?"

"We'll cope, take the roof off."

Chapter 26
Of Learning the Difference: December 1986
Delia

Delia pulled Shirley in the corridor the following day, eyes full of disbelief,

"He said yes."

"I told you. He believes School should be a happy place where kids come because they want to be here, he was never going to say 'No' to a suggestion that increases the good clean fun of life."

"He did a deal with me. Next week, provided we keep a lid on things, Monday to Thursday inclusive, anything goes, like, decorations 'n that, on the Friday."

"Sounds fair."

"He's going to publish the deal in assembly tomorrow. Will you help me to, like, keep the lid on? You know Hopkins 'n such."

Shirley nodded,

"Have you spoken to Rosalind?"

"Not yet, but I will, I'm with her next lesson."

"She'll be all for it."

"Do you really not know why Kim is angry with you?"

"I really don't know."

"Robert fancies you; he's even called your name. Done it more than once. When he was--like, you know."

"Oh dear. Betrayal big time. The apology stands, even though he's got no chance, wrong sex for starters. I'd climb over him to get at Kim."

"Let her know?"

"I didn't mean to eavesdrop, I was asleep, leaning against the trunking, you know how it beefs up the sound, like a loudspeaker. You woke me up, but I'm glad you did." Big Mamma nodded and walked away leaving Delia to pass on the news. The deal that Mr Baques published later in assembly did not mention the Carol Service, only the mode of dress and behaviour.

On their way down to English, Kim found herself being forced to leave go of the wheelchair, as Delia spun herself around and backed into a little-used stairwell doorway.

"What?"

"I've been meddling in your business. I need to, like, own up."

"What?"

"Big Mamma, I told her why you--What she has been doing wrong. She repeated the apology and sent you a message." Delia watched as her friend fought with her annoyance. Eventually,

"What then?"

"She said to tell you he's the wrong sex for her. The rumours are right, apparently, Carly would be much more to her liking, or even you yourself."

"Oh. I thought Anna Monta was straight? I mean she's half-had loads of lads. Not shagged them, everything but though, so I've heard."

Delia shrugged.

"I've heard that too; she might be straight, like, she wasn't mentioned." Kim leaned against the wall and sighed deeply through her nose, after a while, Delia looked at her watch.

"We'll be late."

"Not as late as the troll, though. Okay, let's go."

Down in the prefab, Kim was correct, Mrs Cumpbell and Mr Baggott were even later than they were, so whereas the two other lessons had started, her top set English and Robert's second set were all crushed together in the short corridor outside the rooms. Kim had to push Delia past Robert to get to their class, but she stopped level with him.

"Slapping you was childish and unladylike," she murmured, "I should have just dumped you. So, sorry for slapping you. You're dumped, bye." She walked on down the corridor towards Mrs Cumpbell's room.

The explosion of abuse and shouting of threats, from behind her was truly awesome, prompting the emergence of Miss Fraser, to quell the riot, but throughout it all, Kim stood silent and turned away, holding Delia's hand tightly.

When the cordially detested little runt did finally arrive, the class were instructed to spend the lesson assembling their assignments.

At the exact moment that Kim needed one, Shirley reached over and placed her stapler on the other girl's work, without looking up or saying anything, exactly as she would to Anna or Sally. After a pause of several seconds, it clicked and was placed back down in front of her,

"Thank you," softly.

Shirley looked up, smiled and waved a hand, but again said nothing. Delia smiled, Monta Industries had few problems between Management and Workers, little wonder, with Shirley Jayne Swyfte on the Board, Director in charge of Industrial Relations.

* * *

On the way home with Kim, Delia made the first move in another plan that was slowly forming in her mind,

"Have you stopped taking the pill since --"

"No, should I?"

"No don't, you never know if there's a ship anchored around the next bend. Be, like, a good Girl Scout, prepared."

Kim laughed, the first for some time.

The following day Delia pulled Jennifer,

"I need a boy to give Kim a good seeing to, like, rub out the last four years, any suggestions?"

"A really good seeing to, dragged through a mincer seeing to?"

"She's never come, not with Bob the Poser anyway. I want her to know, like, how it **should** feel."

"Your mates. Richard and Jim, get them to gang bang her. The only thing is, afterwards, she'll really, seriously know the difference. They'll spoil her for mere mortals."

"That's the guys I need. Thanks."

"Richard, can I, like, have a word?"

"Sure." Jim Teale turned to slide away, but Delia held on to his coat.

"You as well," she reversed into the short corridor off the stairwell away from the crush and pulled her boys' heads down to her level. "I want you to take someone out on Saturday night and give her the time of her young life. Bring her home so well shagged she can, like, hardly walk. Can you do that?" She watched them closely; Jennifer would not have lied, but could be mistaken. The reaction was all she could have hoped for,

"We could do i', bu' i' would be nicer for us if we fancied our quarry too."

"Kim Hart."

"Ah. Yes. I was hoping i' migh' be; we heard she'd been cut loose. No problem then," said Jim. "Is she protected?"

"Pill."

"And she won't want long term commitments?"

"She needs a good toasting, commitments or otherwise are between you and her, but she's never come, like, with a boy up her, can you make sure to change that?"

"Do our best."

"One other thing, no matter what you may have heard, she wasn't cut loose, she, like, did the cutting."

"Good for her, I like i'."

"And she might be a bit sticky. Don't, like, take no for an answer."

"We never do. We don't force it, just persuade; we only take good reasons for answers."

"Like Ingrid for instance. I really like Ingrid. I would love to give her a happy time, bu' I've never asked her." Jim shrugged. "Because I know how she feels."

"Jim and Richard have asked us out for dinner again."

"No, they haven't."

"They ha--"

"No, they haven't. They've, like, asked you out. And you're going. You've just come off your bike, upside down in a bramble bush, get out, get straight back on and pedal like crazy."

"But what--How --"

"Do absolutely what you want. All the boys I've ever gone out with wanted to shag me, those I chose to let into my panties, made it well worth my while. My guess is Jim and Richard will be no different and if anyone deserves a night of hair down, knickers down and everything else, like, up and throbbing, you do. You're going out with them, when they go to snog you, you snog them back, have fun and get yourself shagged stupid, for once in your life. Then you'll know. Be able to choose in future. Right? Right!"

On Sunday, she rang her torch bearer,

"Richard, it's Delia."

"Oh, Hello. Mission accomplished, Jim and I had a wonderful time, and Kim said thank you, so I think she did too."

"Good, thank you. That's, like, what I wanted to hear."

"If she's still walking slowly and carefully on Monday, don't ask her why."

"I've heard you're, like, well endowed."

"The one bit of me I'm proud of, until I stand beside Jim. You'll know his nickname. And he knows how to use it; I think we did a grand job, generally."

"Thank you. See ya."

"Bye."

* * *

When Kim called for Delia on the Monday morning, the most important topic of conversation was first to be aired,

"Did you have, like, a nice time on Saturday?"

"Yes. They gave me flowers and even called on Sunday to ask me how I was, both of them."

"That's nice, that's, like, really nice."

"And now I know how it should be done; I'll never settle for

339

second--it wasn't even second best--I'll never settle for indifferent again."

"I'm glad you enjoyed it."

"You know what Hopkins calls Jim, Firehose?"

"Yes."

"Well, now I know why."

"And he doesn't just, like, think it's for pissing with?"

"No. No, he doesn't. You wouldn't think it, would you? I mean they're just nice boys, graceful, but boys, you know, a bit tatty and grubby--"

"The graceful bit is because they are ballet dancers, both of them. And, like, quite good so I'm told."

"So I believe. But if they take you out, they scrub up real nice first, and they're fantastic shags, both of them. I'd never thought of two at once before, but it might not be the last time." She grinned at Delia's stunned face. "It might not even be the last time this year!"

"What happened to the little girl that had strong views about fornication?"

Kim's reply was assertive, barked, almost,

"She got a train pulled on her by experts, who had the courtesy to put her needs first. I still feel strongly, but I now know it's not a simple issue."

Delia and Kim bumped into Richard, for once alone, at break,

"Are you and Jim taking anyone to the Fifth Year Party?"

He glanced down from Kim to Delia, who hadn't been consulted,

"Delia." and

"Me," they said together.

"Would Jim take me and later when you take us home, we'll drop Delia off, and I'll be very co-operative again--Unless," she moved around into Delia's sight and bent over, peering into her eyes. "You want to join in?"

"Take us to the party, Richard, drop me off, take her home and give her a 'Right Royal Seeing To,' I suppose it's only fair she does some catching up."

"Yeah. I'm sure we can manage that."

So for the second party in a row, Delia went with a boy and took some flowers home. And for the second time in less than a week, Kim got thoroughly roasted and took some flowers home.

* * *

The Friday of that week, with six inches of melting snow to flop about in, Timmy was up on the roof again retrieving a younger girl's bag from where Hopkins had thrown it. Rosalind caught sight of him and castigated him again, like a silly little boy, for doing wrong. He tried to get down, slipped and cut his leg jumping to the skip. Miss Ripson didn't even bother to ask Mrs Cumpbell, but whisked him off to the hospital for stitches and missed lessons, one of which was Physics, for which everyone knew, he would be gutted. Mortified at what she'd done and even more devastated when she learned that he was helping a youngster, Rosalind owned up at the first opportunity.

After lunch, when Fred Waston arrived at School looking for his friend, Jennifer stood in front of him and told him generally what had happened and what Miss Ripson had done.

"We were giving him a hard time, I'm sorry."

"You mean Rosalind was giving him a hard time!"

"Yes, it was me, but I didn't mean him to get hurt," said Rosalind unexpectedly from behind Jennifer. "I'm really sorry Fred. Please tell him I'm sorry."

Fred grunted, sidestepped past them and went into school. Jennifer turned to look at Rosalind,

"Meet the new model," she said. "I'm trying hard not to be bitchy any more, help me?"

The redhead leaned forward and kissed her on the lips.

"I'll try," she said.

Where the brilliant, nice, but silly little boy went that snowy weekend is open to speculation, but in his place appeared a brilliant, very nice and confident young man, with Timothy Ebsenter's face. He walked straight up to Rosalind on his way into School on Monday morning and asked her for a date, then politely argued his corner, until she agreed,

"--I reckon we owe each other at least the chance to settle our differences. We couldn't possibly end up any worse off. You never know, we might be able to speak nicely to each other afterwards--I'll be at the end of your road at 6.30, be there--Please." There was a pregnant pause, then a whispered.

"All right, I'll be there."

As he walked away, Jill told her to stand him up. Rosalind's reply made Delia smile inside,

"No, he's right, I owe him that much. The subject is closed. I have the most unexpected date tonight."

The news travelled through the scholastic undergrowth, outstripping any forest fire.

Tim and Rosalind have a date.

That Rosalind would be top of Chemistry in any School Year, other than the one that also contained Timothy Ebsenter was obvious. So her, only occasionally glimpsed, admiration for his ability, coupled with her instant and obvious castigation of his bumbling and gauche clumsiness, most people interpreted as jealousy-fuelled hatred, adding spice, awe and incredulity to the news.

Tim and Rosalind have a date.

5CC and 5JR discussed the date amongst each other in whispers, when they had been dumped, yet again, in the library while feckless staff did other things rather than teach them. When Mr Carpenter called in, saw the students taking care of themselves and took a dozen of them, including the two principals, away for a job, the discussion became open, loud and opinionated.

"He'll not get his oats off her, she--"

"Shut it, Hopkins!"

"Dunno what he sees in her!"

"Or her in him."

"That's because neither of you is looking, like, past your own nose end!"

"Dunno why she said yes. She hates him."

"Huh! She hates everybody."

Delia looked at Big Mamma,

"Like, you or me?"

"I'll do it," said the Company Director and stood up, addressing the entire room. "No! You're all wrong! Rosalind hates only Rosalind. She fell helplessly in love with the first boy who ignored the name and the frustration and treated her kindly no matter what, can't hack it, and copes by hating herself. There are other things too, like the source of the frustration, but that's the main one. I'm delighted for them, they've loved each other since the first year, it's been obvious." She turned slowly regarding the silent room. "Now what we are all going to do is back off, leave them alone and wait. The one thing they don't need is help from anyone here. She could do a lot worse than Ebsenter minor." As she was finishing, the feckless staff returned. Shirley waited, there was a long silence, she glanced at the teachers and sat down.

Tim and Rosalind have a date.

Delia totally agreed with Shirley and wanted to wish Tim luck, but couldn't get him alone. Then Jennifer swooped upon him in the corridor at last lesson change, dragged him into the stairwell, kissed him, a big wet smacker all over his mouth said,

"Well done darling kid brother, best of luck and don't bottle it," and departed as fast as she had arrived.

"I won't, I promise," he called to the disappearing back and got a wave in reply.

What the wobbly-wheelies is going down? They're not even cousins, never mind siblings. But at least now she had the opening.

Kerry got in first,

"Kid brother?"

"Yeah." He grinned as he shrugged his shoulders. "We adopted each other on Saturday, never had a sister before, it's great."

"Oh, best of luck,"

They had heard right after all, but that raised a whole new set of questions, with no time to ask them.

"And the best of luck, like, from me too."

"Thanks."

Delia couldn't wait to ring Warwickshire with the hot news,

"Name, like, who's taking Rosalind out on a date tonight, in one."

"No idea, but I hope it is Timmy Ebsenter!"

"I knew you'd guess right, he walked straight up to--and she said yes--Jill told her to stand him up, but she, like, stomped alower that one--so it's tonight, I mean, like, right now!"

"And about time, it has been obvious from the First Year."

"That's what Shirley said. We got dumped in the Library and--and then the teachers came back to find half their class gone with Mr Carpenter, for a job. It was, like, dead funny because Mr Baggott asked 'Jenny' where they were, and everyone pretended they couldn't hear him until he remembered and called her Jennifer."

"Everybody knows it is Jennifer or nothing!"

"And that's another thing, she kissed Timmy in the bottom stairwell, well, like, snogged him and called him brother. Apparently they--so I was wondering could I, like, have a similar arrangement with--"

Andrew interrupted,

"Of course you can, you can snog him whenever you want to. But tell me if and when you ever cut loose. Please do not leave me to find out from a trouble making gossip that you have been shagging him."

"I do love you, you know."

"Yes, I do know. That is why I feel easy giving you unlimited permission."

That Rosalind's date with Tim had been a success of Olympic Gold Medal proportions became evident the following day when the two met at the gate. They kissed, glued together from toes to scalp; Rosalind hands grasping her boy's coat so tightly, as she hugged him to her, that her knuckles turned white with the effort. Then they separated and largely stayed with their own friends for much of the day, smiling gently at each other when their eyes met and occasionally brushing away specks from off each other's clothes, or exchanging a few murmured words. At every End-of-School from then on, they stood holding hands, making silent love to each other with their eyes for ages, before separating and going home.

* * *

Mrs Cumpbell instructed her Media Studies Sixth Form Class to video her lessons for a day.

"But Miss, it's PE, the inter-form Basketball compe--"

"It's all arranged, permission obtained, you're with me all day." She spun on her toes and set off after some imagined miscreant.

The second lesson that Tuesday morning was the Top Set Fifth Year with Delia, Big Mamma et al. It was the morning after Tim and Ros had got each other sorted out and the boy was emotionally ten years older than when the runt had last seen him, four days previously. So the scene was set for a defining incident when the detested sawn-off had yet another go at him.

Why she picked on Tim so often is a topic for debate, but being widely acknowledged as overall the best scientist in the year may well have had a lot to do with it. The attacks were totally unjustified; his English was excellent and his spelling always acceptable, usually good, but he had a few favourite words that he occasionally got wrong. In his essay he had a character 'recieving a justified reward'.

He sat patiently through her parade of his ignorance finishing up with,

"--only an illiterate-scientist donkey like yourself would be unaware of the rule i before e except after c!"

With the baleful red eye of the video camera on him, Tim nodded gravely at her and enunciating clearly for the microphone, said,

"I'm sorry Miss, we had some emergencies in the height measurements of our experimental species societies yesterday and, until then, I had fancied that my ancient tendencies to being inaccurate had been sufficiently curbed, but I'm either a conscientious, efficient Scientist or I get granted heinous credit for being so, but I acquiesce to you that I am an illiterate and cannot spell consistently well."

The runt of the litter preened herself on her victory and

moved on.

It was a measure of his new self-confidence that the boy apparently felt no need to make any further mention of the 'i before e except after c' incident. It wasn't the end of the matter, however.

* * *

The sorting out of Rosalind's Problems, which had begun in Timothy's arms just before Christmas, was completed many weeks later, at the Spring Parish Committee Meeting.

By pure chance it was the one Madeline would take Delia to attend, so they witnessed everything.

Richard

Naturally, personal relationships were included in conversations between Delia and Richard, during the next one she made her move and mentioned siblings,

"I've got two brothers and a step sister, but nobody, like, my own age."

"I've got nobody. I'd have loved a sister, as I can't have you as my lover, I'd have loved to have you as my sister."

"If you're serious, I'm on. I'll be your sister; you know like Timmy Ebsenter and Jennifer Jackson."

"I'm serious, and it's a done deal, sister."

She held out her hand. He didn't take it.

"Jennifer and Tim kiss when they meet."

She moved over and hugged him and smooched him. His world reeled about him.

"And so do we, but Jennifer kisses many people."

"I know."

Delia looked at him and began to grin,

"I thought so! She's got you into bed as well!"

Richard wriggled uncomfortably.

"Well, was I, like, right?"

"Not exactly in bed, al fresco, on a river bank. Fred and Jim and me, all together the same afternoon, one after another, twice."

"Jennifer never made any secret of her sex drive; just the boys didn't seem to want to know."

"The boys didn't know, and they still don't. That was part of the deal." Delia gave him the eyes and nodded,

"I never thought about more than one person at a time, until I met Amelia. The Boxing day, just before the accident, I went over for tea, and the three of us had a lovely sexy snogging session afterwards; a pretty naughty session it was too. I'd never snogged a girl, probably never will again, But with Amelia, it felt so natural, because I loved her I suppose. So I do understand how more than one could be, like, naughty fun."

"It was incredible. Exciting beyond my wildest dreams,

because it was my first time, but it was fun too."

"First time? Didn't you find it embarrassing?"

"It was Jennifer; she made it seem like the most natural thing in the World. It wasn't embarrassing; it was lovely. Just the wrong girl."

Delia shrugged with open hands giving him the eyes again.

* * *

On the last day of term Delia drew three boxes of a dozen sleigh-bells each from the music stores, one each for herself, Queen Bee and Big Mamma.

Chapter 27
Of Rocking And Revelations:
December 1986 - Easter 1987
Delia/Jean

By Friday morning, the kids had delivered handsomely, now it was their Year Tutor's turn. Mrs Macey had done him proud. The full, fifty-piece Orchestra was assembled on the raised area at the back of the hall, and the seating had been turned around to face them. Delia could see that Mr Baques was trembling with excitement. Behind him, their music stands dripping with tinsel and their uniforms almost hidden under even more tinsel and baubles; the musicians' waited with ill-concealed expectancy. They already had several Gigs of their own in the local Junior Schools, the two local Shopping Malls, plus the official Carol Service two nights ago, in a Church in town, under their belt. This was not to mention having already performed twice that morning, at Nine o'clock and Ten o'clock, after that, there were usually casualties, but apparently not today.

Delia looked around her at the throng, sixty to seventy percent attendance, not bad for the day before a Holiday. The row of animated Christmas Trees, either side of her, had eyes alight with anticipation. Most of the Fifth Year looked interested in the proceedings and a few knowing grins when she got eye contact showed that some at least knew what was really afoot.

Mr Baques had told them to secrete themselves about the hall, but Delia had come back with the information that they wanted to be all together, but Big Mamma and Queen Bee would follow their lead and Rock It Up with them. So he had put them in the front row where he could signal to them, and they could be seen by everyone else.

Most of the Sixth form were already assembled behind them, on the steps to the stage. When Mr Carpenter appeared riding shotgun on the stragglers, their expressions told it all,

'Yet another bloody assembly to get through before we can escape.'

Delia sympathised, there were several teachers that, had they been taking the service, she would at least have considered absenting herself, the troll, Hamish MacNazi, a few others. With luck, their forebodings would pass.

Mr Baques began the Concert and the animated response of the three ginger groups in the hall, plus his own over acted gesticulations, had a decent volume of sound being generated during the Traditional Carols.

Then came 'White Christmas' and he slipped the leash on his wolf pack.

They stood up with shining eyes, raised their Howay The Toon scarves above their heads and swayed like Hula Dancers perfectly in time with the music.

"Well, join them!" Mr Baques' call was directed at the gawping ranks of Sixth Formers stacked up behind his chicks.

At the end of the song, he clapped, and the applause was taken up all around the hall.

Jingle bells was next, Kim darted from her place, grabbed the box of sleigh bells from the front and shot back with them, they were quickly passed along the row. There was activity near Big Mamma and Queen Bee.

Jingle Bells was accompanied throughout by sleigh bells from various parts of the hall; the singing was loud and full of fun and commitment. The applause at the end was even louder and totally spontaneous. Mr Baques stepped forward to announce the next item; several high-ranking Middle Managers, 'D's and 'E's compared to his comparatively lowly status 'C', were standing down the side of the hall. He glanced at them more than once.

Silence, unasked for, enveloped them all, the kids were hanging on his every word; nobody wanted to miss a syllable.

The next song was announced in silence, sung to the rafters and applauded with thunder, garnished with stamps and wolf whistles; and the next and the last, which was traditionally the Christmas Number One in the charts.

Mr Baques and Mrs Macey conferred, Delia clearly heard her say,

"No, stay with it, trust me."

He stayed with it and announced an encore.

They sang through another chorus of the Number One. The applause for the encore made previous efforts seem merely like a rehearsal.

He stepped forward, yet again in absolute silence.

Everyone knew that was the end of the show, but did the Maestro still have something left?

What extra rabbit was he about to pull from the hat?

Delia could see it on every face, from her and her ravers, all the way to the back of the hall, to the ex-World-Weary Sixth Form, every face alive and tuned right in.

"Great. Ladies and Gentlemen, as always, one person's good time is somebody else's hard work. In this case our good time has been paid for by months of hard preparation on behalf of Mrs Macey and the Orchestra. I think you just said, 'Thank You', can you say it again?" He raised his hands, turned to face the Orchestra and clapped.

This time for a solid twenty seconds Delia couldn't hear herself think.

Mr Baques turned back to the kids,

"It's 12.15 pm, remember that School is still in session for the next ten minutes, so don't disturb people, do it quietly and with care, but dismiss now to lunch, I'll see you all next year."

What will they say? Thought Delia, stealing glances at the senior staff. The only comment she heard about it was from one of the secretaries describing it to another one,

"The Staff loved it, the Kids loved it, the Music Department loved it, and people in Oslo probably heard it."

Afterwards, Jean Ripson sauntered along to the Staffroom to collect her lunchtime mail, before joining the Kids for their Christmas Feast. She walked in on a loud and caustic argument!

"It was so noisy and disgraceful I couldn't total my register." The Troll was holding court about something, but Miss Ripson couldn't see through the group clustered inside the door.

"You're free period three on Fridays!" The voice of Bill Carpenter. "You should have been in the hall with your form class, why weren't you?"

When Bill Carpenter Loaded up for Bear most people heard the Gypsy and backed off. Most people,

"I refuse to condone such sacrilege!"

"Speaking as a sidesman and lay preacher of twenty years standing to your six, it was the most spectacularly uplifting Carol Concert I have ever heard. It was full of hope and joy and expectation for the future, the essence of the Spirit of Christmas!" There was a deep rumble of agreement. "And besides which, Jean Ripson does your register; everybody knows that. You were having a skive!" Another deep rumble and Jean found herself shoved aside as Mrs Cumpbell made her exit.

Bill continued, holding a bottle aloft like a sword,

"As the Bard would have said, there are men abed in England, who will consider themselves accursed they were not here when King Stewart roused his naughty girls to raise the roof--" Somebody threw a sandwich at him, and the Staffroom descended into laughter and carnage. Delia's Form Tutor had seen this before; she left in a hurry!

Although it was talked about in his absence, nobody, not a soul, mentioned the Concert to Stewart Baques. Presently he realised that that was probably the highest accolade, collectively, they could pay. When Delia came back for her results in the summer and was no longer a pupil, he told her so and thanked her.

Warwickshire Christmas 1986

Amy

Amy's little face was a comical study,

"I thought that this was the last holiday you go away again?"

"The last Christmas. Easter's the last Easter, then when I come down in the summer I'll, like, never go away again."

"Mummy! The summer! That's ages."

"No, it's not, it's not long at all. I know, we'll get a calendar, a tear-off calendar and you can tear each day off as it goes by. I'll, like, write a little message for you on some of the days, if you promise not to peep."

"I won't peep, I promise."

Tyne-dale Spring 1987

Delia

As expected Delia's Mock Examination Results were impressive, but so were those of everyone else, which had been more hoped for than likely. But, with the urge to succeed coming increasingly from the student population, with the mature girls getting backup and support from occasionally surprising sources among the boys, this year there was more reason to hope.

* * *

There were a couple of training days, which the Kids had off, a few weeks later after the Christmas Break.

When they came back, the troll referred to Tim vitriolically as Mr Ebsenter until February Half Term.

The sixth form Media Studies told everyone why.

On the first Training Day, the English department had been co-opted to be the group leaders for some in-house training on Staff Literacy.

Mrs Cumpbell had used The Fifth Year's lesson as a visual aid in her lecture which she had entitled 'Illiterate Scientists', almost certainly because her group was the Maths, Technology and Science Faculty Staff. Whether she either knew or cared that her audience were fans to a man of neither herself, nor her bullying style, is a moot point, that she intended the lecture as an exercise in humiliation, is not.

The Sixth Formers broadcast the news to anyone who would listen,

"She got us in to run her lecture for her."

"Not content with screwing up the Basketball competition, she took away our day off too."

"But it was almost worth it."

"No almost about it, it was definitely worth it."

"She showed the tape of your lesson--"

"You know i before e except after c?"

"Yes." Accompanied by nods and smiles.

354

"We couldn't believe it; she showed that clip, Timmy's broadside."

Everyone had fallen about, the sixth formers hiding grins behind their hands but the staff openly chuckling, when Tim stuck fourteen examples of her 'rule' being broken legitimately, {seventeen if you count acquiesce, two for societies and both beings} into his one sentence reply to her bullying.

"It was about halfway through his speech when suddenly all the teachers realised by her reaction--"

"That until then she hadn't twigged herself that Timmy Ebsenter had hung her out to dry."

"The chuckles became belly laughs!"

"We nearly pissed ourselves."

"What d'y'mean nearly. I did!"

* * *

Shortly before Easter, Madeline raised the topic Delia had mentioned earlier,

"Are you serious about the Parish Committee?"

"Of course, we go to church every Sunday in Prior's Eastwicke; I'd like to see how a committee works, before I, like, try to join one."

"I'll take you to the next one; I've prepared the way and if you're already there, he'll not be able to say no so readily. Whatever he says, you hear Yes. Sit down, make yourself comfy and take part. He needs a gentle reining in; he's only one vote in ten. He's just about ready for another reminder."

"Pastor Benne?"

"Mine Fürer Benne."

Dave took his girls to Widow Twonky's house for the Parish Committee Meeting and dropped them off,

"Shall I wait?"

"No darling, more leverage, if you are not waiting around the corner. Bye,"

They kissed him and waved him off, as a Police car drew up and out of it stepped a Police sergeant and Rosalind's parents. For a moment Delia wondered if Rosalind's wheeler-dealer dad had finally made a mistake, but quickly realised that the Sergeant was there at the behest of Mr Schelle, not the other way round.

"I didn't know Mr and Mrs Schelle were on the Parish Committee."

"Linda is, but not her husband, and I've never seen the policeman either."

"That's Sergeant Deed, he's hard but fair, I've, like, worked with him before. There's something going down." Several other people slowed at the garden gate, obviously as confused as Madeline, but Mr Schelle waved them in, politely tagging along behind.

The Widow Twonky opened her door to Linda and the other members of the Parish Committee and stood open mouthed without comment as Mr Schelle courteously walked in among them, with a benignly smiling Sergeant Deed in close attendance. Mr Schelle ushered everyone else into the front room, but he and the policeman detained the Widow Twonky outside. Rosalind's Mum began addressing Pastor Benne, even before he had a chance to comment on the stranger in their midst.

"I'm sorry for the short notice Pastor, but can I put an extra item onto the agenda, as item one? There's a visiting speaker who has an urgent appointment elsewhere."

"This is most irregular Linda; I will have to see you in private afterwards about this matter."

Delia was left in no doubt as to the nature of the private meeting and stared at her Dad's girl. Madeline was as horrified as she was. Pastor Benne continued lugubriously, apparently indifferent to the vibes in the room,

"However we will, of course, open the meeting with your visiting speaker, courtesy is vitally important. Item one on the agenda, Linda's visiting speaker." He looked enquiringly at Delia. "Who is?"

"Robertson Schelle, Mr Benne," he said as he stepped into the room. "And I have chosen to accompany me an official who watches me very closely, Sergeant Edward Deed. A friend would not suffice; I need someone who will not only report accurately but will also be believed."

"What is all this? Sergeant, what are you doing here?"

The horse was high and the Pastor on top of it.

"I am here to witness this committee being informed of some irregularities in the behaviour of its members. Please continue Mr Schelle." Rosalind's Dad stood in front of the Pastor, turned his back to him and addressed the committee.

"For more than four years, two of you have been sexually abusing my daughter. Forcing her to strip bare and ravishing her breasts while beating her with a belt, on at least one occasion drawing blood. She disclosed to teachers she trusts, and they told us. My daughter carries permanent V-shaped scars from the cuts inflicted by the metal tip on the point of the belt. The teachers are prepared to give evidence in court, and Sergeant Deed is now taking me down to the Police Station where we will make statements and undertake to press charges against Mr Benne and Widow Twonky." He turned to face the Pastor, whose blustering withered and dried up, as their eyes met. "The London train leaves in." Rosalind's Dad ostentatiously consulted his watch. "Sixteen minutes. Personally, I don't think you can make it, so when I've been to the Police station, I'll be back, alone. Come on Linda, he's changed his mind, he doesn't need to see you in private afterwards, after you Sergeant."

Pastor Benne did make the London train, boarding with what he stood up in, as it was moving out of the station, exactly as Rosalind's Dad had intended. His house was soon up for sale. Widow Twonky went to stay with her sister on the South Coast. Rumour had it that Rob Schelle made a point of tracking the Pastor from pillow to supper and revealing his past to whichever local 'just inside the law Wheeler Dealer' had a vulnerable daughter.

"Pack your case Mr Benne," and occasionally,

"Don't bother unpacking," and very occasionally, how he left Novochester,

"Don't bother packing."

Later back at home Madeline remarked,

"I said he needed a gentle reining in."

"Yes. But you didn't mean it to be, like, quite that gentle."

Madeline was quite taken aback for a moment, then saw the twinkle in Delia's eye and burst out laughing.

The following day Delia pulled Rosalind,

"Madeline, like, took me to Pastor Benne's Parish Committee meeting last night."

"Oh, so you'll know all about my abuse then."

"Yeah. And, like, so does the rest of the Parish."

"You'd better tell us then," she said glancing at Tim, who reached out and gathered her to him protectively. "'Cos Dad didn't."

Shirley began to shepherd the rest of the girls away.

"Don't bother, I don't mind, I'm free now, you might as well stay and listen. And you were right as usual Big Mamma, I did tell Timmy, but I should have told him sooner, but he knows now, so --"

* * *

With Practical Examinations to attend, Coursework deadlines to hit and all the other paraphernalia that accompanies gaining qualifications that are worth having, the Spring Term vanished.

Delia's bags were so heavy with revision books when she came down for Easter that she needed porter assistance at the stations.

Out Of The Bag: Warwickshire Easter 1987
Delia

In the lull, after Easter Monday Bank Holiday,

"Andrew, I want to go to Prior's Richmount, to see loads of people, I want to explore the possibilities of buying the next field."

"What do you want that for?"

"Just doing my homework, ideas. Trust me darling; I won't sign anything until we've discussed it and, like, I've got you to agree."

"What!"

The next field was L-shaped, with a long narrow frontage on the canal, exactly right for building a jetty to moor a large number of narrow boats. The Bryants spent the morning flitting between Freda's and Juliet's Estate Agents' premises, the Solicitors and the NFU branch office. They discussed the project of buying it, guide prices, planning permission and how likely it was to succeed. By the end of the several meetings, it had been agreed to approach the owner and ask if he was willing to sell; or, if not the whole field, perhaps sell the canal-side strip and Delia had found out what she really came for.

* * *

Delia and Amy watched the approach of the baby limousine with interest; few people risked expensive cars along their track, although if the restaurant took off, that would have to change. The car slowed, pulled off the track onto the walled off hard standing on the right and parked up neatly. A pretty little blonde alighted, peering across at their house, which was peeping above the luxuriously rampant hedgerow on the other side of the track.

She was obviously undecided of exactly what to do now.

"Over here."

The blonde head snapped around searching for the source of the call, finally successfully picking out Delia from among the Spring Bulbs around the front of the patio.

"Oh--Er Hello." She stepped out, back onto the track and headed towards the patio. As she cleared the car park wall, a large ginger-pig grunted at her from the other side of a wire fence, right at her side. The blonde jumped up with a little squeal. A saddleback and several other assorted and to city eyes, strange-looking, coloured and spotted pigs were in close attendance.

"That's Tamworth, she's working, ploughing the Long Acre, she's, like, just saying hello."

"Oh, they're coloured--I've never seen a black pig before--Well I've only ever seen white. Are they foreign?"

"There's foreign blood in them, to, like, keep the genes healthy, but they're all recognised British breeds." Delia had to resist a smile as the girl stepped smartly crabwise away from the fence.

"We're interviewing, to see which breeds do well. Work as well as, like, eat."

The irritable gobble of a turkey triggered a small explosion of varied, retaliatory complaints from other farmyard fowl, from just behind the hedge on the blonde's other side.

She accelerated up onto the patio, glancing back apprehensively.

"We're auditioning barnyard fowl too, free-range, hence the, like, unruly hedge bottom."

"Oh--Erm--I'm Carole Friendly, well--it's Henchmow now, but it says Friendly on my card." She approached, it did say Friendly on the card.

"And Press, like, under your fingers?"

"Erm--Yes, does that matter?"

"I'll use the long spoon. I'm Delia Bryant; please sit down."
Carole did so.

"Amy this is Carole, we don't tell her secret things. Say Hello."

"Hello." The little face was a study.

"Hello, Amy."

There was a long pause; presently it became obvious that if Carole didn't break it, no-one would.

"This is a nice place."

"You didn't risk the suspension of your husband's flash car

on our track just to, like, compliment our garden."

"You're not from around here are you?"

"Neither are you."

There was another long pause, with Delia and Amy studying their visitor, waiting.

"I'm researching the late Councillor Mildred Patterson."

"Did you kill her?"

"Well--I thought about it, might have even tried by now, but somebody beat me to it, was it you?"

"I found her, which had me in the frame for a while until they matched up the time of death with my movements that morning. I was several kilometres away, being, like, ridden around my living room, by my husband of a couple of hours. It was accidentally witnessed by the police Sergeant who did most of the legwork. Where were you?"

"Getting a black eye at Hockenheimring, during the race practice, well--Preparing for getting it, not that I knew. I'd have stayed in the press tent had I known that the Piquet supporters were eager to batter the Mansell contingent. The police are satisfied that I was hundreds of kilometres out of range at the time of death."

"Okay, provisionally you didn't kill her, why are you researching her?"

"Well--I was covering a Local Government Junket at Brighton, you know eat, drink and fornicate at the taxpayer's expense and--This mouth was sounding off about how immoral it all was while stuffing lobster into itself."

"And you thought, 'How ironic.'"

"Not at first, I must admit, but an older hack picked up a young cub and straightened her out a bit, professionally, morally--and I'm delighted to say sexually. Councillor Patterson was sounding off about, incestuous relationships, in between spraying flutes of champagne and mouthfuls of lobster over everyone, especially me. I chased the story up. Met a girl called Mary Smith--"

"Mary's a good friend; I'm buying a strip of land from her."

"Ah, well. I met her and discovered that some people are genuinely nice and when I got home, I realised the man who rode me around his bedroom every night, had all the same attributes I'd admired in Mary. So I married him and went after the Councillor instead of her victims."

"Then some inconsiderate knocked her, like, off her perch?"

"Mary rang me to warn me that she'd been questioned and the Police wouldn't be far behind. It allowed me time to organise my thoughts. One of which was, how long a list of suspects did the Police have?"

"Two. Plus East Warwickshire."

"Would you--Help me?"

"It wasn't me, or my husband, or Amy, or Sergeant Maisie Enermouse. And I don't think it was the registrar in Banbury. No more bets please."

"So--You won't help me."

"Oh yes, I will. Whoever killed Mildred, offered me up as their guarantor, I hadn't, like, given permission."

"Where do we start?"

"Prior's Richmount, the only place where I know for certain there is, like, a daisy-wheel printer."

"A what?"

* * *

It was Market Day in Prior's Richmount; the good weather had pulled in everyone for miles around, and Delia had some trouble finding a parking place. Peter waved as she drove past him and a minute later she saw Freda and the Vicar in the distance apparently discussing a sale. Mary and Steven were out together with Steven proudly pushing the pram, so Bobby would probably be selling stock somewhere, or possibly Bill. She'd already seen most of the locals she knew; no doubt she'd see the rest when they managed to park. Right in front of her a pickup began reversing out of a parking slot, Delia paused to give the driver space then slid neatly into the vacant place.

"I'd like to push you--Can I please?"

"If you want."

Delia silently put up with the novice carers mistakes of jerky handling, sudden changes and getting caught against kerbs and was rewarded by the young reporter learning from her mistakes and improving quickly.

"Head towards the Market Place." Through the crush and especially from her lowly position, Delia's view was severely restricted. Every so often, however, in a momentary parting of bodies, she glimpsed people she knew. Amongst others Cade talking to the NFU Secretary; the tall, gaunt, figure of Juliet Means was poised waiting to go into the café, while Sid, Frieda and her solicitor came out; Winston Scuffer was remonstrating with some luckless taxi driver outside the NFU office.

The chair eased as Delia said,

"Over towards --"

She had known before there was no reply, that her chair was no longer being held and suspected that she was talking to herself. She spun around to check. Carole had gone. A few minutes later, she found the reporter in the nearby clothes shop, crouched down behind a rail of dresses. She waited patiently; presently the girl's petrified-deer eyes lost enough of their terror, to allow her to whisper,

"Has he gone?"

Owning Up: Tyne-dale May 1987
Delia

On a Monday a few weeks before their GCE Examinations, while sitting out in the hot summer sunshine, having lunch, suddenly, with no introductory lead-in, Jennifer owned up to having reached double figures!

"Non-virgins own up and what's your score," she said, held her hand up with a pointed finger and continued. "Woman and eleven. I've been waiting since the summer holidays for somebody to ask, I think eleven is too many to continue sitting on."

Although the announcement was received with open-mouthed shock by most, Rosalind and Timmy just smiled, they already knew, and Shirley said,

"Eleven now is it, are you going for the school record, Jennifer?" So Big Mamma knew about some of them before!

"Not intentionally and I'd better point out that it's only nine boys the other two are girls."

"Girls count equal the way you snog them, Sister Dear, it's a genuine eleven everyone, believe me," said Timmy.

"Okay, you lot what's the count then? I'm Virgin, but six ultra-close encounters. Shirley?" said Anna.

"Woman and one."

"Woman and one as well," said Laura, smiling at Sadie.

"Woman and two," said Sadie.

"Woman and one," said Jeanette.

"Woman and two Jeanette and that's even just on what you've told me," said Carly.

"I wasn't counting you."

"Jennifer counted girls too."

"Woman and two."

Carly nodded and added her score,

"Woman and three, all girls of course."

"Woman and one," said Marjorie

"Woman and, well a few, can I leave it at that?" Said Kim.

"Man and three," added Timmy after a pause. With Rosalind

sitting beside him, she didn't even blink.

"Same here," said Fred.

"Woman and five," said Rosalind, to nearly everyone's utter astonishment!

"I think you mean six, little bunny; it's five boys." Timmy leaned over and kissed her on the temple.

"Eeek! Yes! Woman and six."

"Woman and none other than professionally, they don't count, if you are counting it's four figures," said Samantha.

"Woman and one." Put in Jo Keener smoothly continuing from Samantha's calculated analysis and added a bit of her own. "Not the right one, but very nice even so." When it became obvious that that was all she was going to say, everyone looked at next in line, Kerry.

"Virgin, but only because my Dad went to the loo and nearly caught us and I chickened out. So an ultra close encounter."

Shelley was looking to Laura for guidance,

"You say, 'Woman and three'."

"Woman and three," said Shelley confidently and if anyone else had said it smugly, with Shelley it wasn't smugness, relief that she had got it right? Possibly. She resumed fastidiously eating her lunch.

"It's three that we know about, anyway," murmured Laura.

"Woman and two-ish, not three, but nearly," said Delia.

"Woman and one." Finished Jill Keener, looking glum.

Jennifer and Shirley were just looking straight into each other's eyes, there was something going on there, but it wasn't nasty, they were smiling at each other. Then Shirley glanced at Delia, and they swapped grins too.

Jennifer knows who Big Mamma's lover is! That's it, she knows everything else, she knows that as well! She thought.

On the telephone that night Delia couldn't contain her surprise,

"Eleven, in nine months. I mean, like, eleven!"

"Well, remember what she said in the First Year. Virgin only because I have never been asked," replied her man. "I am not that surprised, eleven nice people obviously asked. It is Rosalind's six that has got me groping."

"She's always been friendly with her cousin Mark; he would just ignore the angry comments, the same as Jennifer and wait until she calmed down. And Mark has three close mates, they, like, do everything together."

"She will be calm all the time now, my guess?"

"Yep. Goodbye, Pastor Benne. Hello, lovely girl. Why didn't anyone, like, notice?"

"Sometimes the hardest thing to see is the septum in your own nose."

"Hmm."

"Whom do you think the girl was?"

"Short list of, like, one?"

"Precisely, my guess is Jennifer's list includes Rosalind's."

"Not Timmy surely?"

"Did they not adopt each other as brother and sister the weekend before his first date with Rosalind? The weekend he suddenly grew up ten years and is not his score more than one?"

* * *

MacAuk might occasionally be gullible, but there was nothing wrong with his bottle. While the friends were hanging around at lunchtime a few days later, he came straight over to Tim.

"Ebsenter, w'haven't talked much before, but 'need to know something."

"Yes."

"That day y'sorted Hopkins for the blue dye?"

"Yes, I'll be straight with you Mac, I went to his house specifically to take the bastard apart."

"'not bothered why you went, h'had it coming, besides sorting, did you see h'? See h'as in to look at? Proper?"

"--Yes."

"Was h'covered in sick?"

Tim was obviously taken aback and just stood.

"When Tim was finished with him, yes," answered Fred.

"When y'were finished with h'! Please, it's important. What happened?"

Tim and Fred looked at each other, then,

"No reason not to tell him everything that I can see."

So they did.

"I thumped him, he honked and went down; I rolled him in his own vomit."

"'Was h'own pewk?" MacAuk was still nervous but more with joyful anticipation. This was decidedly not the correct emotion when listening to the downfall of a friend. "H'was clean when h'got home?"

"Yes, pristine, I only hit him the once, in the short ribs, but it had years of payback behind it--"

"Sure did! Y'smashed them. 'mean shattered; they'll never be right again."

"Oh--Well he went down. Honked all over the road, curry and lager, not pleasant. I wanted to do more, I wanted to kick seven bells out of the little shit, I wanted to, but I couldn't do it. Not with him writhing on the floor. So I rolled him, seemed a more fitting, longer lasting punishment. Blue dye on an Art project paid back with multicoloured vomit on his brand new, nipping' clean, white suit, seemed appropriate somehow."

"'was at ten o'clock?"

"Yes, that's definite, I have to be in at eleven, and I wasn't late."

"No way that h'could have been getting a girl drunk and shagging h'silly between ten and ten-thirty in Ryker? While s'was being sick all over him."

"No way Mac, he couldn't stand up, he tried, kept on falling down. And all the sick was his own."

"Knew h'didn't listen, didn't know h'lied so much."

"He can't tell the truth."

The tough little bruiser turned his attention to Delia,

"If you ever think he is, like, get worried, because **you'll** have it wrong, he's a compulsive, pathological liar."

"His brother's girl will confirm that he wasn't in Ryker," said Tim. "His brother hosed him down. I mean really, with a hose in their front path, Mary helped clean him up, she's next door." He pointed. "Next door, that way."

MacAuk nodded,

"'Know the girl y'mean. Thanks." He left.

"What was all that about?" asked Tim.

"Cherchez la femme," said Rosalind grinning.

"Huh?"

"Who is MacAuk sweet on and has he just discovered she's not the easy slag Hopkins claims she is?"

"No more bets please," added Delia nodding.

MacAuk took Hopkins apart that night, re-breaking the ribs Tim had crunched a few months before and adding to that, somewhat more extensive, cosmetic damage. The following day, the tough guy began courting a pale little waif, who lived on the Army's artillery range north-west of Novochester.

* * *

Little Kerry Bobbine came back from her week-long exchange visit in Germany and came over to Jennifer, who was talking to Delia.

" -- and I've got the name too. The Prior's Secret. Several of the local place names are Prior's Whatever, so, like, it fits, and I like it. Hi, Kerry."

"Did you have a successful time in Germany?" asked Jennifer.

"Woman and eight," replied Kerry.

"In one holiday, that's, like, what I call successful," commented Delia.

"Have you been to the clinic?"

Kerry looked straight at Jennifer,

"No. I wondered if you--"

"We'll go tonight, together, I've been meaning to anyway."

"Yes, eleven's a lot more than enough for, like, a visit I would have thought," murmured Delia.

"It's eighteen now."

"Eighteen! How d'y'get to eighteen so quick?"

"Same way you got to eight in a week, told them to be patient, form a queue and everyone would get what they wanted, my guess?"

"Pretty much."

Chapter 28
Of Meeting Old Friends: Tyne-dale August 1987
Delia

The 4x4 swung around in front of the main entrance to West Novochester and parked in a bay. Andrew alighted and surveyed the building.

"Like an old loved suit. Worn out, thread bare and comfortable--"

"Speak for yourself, you cheeky sod!" said a familiar voice and Bill Carpenter, Stewart Baques and the Head came down the steps to greet him. The men shook hands and slapped each other on the back while on the other side of the car Delia surreptitiously slid Amy out and dusted her down.

"Stop skulking around there Mrs Bryant," said the Head Teacher. "Get yourself out here for your bridal kiss."

"Mrs Bryant?"

"He didn't even tell you then? They told nobody Bill, apart from Dave and Madeline, my guess, and of course me for Exam Entries and that."

"Yes, the renegades have been married, bell, book and candle, for over twelve months."

"Not bell, book and candle Ash, that's a local knees up, next

369

week, but we have done the legal bit, Registry Office."

Delia limped shyly around the back of the truck, carrying Amy on her hip, leaning away from the toddler to counter her weight.

"Like, how did you know?" She offered her face for the traditional greeting.

"He knows everything, just don't require him to prove it, because he will," said Stewart, stepping in to have his turn. "Congratulations," he kissed the toddler too. "Hello, Amy. You won't remember me; you were asleep when we last met."

"Don't bet on it," said Andrew

and,

"You're Stewart." The little one replied. "You wear a funny hat."

It took a few moments reflection until it was realised Amy was referring to his canoeing crash hat.

"I'm glad I didn't bet. You're absolutely right." Amy snuggled herself into Delia, smiling.

There was a certain amount of reorganisation as Andrew took Amy and Delia was settled into her chair. Stewart propelled his pupil into school to find her results.

"What do you think of the hot news then?"

"Like, which precise hot news?"

"The other Wedding. You'll have an invite I presume?"

"We've been away, like, on a barge holiday, it might be at my folks home."

"Big Mamma and--"

"John Monta, Anna's Dad?"

"You have got an invite."

"Possibly, she asked about Andrew, Third Year Party day, when I showed her my engagement ring, she showed me hers. I guessed whom, like, in my head, guessed right as it happens."

Jean Ripson was thrilled by Delia's arrival too and took delight in giving to her, her results card.

Straight As.

"Congratulations."

"Thanks, Miss. I was hoping to see more teachers, like, thank them personally."

"I'll pass the thanks on."

* * *

Shirley met Delia in town, bumped into her by chance, free wheeling down the slope, outside ClipArtistes,

"What was all that guff you served up to me last Christmas, like, about Robert being the wrong sex then?"

"Strangely enough Dee, it was the gospel truth. I did a deal with John years ago, I would never look at another boy, but I could go girl shopping whenever I wanted. I don't necessarily want to, but implying that I did--I needed you to believe I wasn't interested in Robert Davison," she waited, watching the pennies dropping. "And I wasn't."

"You weren't lying, you are now, well misleading anyway."

"The absolute truth is that John is the only boy I ever wanted. But the World is full of girls I fancy. Why do you think I never touch anyone, brush hair, help with makeup. I have lots of friends that I want to keep, coming onto them is not necessarily a good way of keeping them."

"Amelia Bryant necked me once. Well, sexy snogged me, twice, Hello and Goodbye, but it was on the same day, less than a week before the accident. I'd never snogged a girl before, never even considered it. But, like, now I understand. I was looking forward to doing it again. But," she shrugged. "Okay you really don't fancy Bob the Poser, I accept that."

"I really would climb over him to get at Kim."

The grin spread wide across Delia's face,

"Okay, I accept that too and like, I gather you'd prefer I kept it secret."

"I'd prefer you kept it all secret, the World will see that I'm not interested in Robert when I marry John. I will not be trying to take Kim's place."

"She dumped him you know, he's told the World he did it, he didn't."

"And now she's making up for lost time, are you all looking after her?"

"Like you lot do with Kerry? Yes. Well, they are, I'm nearly not here."

"I was surprised to hear you got to results day; I thought you were away then. I'm nebbing Delia, sorry, eldest daughter failing."

Although she was still listening, Delia's attention had been on something behind Shirley's left hip,

"Excuse me," the child was looking up at Shirley. "I want to speak to Mummy."

"Yes, Darling." She added to Delia. "All nebbing questions answered, I think."

"Can Daddy have money please?"

Delia selected a note from her purse and gave it to the tot.

"Thank you," she turned and walked purposefully back into the hair salon. Delia watched the girl that called her Mummy, all the way back to the safety of the child's father's embrace, as she replied,

"I'm in the middle of my packing, I'm moving down permanently at the weekend," she transferred her purse to her right hand revealing the rings. They were bright and the plain gold band very new. "Like, he made a legal woman of me last July, we just didn't tell anyone. We're having a Church bash a week tomorrow, but of course, you can't be there."

"And you won't be at mine for the same reason."

"We can think of each other."

Shirley nodded her agreement.

"Even better, let's, like, toast each other. The bride gets to do nothing, yet it's supposed to be, like, Her Day."

"Which is ironic, because if she's a good, innocent girl--"

"She could get a nasty shock that night in bed, like, if she's chosen badly!"

"I pray for Ingrid."

"So do I. How about three o'clock?"

"Absent friends?"

"Absent friends and, like, name each other too."

"Okay. Is sex just as nice when it's legal, not naughty?"

"Oddly enough, yes."

"And as frequent?"

"Oh yes. Yes!"

"Not like in the troll's assembly."

"Hackles no! But, like, Amy's nearly four, so we're trying for a baby before she gets any older." The naughty grin spread wide as she waved at her lap and leaned forward to whisper. "I've got no knickers on under here."

"Has Amy asked any awkward questions yet?"

"She caught us once. Told Andrew not to hurt me, she was upset, so we took her into bed and told her I wasn't being hurt, I was liking it, I used Laura's words, a 'tickle Fight' and she was, like, quite happy from then on. Then, last week, she was playing on the floor, and I had to step over her, and she said, 'Mummy no knickers, tickle fight,' to Andrew. He picked me up, took me into bed and topped me up. She made no further comment, didn't even stop playing with her Pippa dolls."

"With any luck, you've taught her sex is natural and loving, later you'll have to teach her to choose carefully who to do it with."

"One lesson at a time?"

"Exactly. This is probably teaching Granny, but do you know how to calculate your fertile days?"

"Day 14, yes." Delia paused, but this was Big Mamma. "The real truth is we're probably not still trying for the baby. I'm most likely pregnant, like, took the cap out after the exams, came on, on time once, but now I'm a fortnight late, and I'm never late, the top-ups are probably unnecessary, just fun."

"Oh, Delia! Congratulations." Shirley leaned down and hugged the little, reformed tearaway to her and went to kiss her. Delia captured her head and smooched her, just like Amelia had done to Delia herself, all those years ago. Shirley moaned softly and smiled with stars in her eyes when Delia released her. "Thank you--So you're looking at--"

"The end of April." She spread her hand palm down and wiggled the thumb and pinkie up and down. "First week in May. And you?"

"End of May-ish, the dates are exactly right for the wedding night, but if we miss, we'll have lots of fun trying again, topping up 'n that. And if we don't miss, we'll be like you, doing the unnecessary."

The girls parted a few minutes later and when Andrew and Amy joined her, Delia finished her shopping, which included a trip to Quality Greeting Cards.

"What are we looking for?"

"Invitations to a dinner party, that rack there. Look for a Shelley, any Shelley will do, because it's bound to be, like, stunning. They will have Michelle on the back."

"There is no need to look on the back; her work is unmistakable; will these do you, for instance?"

The following day an additional invitation to Big Mamma's Wedding arrived at the Summers' house, supplementing the one for Dave, Madeline and Family; it was for Mr & Mrs Andrew Bryant and Amy. They too were Shelleys, specially commissioned and stunning.

Inside was a note

15.00 hrs.

To Absent Friends and

Delia Bryant/ Shirley, Jayne Monta

'Health, Wealth and Happiness,'

With love,

Shirley

Delia spent part of the morning completing her envelopes and invitation cards, on the bottom she wrote,

And to an important planning meeting afterwards.

Planning To Be Not Hit: Warwickshire August 1987

Delia

Maisie Enermouse climbed out of her impossibly small car, onto the Prior's Secret track, already apologising for her lateness before she stood up.

"It's okay, now you're here, we couldn't, like, hold the meeting without you. Not properly."

The buffet meal in Amelia's Garden was up to the hostess' usual standard, and there was little left when the sporadic skeet of the Insect-cutors became an almost constant crackle with the evening hatch of midges.

"What do you do with the bodies?" asked the Vicar. "That hopper's half full now."

"You know those crunchy pies you like so--"

"That's enough Peter," said Abigail.

"It's nearly as bad," replied Delia giggling. "I feed them to my fish. Midge cake, they go wild, jump half out of the water to, like, get at it. They particularly love wasps and ants. But I think it's time to retreat gracefully."

The Bryants' guests settled into the comfy chairs provided for them and continued the conversation while Amy was made ready for bed. Presently the toddler toured around the room; she hesitated in front of Carole,

"Mummy says I can kiss you goodnight, but I still don't tell you secret things."

"No darling, very wise," said Rupert, next in line. "And you kiss me and don't tell me secrets either."

Amy was taken to bed, and when Delia returned; the atmosphere in the room changed as if a switch had been thrown. Andrew pulled an examination desk out of a corner, unfolded it and set Delia down at it, chairing the meeting.

"Right. To business, to the matters that you were, like, really invited for." She opened a bulky file and withdrew a pad and writing implements. "Matters which nearly cost us a friendship, but actually gained us one instead."

"I'm sorry about the attitude; sadly I'm a police Officer first and a friend second."

"That's okay. Really, I mean it, my favourite teacher, like, apart from him." She waved a negligent hand at her spouse. "Always used to say he was a Teacher first and a Person second. May I ask some questions, specifically about Mildred?"

"You can always ask."

"Criminals have Means, Motive and Opportunity. From where I'm standing I've got none, none and none. Why was I even suspected?"

"From where my Station Inspector was standing you were in the frame and handcuffed to the scaffold, and I'm sorry to say, at first, my view was similar. You had all three, in bold type. It was only when we began to investigate that the simple answer began to unravel. You owned a rifle, and it was common knowledge that you hit what you aim at."

"If it's, like, bigger than a golf ball."

Maisie Enermouse tipped her head in agreement.

"Your gun turned out to be the murder weapon, but it had been discarded, un-cleaned, in a forest. It had been handled and most probably fired by someone heavily made up and fired right handed; you're a lefty." Delia nodded,

"Left eyed."

"A fact of which the murderer seems to be unaware."

Andrew and Delia looked at each other, eyebrows raised. The others waited, but after a short silence, it became obvious that they were not going to reveal, so Maisie decided to continue.

"You had a powerful motive; Mildred was moving Heaven and Earth to get your planning permission overturned. For the café. If she succeeded your life's dream would have gone."

"She had no chance, my brief to the solicitor was it had to be, like, legally fireproof."

"So we later discovered. Opportunity: you were there. Then we got the time of death, and suddenly you were no longer even a remote possibility. You had an irrefutable and completely happenstance, alibi. You hadn't done it; I'm really sorry I thought any different to begin with."

"It's okay, I told you."

"So you weren't in the frame, not my frame anyway, but nor was the only other obvious suspect. At the time of death, Cade was in the Turnpikes, had been for half an hour."

"You had, like, run out of suspects?"

"So we thought. Then they started crawling out of the kindling. Social Services came up with several, one in particular who she'd tried to get libelled in the press recently." She looked from Mary to Carole. "And the young reporter she'd conned into the libel was spitting fire too. Then there are all the projects she's held up in planning, people have lost thousands, for no reason, just because she delayed the permission. Bridging loans cost a fortune, the people that needlessly had to get them, were none too pleased with her."

"But murder, it's a bit, like, extreme. Just because someone's miffed you."

"Depends on the level of miff--It was enough for me to be considering it," said the little blonde and Maisie added,

"People have been killed for refusing to pass the salt."

"Yes, it is a strange solution to the problem, I can not see that they would pass it any quicker the next time they were asked," murmured Andrew.

"So you went from no suspects to, like, far too many?"

"Exactly."

"Let me guess; you're coming back to your original two?"

"Vaguely. Please forgive this, but someone will have to ask you sometime. I know what your answer must be because you would not have relied on a happenstance alibi. But as you've called a meeting and I'm here, now's as good a time as any. Did you have Mildred Patterson killed for you, by someone else?"

"No. I had no reason to do so, and I prefer, like, to outwit, so far that's been sufficient."

"Thank you, we've checked all your known associates, they are accounted for too."

"Have you asked Cade the same question? And checked all his associates?" asked Andrew.

"They were all together in the Pub."

"No they weren't," said Delia, her voice hard-edged.

"They were. Freda, Sid, Peter and the Vicar, the men got pissed off with him telling them over and over, about your meet."

"I checked too, and they weren't. That four were there, which means there were two missing, me, but you know where I was, and the one he denies he knows. But he must know that person, he must, because they both knew the same, not-obvious, inaccurate detail, like, about our house. And that person has access to daisy-wheel printers."

"At first we made the usual assumption, it was such an obvious answer, we never looked past it. Then we met Carole." Andrew nodded at the other couple and paused inviting the continuation.

"When I was thirteen--I was skinny and gawky and pretty unpleasant, even for a teenager. I had braces on my teeth and a dreadful hairdo and a lousy self-image. So--when I met a girl that was at least as unusual looking as I was, but who had done something with it, who offered to show me how to make the best of the nothing I'd got. I happily walked straight into the Minotaur's lair, with my alarm system disconnected. I--I don't remember much of the next few minutes, but I came too, tied up, gagged, blindfolded. And a man--He--He --" Rupert jumped in with the assist,

"He tried to destroy what little self-image a gawky thirteen-year-old girl, with braces on her teeth, still had, by telling her she was ugly, that the only way she would get laid was by being raped, and then he raped her."

"Well--He must have knocked me out again. I woke up in a dingy back lane, in another part of town, I was still trussed up, but the boy who found me kindly released me and dressed me in his jacket. That's all I had on, his little bomber jacket and took me straight to the Police."

Rupert took over as his girl dried, cuddling her and shielding her,

"As the passage of time dulls the pain, she's remembering, increasingly, little details; we keep topping up the file. The girl wears Chanel No. 5; the rapist smells of the goat. Recently she woke up in the middle of the night; she'd remembered she had strange, small, round bruises on the insides of her thighs. They are listed in the Police Medical Report, but nobody could work out where they had come from; until you shed what you have assumed and stick with what you know. Then it was obvious where they had come from, and the identity of the rapist was one step nearer being revealed."

Andrew turned to the Sergeant,

"We have a plan to flush out our villains, but you will have to provide armed backup, Maisie. We are talking excellent shots here, and there is no guarantee that they will not have handguns available, so you have to have an experienced squad of armed men on site."

"We will provide a glittering target to draw all fire away from the populace, but your man has to shoot to disable early, or he won't, like, get the first shot off." She placed a small box on the table.

"Delia you--"

"I've rigged up this little noise-activated switch. As soon as the first shot is fired, we will be plunged into darkness to hide us and you into light to, like, make your arrest--Please, Andrew." Delia threw the switch on the top of the little box; a red light lit up. Andrew moved close to the little box and clapped his hands once, the loud flat 'Bock' of someone that has taken the trouble to learn how to do it properly. The red light went out; a green one came on.

"It's a one-shot switch, to get the red light back again you have to reset it." Delia threw the switch several times; the green light stayed on. "So there's no chance of us being illuminated for a second try. Don't try to deter me, Maisie; it's going to happen."

The police officer sighed deeply,

"Where, when?"

"Saturday, at my Wedding Reception. I've invited everyone, including rapist and murderer and they have all accepted. Your job is to have competent armed guards alert and ready when the birds, like, start taking off."

Richard

Many of the Wedding Guests chose to incorporate Delia's happy day into a holiday break and opted to stay in the area for a long weekend.

The night before, Delia and Andrew took time out of their crowded schedule to have a secret meeting with Madeline, Carly, Kim and Richard in a side room of the Running Pheasant, on the Friday evening, August 28.

"Tomorrow, Mum, Friends and Brother Dear, you have a vital job to do after the wedding breakfast, but before the speeches. At about 2.40 we are going to have a meeting in here with a dozen or so people. It will be very much a fly by the seat of your pants meeting and I must not, like, be distracted."

"We can not stress that strongly enough," interjected Andrew. "What we are asking is really important."

"So Richard will you please ride shotgun on Amy; and Madeline you do, like, ditto on the Summers clan, none of whom are allowed in here until we are finished."

"Carly and Kim can you help where needed and all of you keep your heads down and everyone well hidden and most especially away from this room!"

"Are we allowed to know why?" Asked Madeline.

"I promise we will tell all tomorrow, until then sorry. No."

Richard could see that there was more and was, therefore, unsurprised when Delia linked him, a few minutes later and took him for a walk. She specifically chose a wide open space to whisper to him,

"Cuddle up close brother; this is private."

"Delia this is embarrassing, any closer and I'd be having you. Andrew--"

"You don't have to wriggle, but, Andrew wouldn't mind me dry humping you anyway, Amelia made me dry shag him as, like, a Christmas Present to the pair of us, the Boxing Day before she died and what I have to tell you is secret! Cuddle up."

Obediently he snuggled in; his rampant member pressed tightly between the girl he loved.

"Tomorrow we are taking a big risk."

Richard's heart thumped.

"We have minimised it, like, as much as possible and we will have lots of protection, but it is still a calculated risk."

"Why--"

"Whisper! Don't question me and don't challenge me, just support me. Okay? It has, like, been carefully planned."

He looked into her eyes and sighed deeply through his nose, *Back off Keating a smarter brain than yours is in charge!*

"Okay."

"Brace yourself, you're not going to like this."

"I'm braced."

"There may be gunshots --"

Braced he may have been, but ready for that he wasn't; Richard fought himself back in control,

"Okay."

"If so, hopefully, they will be from the armed police on guard--but it is vital that there are no other targets handy as, like, second bests. So Amy and the rest of my family out of sight. Yes?"

Another deep breath was required before he could speak gently,

"Okay. How long for?"

"Ten, like, possibly fifteen minutes, then you will be told all."

Come on boy, if you cannot have her, at least you can be of service!

"We will guard them better than Cerberus. You make sure that you get your bit spot on. Make sure you're safe."

"If I can concentrate and not worry about my loved ones, I will be, I promise. Now give me a good sexy snog, Brother Dear and, like, take me back."

Chapter 29
Tethered Goats: 29 August 1987
Delia

Just after two-thirty the following day in the side room of the Running Pheasant, Andrew sat everyone down and made sure they had a drink, then peeled his jacket off and dropped it on a chair. A uniformed officer slid in and quietly called for his senior,

"Sergeant."

"Yes." They exchanged a couple of whispered sentences and the constable left. Maisie Enermouse waited until Andrew had finished his chores, then smiled broadly at him as he left the room. Delia sat apart in an alcove brightly illuminated, with Carole standing beside her. A tall, broad and dense, wall of summer pot plants lay before them, while the rest of the frame around the opening was heavily strewn with cascading creepers in flower. The girls looked like a living Victorian Portrait. The photographer set up his tripod directly in front of them and photographed the assembled populace, with several flash-lit shots of his motor-drive. By the time he'd finished, Andrew had joined his girl inside the portrait. Delia addressed the room,

"Thanks for coming everyone. On the day of my civil wedding, I found the murdered remains of the wife of a friend. I thought it was only fitting that on my Spiritual Wedding day, we get justice

for her by unmasking who so callously, like, ended her life."
There were some gasps and the audience perked up.

"Please remain seated everyone. This may take a few minutes," added Andrew.

"The Police were hampered, not because they hadn't any suspects, Cade and I were very obvious ones, but because there were too many. Mary, Bill and Carole, here, are only a few of her casualties on her path of Social destruction. It is possible that Juliet, in her capacity as an Estate Agent, knows several who have suffered due to her planning machinations."

"I do."

and,

"Me!" Exclaimed Juliet and Peter together.

"And me! Added Freda. "I still haven't sold my Aunt's cottage." Delia and Andrew continued their analysis.

"The problem was that either, like, everyone or no-one was in the frame, depending on how you looked at it."

"Means:" said Andrew. "It was Delia's gun, mandated, the difficulty was, it was locked away after the match, Cade made sure Delia saw it was safe. So who could have got to it?"

"It turns out that the answer is anyone! Especially anyone who was, like, there that night and that was several people in this room and many from Prior's Richmount Gun Club. So far we've narrowed the field down to a few dozen candidates."

"Motive: Delia had no motive." Andrew hugged his wife and continued. "Councillor Patterson was never going to overturn her planning permission, that would require an Act of Parliament and Mildred's way of handling things was to beat somebody up, not go to the law. She'd already tried it once with Delia on the first day they met and ended up in custody--Unlikely. Cade had no motive. Despite all her faults, he loved her. Why kill her now, when he had managed to put up with her for the last twenty years? So did any of the few dozen have a motive? No; and this was a real difficulty, the planning committee had passed all her objections on the Tuesday, in her absence, reducing everyone who could have got to the gun to motiveless."

"Opportunity: this was, like, always the biggest problem.

Everybody had a solid alibi because none of those questioned could have been at the scene of the crime when it was committed. Apart from Peter and me, none of those questioned was ever there at all. So could one of the several have been there? Somebody who hadn't been questioned. Was there someone else who should have been questioned? Possibly someone who would have been questioned had all the relationships been known?"

"It was then that we met Carole," said Andrew.

"Now Carole really did want to harm Mildred. Like many journalists and I'm not saying anything I haven't already said to her face, she regarded herself as a guardian of the Public Morality, while dining well, like, off its immorality. Stitching Carole up was a serious, deadly mistake."

"It's true--I did want to stake her out on an anthill, and forget where it was. Rupert had had to persuade me not to try but to kill her with my pen, by revealing her evil actions in an article instead. But, it was only when she turned up dead that I finally decided not to do it for real."

"But, Mildred was only second on her hit list. Carole had a secret tragedy of her own, which she had faced up to and learned to live with until she came to Warwickshire and re-met it, face to face." Andrew put his arm protectively around the blonde. "Would you tell us, Carole? You can edit any details which are too painful."

"I was raped many years ago. The rapist was never caught, and I thought he never would be, but I provided samples and described him in sufficient detail to make the Police confident that if they ever did catch him, I could identify him precisely. And I did. I am talking specifically to you now because you are here in this room. It is why you were invited." All the men in the room looked anxiously at each other. Andrew continued,

"What have rape and murder in common? Well, in this case, motive. The reason we could not narrow the search down to one person was we had not twigged the **real** motive, which was to demonstrate your power of control over someone else. In Mildred's case, ultimate power. Never again would she turn down a planning application."

"So who could have got my gun, not been questioned as to their whereabouts at noon on the 26 of July last year, be a control freak, a good shot and have access to a daisy-wheel printer? Who else but Carole's rapist? We can certainly get you on the rape, and my guess is, like, now that the Police know where to look, the murder will follow."

"The clues you scattered with such profligate generosity will lead back to you, as surely as they cleared my wife."

"I told the Police where to look for a size twenty-odd flowered dress, with perhaps some cushions and a daisy-wheel printer that, like, inflicts specific damage on its wheels."

"Of course they cannot discuss evidence with a witness, but there are many uniformed cats licking their lips clear of cream, so my guess is that they found something interesting."

"And you really should look at people more carefully, if you are going to impersonate them. As far as shooting is concerned, like, I'm a lefty, as one glance my way at the match would have told you. Maisie?"

"Armed Police! Freeze!"

"Very neat. But as far as you are concerned, it's still my game I think," said the suspect and jerked.

The Police Officer behind fired, aiming for the shoulder.

He was too late.

Prior's Richmount Gun Club's Top Marksman had already loosed three shots into the brightly lit alcove at Andrew, Delia and Carole, from point blank range.

Arrested

Maisie

The four shots sounding only like one merged with the plunging darkness in the alcove and the cacophony of exploding glass, in a single, spectacular, prolonged, Crash!

Simultaneously, bright lights came on in the room, and a metal shutter crashed down behind the floral display.

Cade Patterson struggled out of the deep, easy chair, in which he had been sitting.

Sergeant Enermouse helped him and, as he stood up, slid his hands behind his back and snicked the handcuffs onto his wrists.

"Cade Patterson I arrest you on suspicion --."

Cade shrugged free, howling and sank down beside his fallen accomplice who was moaning and twitching, weakly. Maisie was quite dismissive,

"He'll be okay. Eventually. We used rubber bullets; they make a nasty mess, but it's not usually permanent. Mind, I don't know that they will let you share a cell."

Peter had hurled the pot plants out of his way
and was clawing at the shutter,
shouting for Delia.
Abigail grabbed a fire iron
and thrust it into his hand,
he jammed it into the bottom,
trying to lever the door up.

"Don't do that Peter, you'll just have to, like, pay for it, it's only on hire."

Chapter 30
Of Locks and Ghosts and Mis-Direction:
29 August 1987
Delia

"Oh, you minx! You rotten, scheming, conniving, double-dealing, treacherously-thoughtless--"

"Devious?"

"Devious!"

"Sneaky?"

"Snea--"

"We thought you were dead!" exclaimed Abigail bending down to hug the younger girl tightly.

Through the window, Juliet Means and Cade Patterson could be seen being bundled into Police vehicles in preparation for taking them away.

"Like Mr Clements, The reports of my death were greatly exaggerated, unlike Mr Clements that's not in code. But, I'm sorry, we needed to flush our fox out into the open and we, like, planned for her to hit back."

"But how?" exclaimed Mary, her eyes still wide with shock. "We saw her shoot you."

"The same way this whole episode in our lives has been done, Smoke and Mirrors. Why do you think Andrew took his jacket off? Even Freda would have noticed his buttonhole had switched sides. Dazzle with powerful electronic flash, then work Pepper's Ghost, but in the Large Economy Size. We weren't there Mary, just our reflections. We were sheltering safely behind another steel shutter. Pity about the glass, it was quality plate, has to be, or you would, like, see through it."

"No!" cried the Vicar. "That's too much, puns as well! We want explanations. How come Juliet is a rapist? Girls don't rape."

"But, likewise they never visit a public toilet without their handbag, do they?" Peter waited until the heads began nodding. "But, Juliet does, she takes her rifle case, but not her handbag, or at least she did on 25 July last year, the day before Mildred was killed."

"Except that, she was not visiting the toilet. She was stealing the murder weapon. I am thinking that you want an explanation Vicar? Very well, you may have it."

The ante-room was rapidly filling up with the rest of the guests who had been kept unaware of the drama, but alerted by the noise and were now being allowed through by Madeline, Carly, Kim and Richard.

The mantle clock began whirring, heralding the imminent start of its complicated Westminster Chime routine. Delia checked her watch,

"Thank you, Andrew, but, it must, like, wait for a moment. Please pick up a drink everyone." She waved at the sideboard where extra glasses, ready charged, were lined up waiting.

Andrew helped her out of her chair, and everyone else also stood up.

"I'm not the only one getting married today, so is one of my friends from School. We each had to refuse the other's invite, but we, like, agreed to toast each other. So Big Mamma, it's three o'clock." She paused while the chimes reached their climax; the first bong rang out.

"To absent friends and to Shirley Jayne Monta, health, wealth and happiness!" Delia raised her glass and drained it.

The populace copied her and sat when she waved them down.

"Okay, Vicar. Means, motive, opportunity. The means was

easy to identify, it was my gun, anyone who got their hands on the keys after Cade locked up could have, like, run off with it."

"The problem was no-one did. Delia brought the keys straight to me, and they were still in my pocket when the Police came asking for them. So it was either Delia or me and we both had solid alibis."

"So lateral thinking, if no-one got to the keys, could they have got to the lock? What if the lock hadn't, like, been locked at all?

"But," said Freda. "I saw Cade show you it was locked myself."

"The lock is old." Delia produced it from her bag. "It was a quality lock in its day, but it has the same fatal flaw that many of this type have."

"All locks have at least one weakness; someone has to be able to open it," murmured Andrew.

"But early padlocks of the cylinder type, like this one, could be secured in the unlocked position," she clicked it firmly shut between her hands. "Sounded shut tight, didn't it, but the shackle is slid down the outside of the body. To a casual glance, it's locked normally, but all you do to free it is, like, rotate the shackle." She opened her hand revealing the apparently locked, but actually unlocked, padlock and graphically demonstrated.

"And Cade did that?"

"Why else would he draw my attention to it being locked? He never had before. Then he slid it into place and lobbed the keys at me and drew me away. He lobbed the keys, but came, like, straight out to Peter with me. Why did he give me the keys, he never had before? He gave me the keys so that he had filled my hands, but freed his hands to help usher me out."

"It's a bit thin Delia."

"I agree, by itself nothing, I wouldn't even have, like, remembered it, but he'd already marked his card for me, so when the time came to look closely at events, anything he did had to be put in the Double-Check-This box. How would you describe Cade? Honest?"

"Yes."

"Decent, Legal, Truthful?"

"Yes."

"So would I, except that he lied about knowing Juliet when Freda was asking about other Estate Agents. I perked up and gave him, like, a chance to recover if it was just a mistake, he declined, which I found very odd. The second blindingly obvious was Motive."

"We were all looking for revenge motives," said Sergeant Enermouse. "And we were snowed under. It was difficult to get a hold of the idea that there might be a different motive, until Delia took Carole to Prior's Richmount, intending somehow between the two of them to give the Estate Agents daisy-wheel printer the once over."

"We never got to the shop--I saw my rapist--And the cat was out of its bag scent marking everywhere."

"Girls don't rape, not usually anyway. Every time I met Juliet she came on to me, despite being the most butch girl I had ever seen," said Andrew. "I just thought I was the amorous target of a lonely girl--"

"She came on to every man she met," said Abigail, looking around at the heads nodding agreement. "She really annoyed me occasionally. Eventually Peter began to slope off the other way when he saw her coming."

Andrew chuckled and continued his analysis,

"Then Carole recognised her rapist."

"My attacker was definitely male; he'd left semen. When makeup was found in my hair, at first it was assumed it was from the girl, who may or may not have been an accomplice or procurer. But I also had little round bruises on my thighs; it took us a long time to realise they were from suspenders.

"Juliet Means has hidden depths, or to be more exact extremities," said Maisie. "Quite a rare species apparently, a cross-dressing, mostly gay man. Most cross dressers, cross dress, that's their thing. Most gay men are quite happy to be men who just happen to like men. Very few of either cross other boundaries. But a controlling, power-crazed rapist, who basically hates women, who may have murderous tendencies; now there is an animal of colour very familiar."

"Over the years as I remembered little details. Subconsciously I must have realised what had happened, because when I saw her in Prior's Richmount I knew. I knew everything, with complete certainty."

"When Juliet became a subject for investigation, so did her business and her clients, particularly regular clients, not common animals for a provincial Estate Agent. After that, it didn't take us long to turn up Ternimal Investments," summarised Sergeant Enermouse. "Ternimal Investments is Juliet and Cade. And suddenly we were looking at someone else, who was closely but secretly connected with the Pattersons.

"Who hadn't had an alibi checked out, who had had a revenge motive for a time, but now had, like, possibly a whole new one of her, erm, his own."

"Checking movements was going to be problematical, especially as the attempt to blame someone else had been so detailed." Andrew tenderly caressed his wife's shoulder. "It was highly likely that he had prepared an alibi which, after a year, might be hard to disprove. But flushing Juliet from cover, if we were right, would be no problem. A control freak could not sit still and do nothing; he would just have to demonstrate that, even in losing, he had won."

"It was Juliet we saw striding along Berryhill Ridge?"

"Yes. We saw a hat; a flowered dress plumped out with some cushions and a waving stick. We, like, saw exactly what we were meant to see, Mildred."

"The serious, deadly mistake wasn't Mildred setting me up." Carole kissed the girl in the wheelchair.

"No," said Mary shaking her head. "It was attempting to frame Delia!"

"I presume the person we all know as Juliet is in reality John Means. Was there ever a Juliet Means? A sister perhaps, or a wife."

"Yes, darling. Sister. Of whom, nobody seems to know the whereabouts. I omitted to tell you that, didn't want to worry you.

Maisie will be, like, digging up some patios soon, I suspect."

"Only the one. We found what we were looking for under the first one, an hour ago. I can tell you because some sharp-eyed reporter rumbled us, it will be on the evening news, well pictures of the cover we've erected will be anyway. It will be some time before we are absolutely sure who it is, tests and that." The big girl shrugged. "But, as you would say, 'No more bets please'--"

Delia, Chef in a Wheelchair
The End

Jennifer's answers.

'Last lesson:- What was the first thing Mr Baques did after switching on the tape?'

Mr Baques banged twice on his bin

(Two Marks)

'Last lesson:- What was the Last thing Mr Baques did before speaking?'

Mr Baques banged three times on his board.

(Two Marks)

'Last lesson:- Who got the merit mark for saying 'It's Time squared'?'

Sadie Parker.

(Two Marks)

'Last lesson:- What did Sadie get her merit mark for?'

She got it for saying, 'It's time squared.'

(Two Marks)

'Last lesson:- What time did Mr Rickaby run in?'

Mr Rickaby ran in at 13.53 hrs.

(Two Marks)

'Last lesson:- Mr Rickaby's hat had a sticker with 1016 hanging from the brim. Rewrite correctly.'

Mr Rickaby's hat had a note with 10/6 written on it stuck in the band.

(Two Marks)

'Last lesson:- What was on fire?'

Nothing, but a lorry changed gear.

(One Mark)

'Write a sentence about this exercise, stating an important, relevant fact about it.'

Today's tape was last lesson's recording, but edited and changed.

(One Mark)

Karen The Girl That Would Be a Plumber

Due to be released 2017

In the Epilogue as a Prologue at the start of 'Karen' we realise that someone has been killed in an accident -- or was it deliberate?

Who has been killed, by whom and why is the crime fiction whodunit running in the background, throughout the book, of this unusual, coming of age erotic novel. It may well keep you guessing until the end.

Karen is the most knowledgeable plumber around, except that she isn't a plumber. How and why this oxymoron comes about is the foreground theme in this account of the life and loves, testing and success of this feisty Zulu Princess by controversial author, Petra Ceason.

In this latest feel-good story, again, Miss Ceason challenges the hypocrisy of conventional morality, but this time, up front, as well as close and personal.

Enjoy.

Rita--Who?

Due to be released 2017

Although Rita takes the Title Rôle, this is a Searching for Identity, Voyage of Discovery for all eight of the main characters. I have a certain amount of sympathy for some of those that end up discovering to their cost...

When Rita first appeared in a Creative Writing Homework early in 2004, our Tutor was incensed, mainly because the writing was pretty grotty, but also because,

'The Social would have something to say about an under-age working girl.'

I have endeavoured to sort the grotty writing, his area of expertise, but steepled our resolve about the Social, my area of expertise.

My Acknowledgements and Thanks to an early Twentieth Century edition of Boy's Own Paper, for a vaguely remembered story idea, that I adapted to become that of Mary Richards, {and hence Mary Andrew} fighting for her life on the top of a runaway Stage Coach in America's Old West.

My Apologies to Native Americans who, at that time, were portrayed as anarchic savages and thus also in the extract. I do know that contrary to the Hollywood Studio image; you had every provocation to wage war on the invaders. Compared to many of them, you were civilised.

My thanks also to my tutor, Mr E. E. Hughes for the imagination stimulus picture of the four men meeting, from which this crime fiction sprang. My first effort you castigated, so did my Canadian dolly, even I wasn't that keen! I like the finished erotic novel a bit better!

Petra.

SHORT STORIES, UNLIKE MY NOVELS, YOU COULD SHOW MOST OF THESE TO YOUR MAIDEN AUNT.

Collected Short Stories And Pomes {And No It's Not A Typo}

Due to be released 2017

Short stories and Geordie poems {pomes}, that started life as Creative Writing Course Homeworks.

Rather than enter them for competitions, where the meaning of the winning prose is too obtuse for me to fathom, or the successful poetry has neither rhyme nor lyricism; I chose to put them in a book where folk could enjoy them for what they are.

A book of short stories usually contains between five and fifteen stories. You are reading about one with sixty of the little critters, ranging in size from fifty to over five thousand words and believe me, the harder of those two to write, was the fifty!

I was kept under severe restraint while writing these, gagged; manacled; I'm talking SEVERE restraint here!

So Dear True Reader:

The sex is understated and off stage, totally unlike my usual work, but if you like Romance, Crime Fiction, the odd ghost, with just a pinch of fantasy. If you prefer your women feisty, red-blooded, even, when necessary, prepared to do the asking, then this book is for you.

Enjoy,

Petra.

Janie, Mechanic On A Motorbike

Due to be released 2017

Janie Jones is the youngest of a family of two girls and a boy; she is small and plain, ugly is her word, and has large breasts, which combination gets her bullied. She is a Biker and becomes very good at it, earning the title the 'Best Trouble-shooter In The Business.'

Although she is small, she is tough and also pragmatic and naturally very strong, both physically and mentally. Her party trick at the motorcycle club is picking up a power unit with one hand.

Some of Janie's life is planned in meticulous detail, like both her jobs; and some just happens, like her first, unexpected, but torrid love affair and a little act of kindness towards a friend that switches on a complete career change.

For the rich and beautiful, who's main fear is 'Will the media find out?' Janie will be a mystery.

For the other ninety-nine percent of us, Janie is what we'd like the girl in our mirror to become:

Local girl made good.

Enjoy,

Petra.

www.ingramcontent.com/pod-product-compliance
Lightning Source LLC
Chambersburg PA
CBHW020931020726
47495CB00002B/447